They both stared at me as if I had two heads.

"Wait, mitochondrial?" Olsen said. "Nuclear? You lost me."

"You might have heard this before, but I'll review it anyway. There are two types of DNA used in forensics, guys: mitochondrial and nuclear. In the simplest of terms, nuclear DNA is from live cells with a nucleus, for instance when you take a swab from the inside of a suspect's cheek, or semen, vaginal fluid, blood, sometimes saliva, etc. Nuclear DNA can be used to positively identify an individual. *Mitochondrial* DNA on the other hand is not as accurate. It can come from dead sloughed skin cells, or hair without a follicle, for instance. You can use Mi-DNA in addition to your other evidence to narrow down to a probable suspect, but it's not necessarily individual specific." They both looked disappointed. "Hey cheer up, boys. Who knows? We might get lucky." I didn't know how profound this statement would turn out to be.

The three of us were walking down the hallway to the Property and Evidence section so Olsen could book the lens cap and swabs in, when Davis came through the double doors in front of us. His usual sour look was particularly grave this morning.

Without any greeting he asked, "What time did you three leave the hospital last night?"

The question caught us by surprise, as our train of thought was on the cap and DNA evidence. We looked at each other then back at him. I spoke up first.

"Oh, one thirty, two maybe? Not really sure."

The deputies nodded their agreement.

"Well, you got trouble," Davis replied. "Your Indian is dead. This was *your* deal. Get over to the hospital right-the-fuck now! That half-breed K-9 cop is already over there and I'm sure he's sweating it since it was his dog that did the damage, but he was helping you three out. The sheriff is on my ass because the Feds are on his. They want to know why the hell three of our deputies arrested an Indian on The Res without including them. They backed off a bit when the sheriff told them the reservation cop actually made the arrest and it was a hot-foot-pursuit deal, but let there be no doubt, you three are going to be in the shit right along with him if fuckin' Cochise there died from his dog-bite wounds, now *move i*t!"

KUDOS for *Death in the Desert*

In *Death in the Desert* by Douglas Durham, Jason Douglas is a retired cop that gets pulled into dealing with drug dealers and assassins when he has a flat tire in the middle of nowhere in Texas. The only experienced crime scene guy in the area, he becomes the go-to guy for the local sheriff's deputies when Jason's wife finds two skeletons in the desert near where they pull over to fix their tire. Little do they know that they are dealing with much more than simple crime of murder. Jason and his wife Sonya park their RV at a local ranch and Jason goes to work, trying to help solve the crime. Durham's characters are very well-developed and three-dimensional. And he definitely knows his crime scene science. Being a lover of shows like CSI Miami, Law & Order, and Forensic Files, I found Death in the Desert to be on a par with the best of them. It's a fairly long book, about 400 pages, but the pace is fast and the story extremely interesting. – *Taylor Jones, Reviewer*

Death in the Desert by Douglas Durham is a combination murder mystery, thriller/suspense. It's filled with a lot of crime scene science and police terminology, but with the glossary at the beginning, I found it easy for a lay person to understand. I liked the main characters and thought them genuinely well developed. The science is fascinating and I learned a lot about crime scene investigation. The plot is strong and story very fast-paced. And the book has a ring of truth that tells me Durham knows a great deal about crime scene investigation, whether through personal experience or because he did a lot of research, the end result is a book you will find hard to put down. – *Regan Murphy, Reviewer*

He'd finally made it to retirement, but how could he know that a flat tire would lead him to an ominous discovery—throwing him back into a life of violence?

After thirty years of being a cop, Jason Douglas thinks he's through with dead bodies, bloody victims, and nightly gunfire. So when he stops to fix a flat tire in the middle of nowhere, the last thing he expects is to find skeletons in the desert. Nor does he expect to be pulled into a small West Texas sheriff's office as the only available CSI man. Still, he reluctantly agrees to help the deputies process the crime scene. But when people around him start dying brutal deaths, Jason knows things aren't what they seem. Can he find the killer before it's too late, or will he and his wife Sonya become the assassin's next victims?

ACKNOWLEDGEMENTS

I would like to acknowledge the following: My wife Kimberly, whose patience and support was critical in the creation of this story. Several of my closest comrades, Daryl Dellone, Corey Schroeder, Neal Manha, and Michael "Gene" Johnson along with his former K-9 partner "Falcon," one of the most fearless, and fearsome, K-9 officers that ever tread on four paws. All of the Officers, Detectives, Dispatchers, Property Technicians, and Crime Scene Investigators I have had the opportunity to work with on the streets and in headquarters, for without the unique personalities and individual skills of these people, I would not have been able to bring my characters to life. The crooks, gangsters, and thugs without whom I would have no story to tell. Finally, to Lauri, Mike, Faith, Jack, and all of the other great folks at Black Opal Books for giving me the opportunity to tell it.

DEATH IN THE DESERT

A Jason Douglas Novel

Douglas Durham

A Black Opal Books Publication

GENRE: THRILLER/MAINSTREAM/ROMANTIC ELEMENTS

DEATH IN THE DESERT ~ A Jason Douglas Novel
Copyright © 2012 by Douglas Durham
Cover Design by Jackson Cover Designs
All cover art copyright © 2014
All Rights Reserved
Print ISBN: 978-1-626941-06-9

First Publication: FEBRUARY 2014

Published by Black Opal Books **http://www.blackopalbooks.com**

DEDICATION

I have worked with many good men and women throughout my career in law enforcement, all of whom were of great influence in the telling of this story. Some I knew well, others not so much. Most are still with us, some still serving their communities in this selfless and dangerous profession. As they read these pages, I'm certain each will recognize his or her contribution. Others are gone from us now and we mourn their loss. It is to all of these folks and to one fearless K-9, that this book is dedicated.

GLOSSARY OF TERMS & EXPRESSIONS

1:1 ~ refers to reproducing a photograph to actual size scale—one inch to one inch.

10-4 ~ Affirmative.

Adobe Walls ~ Adobe Walls, Texas was the site of two battles, one in 1865 and one in 1874, between buffalo hunters and merchants and the Comanche, Apache, and Arapaho Indian Tribes.

AFIS ~ an acronym for Automated Fingerprint Identification System—a data base for scanning, storing, and sharing fingerprint identification between law enforcement agencies.

AG ~ Attorney General.

AH-64 ~ Designation for the US Army's Apache Attack Helicopter.

ALS ~ Alternate light source.

AO ~ An acronym for Area of Operation, where the mission/battle is taking place, where one is working, or—sometimes—the immediate area.

Article Search Trained ~ Police dogs who are trained to find discarded objects. Examples would be a gun thrown from a moving car, a money bag or ski mask from a robbery, etc. Some dogs become so proficient they can find pieces of disassembled guns thrown in different locations. Most agencies utilizing K-9 dogs have a "slush fund" to pay for accidental bite victims. There is usually a cap on the amount that can be paid out, but it can go as high as several thousand dollars, avoiding many lawsuits as the victims are usually very happy to accept the cash.

ATF (or ATFE) ~ An acronym for the federal law enforcement agency, Alcohol, Tobacco, Firearms, and Explosives.

BMG ~ Browning Machine Gun—originally designed as a heavy machine gun and still used as such today, mainly by snipers, due to its extreme range, accuracy, and ability to penetrate light armor, masonry, brick, and concrete walls.

Ballistic Bubble ~ The bubble or pocket of energy-filled, superheated, compressed air encasing a bullet, which is created as a high-velocity bullet in flight pushes air out of its way. This is what causes the initial damage to the body, first stretching and then shattering tissues, bones, and organs ahead of and to the sides of the bullet itself.

BOL ~ Be on the lookout (for).

The Box ~ A common term for a polygraph examination.

Casa Sobre Ruedas ~ House on wheels.

Cheshire Cat ~ A fictional feline character from Lewis Carroll's *Alice in Wonderland* known for its mischievous—sometimes bordering on evil—grin.

CI ~ An acronym for Confidential Informant.

Code 4 ~ Police code fore no assistance needed.

CODIS ~ An acronym for Combined DNA Index System—an automated, computerized search-and-storage system for DNA samples. Persons arrested for felony crimes now have a sample of their DNA placed on file with this system.

The Comancheros ~ A 1961 western movie starring John Wayne and Stuart Whitman. Wayne portrayed a Texas Ranger Captain using the false name Ed McBain in order to penetrate a group of gun-running outlaws.

Delta ~ An identifying feature inside the fingerprint pattern area.

DNA (Deoxyribonucleic Acid) ~ Genetic strands unique to all living organisms, or in the case of humans, each individual, which can be matched to a particular individual, much like fingerprints, with near 100% accuracy.

Demasiado Facil ~ Too easy.

F3 Nikon Camera ~ manufactured for many years, this 35mm single-lens reflex (SLR) film camera was very popular due to the quality of photos it took and its rugged metal bodied construction.

FAA ~ An acronym for the Federal Aeronautics Administration which is tasked with the investigation of plane crashes.

Fast and Furious ~ code name of a 2009 ATF program with the goal of tracking guns being illegally trafficked across the border into Mexico. The ATF not only allowed, but actually encouraged, several gun shop owners in the United States to sell guns to individuals whom the ATF knew to be straw buyers for the Mexican drug cartels. Almost immediately, the ATF lost control of the program and hundreds of guns disappeared into Mexico without a trace. The failed program only came to light when one of the guns was used to kill a US Border Patrol agent and was found at that crime scene. The United States Congressional investigation, with the help of ATF-agent whistle blowers, revealed that high ranking ATF and US Department of Justice officials, and possibly even officials in The White House, knew of the program's failure and tried to cover it up.

Feather the Prop ~ A term describing the adjustment of the pitch of the propeller so that the leading edge is turned into the wind, creating the least drag—done electrically from inside the cockpit.

FLIR ~ An acronym for Forward Looking Infra-Red—a lens/camera combination, normally attached to law enforcement and military vehicles and aircraft, that detects contrasting heat sources, thus allowing the operator to "see" in total darkness, unlike that of standard night vision technology, which requires a minimum level of light, such as starlight, in order to illuminate the area.

Four-Point Restraints ~ Heavy leather or nylon straps, attached to a bed, which are used to keep violent patients from harming themselves or the hospital staff by securing their wrists and ankles.

Fragged ~ A slang term coined by soldiers referring to killing someone by use of a fragmentation grenade.

Gambaro ~ Thug.

Ghillie Suit ~ A camouflage suit designed to resemble natural foliage, normally made from shredded, colored burlap and commonly used by hunters and military snipers.

Good Stick ~ A term often used to refer to the ability of the pilot of an aircraft—a reference to the days when an airplane was controlled by a vertical column, or "stick," held between the pilot's knees.

Gum-Shoe ~ A common, though not necessarily flattering, name referring to a private investigator.

Gut Bag ~ A term referring to a Native American canteen created from the stomach or gut of an animal.

HEAT ~ An acronym for Help Eliminate Auto Theft—a specialized unit dealing with stolen vehicles and parts.

Hombre ~ Man

Hero Complex ~ A term referring to police, firemen, or other first-responders who plant pieces of evidence or fingerprints, or even start fires and then conveniently "discover" the evidence of the crime so as to be deemed the hero in the case. Some cops have even gone so far as to shoot themselves in their body-armor vest to gain the attention they sought.

Ident-a-Kit ~ A manual picture identification system using clear plastic overlays with different head shapes, facial, and hair features printed on them—used by laying the overlays on top of each other until a composite picture of an individual is created—replaced by a new computer program which performs the same task only much faster.

Javelina ~ A peccary or skunk pig—a medium sized mammal belonging to the Tayassuidae family—looks similar to a pig but is not related to the swine family.

KISS ~ An acronym for the saying, Keep It Simple, Stupid.

Less-Lethal ~ A term referring to shotguns designed to fire small, bean-bag-type projectiles filled with sand, powdered lead, or birdshot, which strike with enough force to incapacitate an individual without causing life threatening injury, though a strike in the head or face at close range can be fatal—also applies to stun-guns and incapacitating chemical sprays, such as pepper spray and mace.

Live-Scan ~ A digital imager, manufactured by several different companies, which is used to scan finger and palm prints of arrestees at the time of booking, for storage in computerized criminal data bases—now used by most agencies in the US and around the world in lieu of rolling a person's prints, using ink and fingerprint cards. Hard copies of the scanned prints can also be printed out from these imagers.

Loupe ~ A specialized magnifying glass used by crime labs for viewing and comparing fingerprints—several other types of loupes are used by jewelers, etc.

Lunge line ~ a rope approximately fifteen feet in length with a halter clip on one end used to exercise a horse.

Marv Albert ~ A well-known basketball sports broadcaster who was arrested for allegedly assaulting his girlfriend by biting her on the back several times.

MOA ~ An acronym for Minute of Angle, which is a "just-under-one-and-one-half inch-sized" grouping of bullets fired from a gun at a distance of 100 yards.

Mojado ~ Spanish slang term for "wetback," or illegal immigrant

MP5 ~ A sub-machine gun, manufactured by Heckler & Koch in both .9mm and .40-caliber, known for its high quality, accuracy, and ease of use—used in close-quarter battle by many police SWAT teams and several nation's militaries, including the Armed Forces of the United States.

MRE ~ An acronym for Meal Ready to Eat, prepackage, single serving, military rations sealed in individual packets.

Ninhydrin ~ A chemical reagent that reacts with amino acids secreted along with the water, salts, and oil from the pores of the skin, turning the acids a purple color, resulting in a purple image of a finger or palm print, normally used on porous, cellulose-infused items such as paper, cardboard, or raw wood.

North Hollywood Shootout ~ An incident that took place in February 1997 when LAPD confronted two heavily armed bank-robbery suspects at the Bank of America in North Hollywood, California, leaving multiple officers and civilians wounded and the two suspects dead.

OHV ~ An acronym for Off Highway Vehicle, such as a quad runner, Jeep, or 4-WD utility.

OP ~ An acronym for Observation Post.

POS ~ An acronym for Point of Sale

Posse Box ~ An aluminum box with a clipboard lid, approximately one-inch thick, used for storing paperwork and/or as a writing surface.

Ranchera ~ Reservation.

RICO ~ An acronym for Racketeer Influenced and Corrupt Organization Act—a set of federal laws created to battle organized crime.

Roll-a-Tape ~ A measuring device used for measuring long distances, consisting of a small wheel on the end of an aluminum handle that rolls along the ground and spins an internal measuring mechanism. The distance is visible through a small window above the wheel.

RP ~An acronym for Reporting Party.

Ruby Ridge ~ An incident that took place in 1992, involving Randy Weaver and his family in a violent confrontation with US Marshalls at their home in the mountains near Ruby Ridge, Idaho, where a sniper with the FBI's Hostage Rescue Team attempted to shoot Weaver from fairly close range, bungling the shot badly, missing Weaver and accidentally killing Weaver's wife, Vicki, who was standing near the front door of their house holding their baby.

SAR ~ An acronym for Search and Rescue.

Slim-Jim ~ A long thin piece of sheet metal notched at one end, used for unlocking car door locks from the exterior via a side window.

Six-P Principle ~ A term meaning Proper Planning Prevents Piss Poor Performance.

Snoopin' and Poopin' ~ A term used by US soldiers and marines, meaning to sneak around, observe, and gather information.

Straw Buyer ~ A person who makes a purchase for another person. It is against federal law to purchase firearms in this fashion.

Spirometer ~ A device used to measure the capacity of air in the lungs.

Topo ~ Short for Topographical. Topo maps are maps published primarily by government agencies like the Bureau of Land Management (BLM) or the US Military, which show in detail the topographical features of the ground in certain areas of the earth, or grids, and normally include longitude and latitude grid lines showing coordinates and colored lines, which indicate the steepness of the terrain. including hills, valleys, peaks, lakes, streams, washes, prominent rock outcroppings, etc. These maps are commonly used by hikers, rock climbers, campers, hunters, fisherman, 4WD/OHV enthusiasts, SAR personnel, etc.

Toyah ~ a small town in southwest Texas, just off I-20 near Pecos

Un-ass this AO ~ A term coined by soldiers in Vietnam, meaning to leave the immediate location.

UC ~ An acronym for Undercover.

VIN ~ An acronym for Vehicle Identification Number, a number that every motor vehicle and trailer has permanently attached or stamped to its body and frame.

W3 ~ The Army rank of warrant officer, Level 3—warrant officer ranks were created during the Vietnam Conflict when helicopter pilots were needed badly and there were no regular-commissioned officers to fill the positions.

Whorl ~ A term that refers to a specific fingerprint pattern.

Wounded Knee ~ Wounded Knee, South Dakota, 1890, was the site of the last major confrontation between the Lakota Sioux and the US Seventh Cavalry.

CHAPTER 1

The Cops

It wasn't so much of a "boom!" as it was a low pitched "thump." Not all that much as volume goes, and really no vibration to speak of, but it jarred the truck. I knew instantly what it was—trailer tire blow-out. *Shit* I thought. *Just what I needed out here in the middle of friggin' nowhere.* Well, it wasn't exactly "nowhere," but close enough that you could see it from here. We were westbound, my wife Sonya and I, on I-20 fifty miles or so west of Pecos, Texas. If you've ever been to Pecos, then you know what I mean by middle of nowhere. The two of us were on the final leg of a "bucket list" trip that we'd been planning for two years prior to my retirement. Up till now, it had been a real hoot and for the most part hassle free.

"*What* was that?" Sonya asked startled.

"Blow-out," I replied. "I need to get off the freeway."

Not far ahead I saw an exit onto what looked like a small country road. *Why would there be a big-time freeway exit onto this apparently little-used, rough-blacktop road,* I wondered. *Probably some local rancher with "juice" and a county supervisor for a buddy.* But I wasn't going to look a gift horse in the mouth. I got the rig slowed down enough to hit the exit without killing us both then cruised down the old road until I found a gravel turnout wide enough to pull out of the way should someone pass by. Looking both ways down this road, I figured that wasn't likely.

We got out of the truck, stretched, and walked back to the trailer. I wasn't surprised when I saw that the center of the three tires on the left side was shredded. *Well at least it hadn't taken the fender with it when it blew.*

"This is going to take a while," I told my wife, "so you might as well get the dogs out of the truck and walk 'em, then you can help me with tools and stuff."

"Okay," she replied.

I could tell by the look on her face she was not thrilled at the pro-
spect of getting her hands dirty by helping me. Even worse, suffering
the most hated of female damage, breaking a fingernail. Mumbling
under her breath, she began to leash up our two dogs for a walk. We
had never had little dogs before. We had inherited these two from our
teen-age daughters who, of course, grew up and drove off to college,
leaving us with these two mutts. It could have been worse, I guessed.
Both were sweet little dogs. They traveled well and didn't yap or
whine all the Goddamn time like so many small dogs did.

I gazed around at the surrounding desert. *Whole lot of fuckin' nothing out here*, I thought, *sand, scrub brush, some scrawny cactus, a few
rattlesnakes probably, and yeah*—I looked down, watching a small
brown scorpion cross the sand in front of my boot—*scorpions. Swell, I
get to crawl around on the ground with bugs that can sting the shit out
of you*!

On the upside, at least it wasn't 110 degrees. That thought actually
made me chuckle as I recalled a line from one of my favorite comedy
movies *Blazing Saddles* when character actor Burton Gilliam says to
all the rail workers as they are laboring away in the hot sun, "C'mon
boys, the way you'z lollie gaggin' around here, you'd think it was a
hunnert'n twenty degrees…can't be mor'n a hunnert'n fourteen!"

Still smiling at that one, I called out to my wife as she started with
the dogs out into the sandy dirt, "Hey, watch out for critters. I just
squashed a scorpion. Keep your eyes open."

Over her shoulder, she tossed me one of her better disdainful *How-
stupid-do-I-look* looks. I shook my head. *Humph! Marital bliss*. With
that I started the unpleasant task of getting the spare tire cranked down.
Crawling under the trailer, I, of course, hit my head straight away in
the process. *Oh yeah, this is going to be some fun*.

"*JAAAY DEEE!*"

My wife's voice was several octaves above her normal tone with
obvious alarm as she yelled my initials, they being "JD," of course. I
had just started jacking up the axle, but as was normal when adrenalin
jolted my system into the "fight or flight" mode, I could move damn
quick without conscious effort. I dropped the jack handle and jetted out
from under the trailer like a torpedo being launched from a tube. I
jerked my "Kahr" PM 9, 9mm pistol from its small holster on my belt.
It was in my hand before I saw her. She was standing frozen like a
statue, 50 yards out into the desert. *Damn*! I thought realizing she was
too far out for a quick rescue. *Why did she go out that far?*

I was running flat out now, but I could already see my worst fears
of her being snake-bitten, or having been surrounded by a group of
drug smugglers, were not a concern—not that my small seven-shot,

auto-loader would do much good if the latter were the case. She was looking down at something, trying to keep the dogs from getting close to whatever she had discovered.

Halfway to her, I slowed. One of the first training officers I'd had so long ago, an old Irish cop complete with food stains on his tie and a pint of Irish whiskey stashed inside his favorite call box, had once told me something I tried never to forget. "Always walk into the mess, boy-o. Never run, no matter how bad things seem. When you run your body will get there quicker than your brain, and that can end badly." This advice had served me well over the years and had actually saved my sorry ass a couple of times. I slowed my running to a walk then to a slow "hunter's stalk," alert for whatever the threat was.

As I got close enough for my wife to hear me, I asked softly, "Are you okay?"

She turned her head toward me and nodded. She then pointed to something on the ground in front of her. It took me several seconds to recognize what I was seeing.

As I did, my brain kicked into a cop's sarcastic overdrive and I blurted out, "Huh, now there's something you don't see every day." Sonya found no humor in that at all. I said to her, "Hon, look around behind you and try to back out of your tracks the same way you came in." Than as an afterthought, I added, "And keep those dogs short-leashed."

Whoops, I thought, *should have held on to that one.* I again got that disdainful look that all women learned how to do in the "Wife Acade-my." *You'd think after 28 years of marriage I'd learn.*

"Ni-en one, one. State yawl's 'mergency pa-lease." The heavy Texas drawl of the sheriff's department dispatcher's voice took me a bit by surprise. I could hear the keys on her dispatch keyboard clicking in the background.

"Yeah, listen," I told her. "I'm a retired cop from California. I'm out here just off of westbound I-20 at exit…ummm, 65. I pulled over to fix a flat tire and I just found something out here that you folks are going to want to know about."

"Yes, suh, and may I have you name and phone numbah pa-lease?"

"Jason Douglas," I replied, also reciting my cell number. I then briefly described what Sonya had found. There was a pause as I heard her speak inaudibly into her head-set microphone.

She came back to me. "Did you say ya'll was a retired offisuh?"

"Yes ma'am," I replied, "from California."

"Are you aahmed?" she asked.

"Aahamed? Oh, *armed.*" I smiled at the accent, knowing how easily I myself had picked them up when I'd lived in different parts of the country. "Yes ma'am."

"A dep'ty is on his way now. Please put any fireaahms you may have away."

"Okay," I said, thinking about them sending just one deputy for this type of call. *Well,* I thought, *maybe it's like that old Texas joke. If there was only one riot, they sent only one ranger, or deputy in this case.*

Southwest Texas along the I-20 corridor was for the most part flat, open, desolate country. Oh, there were the Sierra Madre Mountains to the far south in Mexico and the Guadalupe Mountain Range to the west, but right here where I stood, I could see for miles in every direction. The red and blue lights of the Revas County Sheriff's Department Ford SUV were visible for a good five minutes as it approached. The deputy's vehicle exited the freeway as I had, along that same rough blacktop road. He shut down his emergency lights as he got close. I again thought about them sending only one unit. *They either don't believe what I told them, or hell, maybe they just don't have the people.* The SUV slowed as it passed the rear of our trailer. Now I could see this was a double unit, the two deputies inside watching us where we stood in the gravel turn-out.

As the vehicle slowly approached, I could see they both were particularly interested in where our hands were. Prior to the arrival of the deputies, I'd put my pistol back in the trailer and clued Sonya in on the proper etiquette of how *not* to find one's self on the business end of nervous cop's gun. We were both holding our hands in plain view by our sides, with our driver's licenses gripped in our fingers. I'd also grabbed the paperwork for the truck and trailer right after I'd hung up the phone. As the Sheriff's vehicle slowed, I could see the passenger deputy holding the microphone to his mouth, obviously advising his dispatch of their arrival, our descriptions, and requesting the registration info on the South Dakota plates on our rig. The deputy driving pulled the unit in front of our truck in a classic blocking position. I smiled, thinking sarcastically, *Oh yeah, like we're going to lead all the cops in West Texas on a high speed chase in a pick-up truck pulling a 40 foot fifth wheel.*

Sonya, always the mind reader said, "Be nice."

Both deputies exited the SUV. The driver approached us, the passenger deputy hanging back. Both had their right hands hovering near their side arms. Being a "gun guy," I immediately recognized the weapons as Beretta Storms, thinking to myself, *Maybe 9's, but more likely .40's, since that's the caliber that most agencies like these days.* The approaching deputy was a young Caucasian guy in his early 30s.

He was tall and lean in a muscular way, and even *I* noticed that he was handsome in his tailored khaki uniform. A police recruiting "poster-boy." He was also very pale. My investigator's instincts kicked in. *Either new to day shift, or maybe working over from nights.* I was amused to notice out of the corner of my eye, Sonya checking him out from his boot soles to his shaved head under his brown "Sheriff" ball cap. No doubt she was having a brief "cougar" fantasy moment of her own. That was okay. *We all like to look at good looking people with nice bodies.*

He had on a brand new pair of those streamlined bug-eye tactical sunglasses that all the young-stud S.W.A.T. coppers wore these days. I couldn't see his eyes, but by the slight movement of his head, I could tell he had stolen a quick glance at Sonya's C-cup size and currently bra-less breasts under her T-shirt. He couldn't help himself. Neither could I for that matter. The cool morning air and the adrenalin still pumping through her veins were making her nipples poke at the under-side of her shirt like tent poles. I almost laughed out loud, thinking that guys were the same everywhere.

The passenger deputy was a contrast. Older, probably mid-fifties. Hispanic, barrel chest, with thick forearms. Face and arms weathered brown by the Texas desert sun, his eyes quick and experienced. *Yeah, this guy would be a handful for anyone deciding to try him on,* I decided. His eyes were on both of us, but unlike his younger partner, he was more interested in watching our hands and body language than looking at my wife's tits. His gaze swiftly moved from my eyes, to my hands, to my waistline looking for any telltale bulges under my T-shirt, down over my pockets to my feet, then back to my eyes again. He did the same with Sonya. It was all about officer survival with this guy.

"Hi, guys. I'm Jason Douglas, your RP," I said to them. "This is my wife Sonya."

"Hello," Sonya said, smiling and extending her right hand a bit flir-tatiously to the young deputy.

Thinking more about the front of her shirt than his own well-being, the young cop automatically extended his right hand, his gun hand, and shook hers. *Critical error,* I thought. I caught the quick disapproving look the older deputy shot at his partner, then he turned his attention back to me and we exchanged knowing glances. This seemed to put him somewhat at ease.

"You're retired off the job?" he asked.

"Yeah, central California, Vista P.D.," I replied and showed him my departmental retired ID and badge.

"Deputy Frank Sanchez." He extended his *left* hand. We both smiled. "My not-so-subtle partner here is Deputy James Olsen," Sanchez said.

Embarrassed at being caught boob watching and flustered now, the younger deputy stammered a few words. I was sure he was now thinking about how he was going to explain his voyeurism to his sergeant when I made my complaint about him checking out my wife.

"Relax," I told him, smiling. "First of all, I'm a guy, too. The twins there—" I nodded at my wife's shirt. "—wouldn't have gone unnoticed by me either. Second of all, I'm old school, youngster. I don't beef other cops, within reason anyway." The relief on his face was obvious. "Besides," I continued, winking at Sanchez, "I would imagine your senior partner here will have some additional words of wisdom to impart to you once you guys are alone."

"That's a given," Sanchez muttered under his breath, scowling at his partner.

It was obvious by the look on Olsen's face he was not looking forward to *that* conversation.

With his mind now back on the business at hand, the young deputy asked, "Are you armed?"

"Was," I replied. "I put it back in the trailer just before you guys got here."

He examined our South Dakota driver's licenses and the paperwork for the truck and trailer. "Mind if I pat you down real quick-like?"

"Not at all," I told him and assumed the position against the side of my trailer. "I've got a pocket knife in my right front pocket and a small flashlight in my left."

He removed both, laid them on the ground near his feet, and quickly searched me. I was glad to see he had finally recovered enough of his wits to again start thinking about his own survival.

Sanchez spoke up at that point and said to both of us, "I hope you don't mind, but we'll need to do the same to the young lady. I'm sure you understand. I can call a female deputy to do the search if you'd like, but that may take a while. She'll probably have to come from another agency as we're pretty short on lady deputies these days."

I looked at Sonya. "Honey?"

"I don't care," she said, clearly flattered at the "young lady" comment.

I was sure she was hoping that it would be the handsome young Olsen who would perform this task, but alas it was not to be.

Sanchez shot his young partner a quick *Don't-even-think-about-it* look and took a step forward. "*I'll* take care of it," he said. "Would you turn around, raise your arms out to your sides, please, ma'am?" He then used the backs of his hands to quickly and thoroughly complete her pat-down—armpits, ribs, between her breasts, waist, inner thighs right up to her crotch, front and rear pockets. I noticed he was being overly careful not to allow his hands to spend too much time lingering in any particular spot. Very professional. "My apologies, ma'am," he offered.

"Kind of enjoyed it," she shot back with a playful wink. This embarrassed the older deputy.

Satisfied that we now presented no immediate threat and having heard back from his dispatch on his earpiece that we and our vehicles were not wanted, they were both now at ease. Olsen handed me back our licenses and paperwork and retrieved my knife and light from the ground. "Hey, a 'Fenix,'" he said as he looked at my small flashlight. "I've never seen a small one like this, only their larger tactical lights."

"Yeah," I replied. "I have a bigger one, too, but this one is so handy being pocket size."

As he handed them back, Sanchez said, "Well, let's get to the rat killin', folks. What'd you find out here?"

Turning my head, I nodded to indicate a northeast direction and told him, "It's out there about 50 yards or so. My wife actually found it when she was walking our dogs. We tried not to stomp around too much, but she and the dogs were in close before she saw it. I had her re-trace her steps out, though, so it shouldn't be too bad." Sanchez again started to ask about the find, but I held up my hand. "You have to see it to believe it."

The deputy shrugged and held out his hand for me to precede him. The three of us started walking out into the desert. My wife, having actually picked up a few things over the years from both my work and from watching her favorite crime shows on TV, knew the deputies wouldn't want any more "cooks in the kitchen," so she opted to stay put at the rig with the dogs.

"We'll be out there a while," I told her. "Keep an eye out for any mutants, and keep Pietro close-by."

Puzzled by this Olsen asked, "Mutants? Pietro?"

Sanchez laughed and answered Olsen for me. "Mutants meaning just about anyone who don't have your interests at heart, and Pietro was the inventor's first name, as in Pietro Beretta."

The younger deputy nodded. "Ahh."

"Very astute, deputy," I told Sanchez

"Beretta 9mm?" he asked, referring to the caliber of Sonya's pistol.

"Yeah," I replied, "a full size Model 92."

"Big gun for a girl," Olsen said.

"I know," I answered, "but she shoots it well."

"Cool." The young deputy nodded his approval as we trudged our way through the hard-packed dirt and sand, asking, "So how long were you a cop?"

"I worked the street for about eight years in the Bay Area. Ended up there after I got out of the service. I've been a crime scene guy for the last 22 years in Vista. Supervisor for the last 10."

"Army?" Sanchez asked.

"Yeah, one of the last of the draftees in '70," I told him.

"'Nam?" he asked and I nodded.

"I've heard of Vista," Olsen said "Where exactly is it?"

"Right in the middle of the state," I answered.

"How big is it?" he asked.

"Oh, last census I think the population of the city itself was about half-million, but with all the surrounding and adjoining smaller towns, the whole area is probably closer to 750k."

"Wow!" Olsen said. "That's big. How big is the P.D.?"

I answered as I walked, "When I started we were only about 250 sworn, but in the early '90s, crime got out of control. The streets were literally running with blood. I'm not shittin' you. It was like Chicago is right now. That led our illustrious city leaders to realize that they'd better find some money to hire some more cops or they could kiss their cushy jobs adios, so by 2005 or so, we had about 800 sworn. Now though, with the bad economy and the budget woes, probably only half that number."

"Humph!" Sanchez replied, his aggravation obvious. "I see we're not the only ones having to plug twelve holes in the dike with only ten fingers." He looked me up and down again. "You retired pretty young."

I nodded. "I was tired. Thirty years in this business was enough. More, actually, if you count my Army Military Police time. Too many years of blood, screaming, gunfire, and bodies. Too many shouting suspects, crying victims, and damaged children. Had a bellyful of the politics of the staff weenies and city leaders—you know the story. I was just flat worn out, so I pulled the pin. Wife wanted me out at 20. I hung in there a couple more years, but when that little voice inside me started shouting that it was time to go, I finally listened. We sold the house and everything else, bought the RV, the truck, and the bike, and bailed out of California, destined for the adventurous life of retirement on the road. Hey—" I changed the subject, pointing to Olsen's ball cap. "—I thought all you Texas lawmen wore white cowboy hats?"

"Nah," he said. "That's just the glory boys. The rangers or the junior rangers."

I raised an eyebrow. "Junior rangers?"

"TSDPS," he replied. "Texas Department of Public Safety—highway patrol in California speak."

"Oh," I replied, hearing a bit of animosity, or envy, or maybe some of both in his statement.

As we neared the spot of my wife's discovery, I began leading the deputies in a semi-circle around to the southwest, attempting to pick up Sonya's tracks, explaining that we would approach over the same path, thus not contaminating the scene any more than necessary. I noticed both deputies exchanged quizzical glances, but they nodded their agreement. I related the entire story of our discovery, from the blown-out tire on the interstate, to my wife's near scream, to my armed response.

"What kind of pistol do *you* carry?" Sanchez asked as we approached the spot.

"Depends on the time of year," I replied.

"Oh, you're one of *those* guys, eh?" Olsen inquired. "A gun for every season?"

"Nah," I said. "I own a few, but I generally carry a sub-compact Kahr 9mm in the summer. I carry a compact Smith .45 in the cooler weather."

"Why switch?" he asked.

I was sure he was expecting some complicated "ballistic co-efficiency" answer. "Clothing," I told him. "Summer time I like to wear shorts and a tank and the Kahr is small."

"Mmmmm," Olsen replied, obviously thinking about having only six or seven shots in a small automatic.

I could read his mind. "I know, I know, you give up firepower for size but the object of the game is to *not* get yourself into shooting situations in the first place if you can avoid them."

"Amen to that," Sanchez interjected.

I smiled to myself. I could tell Olsen was still in that *carry-two-guns-and-100-rounds-of-ammo-even-when-you're off-duty* frame of mind, indicative of all young cops. I had been just like him when I was his age. A young, tough, bad-ass cop with a badge and a gun. Instead of that silly "To Protect and Serve" motto so often seen on the doors of patrol cars, it should have read "Don't fuck with me." At least on the cars that young coppers drove.

I found Sonya's and the dog's tracks and the three of us, now single file, turned and slowly made our way northeast along the same path. The tracks ended and we stopped. Olsen seemed taken aback by what he saw. He slowly pulled his sunglass down to the tip of his nose, his mouth agape.

Sanchez simply stared at the scene with an experienced eye, and after a minute he said, "Well, there's something you don't see every day."

I laughed out loud. Both looked at me not understanding why. "Same exact thing I said to my wife."

The scene before us in the sand looked like someone's Halloween porch display. Two intact, sun-bleached and weathered skeletons were laying face down together, perpendicular to each other. Any remnants of flesh or hair were long gone. Partially covering the legs of one of the skeletons were the tattered remains of what appeared to be blue wool pants with a faded yellow stripe, the feet still in rotting leather knee-high, cavalry-style, riding boots, complete with rusted spurs. No clothing of any type was visible on the other, save a small square of leather loin-cloth protruding from under the front of the pelvic girdle. The leather was in surprisingly good shape. Two large heavy bladed and very different, rusted knives were visible, also. One was laying in the sand next to the loin-clothed skeleton. The second was protruding from between the right side ribs of the booted one.

"From the looks of this, we got us one *very* old double homicide," Sanchez observed dryly.

"Will you be calling out your detectives and crime scene people?" I asked him.

Sanchez snorted. "Ol' buddy, you're looking at the only investigation team that'll be responding."

"You're it?" I asked, surprised.

"We're it," he replied. "Like I told ya, times are tough and there's no money to hire deputies, much less any kind of CSI people, so we handle our own investigations."

"What do you do if you run into something you can't handle? Or where do you do any evidence processing?"

Olsen spoke up. "Oh, we can call in the TSDPS crime scene folks for help if we need it. If it's got enough notoriety and enough press interest, the rangers like to take over and get their mugs on TV, but for the most part, it's just us."

"We do have a small crime lab of our own back at the main station," Sanchez said. "Doesn't get used that much, though."

"Wow! Well, good luck," I said to both. "You guys need anything else from me?"

They looked at each other, both wanting to ask, but neither one wanting to be the first to do so.

Finally Sanchez spoke up. "Hey listen, this isn't some gang-banger shot in an alley. We've never encountered anything this weird. We ahhh…"

I looked at him. "You guys need some help getting started with this thing?"

"Well," Sanchez said, smiling, "since you offered and since you are definitely the most experienced crime scene guy amongst us at the moment, it sure would help us out if you could give us some pointers."

"How much you gonna pay me?" I asked him. I could see he was struggling to find a way to tell me that no money would change hands. "Hey," I chuckled. "I'm just kidding you, *but* I do need to run this by the wife before I commit to anything. If she agrees to hang for a while, then yeah I'll help you out, but you should know, the way I see it, this isn't going to be a two hour project. Here's the way it's shaping up to me. It's noon now, and I still have a flat tire that needs to be changed. This scene is going to take some serious time. It'll have to be preserved overnight at least, possibly even longer." Then I asked them, "If the wife agrees and I do stay on and help you out a bit, I'm going to have to find an RV park or truck stop to plant the flag. I have an onboard generator, but I'd at least need water. Any suggestions?"

"This is your lucky day, or maybe this was all just meant to be," Sanchez replied. "As it so happens, there's a rancher I know, big horse ranch, has his place about six miles from this very spot. He's got a big motor home that he parks out near his stable across from the house and he keeps it hooked up there for guests. The parking spot has water, sewer, electric, the works. He owes me one for taking his drunken teenage son home instead of to 'Juvie' one summer night back in July, so if he's around, I'm sure he'd move his RV and let you park there for free."

"That'll work," I told him. "And the price is right for sure, but I can pay him if he balks at the free deal."

"Don't think he'd take any money from any friend of mine," Sanchez continued. "And besides, the guy is rich so it's not like he needs it. I'll make the call."

All three of us then turned back toward the road and our vehicles. I discussed with the two deputies how large an area to tape off surrounding the crime scene. I was thinking about Sonya's reaction to the fact that we might be staying here in the desert for a few days. Surprisingly, when I told her about the deputies' request and the possibility of having a place close by to stay for free, she reluctantly agreed, although I could see she wasn't particularly happy about being stuck in the RV, taking care of the dogs in the middle of nowhere, while I would be out here playing in the sandbox. She *was* placated somewhat when I told her that we'd be staying at a nearby horse ranch. Sonya, like most girls, loved horses.

I then went about the business of finishing up my hour-long, tire-changing chore. Just as I finished picking up my tools and cleaning my hands, Sanchez walked over to me.

"Just got off the phone," he said. "I talked to my rancher friend. His name is Frank Rollins. He's not actually at home right now, but he said it's no problem. He'll have his foreman move his RV and you can park there. I also talked to my lieutenant and brought him up to speed. He's going in right now to discuss all this with the sheriff, including your helping us out, I mean. At first, he wasn't hot on the idea at all. He's concerned about you having to go to court to testify at some point down the road, but I told him I wouldn't let you get into that situation, *and* that with your experience you could be probably of substantial help to us, so he agreed to pitch it to the boss but we'll see. My lieutenant is kind of a dick. He said he'll call me back in a few. Got your tire changed, I see."

"Yeah, what fun," I replied. "Getting damn hot out here now, too."

Sanchez's cell phone rang and he stepped away to speak privately for a few minutes. He then hung up from one call and made a second. After speaking and listening for several minutes, I heard him raise his voice a notch. "I don't care," he said to the person on the other end of the call. "Get hold of whoever is working Toyah today and have him go over to his house, wake his lazy ass up, and get both of them out here pronto! They are our only two reserve deputies and I want them out here like yesterday! "With that he hung up abruptly and walked back over to me.

I hadn't seen Olsen in a bit and I wondered where he'd gone.

"Here's the scoop," Sanchez said. "My lieutenant is on his way here. He said you can help but there's some conditions. No one talks to *anyone* about what we've got out here. The local news guys will get wind of it at some point I'm sure, but as far as anyone is concerned, we've just got another desert fatality and it's 'under investigation.'" He made quotation marks with his fingers then continued. "You're in an advisory position only here. He doesn't want you to take any direct action that could land you a subpoena down the road and, most importantly of all, he wants you to understand there's no pay involved, agreed?"

I frowned, wondering what I was about to get myself into. I was retired, after all, but I'd already agreed so I said, "Okay by me, I guess." I suspected that their wanting to keep this on the "down-low" was a pipe dream, for reasons they obviously hadn't thought of yet.

"I'm also trying to get our only two reserve deputies out here to stand-by overnight," Sanchez continued. "One of them tied one on last night at a wedding and they can't get him to answer the phone but we're going to send someone over to his place to wake him up. Hey, where'd my partner go?" he asked, looking around.

"I don't know," I replied. "Last I saw of him he was out there in the dirt putting out the crime scene tape."

Just then Olsen reappeared at the end of the RV. "Sorry to disappear on you," he said. "Had to take a leak."

"You get that all done out there," Sanchez asked him, nodding toward the scene tape.

Olsen nodded. "Yeah, just like we talked about."

I looked out across the dirt and could see a continuous line of yellow *POLICE LINE – DO NOT CROSS* crime scene tape tied between bushes and cactus surrounding the area. "Patrolling out here in the boonies like you do, you guys should ask your boss if you can get some of those thirty-six-inch, wooden, grade stakes for your tape," I told them. "Then you wouldn't have to look for brush to tie it to."

"Shit," Olsen replied. "We're lucky they still buy crime scene tape for us."

I shook my head, again wondering what I'd gotten myself into.

Sanchez's phone rang. He answered and again conversed in a muted tone for a good five minutes. Finally he hung up and turned to all of us. "Okay, our two reserve deputies will be heading out as soon as they get suited up. Jim, I'm going to ride with these folks over to the Rollins ranch. You stay here and keep an eye on things and when the reserves get here, clue them in on what we need then come pick me up. You remember where the ranch is?"

"Think so," Olsen replied. "Just off 2119 right?" he asked, referring to the designation of a local county road.

"That's it," Sanchez said, "Oh, yeah. One more thing. Remind our guys this is a crime scene out here and not to go poking around, or chatting up their friends or girlfriends about it. Stress that last one more than once. The less people that know about what Douglas's wife found out here the better, and women are not known for their propensity to keep secrets." Sanchez turned to me. "You don't mind if I ride with you folks out to the ranch, do you?" he asked. "I need to leave my partner the unit."

"Not at all," I replied.

Sanchez advised his dispatch over the air what he was doing and where we were headed. As the three of us climbed into my truck, Sonya gave Olsen one last flirtatious smile, knowing full well she was only pouring gasoline onto a fire. I shook my head. *Women.* With Sanchez's directions, I pointed our rig toward County Road 2119.

CHAPTER 2

The Ranch

Fifteen minutes later I turned off of the county road onto a single lane blacktop. After a mile or so, I turned again onto a gravel road which I could now see doubled as a very long driveway with desert on both sides. We passed under an arched sign over the road announcing that we were entering F-R Ranch, Inc. *Not very western-ish*, I thought, looking at the sign.

"Frank's from Los Angeles originally," Sanchez said as if reading my mind. "Made some money in the market in the '80s then left California for the wide open spaces."

"We've got something in common," I told him. "Except for the being rich part."

Sanchez snorted. "No shit, whoops, 'scuse my language, ma'am. All my life I've tried to avoid the pitfalls of the rich and I've succeeded." At that we all chuckled.

Sonya told him not to worry about his language around her. Nodding at me, she said, "I've lived with this gruff old ex-cop too long to be shocked by anything you might say."

Soon we approached several large green pastures on the right side of the gravel road, surrounded by white-painted, steel-pipe fences. Each pasture contained several beautifully groomed, long-legged horses. Roans, chestnuts, bays, and blacks. I was disappointed not to see any buckskins, which were my personal favorite. I was not an equine expert like Sonya. She had owned several horses growing up and had extensive knowledge of the four-legged beasts. I did have some experience with quarter horses however, having worked at a pack station during my summers as a teen and having ridden the horses of friends and rental stock as an adult. Both Sonya and I were comfortable on horseback.

As we drove along, paralleling the pastures, it was obvious these animals were all Thoroughbreds. Show-quality stock.

"They're beautiful!" Sonya exclaimed, thrilled at the thought of staying a few days in such close proximity to these animals. Soon we turned off the gravel road and onto an asphalt driveway leading to the house and stables. I could see Sanchez's buddy Frank Rollins had indeed made a great deal of money in the market. The house was immense. Probably somewhere in the vicinity of 14,000 square feet. It was a well-kept, two-story, ranch-style affair, with a six car garage and a matching guest house off to the side. Both were light tan with white trim and white porch railing. I assumed, correctly as it turned out, the guest house was the foreman's residence. The stables building was also huge and of a matching design and color scheme. It was separated from the main house by several hundred feet of what can only be described as grass-covered park, complete with large shade trees and a pond in the center.

"Wow!" Sonya exclaimed. "I don't think I'll mind hanging out here a few days."

We pulled to a stop and a man approached from the stables, wiping his hands on a red bandana. The man was Hispanic, somewhere in the vicinity of 45 years old, I thought, but it was hard to tell for sure. He wore faded blue jeans; scuffed cowboy boots; and a blue, well-worn western style shirt. A beige, sweat-stained, straw cowboy hat topped his head and leather work gloves protruded from his back pocket. Two rather ominous looking Doberman Pincers came bounding up behind him. The man gave a command in Spanish and both dogs sat down on their haunches. W*ow*! I thought. *Just like the dogs in the movies, or better yet* Magnum P.I.

We all got out of the truck. Sanchez stuck out his hand and greeted the man. "Hello Juan." They shook hands.

"*Hola*, Deputy Sanchez," the man replied. The two conversed briefly in Spanish then continued in English so as not to be rude.

"Juan, how many years have I told you to call me Frank? It should be easy, it's your boss's name."

"Si," the man replied, "but I don't call him Frank either."

Sanchez chuckled at that and turned toward me. "Juan, this is Jason Douglas and his wife Sonya. They're the folks that are going to stay here a few days on the RV site." Sanchez then explained to us that Juan was the foreman of the ranch, which, of course, we'd already figured out.

"Nice to meet you," I said, sticking out my hand.

"*Buenos dias*," he replied, shaking my hand then tipping his hat and nodding to Sonya. "*Buenos dias, senora.*" He turned back to Sanchez. "*Senior* Rollins is gone for a week. He flew his airplane to

Tucson for business, but I moved the *casa sobre ruedas*." He pointed. "Your friends can park right over there."

I looked over at the spot he was indicating near the side of the stable. *Sweet*! I thought as I spotted the site. The high roof covered an oversized concrete pad with a built-in stainless BBQ in one corner. There was an adjoining grass area with two large shade trees near the center. Between the trees was a red brick patio on which sat a large redwood gazebo, complete with matching glass-top table and eight chairs. Subdued outdoor patio lighting had been installed, as had a water mister for cooling the gazebo area. There were full hook-ups for not just one, but two RVs. I hadn't seen the second concrete pad behind the first when I first looked. Best of all, an above ground redwood hot tub sat in a second enclosed gazebo between the two RV pads.

Sonya again exclaimed her approval, "Horses, a great patio, *and* a hot tub? I can live with this for as long as you want me to Jason."

"Sonya," I said to her, looking around, "I've got an idea. Why don't *you* go help the deputies out in that hot, dusty, sweaty desert and *I'll* stay here."

She laughed. "No way, buddy. You go on and do your thing. I'll be just fine here, but if he gets bored—" She smiled mischievously. "—and you don't need him, send that handsome young-stud deputy to look in on me, and tell him to wear a Speedo for the hot tub." As an afterthought she added, "And be sure to call before *you* come back so I have enough time to slip him out the back window."

"You wish," I shot back. "Besides those trailer windows are too small. He'd get hung up by his wood on the way out."

She laughed at that mental picture. I could tell Sanchez wasn't sure what to make of our banter about Olsen. Sonya took him by the arm, assuring him that she was only kidding about his young partner. Together they ambled over to the gazebo to chat while I parked the rig and got it set up

It was late in the afternoon. The sun was nearing the western horizon when Olsen arrived and pulled up next to the RV pad. Sanchez walked over and they exchanged a few words, then both walked over to me. "Okay," Sanchez said. "We're gonna head back out to the scene and make sure our reserves don't need anything else. Do you want to drive out there tomorrow yourself? Or do you want us to pick you up?"

"Pick me up. The earlier the better. I'm an early riser," I replied. "Did your L-T ever make it out there?" I asked Olsen.

"Actually, no," he replied. "And he was kind of pissed when he called and found out you guys left, but after I explained everything to him and reminded him that the scene was secure and nothing was going anywhere, he calmed down a bit. He's kind of a dick."

"Yeah, that's what I heard," I said, looking at Sanchez. "Well, see you in the a.m. then."

With that they both got back in their unit and drove down the gravel road, leaving a small cloud of dust in their wake. Sonya and I settled in for the evening.

"Well," she said. "Quite the day, eh?"

"Oh, yeah," I replied, but I was already thinking about tomorrow.

It was full dark now and after setting up our little camp site, Sonya and I had made brief use of the hot tub. With supper over with and dishes done, I glanced over at my laptop which I had turned on out of habit when the electricity powered up. I was surprised to see all four internet-signal-strength bars full. I walked over and clicked on the Explorer icon. My home Yahoo screen popped up immediately.

"Huh," I said to no one in particular. "Guess I'm picking up this guy's Wi-Fi router from the house."

I wondered if it was password protected. It wasn't. I guessed owning all the surrounding land, this Frank Rollins wasn't worried about anyone poking around with a Wi-Fi scanner. *Cool,* I thought, *internet access. That'll be handy.* I brought up one of the many websites that had information about the Plains Indian Wars.

"What's bugging you," Sonya asked as we crawled into bed.

"There's something wrong with that deal out there," I replied. "But I can't put my finger on it."

"What do you mean?" she asked.

"Not sure," I said, going over the scene in my head

"What do you think those other guys wanted?" she asked.

I looked at her in surprise. "What other guys?"

"Back down on the Interstate overpass," she said. "I was sure you saw them. That's why I didn't mention it at the time."

I sat up. "No, we didn't see them. What were they doing?"

"They were watching you guys through binoculars. They looked my way, too, but mostly watched you guys."

"Did you see a car?" I asked her, now very interested.

"Two Harleys," she replied. "At least, I think they were Harleys. You know me and motorcycles. They sounded like Harley's when they started them, though."

"What did they look like?" I asked her.

"The guys? Or the bikes?"

"Both."

"They were too far off for me to see either very good," she said hesitantly as if searching her memory. "I could just tell that the bikes were dark colored, black maybe, and not like ours, no trunk or hard bags or any of that."

I knew she was referring to our Yamaha being a full-dress style motorcycle. Briefly, I wondered what *that* was all about, but I was too beat to think about it long. *Screw it, probably just looky-loos that saw the sheriff's SUV lights*, I decided. It didn't raise near the concern in my brain that it should have. I clicked off the overhead light and was snoring in less than five minutes.

CHAPTER 3

Bones

Beep! Beep! Beep! Beep! Beep!
I slapped at the alarm clock to shut it off. The luminous hands glowed in the dark. Four-thirty a.m. I lay there for a few minutes, trying to wake up. Finally, I punched the round face of the small, dim, battery-powered LED light on the wall near my head. They said hell hath no wrath like a scorned woman. Maybe so, but I knew for sure hell hath no wrath like my wife if I'd have flipped on the bright overhead light close to her face as she slept.

Pulling myself out of bed, I got the coffee started, showered, and shaved as the coffee dripped through the filter and into the pot. I slipped on my jeans, T-shirt, socks and…*boots, I guess. The desert is not a tennis shoe kind of place.* The elixir of life finally filled the pot. I loved my coffee. I had just finished my second cup when I saw headlights turning into the driveway, the vehicle stopping near the trailer. Our little dogs started going ape-shit, barking and whining. The Dobermans up at the house added their chorus to the symphony.

To my astonishment, Sonya didn't even roll over. After I got our two quieted down, I grabbed my day pack, stuffing it with a couple water bottles, some snacks, and my little Kahr 9mm with two extra magazines. I then opened the door and stepped out. It was clear and cool, but not cold. Stars were still visible in the sky. On the eastern horizon, the sun was getting ready to make its appearance.

The sheriff's department SUV, inside of which both deputies were seated, was idling as they waited for me. Before I stepped over to the unit, I grabbed a couple items out of my truck that I thought I might need and stuffed them in my pack. I then took a moment to look toward the rapidly lightening sky. This time of day, just before dawn, had always been my favorite. I smiled as I thought of all the hunting and fishing trips, and, of course, the camping trips with the kids over the years that had started just this same way. Most of the time I would be the only one up. For those who'd never experienced it, there was really nothing better than a hot cup of good coffee over a campfire in the cool early morning hours of the high country. *Yeah, maybe the desert, too, I guess. Dirt desert like this, not sand desert. Definitely not the beach*! I laughed at myself. I hated sand. Particularly *beach* sand!

One last sip of coffee and I sat the cup down on the gazebo table. I knew Sonya would not be happy I'd left it there, but I wasn't going to go back inside and get our little four-legged noise makers going again. She'd get over it.

"Morning, men. You, too, Deputy Olsen," I said, grinning as I opened the rear door of the SUV to sit behind Sanchez. This morning he was driving. Olsen at first gave me a puzzled look not understanding my greeting. Sanchez chuckled at the old joke.

"Morning," Olsen replied, then he finally got it. "Funny," he replied dryly. "We picked you up some coffee on our way here, but now I'm tempted to throw it out after that crack."

"Don't do that!" I replied. "I have to have my fix. I had some before you got here but I'll always take free coffee."

"By the way," Sanchez advised, "just wanted you to know, our lieutenant called Vista P.D. to check on your bona fides. He talked to your old boss, a Mike Macklin?"

I snorted. "Hope he said nice things about me."

Olsen spoke up then. "Our boss said that *your* boss told him you were a major pain in his ass almost constantly and that you were in hack with him a lot, but he also said you were one of the best crime scene guys he'd ever had and that your fingerprint skills were excellent."

"Nice to be appreciated."

Within the hour, we were back with the bones. After parking, Sanchez walked over to the two sleepy reserve deputies. Both were sitting in the front seat of an older model, dust-covered Ford Crown Victoria patrol car. He conversed with them for a few minutes, at the conclusion of which they started their car and headed back toward the interstate. Olsen and I were standing near the front of the SUV. Sanchez advised us as he walked up, "The guys said everything was quiet as a tomb out here last night, 'cept for the noisy trucks on the interstate. The only action was two guys on motorcycles who pulled off the freeway onto the road down there a-ways," he said, indicating the location with a nod.

This statement immediately caught my attention based on what my wife had related to me in bed. "What was up with that?"

"The reserves didn't know," he replied. "They thought one of them might be having bike trouble or some such, but after about ten minutes, they fired up, turned around, and got back on the freeway."

Coincidence? I wondered. I then filled them both in on what Sonya had told me the previous evening about the two guys on the Harleys.

"Well," Olsen said, retrieving an old Nikon 35mm SLR camera, a camera bag with extra film, and a stack of yellow plastic number stands from the back of the SUV, "it's gotta be coincidence, and if not, there's not much we can do about it now anyway."

Sanchez and I agreed, but I couldn't help but think how much I didn't like coincidences. The three of us turned and started walking out toward the crime scene tape.

"You guys still using film eh?" I asked.

"Yeah," Olsen replied. "They keep telling us one day we'll go digital, but so far nada. I keep hounding the L-T though."

"That's okay," I said. "That old F3 is a workhorse. The last of the metal bodied cameras. It'll take a pounding and still give you great shots. The only bad thing is having to carry and load film all the time." Olsen nodded his agreement. "You like photography?" I asked him.

"Yeah," he replied. "It's kind of a hobby. I took a couple classes when I was in college."

"Good for you. Where'd you go to school?"

"A and M."

"Rich gringo college boy," Sanchez said, grinning.

"Far from it," Olsen replied, aiming a half-hearted kick at Sanchez's butt, but missing as the man dodged. "More like buried-up-to-my-neck-in-student-loans boy. I'll be working out here for eternity just to pay them off."

"Well," I said sarcastically. "Good ol' 'Hope and Change' is promising to make our country a workers' paradise. A real friggin' Garden of Eden to hear him talk. He's gonna change wine into water, etc., etc., so you won't have to ever worry about paying them off." I was *not* a big fan of our current President.

"You one of those TEA Party terrorists I keep hearing about?" Sanchez asked.

"I'm not sure," I said. "If you mean do I think people should work hard and get to keep what they earn, and that we should be able to own guns to defend ourselves, *and* that the government should butt-the-hell out of our lives, then yeah, I guess I am."

Sanchez nodded. "Me, too."

"Me, three," Olsen muttered

The sun was full up, the sky cloudless, and the desert air smelled of sage as we neared the end of my wife's original tracks in the sand.

Olsen set his bag and number stands down. Sanchez immediately began to approach the skeleton duo. When he saw that I had stopped behind him, he paused and turned to me.

"Problem?" he asked.

"Look, this is a bit uncomfortable for me," I said. "I don't know how much you want me to interject, or interact with you guys in the course of your investigation, and I don't want to be stepping on your toes or acting like a know-it-all so to speak."

"Well, I appreciate that," Sanchez said, "but now that we've checked you out and heard you're good at what you do, don't be shy about making suggestions. All will be appreciated."

"Okay then," I told him. "My first suggestion would be for you to back up to me and let's eyeball this deal for a while."

This he did without reluctance, and we stood there, three abreast, looking at the area surrounding the skeletons. *There's still something wrong with this,* I thought, but I couldn't quite put it together. I didn't mention this to them yet. I let my eyes wander across the scene. "If it's okay with you guys, let's work from the scene-tape inward. We'll each take a section for examination so as to not be stepping all over each other. Jim, you take the upper section to the left there. I'll take the middle section, and Frank you take the section to the right."

Both agreed. Being careful not to encroach to closely to the skeletons yet, each of us worked our way around the perimeter, carefully examining the ground and brush. Olsen began taking a few photographs as he walked. He stopped and turned to me with a questioning look about his photography of the scene perimeter.

"You're doing fine," I told him. "Take your perimeter photos inward every few feet like the spokes of a wheel, and be sure to watch your light meter settings when you get around to the other side facing the sun. That can get a bit tricky. Shadows can be a problem also."

I didn't go into that much as I didn't want to overload him with information, but he surprised me with his response.

"You're talking about metering in the shade, not the sun right?"

I nodded. "Yeah, good. You already know about that, huh?"

"Well, we went over it in one of my classes but I haven't done it yet."

"No sweat," I told him. "When you want to take a shot of something that's in the shade, just get the lens into the shade, meter on the item, then back up out into the sun and take the shot without changing the setting. What's in the sun will be somewhat overexposed but the item in the shade will come out perfectly. Moot point now, though."

"How so," he asked.

I looked up at the partially cloudy sky. "No shadows to speak of right now."

He nodded and continued slowly walking, taking photos, and jotting down a few notes in his pocket notebook. After we were all satisfied there was nothing of interest save for the immediate area of the skeletons, we turned our attention to them.

The three of us approached the two, long-dead individuals. Sanchez and I knelt next to the booted one. I had suggested that Olsen stand back from us for two reasons, as I explained to him. The first was so as not to get too many people stirring up the ground near the skeletons, less we stomp on some small evidence items. The second was to have someone to keep the entire scene perspective in mind. This would be particularly important when it came time to prepare a sketch.

"Why sketch it if we have photos?" Olsen asked.

"Always need a sketch to fall back on in the off-chance that something happens to your film or photos," I replied. "It's also easier for anyone who was not at the scene, like say a jury member, to get it clear in their mind what the overall scene looked like. The sketch is almost like an overhead photo, and since you're the scene photographer, you also need to whip out a rough sketch."

"What will he use for some kind of permanent reference points for sketch measurements out here," Sanchez asked as he looked around.

Olsen seemed unsure of what we were referring to and I could tell he was not anxious to try something he'd never done before, but I wasn't going to let him off that easy. I had a solution already in mind. One I'd used many times before.

"When we get to that point," I told him, "I'll just pull my trusty little Garmin E-Trex backpacking GPS out of my pack here and we can use latitude and longitude coordinates as our starting points."

"Well," Sanchez said, "if it isn't 'Inspector Gadget.' I knew you'd come in handy."

As I turned back to the skeletons, I suddenly realized what had been bothering me about them. It was the sand, or more accurately the lack of it. There was no sand *inside* the skeletons, or covering any of the bones or the loin cloth. The skeletons were laying on the desert floor as if they'd died there yesterday.

"Okay, boys," I asked them both, nodding to the long-dead men. "What's wrong with this picture?"

After a few moments of study, Sanchez picked it up. "Son-of-a-bitch!" he exclaimed. "You're talking about why they're not partially covered in sand and dirt?"

"Yup," I replied. "With the wind out here in the desert, these two poor ol' souls should only be partially visible at best. I'm assuming this spot isn't any different than any other desert and is windy at times, yes?"

"Oh, yeah. It gets windy as hell out here many times," Sanchez said.

I reached out and grasped the rusty rowels of the spur on the right boot, gently lifting the remnants of the boot with the foot and lower leg bones inside. *No sand inside the boot either.* A small, tarnished, brass button rolled out onto the sand underneath.

"What about our wearing gloves?" Olsen asked as he saw me lift the boot.

"Not critical at this point," I replied as I gently lowered the boot back down. "Nothing here would be good for prints. Everything is too weathered, corroded, and rough. We *will* need them in a few minutes for handling the bones, clothing, and knives though," I said. "Got any gloves on you?" I asked Sanchez.

He looked in a small, black, basket-weave pouch on his duty belt. "Of course not," he replied. "I forgot to grab some before we walked out here. We have a box in the unit," he added and started to get up."

"Hold on," I said. "We'll get some in a bit. Like I said, not that critical for now, and besides, I have a back-up in case we need it." With that, I reached into my front pants pocket and pulled out an un-used doggie poop-bag, "Which one always carries when RV'ing with dogs since you never know where one of your dogs will take a crap and some grouchy old geezer in an RV park, with nothing better to do, reports to the manager that you didn't clean up after your dog."

Olsen rolled his eyes. "So this is what retirement is like, eh?"

"Better take a couple photos of the button before I pick it up," I told the young deputy. "Get one where it lays and it's relation to the boot it rolled out of." When he was done, I picked it up and exhaled a low whistle. The letters "US" with the numeral "4" directly underneath were still clearly visible stamped on the front side of the small brass orb.

"Wow!" Olsen exclaimed. "That looks like a military button."

"I'm sure it is," I said. "I suspected it yesterday when I saw the pieces of blue wool and these riding boots and spurs," I continued. "I'm a big western history buff so naturally, I did a bit of research on the web last night. Turns out that throughout the 1800s, all over west Texas, the Fourth US Cavalry engaged the Lipan and Mescalero Apache and the Comanche, which, by the way, probably makes our loin cloth guy there an Indian. I'm no real expert," I added, "but I'm going to venture that since it looks like he was only wearing a loin cloth—" I nodded to the leather piece protruding from under his pelvis.

"—and with no medicine-bead chest piece, or any other typical Comanche trappings, this guy was probably an Apache."

Sanchez looked at me with a raised eyebrow. "How do you know so much about Indians?"

"You're not being culturally sensitive, Deputy," I replied with a grin. "Native Americans."

"Whatever," he retorted. "Native Americans then."

"Like I said, I'm a history buff, and I'm also part Ogallala Sioux. Way back, like a great, great, great grandmother or some shit," I told him. "About an eighth or sixteenth as I recall. I got interested in my ancestry some years back and that, coupled with my love of history, led to my interest in the Plains Indian Wars. In particular, Custer's run-in with the Sioux, Cheyenne, and Arapaho at Little Big Horn. I researched the heck out of stuff. Read everything I could find. I even took vacation trips to the Little Big Horn National Battlefield, Wounded Knee, and Adobe Walls. If I'm right, and I'm pretty sure I am, you guys have a much bigger problem than just some old bones laying in the desert."

"How's that?" Olsen inquired.

"Well," I replied, "as soon as word of this gets out, you're going to have everyone and their brother crawling over this place. The US Army, Indian Affairs, local Indian tribal councils, Texas Rangers, archeologists, anthropologists, shit, maybe even the DHS and the FBI."

Without reply, Sanchez stood up and looked at me for a moment, scowling. He shook his head. "Douglas, you really know how to ruin a man's day. Time to call the boss." He then moved back to the well-worn trail we'd all made in the sand, removing his cell phone from his pocket. Olsen and I returned to the SUV for the box of gloves and some water.

It was past noon when the white, unmarked sheriff's car pulled to a stop in the gravel turn-out next to the SUV. The middle-aged Caucasian man that got out was wearing a wrinkled gray suit. Looking at him, I guessed him to be in his mid-to-late-fifties. He was short, no more than five-foot-seven or so, a bit on the heavy side, with a slight paunch. Not really fat, just stocky and carrying a few too many pounds like most of us over the age of 50. He had thinning red hair and a matching red face from sunburn, *or alcohol,* I thought. *Most likely both.* His necktie was pulled down loose, the white, sweat-stained shirt collar un-buttoned. His coat was open and, as he approached our small group, I could see a gold "lieutenant" star clipped to the front of his belt. A stainless-steel, compact, auto-loading pistol of some type rode in a holster farther back on his right hip.

Sanchez and Olsen both greeted him. "Hey, L-T. Hey, L-T."

The man nodded to both deputies, then, unsmiling, he turned to me. "So you're the one making my life difficult, eh?"

"Jason Douglas," I replied, sticking out my hand. He extended his and we shook hands. "Not intentionally," I said, making an attempt at levity. "As you say in this country, I was just passing through, Sheriff."

He didn't smile. "Lieutenant John Davis," he said. "You can call me Lieutenant Davis."

Uh oh, I thought. My "asshole warning light" in the far corner of my brain, which I thought had been disconnected for good when I'd retired and freed myself of guys like this, was flashing madly.

He turned back to Sanchez. "Show me," he said curtly.

Within a few minutes, the four of us were staring down at the two skeletons.

As we stood there, I watched this Lieutenant Davis. I knew his kind well and the look on his face I'd seen many times over the years. I knew he was thinking how his department, and more importantly, how he personally, could benefit from my wife's discovery. Figuring how he could work the Press and stand in front of the TV cameras and microphones and get the lion's share of the credit and who he could throw under the bus if it all went south.

"Shit," I mumbled under my breath. *Some things just never change. Staff weenies are all the same no matter what agency you work for.* I saw Sanchez shoot a quick glance at Olsen and roll his eyes. I hoped Sanchez was savvy enough to realize who the "under the bus guys" were going to be if it came to that. I made a decision right then to "unass this A.O." as soon as possible.

Tired of watching the gears of local politics turn in the lieutenant's head, I let my eyes wander for a brief moment, looking out at the vastness of the empty desert. I tried to imagine what had brought the lone cavalry trooper and the Indian warrior together out here alone where they locked in what appeared to be mortal hand-to-hand combat, if that was indeed what had happened.

I was still contemplating this when a small bright flash of silver light off in the distance caught my attention. It had come from the southwest near the interstate. It had only been visible for a brief second, but I was sure I'd seen it. *Reflection,* was my immediate thought. *Probably the chrome of a bumper or rearview mirror of a moving car or truck.* The light flashed again from the same spot, and this time I could tell it was stationary. Having spent time in tactical combat situations early in my life, I was sure of what it was after it flashed for the third time. We were under observation. The flash was the reflection of the sun off the lens of a pair of binoculars. Someone was watching us.

My attention was then drawn back to the lieutenant as he repeated his question which had been directed at me. "Have you talked to anyone about this?"

"Who would I talk to?" I answered. "I don't know anyone around here."

"No phone calls to anyone? No texts to your retired cop buddies or any of that smart-phone Twitter or Facebook crap?" he pressed.

"I said no one, didn't I?" I didn't need this guy's bullshit. "Look, Lieutenant Davis, if you don't want my help here, I'll bail. I've got no dog in this hunt." Irritation was obvious in my voice.

"Don't get your back up," he said. "We appreciate your help, but I needed to know."

Without waiting for a response, he turned to Sanchez. "I was going to call the Coroner's body pick-up guys from the funeral home out and have them pick up these bones," he said, "but I've changed my mind. I'm going to have one of the reserve deputies who's already been out here come back with our UC van and bring two body bags. I am *not* going to let this turn into a carnival out here and get out of our control. The Press doesn't have wind of this yet and I want it kept that way." Looking at the three of us, he said, "You guys can help him load it all up, and for God's sake don't get the bones mixed up." Rolling the brass button we'd discovered between his fingers and looking at it thoughtfully, he added, "Talk to nobody. You let me worry about the fallout from this little moment in Texas history."

Handing the button back to Olsen, Davis continued. "I want everything brought in with the skeletons. I want it all kept together, so you guys find everything you can and pack it up with them, and I mean *every little piece* of anything that is involved with these two ol' boys. It'll take the reserve a couple hours to get out here by the time we wake him up, *again*, and he picks up the van. That should give you enough time to take plenty of photos and do a thorough search. You make sure the area is scrubbed clean. I want this desert back to being nothing but desert when you leave. Who's taking the photos?" he asked then seeing the camera around Olsen's neck, he nodded at it. "Okay then, Olsen, I want all that film on my desk when you get back. Do not take it back to the state's photo lab. I want this contained to our little group. We clear on all this gentlemen?"

Both deputies replied with a, "Yes, sir."

I just nodded my affirmation to him.

He gave me a hard stare. "Any of this shows up on the six o'clock news and I'll have someone's ass!" He turned abruptly and walked back toward his car. "When you're done here, Mr. Douglas," he tossed

back over his shoulder, "you can be on your way to wherever it is retired cops go for the winter, and ah, thanks."

"Irritating little prick, isn't he?" Sanchez made it a statement more
than a question as soon as Davis was out of earshot.

"Seen lots like him," I replied and couldn't help but think, as I
watched this strutting peacock, that his trying to orchestrate control
over all of this would not end well, particularly now that I was sure
someone else knew we were out here. I had held back that little bit of
information. *Screw it, not for sure about that anyway,* I told myself.
Oh well, hopefully I would be sitting in my folding chair back in Yuma, sipping my "Buffalo Trace" bourbon when this all came apart.
Unfortunately, I would soon learn this was not to be.

With my help and suggestions on camera angles and settings, Olsen
took a lot of photographs. It was a cloudless late afternoon now, and
shadows cast from the surrounding brush and cactus were indeed coming into play. Olsen did get a chance to take photos in the shade, after
all. A breeze had come up, but I was still comfortable in my T-shirt
and jeans. Gloved up now, Sanchez and I carefully moved the bones
aside. Under the skeletons we discovered several additional uniform
buttons, a single rotting moccasin, the remainder of the warrior's loin
cloth, and a remarkably well preserved leather belt and holster, complete with a tarnished brass buckle also embossed with the same US 4
logo. Curiously though, no revolver or ammunition, no rifle, no bow or
arrows, nor any other personal items, just the two knives.

"Odd that some of these guys' stuff is here with them, and some
isn't," I told the two deputies. "And have you noticed the trooper is
wearing his spurs but there's no trace of a saddle, tack, or horse bones?
Which means they were both on foot. Oh, yeah, and no canteen in the
case of the trooper, or gut bag in the case of the Indian. I could maybe
see the gut bag being gone from decomposition, or maybe he never had
one, but the canteen would have been tin, so at least part of it should
still be around."

Olsen spoke up. "Why the hell would they both be out here on foot
in the desert without water?"

Looking at him, I said, "I don't think they were," relaying a suspicion I'd had in my head all along.

Sanchez's puzzled look changed to one of surprise as it suddenly
came together for him also.

"This stuff was planted out here!" he said, looking down.

"Dick-fucking Tracy," I replied. "Now you got it."

After a moment, Olsen asked, "Why would someone go to all that
trouble? And how could whoever did it, be certain someone would find
it?"

I looked at both of them. "Those are the perplexing questions, aren't they?" I mused, thinking that maybe I wouldn't be leaving for Yuma tomorrow, after all. "I don't know the answer to the first, but the second one is easy. All it would take is an anonymous phone call."

"But there hasn't been such a call," Sanchez interjected.

I looked at him. "Maybe we found it before they wanted it found or had a chance to call."

Just before sunset, a light tan Ford panel van pulled into the turnout and stopped next to the SUV. I recognized the driver as one of the reserve deputies I had seen earlier that morning. The three of us had finished searching the area, and Olsen had finished both his photography and, with my help, his sketch. My hand held GPS had indeed worked well for the measurements. Both deputies had been impressed with that little trick, and Sanchez said he was going to try to get the sheriff's department to buy one. If not, he said he'd buy one himself. He turned to guide the driver of the van, not wanting the vehicle stuck in the sand, as it drove out to us. At his direction, the reserve deputy turned the van around and backed across the sand, brush, and rocks to a spot fifteen feet from our skeletons. Sanchez opened the double back doors and, with the aid of the reserve deputy, we began loading the bones and all of the personal effects of the two, long-dead Texans into two separate olive green body bags.

Making certain we had recovered all there was, Sanchez let the reserve deputy depart for the morgue. The man told us before he left that Davis had made arrangements for the bones and other effects to be placed in an isolated biohazard containment room at the morgue, thus guarantying no prying eyes could find them until the sheriff wanted the word to get out.

As Olsen carried his camera, film, sketch, and unused number stands back to the SUV, Sanchez and I broke off large pieces of brush and began to systematically sweep all traces of our tracks, including my wife's and the dog's, from the sand. It was a slow process as we had to walk backward for most of it, but by the time we had worked our way back to the turnout, the desert, or at least this little piece of it, showed no trace that anyone had ever been there.

CHAPTER 4

The Visitor

It was full dark by the time the three of us climbed into the SUV for the trip back to my trailer. As we pulled out onto the old blacktop road toward County Rd 2119, a small red tail light was visible some distance ahead of us. The dim, red glow from the light brightly flared as the vehicle's brakes were applied. *Motorcycle,* I thought, as the rider made a left turn toward the on-ramp to westbound I-20. *Another coincidence*? Sanchez and Olsen, both weary from the day's outdoor chores, didn't realize what they had just seen, but I did.

"Umm guys," I said to them." I think we may have a problem."

Olsen turned toward me in his seat, a questioning look on his face. I saw Sanchez's eyes looking at me in the rearview mirror and knew he was also curious about my statement.

"You see that bike in front of us a minute ago?" I asked.

"Saw it," Sanchez said, "but I really wasn't paying them much attention."

"I didn't notice it," Olsen replied.

"I think the rider might be the one who's been watching us all day," I said, and I proceeded to tell them about the reflection I'd spotted earlier. Sanchez punched the accelerator, and the big V-8 in the Ford SUV responded, pushing us all back in our seats. He made a good try for the spot where the bike had turned, attempting to catch up, or at least catch a glimpse of the plate, but it was in vain. When he reached the intersection a few seconds later, the only tail lights visible were those on the interstate three quarters of a mile south of us. After a brief pause, Sanchez turned the SUV in the opposite direction toward my temporary horse-ranch home.

It was almost 9:00 p.m. when Sanchez pulled up next to my trailer. "We'll get hold of you tomorrow morning after we talk to the lieutenant," he said. "He doesn't see us needing you to hang around anymore.

Personally, I'd like you to stick around a couple days but I'll check with him and let you know."

I nodded and said good night. The bedroom lights were still on as I stepped in.

Sonja was lying in bed reading one of her tabloid magazines. She looked up. "How'd it go today?"

"I really didn't do too much except stand there and act like I knew what I was doing. One thing though, I think there's a lot more to this than finding some old bones in the desert." I then proceeded to give her a brief review of the day's events.

"Wow," she replied. "Weird."

I agreed as I stripped down for a quick shower. "And what did you do all day?"

"Well after my coffee, the dogs and I took a long walk around this place. It is magnificent," she replied. "We were down the gravel road admiring the horses, when that foreman Juan came by in one of those two seat quad-things."

"Like a Rhino?" I asked.

"That's it. In fact it is a Rhino," she said. "Anyway, he came by and we chatted a bit. He's really quite nice. We got to talking about horses and after finding out I'd owned a couple over the years, he asked me if I wanted to go riding."

"Not on one of these million dollar race horses I hope!" I said startled. Visions of one of these animals coming up lame or stepping in a hole while she was riding it was suddenly thrust into my head.

"No silly, I wouldn't have wanted to do that. Well, I might want to but I wouldn't do it. As it turns out, they have some regular riding stock. Several Quarter Horses for the owner's grandkids to ride when they come to visit. He picked out a gelding for me to ride. I had to put him on a lunge line for a while to get the green off of him, but after a bit of exercise we got along just fine. I rode most of the day in fact, and afterward, I helped Juan put out some oats and muck out a few of the stalls in the barn—whoops!" she corrected. "*Stables* I guess rich people call it."

As she told her story, I noticed the bed sheet slipping down and I could see by her exposed breasts she was nude. My wife only sleeps nude for one reason. Being around the smell of horses, hay, and a sweaty cowboy all day had obviously made her horny. Standing there naked by the bed, she could see by my growing erection that I was indeed interested, also. After my abbreviated shower, I turned the lights off, kicked the dogs out of the bedroom, put on some light jazz, and tumbled into her arms, both of us kissing, stroking, and exploring each other's bodies with our fingers, mouths, and tongues—the way experienced lovers do. Our lovemaking was both gentle and rough. Both fast and slow. After all these years together, we knew each other's desires well.

Over the next hour, I was able to make her climax twice before I finally allowed myself to do the same. We lay for a while, our arms and legs intertwined, discussing the possibility of a second go-round, but we were both relaxed now and we drifted off to sleep without bringing it to fruition.

જ⁄ઝ⁄ઝ

As with many animals, mother nature had equipped horses with good defense mechanisms. Powerful hoofs, the ability to run fast, good vision, a particularly keen sense of smell, and exceptional hearing. It was all part of primal survival evolution. These highly tuned senses would alert horses to danger, long before anything seemed amiss to humans. Over the years, many a cowboy's life had been saved by these acute equine powers.

I awoke suddenly in the darkness of the bedroom, at first unaware of what had brought me out of my slumber. A familiar uneasiness crept over me, though it was a feeling I hadn't had in a very long time. Call it a sixth sense, instinct, intuition, or whatever you want. Those who had spent any amount of time in life-threatening environments such as combat or even police work and survived, developed this little voice inside their head—a voice with a simple message, "Listen to me and live. Ignore me and die."

I punched the small button on my watch and the blue Indiglo screen indicated 3 a.m. I took notice of how quiet it was as I lay there in the dark, listening. The quiet was broken then as one of the horses in the pasture at the other end of the stables suddenly whinnied. Seconds later, a horse inside the stables snorted loudly. I heard it's hoof "thump" against the side of his stall. Now I could hear several of the animals in the stables moving around in their stalls. To most people it would mean nothing, but I knew it indicated the horses were uneasy. Sonja was awake now, too.

"Jason, did you hear the horses?" she whispered, their agitation not lost on her.

"Shhhhhhhh. Yeah," I replied softly, listening. "Probably just a coyote."

I tried to play down my concern. Thinking that horses normally do not go on full alert like this for a coyote, as those predators are not much of a threat to a full-grown horse. A mountain lion would set the horses off yes, but I didn't think there were any around here—still, you never knew. Finally, one of the Dobermans up near the house let out a single bark. Reaching down to the black nylon holster attached to the wooden side of the bed, I pulled my Smith & Wesson .45 auto from the holster's grasp. I also picked up my Fenix tactical flashlight and an extra magazine for the Smith, both of which I kept on the floor beneath the holster. I moved the privacy shade on the window next to my head slightly and peeked out. The entire area on this end of the stables, which included the back side of the RV site, was fairly well lit from two large quartz/halogen floodlights mounted high on the front wall of the stables. This made it a pain to get to sleep at times, but I was glad for the illumination now. *Nothing moving out there, but that's not surprising. No critter, or crook for that matter, would creep around close to the front of the stables in that light.* I turned my attention to the other side of the trailer as I walked slowly across the bedroom floor, trying not to make any noise. I knew the two steps down into the living room area would be a problem, as both had a tendency to creak slightly when stepped on

Walking as lightly as my six-foot-two-hundred-twenty-pound frame would allow, I moved to the larger bedroom window just above the dresser, and again, moved the shade aside ever-so-slightly. Looking out toward the tree shaded park with the pond, I caught the faintest hint of movement in the shadows on the back side of the gazebo. The gazebo itself, as well as the table and chairs under it were dark. The patio lights were all on a timer and had automatically shut themselves off at midnight. *Great,* I thought. *As soon as I step out the door, I'll be silhouetted against the lights from the stables. If it's only a coyote, or some other desert critter creeping around out there, no sweat, but if it's a person, this is not the situation I want to be in.* I needed an advantage.

I opened my top dresser drawer and took out my Zenit night vision monocular. I'd purchased the thing several years ago when Big 5 Sporting Goods had it on sale. At the time I didn't know what I'd ever really need it for. It was a gadget, and I just loved gadgets, much to Sonya's chagrin. I smiled remembering how she'd rolled her eyes when I showed it to her, saying I'd "wasted money" on it.

"But it was on sale," I'd told her.

That didn't help. It had stayed under the back seat of the truck since, unused except as entertainment on several camping trips. Two weeks ago on a whim while cleaning my truck, I decided to move the thing inside the RV, throwing it in my top drawer. I now patted myself on the back for doing so, even though it was just a lucky fluke. With the monocular added to my defenses, I moved out of the bedroom, carefully and quietly stepping completely over both steps, and down into the living room.

Moving to the dinette table bench, I positioned myself so as to be able to look out under the privacy shade of the dinette window after I'd lifted it slightly. Placing the monocular to my eye, I focused it as best I could. The landscape of the gazebo and the park beyond came into view and was cast in the eerie green image of the monocular. I couldn't see very far, though. I remembered the little device had an IR—Infrared—projection button on the side of the unit. When the button was pressed, a small infrared beam was projected out from the side of the unit, extending the visual range and clarity dramatically. With the aid of infrared light, I was now able to see most of the park, including the pond. Several ducks were visible roosting in the grass at the near edge of the water. The fact that they were unmoving and quiet led me to the conclusion that I should focus my attention elsewhere. I continued to scan the surrounding darkness. All was still, quiet, and dark.

Honk! Honk! Honk! Honk!

The noise from my blaring truck horn and the flashing of the headlights made me jump a foot into the air. The dim green light of the monocular changed to bright green as the now flashing headlights of my truck shown out into the darkness overloading the diode inside the unit and completely ruining my night vision

"What the *fuck*?" I said out loud, pulling the monocular away from my eye.

Both dogs up at the house were now barking madly, multiple horses were whinnying, and the ducks were now quacking and launching themselves into the water of the pond. Lights came on up at the house. Additional lights came on in the park and on the outside of the stables, all obviously controlled from the central location of the house. *Christ*! I thought as everything lit up like Times Square on New Year's Eve. *What the hell happened*? Several thoughts entered my racing mind simultaneously. I turned then and saw Sonya standing in the bedroom doorway with the truck key remote in her hand.

"I wanted to help," she said sheepishly. "And I remembered what you'd said about using the panic button on the truck alarm." She grimaced. "Did I help or hurt?" She again punched the remote button to shut the truck alarm off.

"It's all good," I said, my heart now slowing to a reliable rhythm. "After all my preaching to you and the girls about using that thing for a personal alarm, I didn't even think of it. Next time though, give me a little warning. I damn near shit myself when that alarm went off."

I flipped on the outside lights of the trailer and threw on my jeans, then stuck my pistol in my waistband, grabbed my tactical light, and opened the door. As I stepped down onto the concrete, I could see the two seat Rhino barreling toward me down the driveway from the guest house. A handheld spotlight was being used by the driver, Juan no doubt, to illuminate the few dark nooks and crannies not lit up by the surrounding lights. The machine stopped next to my truck. Both dogs were in the utility bed of the vehicle, growling now and looking at me with malice in their eyes. With a command, Juan silenced them both. In a rack attached to the dash, within easy reach of his right hand, I also noted the Ruger Mini-14 semi-automatic rifle an Aimpoint, red-dot sight and a high capacity magazine attached. *Gotta love Texas.*

As he pulled to a stop, he turned off the spotlight and stepped out of the vehicle. Sonya, now in her bathrobe, came down the steps behind me, struggling to keep our two killer dogs inside. Juan greeted both of us, and we him. With the combination of Sonya's scent, whom of course they'd been around all day, and Juan's friendly greeting to me, the Dobermans decided they would tolerate me. They turned their attention back to Juan. He gave an audible command, again in Spanish. Both leapt from the bed, gave Sonya and I a quick cursory sniff, then immediately turned and ran into the park beyond the gazebo, their noses to the ground. The ranch foreman took a look around the grounds.

"Animal you think?" I asked him.

"It eeess possible, but I do not think so, *senior*," he replied. "We have, of course, coyotes and *Javelina*, but they do not come near the house or stables much anymore," he said, nodding to the rifle in the rack and then to the dogs. "They learn quickly." Seeing the .45 auto stuck in my waistband, and the flashlight in my hand, he continued. "I see you are prepared for any eventuality, also. I hope you are not a novice in its use?" he asked, clearly trying to determine if I was just another dummy that liked to wave a gun around.

"No, I'm not a novice with a firearm," I said in an attempt to reassure him. "Been around guns all my life. A hunter, soldier, and a cop."

"That eeess good," he replied, "I'll sleep better at night."

I chuckled at that one. I'd already decided Juan was not a "novice" with his rifle either. The three of us stood there chatting for a while as the dogs continued to nose around. Suddenly the Dobermans alerted to something at the far end of the park, near the gate from the gravel road onto the asphalt driveway. The sky in the east was starting to lighten.

"I will drive over there to see what they have found," Juan said. "Would you both like to join me?"

"Sure," I replied, "just let me grab a shirt."

Sonya declined, saying she was going back to bed. A few minutes later the two of us arrived at the gate and joined the agitated dogs. They were sniffing intently at some brush just outside the fence.

"They definitely smell something," I told him.

"Si," he replied. "They run this park every day, chasing the ducks and rabbits for fun. They know all the scents here like they know each other's. This is something new I am sure."

I watched them for a moment then walked out the gate and onto the gravel road. Turning down the road toward the corrals, I examined the surface beneath my feet as I walked. The loose dirt between the large pieces of aggregate was home to a variety of tire tracks. I recognized those of my truck and trailer, and the two seat Rhino. Along the edge of the road on the corral side, I spotted several athletic type shoe tracks. From all my years looking at and comparing shoe tracks from crime scenes, I recognized them as the tracks of Sonya's tennis shoes. It was not just the length of the track, but both the pattern of the tread and the Nike swoosh, which was clearly visible in the ball of one of the shoes. I smiled to myself as the term "class characteristics" came to mind.

Memories of tracks from many past crime scenes came flooding back. Several tracks from the Dobermans mixed with shod horse tracks were visible over the top of hers. I bent down to see if I was still adept at spotting any individual characteristics. *Ah, there it is.* I could see the misshapen imprint in the dirt from the toe of her right shoe that had melted back in June when she propped her feet up too close to a neighbor's fire pit. Standing up, I realized I had not had a chance to take a leak this morning. I turned and walked back to the gate looking for a large bush to water. *Ah, there,* I thought with relief. A spot just past the gate near the white rail fence that was mostly concealed by roadside brush. It was on the other side of the fence from the area where the dogs were still sniffing around, but it was the only nearby cover and I didn't know Juan well enough just to "drop trou" out in the open and piss on his road.

I weaved my way into the bushes, unzipping my jeans as I walked, looking down and trying to speed up the process when I halted suddenly.

The ground was soft and damp from the run-off of the park sprinklers on the other side of the fence. I'd always heard the expression, "There I was, standing there with my dick hanging out," only this time it was not just an expression. I was standing there just so, the need to empty my bladder temporarily forgotten. There at my feet, in a small patch of the bare damp soil completely surrounded by brush, was a near perfect boot track. A heavy lug design on the sole similar to those used on work boots, police duty boots, hiking boots, or—*biker boots, maybe*? I wondered, thinking of the Harley riders Sonya had seen. I tucked myself back into my pants and called out to Juan to put the dogs away and join me.

After ordering the dogs back into the ATV, he walked over. As he approached, I squatted so as to look at the track more closely. The track was pointed away from the fence, toward the gravel road. It had been made by a right boot and was about eleven inches long. There were heavy square lugs on the outer edges and X-shaped lugs on the heel and ball. The very common "Oil Resistant" inlay was plainly visible between the two. I examined it closely, in hopes of seeing something individual as well, such as a missing or gouged lug, or maybe a distinctive wear pattern on the heel or sole. I spotted the latter immediately. The heel was severely worn on the outside rear edge.

Juan worked his way through the brush too me. "I called Deputy Sanchez," he said. "They should be here in no more than a few minutes."

I nodded. "Take a look." I pointed at the track with the beam of my flashlight He looked down. "You always wear cowboy boots don't you?" I asked him.

"Most days," he replied. Noting the type of track it was, he continued, "The only time I wear other boots like that is when I have brush clearing or wood cutting to do."

"Were you over here in work boots in the past couple days?" I asked.

"No, *senior*," he replied. "I have not been over here in weeks, as you can tell by the bushes that have grown out of control. I was going to come over here and cut them back, but I have not had time to do it yet. My boots do not have bottoms like that, and my feet are *poquito*— how you say?—very smaller," he said. Then he asked a question of his own. "Why were you in this brush, *senior*? Did you see something from the road?"

"No," I replied. "I was looking for a place to pee."

"Ah," he said, smiling, then looking back at the track, he clearly noticed it was pointing away from the fence.

I could see from his face he was confused by the direction of the track, so I decided to help him understand. "This track is recent. Most likely from our visitor this morning. What time did you turn on the sprinklers on the grass last night?"

"They are on a timer," Juan replied. "They came on at 1:00 a.m. and shut off thirty minutes later."

"Okay," I told him, "so we know this track was made sometime after the sprinklers shut off at 1:30. See how the edges are sharp and there's nothing in the track like particles of leaves or dirt?" He nodded, so I continued. "It's on the outside of the fence and is pointed toward the road so he, and I'm assuming it was a 'he,' was headed back to the road. The heel of the track is a lot deeper in the dirt than the sole, and the lug marks under the toe are distorted, pushed back sort of. That tells me he was probably running after having come through, or over, the fence." I looked out into the darkness thinking out loud. "Yeah, this was our morning caller."

"Why are there no more tracks here?" Juan asked.

Good question, I thought, taking a minute to gather my thoughts.

"On that side—" I jerked my chin, indicating the inside of the fence. "—the asphalt comes right up to the fence. On this side, this small spot right here is the only bare dirt not covered with brush, gravel or weeds. It's also the only place there was enough water from the run-off to wet the ground enough to hold a track."

Juan looked around accessing my hypothesis, then turned to me and nodded. "You are smart at this, *senior*," he said. "Do you think you could match this track to someone like they do on TV?"

"Not at this point," I responded with a chuckle. "First of all, I'd have to have special photos of this track, or a plaster cast of it, or preferably both. Then I'd need the boot to compare the track with. I could say it was the same approximate size and had the same pattern of sole and similar heel wear. Hell, I could even say the dirt found on the bottom of the boot was similar in texture, color, and consistency to this dirt here. But without anything else to go on, I could not say it was an exact match. It just doesn't work like they show on TV. Besides," I continued, "we don't know *for sure* this track was from our early morning caller. I, myself, am pretty sure, but there's lots of people that wear boots with soles like this. Could've been someone just out hiking."

Juan nodded but by his skeptical expression I could tell he didn't believe that for a minute. That was okay, neither did I.

The sun was full up as we pulled back up to the RV. Sonya considered herself presentable as she was dressed in her usual tight jeans and T-shirt with her hair combed and her lipstick on. She had made some coffee and the three of us were enjoying a cup. We were still talking about the night's events when the sheriff's department SUV with the two now-familiar lawmen inside turned off of the gravel road onto the driveway, stopping next to our rig.

"Morning folks. Got here as quick as we could after we logged on," Olsen said as both deputies got out of their vehicle. Today he wasn't *quite* as obvious about staring at Sonya's T-shirt. Both deputies were, however, staring at the dogs in the back of the Rhino. Both Dobermans silently watched them in return. Dogs didn't like uniforms.

"They know me but they still scare the shit out of me," Sanchez said, nodding to the dogs.

"They like you," Juan returned.

"Yeah," I snorted, "they like you for breakfast."

"They'd like us as a doggie breakfast burrito," Olsen chimed in, casting a wary eye their way.

"Well, I think they're sweet," Sonya said as she walked over to them and began to scratch both their ears. At this, both dogs dismissed the deputies and competed for her attention. Our two little mutts didn't like the uniforms either. Both were barking at the deputies. *Dogs are funny,* I thought. The Dobermans could have had our dogs for a snack, but after Sonya had "introduced" them to each other the previous day, the four canines had gotten along just fine, even playing together in the park for a bit.

Noticing the pistol stuck in my belt, Sanchez asked if we had found any indication whether our early morning visitor had been man or beast.

"Maybe," I replied. "I found a good boot track over by the gate."

"Really? Let's check it out," said Olsen.

As Juan and Sonya continued to fuss with the dogs, the two deputies and myself walked to the gate.

"How the hell did you find it in this brush in the dark?" Sanchez asked with a bit of suspicion in his voice. I knew he was considering the "hero complex."

"Don't worry, Deputy," I told Sanchez. "I know what you're thinking, but it isn't one of ours. While Juan and I were checking the area, I was looking for a spot to take a leak and those were the only tall bushes around."

"Where was Juan when you found the track?" Sanchez asked, not quite ready to let it go.

"Right there with the dogs." I indicated a spot on the grass only twenty feet from the track. "He was pretty much watching me the whole time, until I unzipped my fly that is. Couple seconds later I called him over here. He's wearing cowboy boots by the way, and as you can see I'm in 'hikers.'"

This seemed to satisfy his questions. Olsen asked Sanchez if photos of the track were in order.

Sanchez looked at Juan and asked, "You want to make an official prowler report, Juan?"

"I do not think so, Deputy," Juan replied, looking at me for some possible guidance. I didn't respond so he continued. "Mr. Rollins would not want it, I think, unless something worse had happened."

"Just as well," Sanchez replied. "If we took a report, we'd need to take photos of the track and we don't have any shoe track photo equipment."

Juan shrugged and the two of them walked off, talking, leaving Olsen and myself looking down at the track.

I was puzzled, so I asked Olsen, "So if you guys get a crime scene that *does* need shoe track photos taken, what do you do?"

"Oh," he replied, "we usually call in the state cops' crime scene guys."

"What if they are busy?" I asked him.

"Then we wait, or we blow it off," he said.

"That's a fucked up system," I told him.

"Yep," he replied

"Okay, shoe-track photos 101. All you need is a camera with a detachable flash, which you've already got, a flash sync cord so you can hold it out to the side, some black and white film, and a tape measure."

"But what about a special stand to hold the camera?" he asked, "and why black and white film?" he added as an afterthought.

"Man, this is like playing cards with my brother's kids," I said, smiling and shaking my head. "A camera stand, or even an adjustable tri-pod that can point straight down for that matter, definitely makes it more convenient, but it's not absolutely necessary. A stand gives you a fixed and known distance from the track to the lens when you print the photos out for a 1:1 comparison later, and it frees up your hands when you're taking your photos, but you don't *have* to have it. You can just free hand it as long as you have someone to help you hold all your stuff like the flash unit. The black and white film offers better contrast in the photo, again for comparison purposes."

Olsen nodded, but I could tell he did not fully understand the entire process. Engrossed in the conversation, neither of us noticed that Juan and Sanchez had walked up behind us, listening.

"Do you have anything in your camera bag in the SUV, besides just your camera?" I asked Olsen.

"Just a flash sync cord which I've never used," he replied.

I looked around at Sanchez. "You have any objection to me doing some shoe track training with your young partner here on this track?"

"Not at all," he replied. "I'd like to see how myself. I haven't done anything like it since the academy and we've got no calls holding right now. Before I forget, though, we had another reason for coming out here besides Juan's phone call." I looked at him, raising an eyebrow. "We got a BOL over the wire last night. There were two thefts that I think you'll find interesting. The first was ten days ago from the Texas

State Cemetery. Someone dug up the remains of a Fourth US Cavalry trooper." "The second was—"

"Let me guess," I interrupted. "Indian remains?"

"Yep," Sanchez replied. "Apache, but not from that Texas cemetery, or any other in this state, for that matter. These remains were dug up and stolen, two days after the trooper, from the Apache Cemetery at Ft. Sill Oklahoma."

"No leads I suppose? Or any indication as to why they would turn up in the desert outside of Pecos?"

"Nope," he replied. "But Lieutenant Davis is already setting up a press conference about our office's remarkable recovery of both sets of remains."

Shaking my head, I turned and walked toward my truck to gather a few items to help Olsen learn about shoe track photos.

"Hope he spells my name right," I shot back over my shoulder.

"I said *RE*-covery, not *DIS*-covery," Sanchez replied. "I seriously doubt anyone's name but his will come up."

"Humph!" I grunted. "What a surprise." As Olsen retrieved his camera from the SUV, I told him, "I've got some stuff that'll help us in my tool box. It's' too bad you don't have any black and white film in that camera case, but we'll just have to wing it with color film. I'll be right back," I said, walking away.

Within minutes, Sanchez, Olsen, and I were again standing next to the shoe track. Juan, accompanied by the Dobermans, had driven off to the stables to start his daily chores of caring for the horses. Sonya opted to go with him to help feed and curry the animals. She didn't consider that a chore at all.

Removing a steel tape measure and a small steel ruler from my pocket, both of which I had retrieved from my tool box, I began explaining the finer points of taking crime scene shoe track photos to the two deputies. Over the next hour, I explained things such as what focal length setting on the lens would reproduce the best photographs and how to use the tape measure to find the desired height of the camera over the track if you were without a camera stand. I demonstrated how to place the ruler next to the track to show the proper scale and how to operate the flash at an angle when it was detached from the camera. I showed them how to draw a small north arrow on a piece of paper and place it next to the track so it would be in the photo to show direction. I even showed them how to shade the track with a piece of wood or cardboard, so as to make the flash effective in bright sunlight. Olsen made notes to himself the entire time, and I found I enjoyed imparting my knowledge to them, more so than I would've thought. When we finished, both deputies were impressed.

"I guess you do know a lot about this crime scene stuff," Sanchez said, Olsen agreeing.

I took a dramatic bow and held my hands over my head and, to an imaginary audience, said, "Thank you. Good Night."

"Wise ass," Sanchez mumbled.

CHAPTER 5

Bikers

Real life descendants of the Lipan Indian tribe, Benny "Teo Feathers" Johnson and Lyle "White Horse" James had grown up together on the reservation. They had dropped out of high school, neither really seeing the need for an education since they lived on both state and federal assistance programs. Neither had any desire to learn a trade and work for a living. Their desire for additional income led Benny and Lyle to supplement their monthly government checks with theft, burglary, and marijuana sales, the latter of which they grew themselves in their grandmother's corn patch. This made it ridiculously easy for the bikers to grow and sell their own blend of what they liked to call "Cactus Whacktus." It was a name Lyle had come up with after a night of pot smoking and tequila drinking. So far their endeavors had generated enough profit to keep them in tequila and dope, and to buy two used black Harley Dyna-Glides and two stolen Glock .9mm pistols. Most of the time the two commuted to the surrounding towns of Van Horn and Pecos on their Harleys to steal what they could, drink tequila at the local bars, and sell their pot to the Mexican laborers.

Like most crooks, Benny and Lyle were not all that smart. They smoked too much of their own product, drank too much tequila, and talked too much about their "work." On one of their recent sales trips to Pecos, both were sitting in a bar negotiating a deal with a local drug dealer, attempting to unload two pounds of marijuana. The dealer wanted it on consignment, but that was a non-starter with the two bikers. The dealer was pissed. After all, these two had let him consign dope in the past.

Lyle was getting pretty drunk. Soon he let it slip that he and Benny were going to expand their growing operation to include their aunt's corn patch, thus doubling their output. They were therefore interested in expanding their sales area to include towns outside of Pecos and

Van Horn. They figured Odessa to the east would be a good market, or maybe even as far west as El Paso. It would be a good move for them, or so they thought. They could double, or even triple what they were selling now.

"Then we won't need your cheap, sorry ass," Lyle drunkenly told the dealer.

"Hey, shut up, Lyle," Benny admonished. "We need this man's business."

But the damage was done. Lyle's insult really pissed the man off, and the information about the expansion of business was not lost on him as Benny and Lyle were not the only suppliers he did business with. In fact, they were more like back-up suppliers to him when he got low on product. He got the majority of his product from some particularly nasty folks in Ciudad Juarez, via El Paso, whom he was sure were connected to the Zeta Drug Cartel.

Always the opportunist, the dealer was equally sure the cartel would pay handsomely for information about outsiders attempting to sell drugs in their territory. They defended their turf viciously, as evidenced by the 35,000 murders in northern Mexico over the past few years. They would not normally trouble themselves over two small-time punks slinging dope in the punks' own neighborhood, but when they learned that these two planned to expand distribution to several towns, they would probably want to curtail such a plan. Of course, the dealer would have to be cautious in his approach to these folks, less he end up with *his* head in a bag, but if he played his hand just right, he felt confident he could quickly turn this information into some extra cash. He smiled to himself and continued to negotiate with Benny and Lyle, who's rude comment to the dealer had just sealed their fate. That was three weeks ago.

The two Indian bikers were currently sitting at a table at the Subway sandwich shop inside the Flying J Truck Stop, just off the interstate in Pecos. They were discussing amongst other things, Lyle's visit to the Rollins' ranch early this morning and Benny was not happy about that.

"What the fuck happened, dude?" Benny demanded.

"Oh, those Goddamn horses gave me away. Then those two big fucking dogs started barking and then their fucking truck alarm went off, lights, camera, action, dude! I had to get the fuck outta there so I ran back down the road to my bike. I didn't want to start it or they would-a heard me so I pushed it like about a fucking mile before I could ride it."

"Why'd you go out there anyway, man?" Benny asked

"I wanted to see who this guy is."

"Yeah? Well, you didn't find out anything did you? And you almost got caught, you stupid fuck."

"Not really, just what we knew already from watching them. He's some kind of cop I guess, and his ol' lady has big tits." Lyle laughed. He had always been a boob man.

"Look, man," Benny growled. "We can't fuck this up. Don't go out there again. If he's a cop you know he's got a gun. Shit, maybe his ol' lady has her own gun, too, you stupid fuck. You ever think of that?" Lyle considered that for a moment and then shook his head. "And when we been ridin' out by there before," Benny continued, "we seen that Mexican dude in that jeep-thing always has that fucking rifle with him and those big fucking Dobermans in the back. Now we've those two county pigs sniffin' around, too. Our new deal is too important to get caught screwing around out there lookin' at titties! You are one dumb son-of-a-bitch, Lyle!"

Lyle, trying to defend himself from Benny's verbal onslaught, shot back, "I wasn't just lookin' at titties. Look, Benny, you're the one who said once the cops found those fucking bones we stole, there'd be such a fuss out there for a couple weeks that we'd be able to move a lot of dope to the storage shed in El Paso without any cops on the road to hassle us."

"Yeah, I know." Benny shrugged. "I thought sure that every cop and Fed and newspaper reporter within 200 miles would be camped out there for days trying to figure that shit out. I didn't count no white-boy trailer trash cop and his ol' lady stumbling across them two skeletons before we had a chance to call it in. What I can't figure out is why the cops just hauled them bones off. I mean that's a big fuckin' deal, ya know? Like finding' a fucking dinosaur or some shit."

"Yeah?" Lyle retorted. "Well, all I know is we spent a week, a lot of sweat, and a lot of goddamn gas money diggin' those two dead fuckers up and hauling them back here and it didn't amount to jack shit! By the way, my uncle is pissed we didn't get his truck back to him when we told him. Says we can't ever borrow it again."

"We'll just have to think of something else," Benny said, lost in thought. "But in the meantime, Lyle, don't go back out there. I'm serious!"

"Aw-right," Lyle replied.

But Benny had his doubts. Lyle pretty much did what he wanted. *Stupid fuck*, Benny thought as he looked out the window and saw something he didn't like.

DEPARTMENT OF PUBLIC SAFETY was printed boldly on the door of the dark blue and white 4 door sedan along with a likeness of the state of Texas. The patrol car pulled into the parking stall just outside the window where Benny and Lyle sat. Two state troopers were seated inside.

"Shit!" Benny said, spotting the car. "Let's get the fuck outta here."

Fortunately for the two outlaws, their bikes were parked at the other end of the truck stop so they were able to leave through the side exit of the mini-mart, thus avoiding walking by the troopers' sedan. With a rumble, they started their Harleys and turned out onto the frontage road that led to the on-ramp of the interstate.

As the two Harleys made the turn onto the on-ramp, Benny shot one last glance back in his single side view mirror to see if the troopers' car was still parked at the truck stop, which it was, both state troopers now inside the mini-mart buying coffee. What Benny *didn't* see in his side view mirror was the silver Ford Explorer, which had been parked between two semi-trucks in the gravel lot of the overnight truck parking area, pull out to follow them. The Ford was covered with dirt and mud. The silver paint had long ago faded in the desert sun and was now a flat, dull gray. The chrome bumpers and side reflectors were rusted and dirt covered. It was by design. All of the shiny or reflective surfaces on the Explorer had been rendered dull by either layers of dirt and mud, rust, or in some cases even strategically placed duct tape. It was excellent urban camouflage for both Mexico and the west Texas plains, particularly at night.

CHAPTER 6

The Mexican Man

The sole occupant of the Ford Explorer was a Mexican man. He was well dressed in an expensive tailored suit, which was at odds with the vehicle he drove. In his mid-thirties, he also looked to be in very good physical shape. Behind his Ray-Ban sunglasses the man's brown eyes were quick and observant. They also were cold and emotionless. A black nylon equipment bag sat on the passenger seat next to him and there was a slight bulge just beneath the left armpit of his coat. The Explorer pulled onto the interstate a half mile behind the two Harleys. This pattern would repeat itself throughout the day as the two bikers made several stops to sell varying amounts of their pot.

As the Mexican man followed the two, he was surprised and somewhat amused at Benny and Lyle's lack of attention to their surroundings, particularly considering they were dealing drugs in Texas, a state known for its lack of tolerance for overt criminal activity. As a former Mexican Army Special Forces member, the training he'd received from his US Army Green Beret and ranger advisors had stressed the critical importance of maintaining one's "situational awareness." These two *idiotas* had none.

Living in El Paso now as a Mexican businessman, he maintained the dual citizenship of both the US and Mexico. This had allowed him to perform private "contract work" on the United States side of the border for the Zeta Cartel, without detection for the past five years. Best of all, he was still alive which, to be honest, surprised him. His handlers in Juarez had wanted to send a back-up man to assist him with this particular job, but he had convinced them it would be easy and quick. He hoped it would be so. He'd told them there was no reason to risk sending someone across the border with the US Border Patrol so active these days.

"I've got this," he'd told them using a current and popular American expression. What he did not tell them was that he had no desire to share his high five figure compensation for this job with someone else. Now as he followed and observed the two bikers, he smiled. *This will be even easier than I thought.* Unfortunately, he didn't remember another important item from his Special Forces training. It was a quote by German Field Marshall Helmuth von Moltke. "No battle plan survives first contact with the enemy."

∽∽∽

As Benny and Lyle, followed by their uninvited escort, made their rounds in Pecos, Sonya and I were once again getting the truck and trailer hooked up ready to finish our quest westward. That morning, a local truck-tire shop that Sanchez had recommended sent a service truck out to the ranch and replaced our shredded tire with a new one. Davis had also driven out to the ranch that morning and asked us a few more cursory questions, but I could tell he was just going through the motions. He was much more interested in getting back in time to preen himself for the big press conference, which was scheduled for 3:00 o'clock that afternoon, and quickly bid us a curt, "Goodbye," and an unenthusiastic, "Thanks on behalf of the sheriff," for our help. Then he suggested we be on our way.

The sooner the better, I was thinking. By mid-day, Olsen and Sanchez had bid us farewell and gone back to their normal beat duties.

Since it was almost 3:00 p.m., I turned on the TV one last time and tuned into one of the local channels. Regular television programming had been preempted for the press conference. It was quite the gathering. Davis was there, of course, in his role as "lead investigator" standing behind the sheriff. Also present were representatives from the US Bureau of Indian Affairs, the Apache Tribal Counsel, the Texas Governor's office, the Texas State Department of Public Safety, the US Bureau of Land Management, the Oklahoma Governor's office, and even a representative from US Army's current Fourth Cavalry Brigade all the way from Ft. Knox Kentucky. The sheriff made a statement about the thefts and the on-going investigation, and how he was sure there would be arrests in the case very soon. He then spoke of the tedious and careful recovery effort ensuring the remains were not damaged. Both of these two statements made me laugh out loud.

No wonder that prick Davis wants us out of here so quick. Doesn't want anyone telling the press about him having us throw those bones around like bags of trash and then hiding them out until he figured out a way to make himself look good. He'd probably also threatened

Sanchez and Olsen with banishment to some remote beat on midnights or permanent assignment to the Property Room if *they* said anything.

The sheriff droned on about how the stolen remains from the two cemeteries would be re-interned at the earliest possible moment, blah, blah, blah. He did actually mention that the remains had been discovered by "two vacationing tourists hiking in the area," though neither Sonya's nor my name came up, which of course was no surprise. When you work as a crime scene investigator, you get used to doing the majority of the work while the staff weenies take the credit. It was the same in Sonya's line of work as a nurse, with nurses doing all the work and the doctors taking the bow. *I wonder when the clowns and jugglers are going to show up,* I thought as I watched the TV circus.

Just as the press conference ended, there was a knock on our trailer door. I looked out the window to see Juan standing just outside. "Good afternoon, *Senior* Douglas," Juan greeted me as I opened the door.

"*Hola*, Juan, *que pasa?*" I asked

"*Senior*, I just wanted you to know that you can stay another night if you wish. It is getting late and I thought you might want to wait until tomorrow to leave."

"*Gracias*, Juan," I replied. "I'll talk it over with *El Jefe*—" I nodded at my wife. "—and let you know."

He looked puzzled. "Ah, *si*," he grinned, finally understanding the joke about Sonya being my boss.

As he turned toward the house, walking away, I wondered where the Dobie's were. He was rarely without the dogs.

Sonya had been in the shower when Juan knocked. "Who was that?"

"Juan," I told her. "He said we could stay another night. I'm glad he offered since I was thinking of asking him anyway. We wouldn't get far tonight before I'd be too tired to drive."

Sonya nodded and went in to dry her hair. I watched her walk into the bedroom wearing just a towel and I couldn't help but think to myself how great she looked even after all these years of living together.

I slipped out of my jeans and T-shirt, walked up behind her, and pulled off the towel. "Let's chop some wood."

"You're so romantic, but no way," she replied. "I have to dry my hair." She made a half-hearted effort at pushing me away, but I could read the signs. She was in a playful mood. "Besides," she said, "that Deputy Olsen is going to sneak over later and I have to save some for him."

"Shit, that kid may have lots of muscles but you know those young guys can't screw worth a damn. They're strictly three-minute-drill boys." With that I pushed her back on the bed. "Besides," I continued, pointing down, "there's no way he could match this."

Sonya glanced down, smiling. "Yeah, that one's going to be tough to beat."

And she reached for me. I began kissing her face and lips, then I slowly kissed my way down the front of her body.

☙☜☙

Lyle was sitting in a dilapidated lawn chair outside his grandmother's shack, making a fateful decision. He sucked hard on the end of the joint, making the ember at the opposite end of the small hand-rolled cigarette glow bright orange, then he drank down a final shot of tequila. He was going to ignore Benny's warning not to ride back out to the ranch. Lyle wanted to see if that trailer-cop and his big-titted wife had left, or what. There was something about the guy that bugged Lyle.

Out in the desert two days prior, as he and Benny had watched them through their binoculars, they had observed that this guy appeared to be directing the two deputies. Telling them what to do. In Lyle's mind, this made him a threat and he wanted the guy gone one way or another. Lyle never watched anything on his grandmother's old portable TV. If he had, he might have caught the press conference, or at least some reference to it, and thus come to the realization that, with all the excitement about the two skeletons over with for now, the "trailer-cop" would probably be pulling out.

Undaunted and uninformed, Lyle walked over to his Harley. Three kicks and it started. He rolled down the back roads toward the Rollins ranch at breakneck speed. The motorcycle's single headlight cast a dim yellow beam down the road. Lyle noticed there was no moon tonight and the stars lit up the night desert sky. It reminded him of a planetarium in Dallas he and Benny once visited, after getting stoned of course. As he made the right hand turn from the reservation's dirt road onto the single lane county blacktop, Lyle didn't notice the silver Ford Explorer with its lights out, detach itself from the desert landscape and follow him.

The Mexican man driving the Explorer was a believer in taking advantage of any opportunity that might present itself only once. That was why, after following the two bikers to the reservation turn off earlier in the evening, he'd decided to back the SUV into the desert between some brush not far from the intersection and watch the reservation road. The Mexican man knew one or both of the bikers would be starting their day off like every other, and he was fully prepared to spend the night right here in his vehicle watching until the two rode out in the morning. After all, he'd slept in places much worse than this. He knew the chances of a cop spotting him parked here were slim to none. He'd done his homework and knew that the sheriff's night shifts were assigned the fewest deputies, and that the reservation police had only one officer who didn't work at night unless called out.

The Mexican man had never understood this. It was the same with American police all over the country. The busiest time for the police was at night, and they always had the fewest officers working. *Maybe it is a union thing,* he thought, smiling to himself. *Or maybe the police bosses want more cops to be seen during the daytime by the citizens so they can keep their cushy office jobs.*

He didn't know how right he was with this last thought. Either way, it had always served him well knowing that his American police adversaries were constantly shorthanded, particularly in the hours of darkness. Should a deputy happen to wander by, he would just explain that he'd had a bit too much to drink and was sleeping it off. To this end, he always kept four empty cans of Tecate beer on his back floorboard as props.

The Mexican man was alerted when he saw the single motorcycle headlight coming toward him down the reservation road. When he was sure it was one of the bikers he'd been following, he thought to himself, *Si, demasiado facil.* He reached into the equipment bag, pulled out a set of ATN night vision goggles, and pulled them over his head. He waited until Lyle made the turn onto the road away from him to switch them on, less the headlight on the motorcycle cause the goggles to "flare" and blind him.

As the Mexican man pulled the Explorer out onto the blacktop road with the goggles now switched on, he could see very well in the nearly complete darkness, though it was all cast in an eerie, green glow. The black ribbon of the roadway, the nearby bushes and cactus, even a cotton tail rabbit darting across the roadway were visible in every detail. The motorcycle ahead of him generated bright halos of green light. With his own headlights off and nothing to reflect on the Explorer's exterior, he was certain he was nearly invisible in the vibrating rearview mirrors of the motorcycle.

As he drove, he reached into the equipment bag a second time removing two additional items. The first was a pair of thin black leather gloves, which he put on his hands. The second was a sawed-off shotgun. The weapon was wrapped in clear plastic food wrap, having already been loaded and sanitized by him for fingerprints and any possible DNA deposits. The shotgun was an older model 12 gauge side-by-side "coach gun," complete with dual triggers and exposed hammers. The stock and both barrels had been cut off and, as such, its total length was less than twenty inches. Like many shotguns manufactured prior to the Federal Firearms Act of 1968, it had no serial number.

It was untraceable and disposable. One chamber of the weapon was loaded with a 12 gauge BB-sized buckshot shotgun shell, the other with 00-sized buckshot which was commonly referred to as double ought. Each of the shotgun shells were extremely deadly in their own right, but by combining the two different sizes of the buckshot, they created a blast pattern that all but eliminated the possibility of missing his target at close range. Moreover, anyone could legally buy this type of ammunition over the counter at any sporting goods store that sold guns and ammunition. This was an advantage when trying to cover the tracks of such a purchase, and the Mexican man was an expert at covering his tracks…

❦❦❦

Several days prior to beginning his observation of Benny and Lyle's daily routine, the Mexican man had made his preparations. Using cash and an assumed name, he'd checked into a local cheap motel. After he had changed clothing into non-descript jeans, T-shirt, boots, and a straw cowboy hat, he looked like any other local resident. He drove to a nearby sporting goods store and purchased a single box of the BB-buckshot shells. Although he maintained a legitimate Texas driver's license, several in fact, he was not required to produce it to purchase the shotgun shells. Unlike most anti-gun and anti-hunting states such as California, Texas did not require an ID to purchase ammunition providing there was no question about one being over the age of 18. He then drove several miles away to purchase the 00-buckshot shells at a different store.

The man parked half a block from each of the stores and walked to each to make his purchases, ensuring his vehicle was never seen parked at either.

As he made his purchases, he also made sure that both boxes of shells were of the same Winchester Super-X brand. This brand was common and was sold not just in sporting goods stores, but also many Wal*Marts across the country and even some local mini-marts. This made his purchases that much harder to track. He was careful to ensure that at each store, only the store clerks handled and bagged the shotgun shell boxes. The Mexican man considered himself a professional at his work. He kept up with any publications and internet articles he could find on forensic evidence. He was well aware of the advances that had been made in recent years in the fields of criminal DNA analysis and fingerprint development techniques. It was critical that he took precautions so as not to leave any traces of his own fingerprints or any DNA deposits on the boxes, the shotgun shells, or the weapon.

Back in his motel room, he first "sanitized" the weapon. Wearing surgical gloves on his hands and a disposable paper dust mask over his nose and mouth in case of an accidental sneeze or cough, he first scrubbed the shotgun with paint thinner. He knew that one of the ingredients of the thinner was toluene, which would destroy any DNA traces. After drying it as best he could, he sprayed it in its entirety with lightweight WD-40 lubricating oil, inside and out. After letting the WD-40 saturate for an hour, he sprayed it a second time then wiped it down thoroughly with a clean rag. Removing two shotgun shells from each of the boxes, he loaded the two chambers of the weapon. He placed two extra shells in a plastic sandwich bag, which he, in turn, placed in his equipment bag. He was confident he would need no more than the four shells. With this task completed, he wrapped the weapon in one layer of the kitchen wrap. The thin plastic wrap was an additional precaution. It guarded against not only his accidentally touching the weapon without his gloves, but would also help contain any gunshot residue when the weapon was fired. The wrap was thin enough not to hinder the cocking and firing of the weapon. With his preparations complete, he checked out of the room and drove to a remote spot in the desert 15 minutes away.

So as to not have any of the unused and matching shotgun shells in his vehicle or on his person, he started a small campfire intending to destroy them in the flames. He knew that, unlike ammunition manufactured using brass casings which would explode when subjected to extreme heat, the plastic casings of the shotgun shells would simply melt in the fire, the gun powder contained within them burning up with a bright yellow flare. Providing he fed the shells into the fire one or two at a time, the primers in the shells would merely "pop" no louder than a child's cap pistol. The brass ends of the shotgun shells would remain in the ashes of the fire, of course, but the man was not concerned. They would be charred and misshapen by the heat. It would be nothing short of a miracle if they were ever found at all, given the remote location of the campfire, and they would not be of any value as evidence if they were. He followed up by also burning all of the sales receipts, the shotgun shell boxes, the box of remaining kitchen wrap, and the shopping bags. It took somewhat longer than he had anticipated, but once satisfied that nothing remained in the ashes that could point back to him, he was ready to return to his observation of the two bikers, which brought him to this point: following Lyle along the blacktop road in the darkness.

If there was one weak point in the Mexican man's operational plan, it was the unknown geography of this road, particularly at night. After following both of the bikers for several days, he was now familiar with their daily routes and stops. Humans were creatures of habit, particularly if they did not detect a threat or were just plain dumb, which he was sure of in the case of Lyle.

The Mexican man was puzzled now though. Up to this point, the two Indians were always together when they'd ridden off the reservation. Lyle being out by himself tonight was something new. *Where are you going amigo?* the man wondered as he followed Lyle. *Chasing down some puta, maybe?* Then another thought popped into the man's head. *Maybe he's selling behind his partner's back, making some side money Benny doesn't know about.* He hoped the latter was the case. A woman, in particular a regular girlfriend, could complicate things if that was indeed where Lyle was going. The man shortened the distance between his SUV and the bike, not wanting to suddenly lose sight of Lyle should he unexpectedly turn off on a side road. Suddenly the brake light of the bike flared green in his night vision goggles. Then both lights on the bike disappeared. Fearing at first that Lyle had indeed turned off or gone around a curve, the Mexican man sped up. Within seconds, however, he realized this stretch of the road was straight and that Lyle had stopped.

Have I been spotted? No, he didn't think so. Not wanting his own brake lights giving him away in the darkness, the man slowed the SUV to a stop on the shoulder of the road by using the emergency brake.

Having already disconnected both dome lights, the man stepped out of the SUV still wearing the night vision headgear and silently closed the door. He could see the parked motorcycle on the side of the road a hundred yards ahead. *So you have indeed stopped, my friend.* After taking a few quiet steps closer, he saw Lyle walking up the embankment next to the parked motorcycle. He disappeared over the top. *What is the Indian up to?*

The Mexican man retrieved the shotgun from his equipment bag, placing the baggie, with the two extra shotgun shells inside, in his pocket. *If an emergency arises,* he thought, but he was confident he would need only the two shells already loaded in the weapon. He carried a revolver in his shoulder holster also should the need arise, but he was a careful man and avoided "emergencies" whenever possible. Still, one never knew, which is why as a Texas resident he had long ago obtained a concealed carry permit for the handgun and used a revolver as opposed to a semi-automatic pistol for the simple reason that the revolver didn't spew shell casings everywhere when fired. Being an excellent shot, he also did not need to carry a handgun that held a dozen or more cartridges like so many people did these days. His revolver was a Smith & Wesson Model 620. Unlike most large caliber revolvers, this model held *seven* shots as opposed to the standard six. Polishing of the internal parts made it fire smoothly and flawlessly, and he had upgraded the factory sights. Although it was chambered for the .357 magnum cartridge, he kept it normally loaded with .38 Special +P Glaser personal defense ammunition. This made the weapon much easier to control and, more importantly, reduced the amount of muzzle flash in low light. The bullet from the special cartridge fragmented into many small pieces when it struck its target. Although it would not penetrate a hard surface like a door or wall, it was unbelievably devastating to human tissue. Best of all, after the hit on the body, there were no pieces of the bullet left intact that were large enough for the police to use for any type of ballistic comparison. He practiced with the revolver regularly, but would use it only as a last resort.

The Mexican man moved swiftly along the shoulder of the roadway now, first to the handlebars of the Indian's parked motorcycle where he paused for a few seconds, then to the top of the embankment. He scanned the area with the NV goggles. *There!* He saw Lyle walking on what looked like a gravel road which paralleled the blacktop road behind him. Only 100 yards separated the two. Lyle appeared to be walking slowly, carefully, stopping every few yards.

The man's curiosity level was rising. *Que pasa?* the man wondered. He followed Lyle at a distance, being careful not to make any sound. The desert soil under his feet made for fairly quiet walking, and the NVG's helped him avoid any dry brush or grass that would crack under his weight. The man shook his head slightly at the biker's ineptness. Even at this distance, he could hear Lyle's feet on the gravel surface of the road. The heavy-soled motorcycle boots Lyle wore might have looked cool when riding his Harley, but they crunched nosily on the gravel every few steps. And the biker didn't have the sense to walk on the softer dirt on either side of the road.

The Mexican man could now see the lights from what looked like a large ranch. With the aid of the goggles, he could make out a large house and stable with a large, fifth-wheel trailer parked next to it. At least an acre of grass and trees separated the two. There were several horses standing in the adjacent corrals. This concerned him. He knew if they got much closer, the horses would get their scent and become alarmed. *Whoever lives here will undoubtedly have dogs and a gun or two, also.* Another possible complication he did not need.

Just as the man was considering turning around and staking out Lyle's bike for his inevitable return to it, the biker stopped on the far side of the gravel road and squatted down. As the man watched, Lyle produced a pair of binoculars and began to watch the ranch area. The man could not tell from this distance whether the binoculars Lyle held to his eyes had night vision capability or not. He didn't think so, as most NV binoculars were larger than what these appeared to be. Still, the man could not take the chance. He noted he was downwind from the animals. *Good, the horses could not smell either of them.* The man silently circled around behind Lyle then crossed the gravel road.

Moving slowly, he crept up to within a few feet of the biker and quietly slipped off the NV goggles. He could see well enough in the darkness now and didn't need them. It was a warm night and the man was pleased to see that Lyle had worn only his thin leather vest over a T-shirt, as opposed to his thick leather motorcycle jacket. Thick leather can be a tough opponent at times. The man now had the shotgun point-ed at Lyle's back, both hammers cocked, but he was a professional. His fingers were not on the set of triggers—yet. Lyle was so far oblivi-ous to his presence. It was due to this that the man now considered using his knife to bring Lyle's life to an end. The Mexican man always carried his Boker spring-blade, tactical knife with him. It was fairly large for a folding knife but still fit in his pants pocket well, held in place by the clip on the side of the grip. The man kept it so sharp even *he* had to handle it carefully. He was never without it. He could easily and, more importantly, silently dispatch the biker with the knife, but not by cutting his throat as was always depicted on TV. That was nei-ther silent nor clean. A wound such as that, although indeed fatal, would leave Lyle kicking and thrashing around on the ground, noisily gagging and spewing blood like a lawn sprinkler. There was a much better way to use his knife if he could get close enough and he went over it in his mind: *Left hand firmly and suddenly clamped over the mouth and nose, slightly pulling the face to the left, then drive the knife blade in its entirety upward into the soft tissue at the base of the skull. One harsh twist severing the brain stem and Lyle would be a rag doll. No noise and very little blood.* He'd done it enough times to be adept at it and he started to reach for his pocket. However, before the man's right hand moved from the shotgun, the biker made the decision for him.

As Lyle had squatted there watching the ranch with his binoculars, he knew he just couldn't get closer without all hell breaking loose from those animals. The ride out to the ranch in the night air and the hike to this spot had sobered him up some. He was thinking a bit more clearly and starting to agree with Benny that he shouldn't be out here alone.

Fuck it, Lyle decided. *I'm outta here.*

Without warning, the biker suddenly stood up and turned around. He looked shocked to see the dark silhouette of a person standing so close behind him. "Who the fuck are you?" Lyle barked and reached for the pistol stuck in his waistband.

He was too slow by half. The Mexican man didn't hesitate. With practiced training, he closed one eye protecting it against the loss of sight from muzzle flash, and squeezed both triggers.

The combined buckshot from both barrels of the shotgun struck Lyle from mid-thigh to his forehead, penetrating every major organ of his body as well as his skull. The blast knocked him back five feet. A few of the buckshot even exited the back of his throat and arms. He was dead before he hit the ground. The noise of the blast spooked the horses and all were now whinnying and snorting. The dogs in their kennel outside the house started barking furiously.

The bright flash in the darkness ruined the Mexican man's night vision in the eye that he'd kept open. The closed eye was fine. Moving swiftly, the man unwrapped the plastic wrap from the shotgun and dropped the weapon into a bush next to Lyle. He removed the baggie from his pocket and dumped the two extra shotgun shells next to the shotgun. He then placed the baggie and the plastic wrap back in his pocket. He knew that none of the items could be traced back to him, and he did not want to have the weapon or the extra shells on him should he be randomly stopped by some cop. Retrieving his NV goggles, he began his trek back to the Explorer.

Lights came on at the house, the park, and the RV. *Interesting*, he thought as he moved through the darkness. *Someone is living in the trailer.* He had briefly entertained the thought of cutting off Lyle's head, a definitive calling card of the people he worked for, and he would have done so had he been able to kill Lyle silently, but there was no time for such pleasures now. He turned and quickly crossed the gravel road, making his way across the desert to his SUV.

At the top of the embankment, he paused and looked in both directions. He wanted to ensure that the blacktop road was still deserted, which it was. With the NV goggles still in place, he started the Explorer, made a U-turn and drove back toward the reservation.

The man had hoped to take care of both Indians at one time, but this opportunity had been too good to pass up. He would now have to wait for a second opportunity to take out Benny. The shotgun was gone now of course, but he would figure something else out. Through his NV goggles he could see he was nearing an intersection with a larger road. This one actually had some cross-traffic on it. As he approached, he removed the goggles and placed them back in his bag. Waiting until there were no vehicles in sight, he turned on his headlights and made a right hand turn.

ɛ/ɔɛ/ɔ

I was dreaming, deep in sleep. The distant muzzle blast from the shotgun had become part of my dream for just an instant, as sometimes happened, then I awoke with a start, glancing at my dresser clock. 1:00 a.m. Fully awake, I knew now that I'd actually heard the small explosion and not dreamed it. Old instincts told me it had been a gunshot. The alarmed state of the horses and dogs confirmed it. Once again in the middle of the night, I threw on my clothes as outside lights came on. With that blast stirring up the animals as it did, and Juan turning on every light *he* could find up at the house and in the park, it was not a time for stealth.

Since I was going to go barreling out of the trailer into who knows what, I stuck the Smith .45 in my belt and grabbed for my shotgun which I also kept close at hand by the side of the bed. It was a Benelli short-barreled M4 auto-loader. It's nine-shot capacity would level the playing field nicely, no matter what, or who, was out there. Sonya was, of course, awake now. I told her to keep the inside lights off and that I was headed outside. I could see the concern on her face, but she said nothing.

I readied the weapon, then threw open the door, and jumped over the steps and to the ground all in one motion. I'm no ballerina. I landed hard in a crouch with the trailer at my back. I quickly scanned the immediate area. *I'm too old for all this jumping around shit*, I thought as my back and ankles now felt the impact of the three foot descent. The entire area was now lit up like a football stadium. I lowered the shotgun as Juan again came rolling up in the Rhino with the now highly agitated dogs.

I nodded a greeting. "I take it you heard the shot."

"Yes, I heard it. I was still up doing some paperwork for *Senior* Rollins. I thought you had shot at someone maybe?" he replied.

I shook my head. "Could you tell where it came from?"

He pointed down the gravel road. "Somewhere down that way."

"Well, we might as well go see," I told him as I got into the ATV.

Both dogs sniffed at the back of my neck. Their noses were cold but both were panting with anxiety, their breath hot. I checked the shotgun to make sure the safety was on. I noticed the Ruger rifle was lying across Juan's lap. He drove slowly down the gravel driveway and out through the gate while I operated the spotlight. We made several passes up and down the road in both directions, but saw nothing suspicious. The dogs whined and stood up as we passed one particular spot, but they didn't actually "alert" so Juan would not let them out of the Rhino, telling me he didn't want to have to wait on them while they chased a rabbit for an hour in the dark. In the distance, we could hear sirens on the interstate, a lot of sirens, but they were fading. Definitely not headed in our direction, and within a few minutes the sound was gone. After 45 minutes of searching, Juan and I called it quits

"I'm headed back to bed," I told him, "we're outta here early."

He nodded. "I, too, will go back to my siesta."

CHAPTER 7

Discovery

By 7 a.m. the next morning, Sonya and I were ready to roll out. Juan, of course, was already up and attending to the horses. We said our goodbyes to him and the dogs. I pulled the rig out the gate and headed down the gravel road. At the intersection with the old blacktop, I stopped and looked left, then right. A minute went by.

Sonya looked up from her writing in her checkbook to see why we were still stopped. She noticed I was staring down the road to the right. Seeing there was no cross-traffic, she asked "What?"

"There's a motorcycle parked down there," I answered.

She took off her reading glasses and looked down the road to the bike parked on right shoulder. "Yeah, so?"

"It looks like a Harley—a black Harley," I responded.

She repeated herself, "Yeah, so?"

"So what do you think the odds of us being scoped out by guys on dark colored Harleys and now a black Harley being parked here?" I asked.

"You're paranoid," was her reply.

"It's been said of me, but I'm still going to walk down there and check it out." And with that I shut off the truck and stepped out.

"You gonna take your man-purse?" she asked, referring to my camouflaged shoulder bag.

The bag had been a gift from my son-in-law several months prior. Currently a soldier with the First Infantry Division "The Big Red 1," he had seen the bag in the PX at Ft Riley. Knowing I rode a motorcycle, he'd thought it would be a good way to carry essentials while riding, and he was right. It was particularly handy for carrying my wallet, my cell phone, *and* any one of my pistols.

"Yeah, thanks, hand it to me," I replied.

After placing it over my shoulder, I began walking the quarter mile to the parked bike. I stayed on the asphalt as I walked. The shoulder of the road was wide with soft lose dust and I didn't want my brand new white tennis shoes to get filthy. I noticed the dirt shoulder was edged by a ten-foot-high embankment. I'd walked only a hundred feet or so, when I noticed fresh car tire tracks and shoe tracks in the dust. *Old habits die hard*, I thought as I stopped and took a closer look. *Cowboy boots.* The print had a smooth sole, pointed toe and deep heel. After twenty-two years as an investigator, you just can't turn it off. From the track I could see that someone had pulled over here recently, got out, and walked around, then climbed up the embankment. *Odd*, I thought. *Why go up there? Maybe they just wanted to see what was up there.* Curious now, I did the same.

At the top of the embankment, I could see the shoe tracks leading across the small stretch of desert toward the parallel gravel road to the ranch.

"I'll come back to you in a minute, whoever you are," I said to myself.

I turned back down the embankment and continued on to the Harley. When I got close, I could see it was a black Dyna Glide. At first glance, it appeared undamaged. There was no visible evidence of a breakdown such as oil leaking, a flat tire, or a broken drive belt. Being a motorcycle guy myself, I examined it more closely. The kill switch on the handlebar had been broken off.

As I walked around the bike, heavy-soled boot tracks were clearly visible in the dirt of the shoulder. I could clearly see that the rider got off and walked around his bike. I couldn't see any tracks on the embankment here though, as it was rocky and covered with brush. I bent down to examine one of the boot tracks near the bike more closely. *Shit, this looks just like the boot track we found day before yesterday by the gate. Same heavy-lug sole pattern. Even the same Oil Resistant sole insert.*

I looked back and forth between the spot where I'd just seen the car tracks and the bike where I was kneeling. I was trying to put it together in my mind. *Had they arrived together? Was the car driver here to pick up the bike rider? If so, why park so far apart? Had someone in the car been following the bike, or visa-versa? But if that's the case, who was following whom and why?*

More questions than answers. I climbed the embankment directly overlooking the Harley. Sure enough there were the same heavy boot tracks at the top. They led off in the direction of the parallel gravel ranch road. Lost in concentration, I was startled when my cell phone's obnoxious ring tone sounded. It was Sonya. She was growing impatient, sitting in the truck waiting for me.

"Where'd you go?" she asked.

"I'm up here on this embankment just above the Harley."

"Oh, okay, I see you now. What are you doing?"

"I found something I need to check out, gonna be a few."

She sighed. "What is it?"

"I'll explain in a bit."

"Okay, she replied, "but try to hurry. It's getting warm in here even with the windows down. I'll get out and let the dogs run around a bit."

"Okay, but don't go far and don't come down this way. I'll be back in a few minutes." I'd already decided I would leave this mystery to Sanchez and call him as I drove away.

"Why not?" she asked.

"There's a bunch of tire and shoe tracks in the dirt here and I don't want the dogs running around and screwing them up."

"So there's tire and shoe tracks, who cares, Jason? Let's go."

I was growing impatient. "Just humor me for bit please."

"Okay, but hurry up," she replied with *that* tone in her voice.

As we hung-up I could see her opening the truck door. I turned and started following the boot tracks. Just as a precaution, I unzipped a pouch on my bag, the pouch that held my little Kahr.

It is getting warm, I thought as I walked. I was perspiring under my baseball cap. The biker boot tracks, which is what I was referring to them as now, were clearly visible in the dirt and it was easy following them across the small patch of desert. As I neared the gravel road, I could hear the loud buzzing of flying insects. At the edge of the gravel road the boot tracks disappeared and I stopped. Obviously whomever walked here had crossed the hard packed road, the tracks leaving no trace on its hard surface. The buzzing of the insects was annoying and now drew my attention. I could see a large cloud of horse flies hovering over some bushes fifteen feet on the other side of the road near the barbwire fence. I looked for any other large gathering of the insects that might indicate this was normal, but could see none. The gunshot last night, the flies circling here. *Oh man, I really don't want to walk over there.* I suspected the flies were an indication of what I was going to find when I crossed the road.

After taking a quick look around to ensure I was alone, I slowly crossed the gravel toward the brush, my right hand now gripping the pistol in my satchel. I caught a faint whiff of a scent I'd smelled too often in my life. It was the stench of death. I stopped short when I could see into the brush and rolled my eyes upward. "You gotta be shittin' me," I said out loud to myself, my suspicion confirmed. *Another ghost to add to my collection*, I thought as I looked down at the very dead biker.

He was lying on his back, his dilated eyes half open. Most of his blood had already saturated the ground beneath him leaving him very pale. I noticed a few of the small holes in the exposed areas of his flesh and T-shirt, some larger than others. *Shotgun, had to be. Two different sized shot maybe*, I thought as I looked at the damaged flesh. The smell was most unpleasant. It wasn't just the coppery smell of blood. There was also the body's release of excrement as it had relaxed with the first stages of decomposition being hurried along by the warm sun. *Wish I had a cigar, or some Vicks to smear under my nose.* Breathing through my mouth against the smell, I squatted next to the body, reached down and raised his wrist. His arm and body were stiff. *Okay, rigor has fully set in, so call it eight to ten hours ago, that makes it the shot we heard last night. Aw man, fuck this! I should have left yesterday.* It was then that I saw the shotgun and the two live shells laying in the brush next to the body.

The biker had one of those leather trucker's wallets on a chain attached to the right side of his belt. The wallet was laying in the bloody dirt at his side. I had no gloves, but I wanted to see if there was any ID. I checked my fingers to make sure I had no small open cuts, then avoiding the blood as best I could, I flipped the wallet over with a small stick. Using my fingertips I unsnapped and opened the flaps of leather. As luck would have it, the biker's Texas driver's license and a food stamp card was tucked in the first slot. I pulled it out by the edges.

"Lyle James."

I noticed the license was expired. *Well, Lyle*, I thought, looking back and forth between his dead face and the license photo. *You've looked better.* I replaced the license leaving the wallet unsnapped. Lyle's vest was askew and I could see the butt of a pistol protruding from his waistband. I reached over with the stick and lifted the left side of his vest. *Well, well, well, a Glock. Didn't do you much good though, did it, pal?* Wiping my fingertips off on my jeans, I stood up.

Lyle wasn't going anywhere in the immediate future, and I wanted to follow up on another hunch before I called the authorities. I called Sonya's phone. She answered after a few rings.

"We've got a situation here," I told her. I then proceeded to explain everything I'd seen and done over the past 30 minutes. She listened in shock.

"Do you want me to try to drive the rig over there? Or call someone?" she asked.

"No, not over here, no, but do you think you could pull down the blacktop road toward the Harley?"

"I think so," she replied, her voice a bit uncertain.

"Okay, in a few minutes you'll see me standing back at the top of the embankment. When you do, I want you to drive the rig down to me, but be sure to stay on the road. *Don't* pull off on the shoulder, and don't forget to swing the rig wide when you make your turn there at the intersection. Watch me and when I wave that's where I want you to stop. I'll tell you what to do when we meet up."

"Okay," she said.

As I turned back to Lyle's body, movement near the stables caught my eye. It was Juan in the Rhino. I could see he was driving toward the gate, having already seen me standing in the gravel road, though I was certain he hadn't recognized that it was me from that distance. I was equally certain his Ruger rifle would be within his reach and I wanted to make sure I was recognized. I began walking toward him, waiving my arms. He stopped when he got close enough to see that it was me. I was glad the dogs weren't with him. I didn't want them jumping out and running around everywhere either.

"*Senior* Douglas?" he said, puzzled. "I thought you left."

"I did. I'll explain it all in a bit. You know that shot we thought we heard last night?"

"Yes?"

"Well there's a dead guy right down there," I said, pointing back down the road at the bushes.

He looked down the road and then back at me. "You are *disfortunado, senior*. Trouble, it follows you."

"It's been said of me," I replied as I climbed into the ATV beside him.

I directed Juan down the road a short distance from the body. As we looked at Lyle from the edge of the road, I briefly explained to Juan how I came to find him. He shook his head and looked back at me.

"Trouble follows you, *senior*," he repeated.

"Yeah, you said that already. Juan, I need you to go call the sheriff's office, no wait, call Deputy Sanchez direct. You still have his cell number?"

"Yes. Okay, call him and tell him the whole story. Everything about us hearing the shot last night and me finding the body. Everything right up to now. Let him decide how to handle it and who he wants to tell what."

"*Si, senior*, but what are you going to do?" Juan asked.

"I'm going to walk over there and see if I can find anything else. Can you stay here by the body until I get back? Or does it bug you?"

"*Senior*, I grew up in one of Tijuana's worst slums. The dead are not new to me."

I nodded and turned back across the desert, following my own tracks. As an afterthought, I turned back to Juan. "Do you think Mr. Rollins would care if we stayed a few more days in the RV spot? Or should I look for something else."

"No, *senior*, he won't care. He called me last night to say he was flying to Kentucky to look at some horses. He won't be back for at least a week. Of course, I don't know what he would say about all of this, but there is no need to trouble him with it until he returns."

Nodding I said, "Looks like I might be here a couple more days so I'll pull the rig back around later." *This is like some bad dream I just can't wake up from.*

I hiked back to the top edge of the embankment overlooking the Harley. Turning, I began slowly walking along the edge back toward the car tire tracks on the shoulder below, trying now to find the shoe tracks of the car driver. I was fairly certain at this point that the driver of the car had been the one that followed the biker, and probably the one that shot him, so he would have had to climb the embankment as Lyle had. So many questions. *Why had Lyle James been snooping around the ranch in the first place? Why had the driver of the car followed Lyle and shot him? If that is indeed what happened.* I looked around. *How had the guy managed to follow Lyle in all this open country without being seen? Who was the shooter and why Lyle?* Now I was somewhat fascinated.

Sonya had seen me reach the embankment and was now driving slowly toward me on the blacktop road. *Good, she made the turn without tearing off the side of the trailer on the STOP sign.* She had just about pulled up even with me when I found the shoe tracks, or more accurately cowboy boot tracks, I was searching for. I waved my hand.

She stopped and rolled down the passenger side window. "This where you want me?"

"Yeah," I replied. Looking down at the car tire tracks on the shoulder of the road below me, I could see our rig blocked access to them from the roadway. "Park it and turn the flashers on and sit tight. I'll be right back."

I turned away and followed the shoe tracks into the desert. I noticed that after topping the embankment, this set of cowboy boot tracks paralleled the tracks left by Lyle, maybe 50 yards apart. After a short distance the cowboy boot tracks began to angle toward the biker's tracks. *So the shooter corrected his course as he stalked Lyle. That means he either knew where Lyle was going to be, or he could see where Lyle was going. How would he manage that in the dark without being seen?*

Thinking back to when Juan and I were searching last night, I couldn't remember if the moon had been out. I pulled out my phone.

Good signal, excellent. Smart phones do come in handy once in a
while. Mine was an IPhone. I pulled up an internet page that showed
phases of the moon for this month. There had been no moon at all last
night. *Okay, so with no moon it was dark, as in damn near pitch black.
That made the odds of the shooter finding Lyle hiding in a particular
spot without alerting him, near impossible. So he was following him,
which means he could see him. How could he have seen Lyle well
enough in the dark to follow him? Lyle could have been using a flashlight, but that is unlikely since it would be visible from the ranch, and
hopefully even Lyle was not that stupid, but hey, you never know.* I
snorted. The answer came to me suddenly. *Has to be NVGs.*

I had been fascinated by all of this, but now I was totally hooked. I
could see as I followed the cowboy boot tracks, they did indeed lead
right to the edge of the gravel road, not far from the body. Juan stood
there watching me, trying to stay upwind of Lyle. While I found nothing on the gravel surface of the road, I knew the shooter had to have
left a set of tracks returning to his vehicle. It didn't take much looking
to find them.

This second set of cowboy boot tracks crossed the small patch of
desert, back to the embankment, thirty feet from where he originally
came upon Lyle. The tracks of his return trail were not as clear as the
first. Here the soil was rocky and there was more brush. I walked back
to the embankment overlooking our trailer and could now hear a siren
approaching in the distance. Elevated as I was, I could see the emergency lights of the sheriff's department SUV approaching along the
country road. *Deja vu.*

As the vehicle neared the turn-off onto the ranch gravel road, the
SUV stopped. I knew the deputy, or deputies as it were, were looking
in my direction, probably trying to decide where to go first. Our rig,
the Harley, and myself were all clearly visible from where they sat.
After a few seconds, the SUV turned slightly and came my way. I was
hoping it was Sanchez and Olsen, or at least one of them. I didn't want
to go through the whole establishing myself again. As they got closer, I
was relieved to see both familiar faces behind the windshield. Sanchez
was driving and he parked the SUV behind the trailer. Both deputies
stepped out.

"Mind the shoulder, boys," I called to them. "There's some tracks
there in the dirt that I'm sure are involved."

"What the hell is going on?" Sanchez shot back. "Juan called me
on my phone a little while ago and said there'd been a shooting, and
just what the hell are you still doing here anyway?"

I could see he was a bit testy this morning. "We were leaving. I
was literally in the process of pulling out onto this road when I stum-

bled across this whole deal. You're a bit grouchy, Frank. Haven't had your coffee yet? Or not get any last night, or what?"

Sanchez was about to respond, probably to smear my lineage when Olsen jumped in. "We got called out early to cover the night guys. Some big shoot-em deal up down south in Van Horn. Everyone is down there, our guys, Davis county guys, the TSDPS, the Border Patrol—shit, everyone and their brother is down there. Don't have all the particulars yet but it was a real North Hollywood type deal we're hearing."

"When it rains it pours," I told them. "You've got a bit of a mess here also." And with that I walked down the embankment to them, making sure I was well clear of the tracks in the dirt.

Sonya got out of the truck and the four of us began slowly walking along the road toward the Harley, Sonya a few steps behind us. I talked and they listened. I filled them in on everything I'd found, and how I had come to find it. I tried to stick to the basics at first, not interjecting my own conclusions yet, but I could still see they were a bit overwhelmed by the sheer amount of information I was laying on them.

"Wait!" Sanchez interrupted with alarm as I neared the end of my tale. "Juan is the only one back there standing by this dead guy?"

"Yup, but not to worry. The stiff isn't going to jump up and run off, and there's no one else around," I replied.

Sanchez turned to his partner, "Jim, grab the car and get up there and let Juan get out of there. Stay there till we get up there."

"Frank, you might want to get another unit or two out here to help you with scene security," I told him. "As you can see, it's pretty spread out."

"We don't *have* any other units," the deputy replied testily. "We told you, everyone is either down south or covering for those who are!"

Now I was getting pissed. "Hey, bud, step off a bit, I'm on your side remember."

"Sorry, Jason," he apologized. "I got out of bed on the wrong side this morning and it hasn't gotten any better."

"No big," I replied.

Sonya spoke up then. "Why don't we go park the rig back at the stables, and we can drop off Deputy Olsen where Juan is on the way. That way Deputy Sanchez can stay here and keep his unit thingy here until you guys are done?"

"How do I get back here after dropping Olsen and the rig?" I asked her.

"What do you mean?" she replied. "You walk, of course. You've already walked it like three times this morning."

She looked at me smugly. The three of us all looked at her then at each other.

I shrugged then turned to the deputies. "Man always bows to the wisdom of the female of the species."

Both men nodded in agreement.

Once again, three of us climbed into the truck, leaving Sanchez by the Harley at the side of the road. I had to drive up the road some to turn around, but within a few minutes we had dropped the deputy off with the body, picked up Juan, and again parked the truck and trailer back next to the stables.

"This feels like that old episode of *Twilight Zone's* Centerville. I told Sonya. "You know, the one where the guy keeps getting on the train departing Centerville and the train just keeps arriving back in Centerville."

As Sonya once again prepared the trailer for our extended stay, Juan, driving the Rhino now, took pity on me after seeing me trudging down the gravel road and gave me a ride back to Sanchez.

"I just talked to Lieutenant Davis and you're drafted," Sanchez advised me when I stepped out of the ATV.

"Wait, what?"

"Davis and the sheriff talked it over. Davis is going to be down in Van Horn for who knows how long on that shooting deal. Every crime scene guy for 100 miles is down there too, including the state guys and the Feds. You are the only experienced crime scene guy available, so I've been ordered to 'deputize' you, temporarily that is."

I considered this for a minute. "What if I don't want to be deputized?"

"You don't have any choice, mi amigo. Texas law from the old days about appointing a posse or some such horseshit. It's an ancient law, but it comes in handy on occasion. And here's the funny part, we can actually throw you in jail if you refuse. See? Told you it was the funny part. Don't worry, the whole 'deputize' thing is CYA in case you get shot or some other bad thing happens to you. *And* if you're a deputy, even a temporary one, I might be able to get you some petty cash for gas and such. Maybe even a county car to run around in."

I shot him a disdainful look and imitated a child's voice. "Oooh, Uncle Frank, can I turn on the lights and siren, too?"

"It would be an *un-marked* car," Sanchez replied acidly.

"Forget that crap," I shot back. "I'll ride around with you for the most part, but some gas cash would be nice though."

"I'll work on it." He handed me a gold-colored, seven-pointed star. "The L-T said I can give you an 'auxiliary deputy' badge if you want it."

I conjured up my best Mexican accent saying, "Badges! I don't need no stinking badges!"

The humor would have been lost on Olsen. Not old enough to know who Humphrey Bogart was. But Sanchez chuckled. "You make a terrible Mexican."

I took the badge from him and looked at it. "Sounds kind of lame to me. 'Auxiliary deputy' sounds like I should be riding a horse in a parade in one of those orange 'sheriff's posse' shirts."

"Actually our posse wears white shirts for parades," Sanchez corrected. "And FYI, it puts *me* in charge of *you*." He was in a better humor now that he had someone that *he* could fuck with, namely me. "That badge is just like ours." He pointed to the upper left part of his shirt. "Can't really see the *Auxiliary* on it unless you look close. Davis said it might open some doors for you."

"It might get my ass kicked, too." I wondered where he had come up with it. "So do you give these out to so many people that you have to carry extras around with you?"

"Not usually," he replied. "We had a search and rescue a couple months ago and one of the volunteer posse guys forgot to turn his badge in. I went out to his place to get it several days ago and I still had it in my bag."

Still looking at the badge, I asked, "So do I need an ID card or a secret decoder ring or anything? Maybe need to know the secret handshake?"

"Don't be a wise-ass, Douglas, you want it or not?"

"I'll hang onto it for now," I told him, looking closely at the brass star.

A large banner reading *DEPUTY SHERIFF* spanning the top overshadowed the small *Auxiliary* banner near the bottom. *STATE OF TEXAS* was printed on the large banner across the bottom. There was no badge number, just the letter *A* in the small flat spot reserved for the number.

"Just replace your retired VPD 'Retired' badge with that one in your wallet. That should be all you need."

I looked at him and in the best Texas drawl I could muster replied, "Sure thang, Maaarshal Dillon."

Sanchez rolled his eyes. "That was Dodge City, Kansas, asshole. So now, 'Mr. CSI,' what are we going to do first?"

I was starting to like this guy. He was as sarcastic as I was. I turned back to look at the embankment. *Good question*, I thought, getting back to matter at hand *Dead guy over there, tracks and Harley over here, and tracks across that patch of desert.*

Making my decision, I told Sanchez, "We'll split this up into three parts. The shoulder of the road, all along here where the tracks are, and the embankment adjacent there will be one part. The desert between the two roads will be the second part, and poor dead Lyle over there will be the third part. He's not going anywhere, and we're fortunate there's no one else stomping around out here, so let's take care of this area first. I'll get the scene and track photos out of the way."

Sanchez nodded and said he'd call for a tow truck for the bike. "I'm assuming inside storage?"

"Yeah, somewhere secure," I replied. "You guys have an impound somewhere?"

"We do but it's only an outside deal. I'll see what I can find." Apparently knowing the bike had to be secured out of the weather so I could process it for prints later, Sanchez got back on his cell phone.

"Hey!" I called to him, "make sure the tow driver knows not to touch the thing without gloves on."

He nodded his understanding back at me. Off the phone several minutes later, Sanchez advised me the Harley was going to be towed to the county maintenance yard and locked in the enclosed metal shop that was also used to store stolen bicycles and other stolen equipment. It would also be marked with some crime scene tape by the tow driver. Sanchez then called Olsen, catching him up on our status. The two of us then began placing yellow plastic number stands, with me explaining my numbering logic as we went. The first of the stands were placed at the car tire and cowboy boot tracks, then the biker boot tracks on the shoulder down the road around the Harley. I was pleased to see that the stands they carried in the SUV were numbered up to 100, instead of the usual set of 50. We would eventually need them all.

We placed stands at every track we could find, but I intended to photograph *only* a few of the best tracks of each of the feet from both the shooter and Lyle. Sanchez inquired as to why.

"We can tell by the tracks there were only two people out here," I explained. "The scene photos need to show where they came and went as best we can using the number stands, but we only need a few good photos of each right and left for comparison since we're only dealing with two pairs of footwear. I'll take three photos of each from three different angles, but if we try to take track photos of each and every single track, we'll be out here for days."

Satisfied with this answer, he returned to the SUV and retrieved the camera, returning with a surprise. "After our conversation the other day about cameras and film, Olsen was actually able to talk the sheriff into springing for a new digital SLR camera. Man, you shoulda' seen Jim yesterday when he picked it up. He drove up to Odessa to get it from the camera shop up there. He was like a kid at Christmas that just got his favorite toy. Only problem is, he hasn't figured it all out yet. It's supposed to have a black and white mode."

Oh crap! I thought as he spoke. *This really isn't the time to be trying to figure out a new camera.* Sanchez pulled the camera from the case. I was immediately relieved to see it was only a newer version of the Nikon D300S. The same camera my bureau had switched to a year before I retired.

"Excellent," I said and took the camera from him.

"You already know how to use this thing?" he asked with a surprised look on his face.

"Think so," I replied.

"Damn, dude, is there anything you don't know? You friggin' Superman or what?"

"Nah." Again I replied with the Texas drawl as I stood super-erect with my hands on my hips, staring off at the horizon. "Out here in the west, they just call me, The Lone Ranger."

Sanchez shook his head. "So I guess that makes me Tonto?"

"Yup."

"Screw you, Ke-mo Sa-bee."

We both got a laugh out of that one.

I took overall photos of the scene from every angle, distant, mid-range, and close up. I then busied myself with the shoe, boot, and tire track photos. Placing a plastic ruler Sanchez carried in his posse box, and a small hand-drawn north arrow on a piece of paper next to each track, I detached the flash unit from the camera and, with Sanchez's assistance—him holding a floor mat out of the SUV over the track to shade it for the flash, I finished the track photos, also. Sanchez had previously radioed his dispatch and checked the plates on the Harley. The bike came back registered to a Lyle James with an address on the local Indian reservation. There were also two outstanding traffic warrants for unpaid speeding tickets. *That's money the county will never see. Well, maybe when they auction the bike off down the road.*

Two hours later, I had finished taking all the scene and track photos. I grabbed a yellow legal pad out and the Roll-a-Tape out of the SUV and was drawing up a rough sketch when the tow truck arrived. Under Sanchez' supervision, the bike was loaded up, strapped down, and hauled away.

The deputy stood watching me take measurements from the edge of the asphalt. "No Garmin this time? For your measurements, I mean."

"Nope."

"Where are you going to get the second measurement from?" I pointed to the Stop sign back at the intersection. He nodded. "Okay, but isn't that a bit far for the Roll-a-Tape?"

"Probably," I replied as I started hiking back to the intersection, "so I'll pace it off which will be close enough for our purposes. Not going to get it exact out here in the brush anyway."

With the sketching chore complete, Sanchez and I stood at the top of the embankment looking across the small patch of desert toward the gravel road. I could see that using the number stands on the ground here would not be of much use. I explained to the deputy that the stands were not tall enough to be seen in the photos in the brush, but we needed to figure something out since it was critical that we show the locations of both sets of tracks crossing the desert and converging at the gravel road. I was trying to figure out how we could do this. What we needed were some evidence marking flags that were made just for this type of situation, but we had none.

After a few minutes pondering the problem, Sanchez said, "I have an idea. I'll be right back." Leaving me standing there, the deputy walked back to his SUV, got in, made a U-turn, and drove off at a good clip. I could see the SUV make the turn onto the main road a mile or so distant, then it disappeared out of sight.

Ten minutes went by before I saw the SUV make the turn back on-to the blacktop road toward me. When it pulled to a stop, Sanchez got out, walked around, and opened the rear cargo door. Reaching in, he came out with a large bundle of very weathered, wooden, construction-grade stakes, complete with faded orange plastic flag strips tied to their ends. They were all about 3 feet long.

"Where'd you come up with those?" I inquired.

"There's a subdivision that got put on hold down the road a ways," he advised. "When the economy went bad, everything just got left out there. Will these work for marking the tracks?"

"Any port in a storm," I said. "Should work." *The orange strips are pretty faded, though. Going to be hard to see, that gray/brown wood against a gray/brown background.* Then it came to me and I turned back to him. "We'll put the number stands on the top ends of the stakes. They'll show up good. There's no wind today so they should stay on the stakes just fine."

Our ideas now combined, we set about the task of marking both sets of boot tracks across the dirt with the stakes and stands. It worked well, and once again I repeated my scene and track photos and roughed out a sketch.

"There's no fixed points out here for your measurements this time," Sanchez ventured.

"Not to worry," I replied as I pulled out my small GPS, again holding it up for him to see.

"Yeah, yeah," he muttered, shaking his head. "Super-friggin' CSI man."

For two guys who hadn't known each other a week ago, we were forming quite the bond. As I began writing down grid coordinates the Garmin was providing me for the two trails, Sanchez advised that he was going to pull his SUV around to Olsen on the gravel road near the body.

As he walked toward the top of the embankment, I shouted after him. "How long does it take your coroner to get here after you call him?"

"Oh, usually about an hour or so," he replied.

"Think he'll come out and do a liver temp for us any sooner than that?"

"He might. I'll call him when I get to the car," he yelled back as he disappeared down over the edge.

Ten minutes later I saw his unit pulling up to Olsen on the gravel road.

CHAPTER 8

Benny

B enny was pissed. Lyle had not been seen by anyone on The Res that morning and his Harley was missing. He'd tried to call Lyle's cell phone, but that had been of no use. Turned out it was laying in the dirt next to the lawn chair where Lyle had dropped it the night before. Benny suspected Lyle had ridden back out to the Rollins' ranch.

Lyle's grandmother all but confirmed it when she told Benny she'd heard Lyle's "motorbike," as she always called it, start up and drive away in the middle of the night. Benny unlocked the shed behind her house, and then did the same with the heavy steel locker sitting on the floor of the shed. It was actually a large steel tool box the two bikers had stolen out of the bed of a parked truck at the Flying J Truck Stop late one night. They'd bolted it to the floor of the shed and converted it into their "stash" locker after selling off the stolen tools inside of it. Several kilos of high quality marijuana were now inside.

After making sure they were all accounted for, Benny sat on the locker, trying to decide what to do. He was growing concerned that Lyle had piled his bike up somewhere. Should he go look for him? He figured he'd better but he didn't know where to start. Benny was comforted somewhat by the fact that if Lyle had crashed and the cops were involved, they would already be here by now, confirming Lyle's address and talking to Grandma.

On a whim he walked over to Lyle's uncle's shack and pounded on the door. The 70-inch, flat-screen TV inside was blaring a re-run of *The Price is Right*.

"What the fuck do you want?" Lyle's uncle, Thomas "White Feather" James, asked when he opened the door. He was in his usual daily attire of jeans with no shirt or shoes. He had a beer can in his hand which was also part of his usual daily persona as evidenced by his protruding beer belly.

"Hey, Tommy, just wanted to know if I could borrow your truck?"

"Fuck you! You and that worthless piece-of-shit nephew of mine didn't bring it back when you told me—that would be the last time you borrowed it—and you sorry fucks left the gas tank empty when you finally got it here!"

"That was Lyle," Benny insisted. "He told me he was going to bring it back right away after he dropped me off. I didn't know he was going to use it for two days while his bike was in the shop. I'll bring it right back, I promise. I think Lyle may be broke down somewhere."

Tommy belched and looked at Benny with a cocked eyebrow. "Why do you need my truck? Ride your own fucking bike!"

Benny thought quickly. "If Lyle's broke down, I'll need the truck to bring his bike back." Benny was lying of course. Just in case Lyle *had* done something stupid like got caught snooping around the ranch or crashed, Benny wanted to scout it out without being seen on his Harley.

"How long?" Tommy asked.

"Couple hours, maybe three, tops."

Tommy considered it then turned and removed the truck keys from a hook on the wall near the door. "Three hours, asshole! If it's not back in three hours…" He let the threat hang without finishing it. "The gas tank better not be empty and you own me a 12 pack!"

"I'll have it back," Benny assured him.

Tommy James slammed the door before Benny could say anything more. After pulling his Harley around into the shade by the side of the shed, Benny climbed into the old, beat-up, brown and white Chevy Cheyenne pickup truck and headed out onto the reservation road. His plan was to first drive by the Rollins' ranch. If that didn't pan out, he would begin checking with their friends and then Lyle's favorite local haunts.

CHAPTER 9

Watching

The saying was, "Patience is a Virtue." If that was true, the Mexican man was *very* virtuous. He had the patience of a clam. After eliminating Lyle earlier that morning, he had decided that when it was light enough to see anything from a distance, he would try to find a good place to observe the proceedings if and when, the cops discovered the biker's corpse. The man was in no hurry. He wanted to gauge the response and thoroughness of the local sheriff's personnel. There was no need to rush back to kill Benny. The man knew Benny would not go anywhere. He wasn't yet aware he was being hunted. If the Mexican man planned it correctly, Benny never would until it was far too late for him to save himself

Several hours until daylight, the man thought as he looked at his watch. He decided to get some sleep. He drove several miles back to the interstate and parked on the gravel shoulder, well away from the traffic in the slow-lane. He got out and raised the hood. While still outside the car, he also concealed his equipment bag in some desert brush 20 feet from his vehicle. Should a curious cop happen by, the raised hood would explain his being parked here—mechanical difficulty, waiting for a tow truck—but he didn't want to have to explain the contents of the bag. Once he was confident the bag could not be seen from the shoulder of the road, he climbed back into the driver's seat.

Taking off his cowboy boots, he put on a set of tennis shoes. He knew the soles of the boots were smooth and non-descript, but he took no chances. He would dispose of them later today. They were new boots purchased just for this occasion. He was certain that if he left them sitting on a curb somewhere, they would soon afterward be on the feet of a "Border Brother." The man then laid his head back and closed his eyes. Soon he drifted off into a light sleep.

Just after dawn, the Mexican man's "internal alarm clock" woke him. The traffic on the interstate was light. *Not even many trucks*, he noticed. He double checked the highway in both directions for any errant state troopers. He was surprised that his presence here on the side of the road hadn't been questioned. Seeing all was clear, he got out and quickly retrieved his bag from the brush and slammed the hood shut. He then started the Explorer and drove back to the general area of the ranch.

Finding a small rise just over a mile distant from the spot where Lyle's body lay, he parked the Explorer at the bottom where it could not be easily seen. Retrieving a set of Leica 10x42 binoculars from his bag and a small, folding camping stool from the back of the Explorer, and being careful not to silhouette himself against the rising sun at his back, he climbed the short distance to the top of the rise and checked the surrounding area. The morning was clear and cool. The hill, though it didn't rise very high above the desert floor, was positioned perfectly. It was directly in line with both the gravel road and the old blacktop. From here he could look straight down both roads toward the ranch. Making a 360-degree sweep, he was pleased he could also see the surrounding desert for miles The sun was rising at his back, which would all but eliminate any reflection from the glass of his binoculars should anyone be looking this way from the ranch. He had chosen his OP well.

The man unfolded the stool and sat down. With the powerful binoculars, he could clearly see the corrals and horses, and the fence near Lyle's body, though he couldn't actually make out the dark shape of the body due to the distance and the brush. He could also see a good portion of the house, the stables, and the small park in between. *Casa bonito*, he thought, *mucho dinero*. Lyle's Harley was clearly visible parked on the shoulder of the old blacktop road. The man wished he'd had the time to do something about the bike after killing Lyle. Then he shrugged. *Por nada.*

He was admiring the clarity of the high priced binoculars when he noticed movement in the ranch driveway. A maroon pickup truck pulling a large fifth-wheel trailer was pulling out of the gate and onto the gravel road. As he watched, the truck and trailer approached the intersection with the old blacktop road. The Mexican man recognized it as the same trailer he'd seen parked near the stables earlier that morning when all the lights came on, though in his haste he hadn't noticed the truck. The rig came to a stop at the intersection and he could see a white man and woman in the front seats. The Mexican man was puzzled when the truck sat un-moving.

As he watched, the gringo got out of the driver's seat. After exchanging words with the woman, the driver put a satchel over his shoulder and began walking toward the parked Harley. He stopped halfway to the bike, bent down, and began to examine the dirt on the

shoulder. *Who was this*? the Mexican man wondered. Then it dawned
on him the gringo was looking at the tracks he'd left in the dirt when
he'd followed Lyle. Over the next hour, he watched the gringo walk
from the top of the embankment down to the Harley then back up the
embankment and across the small patch of desert to the gravel road. He
noticed the man examine the ground everywhere he went. He saw the
woman move the truck and trailer, and he was watching when the
gringo discovered Lyle's body.

Soon a two-seater, all-terrain Rhino drove out of the gate and down
the gravel road. The ATV stopped next to where the gringo was standing and a Hispanic man got out. Both men stood together talking and
looking at the dead biker. It was obvious the man driving the Rhino
was an employee of the ranch, *But who was this gringo*? the Mexican
man wondered. *He acts like some kind of a cop. But why would he be
staying at the ranch in a trailer*?

The Mexican man had not watched the news or read a newspaper
in over a week. He now wondered if he had missed something important. As the Mexican man continued to observe, the gringo walked
back to the embankment above the blacktop road and was soon met by
an arriving sheriff's vehicle with its lights and siren on.

The spectacle became even more puzzling. Watching intently now,
the man saw both deputies greet the gringo. It was immediately appar-
ent this was not the first time these three had met. After a conversation,
one deputy then got into the pickup truck with the gringo and the
woman, and together the three of them drove back to the body. The
other deputy stayed near his vehicle on the blacktop road. The Rhino,
accompanied by the truck/trailer rig, then moved down the gravel road
to the ranch, leaving one deputy with the body. This was most curious.

The Mexican man longed for a long range hyperbolic directional
microphone. He would have liked to listen in on these conversations.
He made a mental note to try to obtain such a device from his employers. One never knew when it might come in handy again.

Certain that he'd left nothing at the shooting scene that would connect him to it, the Mexican man was now more curious than concerned
as he watched the proceedings. He knew he was overstaying his wel-
come on the top of the hill. He'd been watching the gringo and two
deputies for almost three hours now. The sun had climbed high enough
in the sky to start becoming a reflection threat. He had been lucky so
far. Only three cars had driven by on the road near the base of hill, and
none had showed any interest in his parked Explorer. It was time to
leave.

He picked up his stool and walked back to his SUV, started it up,
and made a U-turn. He needed to drive to a tire shop in Odessa, buy a

new set of tires for the Explorer, and get rid of these four. He didn't think there was enough tread left on these to leave much of a tire track, but it paid to be careful. And *after all*, he thought with a wry smile, *I do want be a safe driver.*

As he made the turn onto the main county road, an older brown and white Chevy Cheyenne pickup truck passed him traveling in the opposite direction. He hadn't seen the pickup turn off the old blacktop road near the ranch and it caught him by surprise. The Mexican man thought the driver looked familiar, but couldn't immediately place him. This bothered him.

CHAPTER 10

Lyle

I was standing with the two deputies looking down on Lyle's body when the female deputy coroner arrived. She parked her unmarked county car behind Sanchez's unit and stepped out. *Mmmmm, not bad*, I thought to myself as she walked up to us. She was a shapely Hispanic woman, in her mid-thirties with shoulder length black hair and brown eyes. She was wearing a gray-skirted business suit and carried a leather satchel similar to the kind pilots use. She placed it on the gravel of the road as she reached us.

Frank greeted her. "Vicki."

"Frank, Jim." She nodded to both deputies then turned toward me.

Sanchez introduced us. "Vicki DeLeon, this is Jason Douglas."

I extended my hand. "My pleasure."

She shook hands. "So you're the big CSI guy I've been hearing about for the past few days?"

"I don't know about that," I said, trying my best to not let her see me checking out her shapely legs. *Men truly are pigs*, I thought to myself, smiling at her.

"That's what I hear anyway," she said, smiling back at me.

Sanchez jumped in. "Don't buy the humble act, Vicki. This guy is the real deal. Very good at it. You just come from a date?" he asked, clearly referring to her semi-formal attire.

"I know, huh?" she replied. "I was supposed to be in a meeting with your boss and the state AG this morning, but then the shoot-out down south happened, you heard?" We all nodded, so she continued. "And the meeting got shelved, but no one got the word to me until I walked into the office and was handed your deal, so here I am." She struck a pose

"Business Barbie," Sanchez started to say, "All dressed up and—"

"*Don't* say 'no one to blow,'" she snapped, cutting him off, "or I'll kick you right in the balls."

Turning to me, she said, "Forgive me, I'm not usually this crude in front of strangers, but Frank here is my uncle on my mom's side, so I take liberties."

She put on a pair of latex gloves and bent over Lyle's body.

"I'll bet the guy who invented the meat cooking thermometer never thought it would be used for this," I offered as Vicki shoved the sharp point of the thermometer probe through Lyle's side and into his liver. I'd seen it done hundreds of times over the years, but it always made me wince.

She broke the rigor mortis in Lyle's fingers. Each one "snapped!" as she forced them open. After a few minutes she looked at the thermometer and made a notation on the legal pad she had removed from her satchel. She looked up at me. "Sometime around midnight or 1:00 a.m.," she said, referring to the time of Lyle's untimely demise.

"Yeah, that matches our time line," I replied.

Apparently she hadn't been informed of the gunshot that had awakened me earlier that morning. I quickly filled her in.

While she had been waiting for Lyle's liver temp reading, I had taken photographs of the body and the surrounding area. Observing me, Vicki then pulled her own digital camera out of her satchel. *No neck strap*, I noticed. *Need to mention that to her.*

As she was adjusting some of her camera's settings, she began telling anyone who'd listen, "I just bought this camera. It's really neat."

"You buy it just for your work?" Olsen asked. "You usually just get copies of our photos."

"I know but I wanted my own set so I can look at them right away," she replied. "It's a great camera—" She stopped in mid-sentence because she'd just dropped it onto the hard surface of the gravel road.

"Not anymore," Sanchez blurted out sarcastically.

Olsen snorted at that one.

Oh shit, I thought. *I put the bad mojo on her with the neck strap thing.*

Startled, she exclaimed, "Oh shit!" She picked it up she looked at me. "You think it's ruined?"

"Might well be. Not many digitals can take a shock like that."

Sure enough, it didn't work when she tried to turn it on. Looking forlorn, she stuffed it back in her bag. She would need our photos, after all.

As was common in many places across the country, one of the local funeral homes was contracted by Revas County to transport bodies to the morgue. Vicki had called for the body transport not long after she'd arrived. I bent down and removed Lyle's pistol and the extra magazine from his vest pocket. I also grabbed his wallet, the hunting knife from the sheath on his belt, and his boots. A quick search of his clothing for a cell phone came up empty. The two funeral home employees, or "meat bees" as I'd always called them, arrived. When Vicki gave them the okay, they zipped Lyle into a body bag, loaded him up in their van, and drove off. The deputy coroner made notes of the personal effects of Lyle's that we had removed, then she too packed up her satchel, said her goodbyes, and headed out. She assured Sanchez before she left that she would forward copies of the autopsy photos and report to the sheriff's office, though we all knew the cause of death would be Lyle's acute case of lead poisoning.

"Looks like we caught a break, the shooter leaving his shotgun behind," Olsen ventured as we looked at it and the two lose shells laying in the bloody dirt.

"Not likely," I told him. "I'd be willing to bet it won't have any value to us at all, other than we can be reasonably sure it was the murder weapon."

"Why not?" he asked. "After all, we've got the gun with spent shells in it and live shells laying right there. We can get prints and DNA off of everything."

Sanchez shook his head. Looking at me, he asked a one word question, "Professional?"

"I'm thinking," was my answer.

"I don't understand," said Olsen.

What was that phrase Obama was so fond of, ah yes, this would be a "teaching moment," I thought as I began running it down for the young deputy. I told Sanchez to jump in if he thought of anything I missed.

"Okay, Jim, here's the deal. I'm fairly sure the shooter followed Lyle out here because of the locations of the tire tracks and their relation to the bike. It would not be an easy thing to do at night without Lyle knowing he was being followed, so how would the shooter be able to do that? After finding both sets of shoe tracks out there and figuring out who was following whom, I'm certain the shooter had to be using some kind of night vision gear, *and* it would have to be the type he was able to wear, like goggles, because he needed to have his hands free. Those are expensive. Definitely not your $100 sporting goods store variety. That tells us he has the money to buy that kind of stuff. He wore shoes, or more accurately cowboy boots, with no sole design on the bottoms, which I'm certain was deliberate, and he's probably already ditched them. Speaking of tracks, or more specifically tire tread designs, the tire tracks over there by the embankment showed that the tires on what I believe to be the shooter's car were almost bald. Again, probably intentional. Just enough tread on them to keep from getting stopped by a traffic cop. I went ahead and took track photos of them but they're not going to be comparable. Just not good enough. He's probably got plans to change the tires out anyway if he hasn't already done so. Also, when I examined Lyle's Harley closely, I noticed the engine 'kill switch' next to the throttle was broken off."

"It's a used bike," Olsen said.

"Not *that* used," I countered. "Go Look at it. It's well cared for and from what I could tell there was nothing else broken or missing from it. The switch was broken off in the 'kill' position, which means that in all likelihood it had been broken off *after* the engine had been shut off. I'm sure the shooter did this after Lyle walked away from the bike in order to keep him from leaving, should it come to that. So the shooter follows Lyle across the desert in the dark using his NVGs to this spot and blasts him. What I can't figure out is why he would shoot him, making all that noise this close to the ranch when he could've in all probability silently killed him.

"Maybe he likes the powerful statement a shotgun makes, or just likes these sawed-off shotguns," Sanchez offered.

"He couldn't have liked this one too much," I replied. "He didn't hesitate to leave it here."

"Well, maybe he just likes shotguns in general, or didn't have a knife, or has an aversion to using knives." Olsen shuttered. "I know I would."

"Maybe, but this guy kills people for a living and he's good at it, I think, so a good knife would be a tool of the trade. Indeed he might like shotguns. What's not to like? They're deadly if you can get close. They can be purchased anywhere. They don't leave rifling marks on a bullet that can be traced and, most important of all, older ones like this can't be traced because a lot of them don't have serial numbers."

Seeing the questioning looks, I explained why to both deputies. "Before the Federal Firearms Act back in 1968, shotguns and .22 rifles were not required to have a serial number, but back to the knife thing. If the shooter is indeed a pro as I suspect, I'm sure he would carry a good *sharp* knife at least as a back-up weapon and would most likely *not* be shy about using it when it suited him. No boys, this guy is smart, careful, well equipped, and apparently well financed. He wouldn't be the type to take unnecessary chances unless he saw no other option. I'm betting Lyle did something to force the shooter's hand before he could stick him or cut his throat. I'm equally sure that after all his preparation, our shooter didn't just accidentally drop his shotgun and shells with his prints and DNA on them. That only happens on TV. He dropped it all right—here, deliberately."

"Why would he do that?" Olsen asked.

"Murphy's Law," Sanchez interjected thoughtfully.

"Exactly," I replied.

"Huh?" Olsen was now thoroughly confused.

I turned to him. "Murphy's Law states that if something can go wrong, it probably will. If you had just murdered someone and drove away, what might be something random that could happen to you? Something that you certainly would not want to happen if you were still in possession of a sawed-off shotgun?" I could see the light bulb above Olsen's head light up,

"A traffic stop, or a TA?"

I nodded. Olsen looked back at the items on the ground, fully understanding now.

"I absolutely would not want to be driving around with the murder weapon, or anything else that could connect me to it," Sanchez interjected as he stared at the extra shotgun shells laying on the ground.

I winked at him. "You get a cookie."

"Goddamn, you are *such* a wise-ass," Sanchez told me for the fourth time today.

"We'll collect this stuff, of course," I told them both, "and I'll process it for prints in your little lab, but I'm not going to hold my breath." *I might have a trick or two up my sleeve regarding the shotgun,* I thought to myself. *But there's no sense getting anyone's hopes up yet.*

CHAPTER 11

Missing

Benny was really worried now. He had driven the truck around longer than the three hours Tommy had dictated, with nothing to show for it. Benny had stopped at several of the local bars that he and Lyle frequented. He made calls to all their friends, and even a couple of skanks that traded sex for dope with Lyle once in a while. Benny even called some of the people they sold pot to. No one had seen Lyle, at least so they said. He'd called the Harley shop with no luck either. Benny finally called the local hospital and pretended to be a relative of Lyle's to ask if Lyle had been admitted. He hadn't. Soon he would have to get the truck back to Tommy. After making a call to Lyle's grandmother just to see if Lyle had shown back up at the reservation, which of course he hadn't, Benny decided he would try to drive out near the ranch as a last resort. He turned off the county road onto the old blacktop. As he got close to the intersection with the gravel ranch road, Benny slowed, hoping to make the turn and drive down to the ranch gate and back, but instead he braked to a sudden stop.

What he saw was not encouraging. A sheriff's department SUV was parked on the gravel a half mile from him facing the opposite direction. It's red and blue lights were flashing. There was a smaller unmarked car parked behind the SUV. As he watched, he saw three men and a woman standing off to the side of the road in front of the SUV. Two of the men wore uniforms, and one was in street clothes as was the woman. Benny was too far away to hear their conversation, of course, but he could see they were all looking at something in the brush on the side of the road, and he just knew *that* couldn't be good. Instinctively somehow, he knew it involved Lyle.

Benny wished he could drive past them for a closer look but he was aware, as was everyone else that no one else lived out this way, that this gravel road was a private driveway for the ranch and it was a dead end. If he drove down that way he would draw attention to himself and to Tommy's truck. *That* he didn't need.

Benny sat there for a few minutes trying to decide what to do. The woman made the decision for him. She was now walking back to her car and was looking in Benny's direction. Benny made a casual U-turn and headed back toward the reservation. At the intersection with the county road, he made a left turn and accelerated. *Gotta get the fuck outta here before she gets a good look at the truck. I'll go into The Res the back way.*

"What the fuck did you get yourself into Lyle?" he said out loud. He was so distraught at this point, he barely noticed the dirty silver Ford Explorer pass him in the opposite direction.

CHAPTER 12

The Lab

It was late by the time the deputies and I finished up the measurements for the last of the crime scene sketches and picked up all the number stands. The sun was on the horizon. We had already bagged up the weapon and shells and we were beat. Sanchez advised that they were going to take all of the items we'd collected back to their lab, download the photos into one of their desktop computers, burn them onto a disc, then head home for the night. I gave them their camera, asking if they needed help with the photos. Both were confident they could handle it, and Sanchez asked if I wanted to come down tonight to process the weapon and shells in their crime lab, but I declined.

"Too damn tired," I told them. I did agree to join them there the next morning at 8:00 a.m. They told me it would be a thirty-minute drive from the ranch, so I wrote down the address of their office and the directions they gave me. I then bid them farewell and turned down the gravel road, walking through the ranch gate to my trailer.

Sonya fixed a quick meal, after which I grabbed a cigar and a snifter of bourbon. We soaked in the hot tub for an hour. *It has been one hell of a day,* I thought as I lay down in the bed. I wouldn't have any trouble falling asleep tonight. I only hoped there wouldn't be another "after-hours" interruption. There wasn't. Dreamless sleep came quickly.

ессея

After an early shower and coffee, I punched the address that the two deputies had given me into the GPS on the dash of my truck. Their office was located in the town of Pecos, 40 miles from the ranch. Sanchez was right on with the driving time. Thirty minutes later I pulled into a parking stall in front of the building. As I walked into the lobby, I saw Olsen standing behind the Plexiglas counter barrier talking to a woman in civilian clothes seated there. He saw me and nodded, indicating he would be right with me. The woman looked my way then turned back to Olsen. I glanced around the lobby then around the room in which the two were standing. Obviously this area was part of their records section. The woman wore a tan plastic ID badge announcing she was an "Administrative Clerk."

Finished with their conversation, Olsen motioned me to a door that allowed access behind the counter and "buzzed" me in. He introduced me to the woman Dolores, as a courtesy, then motioned me toward another door at the end of the room. The place seemed deserted. We walked down a long corridor passing several small offices boasting names and titles on their doors. I read them silently as we walked by, *Sergeant Oliver, Sergeant Sandoval, Sergeant Ball, Lieutenant Maguire, Lieutenant Davis.* The offices appeared to be empty at present. I could even tell the larger offices of the sheriff and undersheriff which were both at the end of the hallway, were closed and locked.

"Where is everyone?" I asked Olsen. "Place looks deserted."

"Different places. Couple of the sergeants are out in the field. Most of the staff is down in Van Horn again today 'cept for Lieutenant McGuire. He's on vacation in Hawaii, the lucky bastard." We turned a corner and passed through a set of double doors. Their crime lab, fingerprint dusting room, and AFIS room were all located in this corridor. Sanchez was standing in the hallway waiting for us. We greeted each other and he pointed out the coffee pot in the AFIS room. After pouring myself a cup, the three of us entered the lab.

Not bad, I thought to myself as I looked around the room. It wasn't *that* small and, at first glance, it looked well equipped. The room was forty-feet-by-sixty-feet with a long examination/work table down the center. Along the right wall I saw one large and two smaller Superglue fuming chambers, two air-tight clothes drying cabinets, complete fans and biohazard scrubbing filters, and a bank of steel evidence storage lockers. Along the opposite wall were two large stainless steel sinks set in a room length counter with a steel chemical storage locker at one end. An enclosed hooded vent-fan covered one of the sinks. On the back wall there were evidence storage lockers mounted above a long counter. A fingerprint enhancing ALS or laser, as some mistakenly referred to it, was sitting on one end of it along with an accompanying camera and tripod.

My eyes opened wide when I saw the device sitting at the opposite end of the counter. It was an elongated steel chamber fourteen inches in diameter. There was tubing and wiring attached to the sides. I immediately recognized it as a Vacuum Metal Deposition chamber, or

VMD. It was used for obtaining fingerprints off of evidence, primarily when other methods have failed, and was normally reserved for use in major cases. They were not often seen, due to the cost involved in both their purchase and operation, the latter due to the fact that a super-fine dust of real gold was one of the primary ingredients used.

"Holy crap! A VMD," I blurted out. "Thought you guys didn't have any money."

"We don't," Sanchez replied. "Got it with grant money, but we've only used it once. We have to get Davis's permission to fire it up, so it rarely gets used. I don't even know if we can remember how. The one time we did use it though, it worked pretty good. Got some prints off of a knife handle in a who-done-it homicide three years ago."

I was impressed with their lab and I told them so. "You guys have basically everything you need here to do most stuff."

"Yeah," Sanchez replied. "Now if we just had the people and the time to use all this neat crap!"

The three of us donned surgical gloves and Sanchez retrieved the shotgun and the four shells from one of the evidence lockers. "What about Lyle's pistol and knife?" he asked me.

"We'll throw them in the Superglue tank, along with the magazines and cartridges," I told him nodding at the fuming chambers. "Even though we know all that stuff *was* his, some attorney down the road will for sure make a big deal about us not processing it, and Lyle's Glock is probably stolen, so you never know. We might get a print off of it that belongs to someone else and get you a lead in an unrelated case. Before you put it all in the tank, we need to swab the guns, mags, and ammo, again, just to say we did. I'm not optimistic about DNA on the shotgun or shells, but you never know on the pistol stuff."

Olsen pointed out some distilled water and sterile swabs on the shelf above the sink. Sanchez unloaded the pistol magazines. After putting a drop of the water on each of the swabs, I gently rubbed the triggers and grips of both guns, the hilt of the knife, the floor plates of the magazines, and all of the ammunition, including the shotgun shells, each with their own individual swab. When I'd finished, Sanchez spread all of the items on shelves in the large fuming chamber. Olsen retrieved a squeeze bottle of Superglue from the chemical locker, put a quarter-sized blob in a small aluminum foil cup, then placed the cup on the heating element of the chamber. Latching the air-tight door, Sanchez checked to make sure there was water in the humidifier attached to the side of the unit then flipped the "on" switch.

"I've used this before," Olsen said, "but I really don't understand how it works."

"Pretty simple really," I explained. "The Japs—whoops sorry, there I go being culturally insensitive again—Tokyo cops discovered it totally by accident back in like '77. Your fingers and palms extrude moisture through pores in the ridges. It's a combination of water, fats in the form of oil, salts, and amino acids. I could quote the percentages of each for you, but that's not important right now and it would just clutter up your brain, so for now let's just call it all "moisture." When you touch something with your fingers, palms, or your feet for that matter, that moisture, in most cases, stays on the surface of whatever you've touched in the pattern of the friction ridges."

Sanchez' eyebrows went up. "Friction ridges?"

"Mmmm, okay, I'll start over," I said patiently. "All of us good ol' primates have friction ridges on our fingers, hands and feet." Both deputies looked at their hands which made me smile. *Everyone does that*. "The ridges allowed our ancestors to swing from trees without falling into the open mouths of a Meat-a-saurus on the jungle floor, and these same ridges keep you and me from dropping our coffee cups onto *this* floor. In other words, friction ridges are for gripping, hence the name. Anyway, to keep it simple, as the Superglue heats up in the little container in there—" I nodded to the chamber. "—the main chemical compound in it called cyanoacrylate vaporizes. The chemical vapor then drifts around and attaches itself to the moisture from the print, thus crystallizing and hardening the pattern left by the finger, or palm, or even soles of feet and toes. The humidifier just adds moisture vapor to the inside of the chamber which hurries the process along."

Twenty-five minutes later, the chamber vented itself and we were able to retrieve the items. All of them had a thin layer of hard white residue on them to some extent. Several partial fingerprints were visible on the sides of the pistol magazines and on two of the live cartridges. Nothing was visible on the knife, the Glock itself, the shotgun or the shells, which came as no surprise.

"Why is there white residue visible on all of the items except the Glock," Sanchez asked.

"Glock pistols have a polymer, or plastic if you will, frame," I explained. "Superglue works well on some types of plastics, but not others. Look at the plastic ends of the shotgun shells, same thing. The slide on the Glock is metal not plastic, but it has a special matt finish. Rough, like fine black sandpaper, and that's also a bit resistant to Superglue."

With that explanation out of the way, we turned our attention to the shotgun. It was as I'd suspected—nothing. I could see the disappointment on the faces of both deputies as I turned the shotgun upside down.

"We haven't struck out quite yet," I told them. I grabbed the leading edge of the wood fore-grip and pulled downward. The fore-grip snapped off the weapon into my hand.

Surprised, Sanchez asked, "How did you do that?"

"The fore-grips on most double and single barrel shotguns are held in place by a strong spring clip on the underside of the wood," I explained as I showed him. "Once in a while you run into one that has a screw, but most just pop off like this one did."

Looking closely at the wood surface on the underside of the fore-grip, I saw faint ridge detail from a fingerprint on the edging surrounding the metal clip. "Well, well, well—maybe someone did leave us an early Christmas present," I said as I showed them.

"Oh, man, *my* hero," Olsen cooed and batted his eyes.

"Let's not get carried away just yet," I told them. "We need to see if we can enhance it, and remember this could be anyone's print. But it's a place to start and we might get lucky. I guess we need permission to use the VMD?"

"Fuck that!" Sanchez said "It's just like being married. It's always better to ask for forgiveness that for permission."

I grinned at him. "You are *so* right, my married brother."

Three hours and a half gram of gold dust later, I retrieved the fore-grip of the shotgun from the VMD chamber. The partial fingerprint on it now stood out well. Using the digital camera in the lab I photographed the print. It had taken me a while to get the settings and lighting the way I wanted it, but after 30 minutes of tinkering I was satisfied with the outcome. The partial fingerprint was better than I first thought it would be. I could tell it was a "whorl" pattern with the left "delta" clearly visible. The three of us walked down the hall to the AFIS room with the photograph.

The female AFIS operator's name was Tracy. Like so many others in these lean times, she was working as a "Jack of all trades." Originally hired as a dispatcher five years earlier, she had also been trained as the department's Law Enforcement Teletype Operator, so it was a natural jump for her when the sheriff was looking for someone who wanted to learn to enter and retrieve fingerprints from the AFIS system. She told me she had spent three weeks with the state lab folks learning the basics of fingerprints and their AFIS system, and the rest she just learned as she went. I could tell she was a smart woman and picked up things very quickly. It took us a bit, but between the two of us, we figured out how to do a direct entry of the print into the AFIS computer.

Ten minutes later she handed me a digital print out from the data base. To the layman, the printout was just a jumble of numbers accompanied by a black and white depiction of a partial fingerprint, but to both her and me, it was the potential identification of a suspect.

"The score is high," she advised me, referring to the numerical score the data base assigned to the list of the top ten fingers that the entry "hit" on. "It's not a 999, but it's a 620 and the next closest is 230."

"That's encouraging," I said.

"I don't *even* know what you're talking about," Sanchez interjected.

Olsen was also lost I could see. Tracy asked if she could explain it to them.

"Absolutely," I told her. "You know your system better than I do."

She held up the printout for both to see. I could tell she wanted to keep it simple to understand, without patronizing them.

"There's a list of ten numerical scores here from the fingers of ten different people or "candidates," she explained. "When the computer searched the data base, it found ten candidates' fingers that *could be* a match, with some closer to a match than others. It assigned a numerical score to each candidate in the order of how close of a match each finger was to the print we entered. If the scores are all low and they are all close to each other in numerical value, that isn't good. If the first candidate's score is a perfect one of 999, or even close to perfect, that is *very* good. If there is a big numerical separation between the scores of the first and second candidates, that can be good also, and that's what we've got right now."

"So who's the suspect?" Olsen asked.

"We don't' know yet," she replied. "I will print out the fingerprints of the first candidate using the guy's State Identification Number, or SID number. Once Mr. Douglas here compares the print from the shotgun to the prints of the first candidate and tells us it's a match, I'll enter the SID into teletype and get a criminal history on the guy, and *then* we'll have a name." She turned to me for any input I had.

"I couldn't have explained it any better, and call me Jason by the way."

Within just a few minutes she handed me a digital set of finger and palm prints she'd retrieved from the data base. I grabbed a fingerprint magnifying loupe she had setting on her desk, sat down, and began to do a quick comparison of the two sets of printouts. It didn't take too long for me to see that the print from the shotgun fore-grip matched the right middle finger of candidate number one. Tracy took both printouts and left the room headed for teletype, wherever that was. Fifteen minutes later she returned, walking down the hall and chatting it up with my good buddy, Davis, himself just getting back from the shooting scene in Van Horn.

He stuck his head in the lab and in his best stern lieutenant's voice said, "You still here, Douglas?" Without waiting for an answer he looked at Sanchez. "I expect an update forthwith gentlemen."

Sanchez nodded. "Ten minutes L-T."

Davis frowned, "Not a minute longer, Deputy." He turned and headed back up the hall to his office.

"Your guy's name according to his sheet is "Fernando Lopez." Tracy addressed the three of us reading from the "crime-history" printout as she walked through the door of the lab. "Convicted for selling stolen property, a gun used in an armed robbery. Sentenced to two years, he's out and about now on parole . His last known address was in Sierra Blanca."

"Where's that?" I inquired.

"Down I 10 South of Van Horn," Olsen replied.

I heard footsteps coming down the hall at a rapid pace. Davis walked into the lab.

"What name did you just say?" he asked Tracy.

Startled by his sudden re-appearance, she repeated herself. "Fernando Lopez."

"What's the DOB?" She told him. "And how is he connected to what you're doing?" he inquired of us, clearly interested now.

I spoke up and briefly explained how we came to generate his name.

Addressing the two deputies and myself, Davis said tersely, "In my office now," and walked away. All four of us looked at each other.

"Better you than me boys," Tracy ventured.

"Guess we should have asked permission to use the VMD first," I said.

Christ, I don't even work here and I'm gonna get a beatin', I thought to myself. The three of us trudged down the hall like kids that were being sent to the Principal's office.

Davis had arranged three chairs so we could sit in front of his desk. As we entered he motioned Olsen to shut the door. Olsen was nervous, I could see. Sanchez had put on his talking-to-the-boss face. I wasn't bothered and it showed. I could tell Davis didn't like the fact that his position didn't intimidate me. *Tough shit*, I thought. *This isn't my first rodeo, cowboy.*

"First catch me up," he said, addressing Sanchez.

The senior deputy briefed him on everything that had happened from the two deputies arriving and meeting me out at the ranch, right up until a few minutes ago. I filled in the holes. Olsen didn't say much.

Davis listened and when we'd finished, he got on Sanchez's ass a bit for using the VMD without calling him, but not as bad as I thought he might. He seemed distracted as he then changed the course of the conversation. "First off, Mr. Douglas, I want to thank you for your help." His change to a more conciliatory tone surprised me. "Being as shorthanded as we are, we don't have any of our own crime scene people right now and the state guys are all tied up on this Van Horn deal, so your help and obvious expertise is appreciated. I'll see if I can swing some gas expense money your way when this is all done. You two," he said to Sanchez and Olsen, "can forget your patrol duties until this case you're working on is finished. You're on it full time as is Mr. Douglas here."

We were all surprised at that. I'd figured he wanted me gone.

Davis continued. "There's a reason. Now all of you keep what I'm about to tell you to yourselves and I mean it. The only reason I'm telling you at all is because of that name you generated out of AFIS. The guy whose fingerprint you got off the shotgun was arrested for a parole violation coming through one of our checkpoints down near Van Horn after the shooting deal down there."

"Why was he arrested?" I asked.

"Possession of a firearm," Davis said. "Actually firearms I should say, as in plural. Two stolen handguns, three deer rifles, two AR-15s and…" He looked down at his notes then back at me. "…two sawed-off double barrel shotguns."

"The gun we recovered out at the dead biker was a sawed-off gauge," Olsen blurted out.

Davis looked at him disapprovingly. "What's with this gauge bull-shit? You a gangster now or what?"

Olsen looked back at the lieutenant with a sheepish smile. "Sorry L-T. I heard that term from a suspect and thought it sounded cool."

"Yeah? Well, drop it. You're a professional sheriff's deputy, not a street thug." Davis then turned to Sanchez. "What all do you have still open here?" He nodded toward the crime lab.

"We're done processing everything," Sanchez replied. "We just have to book all this crap into the Property Section."

Davis thought a moment. "Call that guy over in Property, what's his name, David something?"

"Dave DeLeon," Olsen said. "You know him L-T, he's the one that's married to Sanchez's niece, the coroner chick."

"Whatever," Davis replied. "Call him over here and have him book all of it for you. And by the way, Deputy Sanchez, it's evidence, not 'crap.' I want you three guys to go over to the jail and see if you can get anything out of this Lopez character that will help us. Who knows, maybe *he's* the guy that shot your biker." The lieutenant seeing the quick look Sanchez shot my way addressed me. "What?

I looked back at him. "Lopez isn't our shooter, Lieutenant." It was plain he was going to jump on me for my "assumption." *Back in his Lieutenant Prick mode again, I see.* "Hold on, Lieutenant," I told him, holding up my hand, "don't get your shorts in a wad. I'm not saying Lopez is not involved somehow, but whoever blasted Lyle James was a pro, not some half-assed gun peddler."

"And what makes you so sure?" he responded snidely.

"Look, Lieutenant, I've been doing this job a long time and I'm fairly good at what I do. This guy is a ghost. He came and went without leaving any trace to tie him to killing Lyle James. I saw some things out at the crime scene that told me our shooter had knowledge of surveillance techniques, maybe even formal training in it. He had specialized night vision equipment and used a weapon and ammunition that can't be traced, not directly to him, anyway. He used tactics that allowed him to sneak up and kill James, who was armed and probably alert himself, with no confrontation or struggle. Most important of all, our shooter killed James at close range, eye to eye, without hesitation. That tells me he's done it before. Does that sound like some penny-ante crook like Lopez?"

Davis thought about this for a moment then turned to Sanchez. "Go interview Lopez and see what you can find out. Take Olsen with you. He might learn something other than how to talk like an LA gangbanger." Davis seemed to have forgotten about me altogether. *Probably just hopes I'll ride off into the sunset,* I thought. "Get out," he said which ended the conversation.

As the three of us walked back out into the hallway, Sanchez asked me, "You wanna go with us over to the jail?"

"Nope," I replied. "This isn't an episode of *CSI Miami* and I'm not that goofy red-headed actor who runs around kicking down doors, waving his gun around, and then gets the suspect to confess by wearing his cool sunglasses and spewing smart-ass remarks. You two guys are the *real* cops here. I'm just the 'temp,' remember. A retired has-been detective."

"Yeah, right," he shot back. "You think I should bring up the fingerprint on our shotgun to him?"

"Up to you, but I wouldn't just yet," I told him. "That's the strongest leverage we have on him and you need to play that card at just the right time."

Sanchez cocked his head sideways in the direction of the jail. "Okay, but what are you going to do while we're over at the jail?"

I looked at both and winked. "I think I'll go back to the trailer and spend some time with the ol' lady. Might get lucky *if* she's obliging. When you're done playing 'pat-a-cake' with this Lopez ass-wipe, call me and let me know if you get anything useful out of him."

"Will do," Sanchez said.

As the two deputies turned to walk the other way down the hall, Olsen mumbled, "I wish I was headed back to my place to 'get lucky.'"

Sanchez stopped and looked at him. "I hope you aren't referring to Sonya."

Olsen looked shocked. "No way! Figure of speech. I just meant I'd like to be headed home to *my* girlfriend."

"Yeah, pussy is a paradox," Sanchez said as he started walking again.

"How's that?" Olsen asked.

Sanchez looked at him, smiling. "You spend 9 months waiting to get out of that thing and then the rest of your life trying to get back in."

CHAPTER 13

Traces

The Mexican man was now driving back toward the reservation. Several hours after he had unknowingly passed Benny on the rural county road, the man had completed his visit to every tire shop in Odessa looking for two things, tires with a generic nondescript tread design, and a shop that would accept a cash purchase with no computerized POS entry. His personal ID information was all false of course, but a credit card or debit card purchase was a thread that could be picked at. He didn't want *any* electronic information about him out there, false or not.

The man did not own a cell phone or a computer. Both were too convenient to use and they each stored even the most innocuous information. He was well aware of the privacy and tracking dangers of social networks such as Facebook, Google, and Twitter. He knew that cell phone conversations were monitored on a regular basis by the large Cray computers at the National Security Agency, and that phone text messages were stored on carriers' servers for months and even years in some cases. He knew that cell phones gave off constant tracking signals, even when turned off. The only cell phones he had ever used were of the pre-paid, disposable variety, but even those could pose a threat if not discarded quickly.

His Special Forces training had taught him that information stored on the hard drives of computers and the chips in Smart Phones could never truly be deleted or erased, except with the use of shadow programs which were available only to law enforcement. He also knew that bits of information could be recovered by law enforcement from computer hard drives and phones that had been deliberately damaged by such efforts such as fire, pounding with hammers, and corrosive liquids.

The Mexican man had finally settled on a set of semi-aggressive mud and snow tires he'd found at a small tire shop owned by a local.

The owner was more than happy to take cash with no receipt exchanged. The Mexican man would obviously need to use this vehicle to keep his "appointment" with Benny whenever it came, but he would now have to use care where he parked. These aggressive tires would leave definitive marks in loose dirt and sand. True he was going to switch vehicles and burn the SUV when his task was complete. In this line of work, you didn't evade US law enforcement for long if you were not very, very careful, but for now he would keep the Explorer.

Along the same lines of thought, the man hadn't wanted to stay in any motel another night, but it looked like he would be forced to. From what he'd observed, the sheriff's department here seemed to have what appeared to be a competent crime scene unit, which he would need to avoid. This surprised him considering the Revas County Sheriff's Department was not a large and well-funded police agency.

The Mexican man picked out a different low-end motel this time, but one still close to the Interstate. After parking the Explorer in the rear parking lot, he checked in and once again paid cash for a room. He told the desk clerk he did not know how long he would be staying, but that it would be several days and gave the man enough cash to cover the upcoming week, telling him if he finished his business sooner the clerk could keep the remainder of the money. This was fine with the clerk and again, no paperwork changed hands. After he'd showered and shaved, the man checked his revolver and placed it under his pillow. He also examined the other equipment in his bag for any damage. He was glad he had decided to bring a change of underwear and socks.

Satisfied that all was in order, he turned the TV on to a local news station. It was only then that he learned of the bank robbery and shoot out with the police near Van Horn Texas. Both of the robbers had been shot dead after an extensive car chase. Three cops had been wounded in that fight, as well as one shot and killed just outside the bank in Van Horn. The news also reported several others were arrested at "safety checkpoints." The Mexican man smiled. *A nice word for "roadblock,"* he thought. It was not known if any of those arrested were connected to the robbery. *Idiotas*, he thought as he listened to the reporter revel in the details. Did these three morons actually think they could kill a cop in Texas and then just drive away? *Or maybe they'd had glorious images of themselves as Butch and Sundance, or Billy the Kid, eh*? What was of more concern to the Mexican man was the hornet's nest of cops the chase and shootout had stirred up. That could make getting back to El Paso on the interstate difficult if it didn't all die down soon. *Wait! What name did that reporter just say?* The man turned up the volume.

"Texas State Department of Public Safety arrested one Fernando Lopez, as he tried to pass through a safety check point with several guns in his possession," the reporter reiterated. "A department spokesman said that Lopez, a resident of Sierra Blanca, Texas, was on parole for past criminal activity. Authorities are investigating whether Lopez has any connection to the robbery or the two deceased suspects. Also today, the Revas County Sheriff's Department said a body of a man has been discovered on property owned by a Toyah area horse rancher. Sheriff's spokesman Lieutenant John Davis identified the man as Lyle James, a local resident. Davis said the cause of death is unknown, but it is being investigated as suspicious. The rancher is said to be away on business and is not a person of interest in this case. In other news…" The Mexican man was no longer paying attention.

Although he had never dealt directly with this Lopez *vato*, he knew the shotgun he'd used on Lyle had originally come from him. The Mexican man made a point of knowing where the tools of his trade originated. This Lopez was just one of many sources for the illegal weapons his employers furnished him. He also knew that Lopez purchased guns from a "straw buyer" in Arizona, and then sold them in Mexico for twice or three times what he'd paid. The Mexican man was *fairly* certain the cops could not connect him to Lopez, but "fairly certain" was not "certain." It was a thread that the police could start to pick at. All the more reason to finish his business and get back to El Paso as quickly as possible. He would visit Benny first thing in the morning.

CHAPTER 14

Confirmed

I told you three fucking hours! Not all goddamn day!"
Tommy was yelling and holding up three fingers. He was so pissed
that spit was flying out of his mouth as he spoke. Benny was standing on the porch with the keys. Tommy, as usual, was drunk. His TV
was blaring the news in the living room. Benny had known he'd be
pissed off about him keeping the truck all day, but time just got away
from him in his search for Lyle, and at this point he really didn't give a
shit about Tommy's tirade.

Benny was worried sick about Lyle. "Listen, Tommy, goddamn it!
I was out looking for Lyle, man. No one has seen him all day. Doesn't
that bother you?"

"Fuck him!" Tommy shouted. "He's probably off drunk somewhere or over bangin' one of those ugly bitches in Toyah he calls his
girlfriends!"

Benny tried again. "You're not hearin' me, man! No one has seen
him, *no*-fucking-body! I've been everywhere and talked to everyone."

Tommy wasn't listening. "Yeah? Well, like I said, fuck him and
fuck you, too! That's the last time you use my truck, you little shit!"
Tommy grabbed the keys out of Benny's hand. "Now get off my
fuckin' porch 'fore I kick your skinny ass!"

Just as he started to slam the door, Benny heard a blurb from the
news anchorwoman on the TV. Benny put his hand on the door and
pushed his way into Tommy's living room.

"Hey, what the fuck do you think you're doin'?" Tommy shouted.

Benny was tired, dirty, and worried. Now *he* was getting pissed. He
wanted to hear the news story and he wanted Tommy to shut the hell
up. Tommy made a grab for his arm. Benny, in one quick motion, spun
and jerked the Glock from his shoulder holster in a move he and Lyle
had been practicing for months. He shoved the pistol barrel in Tom-

my's face. To Tommy, the end of the barrel must have looked as big as a fifty-five-gallon drum.

"Shut the fuck up, Tommy, or I swear to God, I'll turn your head into a bowl! I'll be outta here in a minute. I want to hear this, now *shut the fuck up!*"

Tommy, for all his bluster, was in reality pretty much a coward when it came to actual violence. Shocked by Benny's sudden threat, he closed his mouth and faced the TV. Benny holstered the weapon and did the same.

"Texas State Department of Public Safety arrested one Fernando Lopez, as he tried to pass through a safety check point with several guns in his possession. A department spokesman said that Lopez, a resident of Sierra Blanca, Texas, was on parole for past criminal activity. Authorities are investigating whether Lopez had any connection to the robbery or the two deceased suspects. Also today, the Revas County Sheriff's Department said a body of a man has been discovered on property owned by a Toyah area horse rancher. Sheriff's spokesman Lt. John Davis identified the man as Lyle James, a local resident. Davis said the cause of death is unknown, but it is being investigated as suspicious. The rancher is…" Benny was no longer listening.

Tommy stared at the TV in disbelief. Benny just turned and walked out the door pulling it shut behind him. *Lyle's dead. What the fuck happened? The sheriff's guy said it was "suspicious" and they didn't mention Lyle's bike, so it wasn't a wreck. Had Lyle sold pot to someone and it went wrong? No, not even Lyle would have gone out by the ranch to make a dope deal.* Benny's mind was racing. *Suspicious, they wouldn't have said that if the rancher, or that foreman, or that trailer cop guy had killed Lyle as a prowler would they? And what about Lopez? He's the guy we bought the Glocks from. Was he somehow connected to Lyle's death? Wait, no, the news said he had been arrested down by Van Horn. That is a long ways from where Lyle was found and he was commin' this way, not runnin' south.*

Benny's head hurt. He needed a drink, a joint, and some sleep. He was hoping that tomorrow would bring some answers as to why his lifelong friend and partner was lying in the county morgue.

CHAPTER 15

Lopez

Fernando Lopez was not an illiterate street thug. He'd been raised in Las Cruces New Mexico, the youngest of three sons of an upper middle class Mexican family and, unlike so many of his friends, he'd actually graduated high school with a decent GPA. His parents had wanted him to go to college, but he'd decided that criminal enterprise was an easier way to make money.

After high school, he had dabbled with stealing cars, stripping them, and selling their parts but that took a lot of time and the profit margin was small. He also tried some narcotics sales, though not being a drug user himself, dope sales never really interested him as a long-term business, and dopers as clients were notoriously unreliable. They were always ready to give someone else up to the cops if it meant them walking on a distribution charge. Lopez then got into buying and selling stolen property from local burglars. This turned out to be fairly profitable since most of the thieves *were* dopers and he could buy low and sell high if the items were valuable enough.

It was his involvement in this last endeavor that had shown him how profitable guns could be. Unfortunately, before Lopez could reap many of the rewards from his new found venture, one of his "customers" had been shot and wounded during an armed robbery attempt. The cops had offered the guy a deal if he gave up whomever had sold him the gun, namely one Fernando Lopez. The District Attorney tried to convict Lopez as an accessory to the robbery, but his attorney had pled it down to a charge of selling of stolen property. Due to the fact that the property had been a gun, Lopez was sentenced to two years in the state prison, however, overcrowding and no money led to his early release on parole after 14 months. While in prison, Lopez met people. People who gave him the idea of establishing a gun pipeline to the Zeta Drug Cartel thus eliminating his having to deal with ignorant thugs like the one that got him busted. It would be dangerous sure, but he could make a *lot* of money quickly and then retire from gun running, or so he hoped

Upon his release, Lopez went about setting up his own straw buyer network, using three of his cousins who lived in Arizona. At first none of the three wanted to get involved, but once he showed them how much money they could make and instructed them on how to protect themselves from the authorities, they agreed to help, albeit somewhat reluctantly. So far it had been profitable for all concerned. There were risks, of course, but as he'd told them, "Risks were a part of any business venture, legal or illegal."

He knew it was dangerous dealing with the cartel on one hand and dodging the Alcohol, Tobacco & Firearms cops on the other, but the truth be told, he was much more fearful of the cartel than the ATF. That federal agency was much too distracted by problems of their own making now.

Since the ATF's colossal blunder with their "Fast and Furious" gun-walking operation had come to light, they had backed off the gun shop owners in Arizona, New Mexico, and Texas, making Lopez's purchases and his subsequent sales that much easier. One other thing Fernando Lopez thought he now knew well was the American legal system. When Sanchez and Olsen arrived to interview him, all three were ushered into a small interrogation room by jail staff.

At first Lopez had tried to pull the "*no habla*" routine, but when Sanchez played a recording of his voice from the conversation at the check point with a state trooper, Lopez realized that was not going to fly. Suddenly and miraculously he became bi-lingual, although all he would say was, "I want a lawyer."

Sanchez continued to press him but was getting nowhere. He decided to try another angle and stared at Lopez across the table. "We saw some of your handy work yesterday." Lopez said nothing. "Guy got killed with a sawed-off double barreled shotgun. A shotgun just like the ones the state troopers found in your car. A witness saw you driving away."

Lopez's eyes wandered around the room, giving the deputies his best this-is-so-boring impression, but his mind was racing. *Shit, I shouldn't have stuck those two shotguns in with my other stuff.*

Lopez didn't directly deal with *stolen* guns much at all anymore. He preferred selling guns that had been legally purchased. True there had been those two stolen Glock pistols he's sold to those two lame-ass Indian bikers and, of course, the two sawed-off shotguns he'd been caught with, but the sales of the Glocks had been a favor for a friend out on the reservation, and the shotguns were a special order to be delivered to a man in El Paso next week. It had not been the first time his cartel contact had requested these specific types of altered weapons. Lopez suspected they'd been ordered for a specific job, or a person with specific tastes, or both. It had just been plain bad luck that Lopez had decided to pass through the Van Horn checkpoint on his way to deliver the shotguns so soon after the chase and shoot out.

When Sanchez threw out this last accusation, Lopez couldn't resist answering him, "Fuck you. No witness saw me anywhere around here yesterday or any other day. I been in Odessa for a week and I got people who will swear to that, so fuck off!"

Sanchez really wanted to punch this guy's face in. *Too bad water boarding isn't an option.*

He changed directions again. "Look, Fernando, you're screwed. You're on parole and caught with not just guns, but *stolen* guns that have been cut down. Tell me who you were taking them to and maybe we can cut a deal."

"Fuck you. Those weren't my guns and that wasn't even my car. I didn't know they were even in the trunk."

This information caught Sanchez off guard though he tried not to show it. Davis had not said anything about who the car Lopez had been driving belonged to.

"Yeah? Then whose car was it?"

"Fuck you! I don't gotta tell you nothing 'cause I know my propositions!"

Olsen snorted and almost laughed out loud. Lopez's mastery of the English language was less than perfect. Sanchez got up and stretched, telling Olsen he needed some coffee since this was obviously going to go on a while.

"Want some?" he asked Olsen.

"No thanks," Olsen replied, wondering what Sanchez was really up to.

"How about you, Mr. Lopez, want a soda or water or something?" His question was met with silence, so he turned and tapped on the door. A corrections deputy soon opened it from the outside and Sanchez stepped into the hallway reaching for his cell phone.

෴

I answered mine after the fourth ring.

"You out at the ranch?" he asked.

"Actually, I'm over at Wal*Mart. Sonya called me right after I left you guys and wanted me to pick up some stuff. Why? What's up?"

"I think we're going to have to jolt this asshole with the fingerprint we found. He's not a novice at this game and he's not giving us anything. He lawyered up right off the bat," Sanchez advised.

"You call a lawyer for him yet?" I asked.

"Not yet. Just getting ready to."

"I guess we can throw the print out there if you're really thinking you need to," I told him.

"I would, but I'm not versed enough in fingerprint lingo to make a believer out of him if he hits me with something I've never heard of. This guy's not as dumb as most. He already blindsided me with some information about his car."

"What about his car?" I asked.

"It's not his, according to him, and I believe him," he replied.

"You're shittin' me!"

"Nope. He won't say whose it is, and by the way he's sitting' there all smug with that shit-eating-grin on his face, I can tell he's not lyin' about it. He says it belongs to someone else and he didn't even know the guns were there."

I could tell Sanchez was growing exasperated. I shook my head as I looked at my shoes. "Nice of Davis to let you know beforehand, eh? Okay, I'll come over to the jail. Do you have the photo of the print with you? We'll need it and his AFIS print out?" Sanchez said he did. "Good. Before I get there do me a favor." I related my request then hung up.

Looking down at the shopping cart full of merchandise I had already accumulated, I thought, *There will soon be a Wal*Mart associate that is not going to be happy with me.* I turned and walked out to my truck leaving the cart where it was. *Sonya won't be too happy either.* I hit the speed dial to her phone as I turned out onto the highway. Fifteen minutes later, I pulled into the county jail's employee parking lot.

My "deputy" badge actually came in handy when I was stopped at the gate to the lot by the security guard. One glance at it and he waived me through. I flashed it again to the lobby corrections deputy, who'd been told to expect me. He buzzed me into the main jail's in-processing area where Sanchez was waiting to guide me back to the interrogation room. He handed me several sheets of paper he had retrieved from the booking area, per my request. They were digital printouts of Lopez's finger and palm prints from the Live-Scan used by the jail and a mug photo of Lyle James, taken the last time he was arrested.

"You my lawyer?" Lopez asked when he saw me walk into the room. I said nothing "Who the fuck are you then, *vato*?"

I quietly walked over to the table and sat down. I still said nothing to him. I just stared into his eyes. This unnerved him somewhat which, of course, was my intention. I slowly placed each sheet of paper in front of him one at a time, turning them so he could see them.

"What the fuck are these?" he asked, raising his voice.

In 1976, the movie *Marathon Man* starring Dustin Hoffman was released. In the film, the actor Sir Lawrence Olivier portrayed a calmly evil interrogator. His passive demeanor and his quiet, yet extremely disturbing tone of voice as he repeatedly asked Hoffman's character, "Is it safe?" stuck with me all through the years. I used my best imitation of that voice and demeanor now.

Keeping my tone low and even, I said to him, "These four pieces of paper are going to put you in prison for many years to come, Mr. Lopez. They may even land you on the lethal injection table."

He was looking back and forth between the printouts, the photograph, and me.

"Do you see this particular photograph, Mr. Lopez?" I asked, holding it up for him to examine. I looked at it and smiled. "This is a photograph of a partial fingerprint. It's your fingerprint, Mr. Lopez. Do you want to know where we found it? We found it on the shotgun that was used to kill this man." I showed him a mug shot of Lyle James, which up to now had not been part of the display on the table. I saw him twitch ever-so-slightly, and right then I knew he'd recognized the photo of James. Looking at Sanchez and Olsen I asked them, "Did you hear that?" Neither was sure how to answer so I did it for them. "That was the sound of Fernando's asshole slamming shut when he saw Lyle's photo here." I tossed the photo on the table.

"Never seen him before," Lopez said, though I could hear the uncertainty in his voice now.

"We all know that's not true, now don't we, Mr. Lopez? It won't be hard to find the connection between you and poor dead Lyle here, and now we can absolutely put your finger on the gun that killed him. Yours is the *only* fingerprint on that gun, Mr. Lopez." I could see he was nervous now.

"I want my lawyer," he repeated again.

"Let's not worry about the lawyer right now," I told him.

"Hey! You can't do that!" Lopez yelped.

I continued in the same low tone. "Actually, since the three of us are the only ones in this room, I can do anything I want."

"I'll file a complaint!" he shouted.

"That's entirely up to you, Mr. Lopez, but who do you think will be believed? A convicted felon suspected of murder, or three esteemed officers of the law with flawless records?"

Lopez sat there in confusion. I could see beads of sweat starting to form on his forehead

I pressed on. "You sold Lyle James here the stolen pistol he was carrying, and when he didn't pay you for it, you followed him and killed him. Isn't that so, Mr. Lopez?"

The mention of the pistol now totally threw him off his game. I had no idea where James had come by his gun. I was just fishing. When we'd been in the lab, I had attempted to show the two deputies how to try to restore the Glock's scratched out serial number using one of the more common methods of Fry's Reagent, some emery paper, and a low voltage power source, but the numbers on the weapon had been too badly damaged. All we had been able to recover was the letter G and the numerals 29. Not enough for a computer search of the original registered owner, but Lopez didn't know that.

I smiled at him. "We know when the gun was stolen, who stole it, and how you came by it. We know it all now, don't we, Mr. Lopez?" Before he could answer this question, I hammered him again. "Now I know there's a very slim possibility a good lawyer *might* get you out of a first-degree murder charge. You could claim it was self-defense or some such nonsense and your lawyer might get you a plea deal, maybe second-degree murder if you are lucky."

Sanchez glanced at me. He was obviously afraid I was giving this crook ideas, but I knew where I was going with this. I gave Sanchez a wink and continued.

"Either way, you will still have to do a substantial amount of prison time, yes? What would happen, do you think, if through a series of well-orchestrated events on our part, word got back to certain people south of the border that you were working with us? Giving us names and places and dates, and that in the spirit of multi-national coopera-tion, we were of course going to pass this information along to the Mexican Federal Police?"

Lopez's eyes widened. I slowly stood up and walked around the ta-ble behind him. Without warning, I suddenly grabbed him by his hair and jerked his head back and at the same time slapped the table top hard with the palm of my hand. Startled by the noise, Sanchez and Olsen both jumped.

Still grasping his hair, I placed my mouth next to Lopez's ear and spoke very softly. "I'll tell you what would happen, Mr. Lopez. Some dark night, another prisoner will come to you." I whispered now. "And he will come to you on tiptoes, so you ain't never gonna hear him. He'll have a shiv, freshly sharpened on the stone wall of his cell. He'll cover your mouth, so you can't make a sound, and then slice open your throat. You'll bleed out in a little over a minute. When that's done, he's going reach in through the gaping hole in your throat, pull your tongue out through your neck, and let it just hang there. It's called a Columbian Necktie, and it's a message to others about talking out of turn, like to the police."

I slowly drew my thumbnail across his exposed throat then let his hair go. His head stayed back for a few seconds as he tried to clear his head of the mental image I'd left him with.

I couldn't help myself. I bent down and whispered in his ear, "Is it safe?"

"Huh? What?" he asked, confused and uncertain now. He hadn't really heard me. I sat down next to him, took his right hand in mine and grasped his elbow with my left hand as a good friend, or a mentor might. I was now in total control of not only his arm, but of his emotions.

I looked at him directly in the eyes and said, "Mr. Lopez, I'm actually very certain you *didn't* shoot Lyle James, but we have two ways this can go. I will put you in prison for his murder and I will see to it that word leaks out you're a rat. Or I can help you. You are a criminal but not a murderer. I can help you get your life back in order. Do you want to live out your life in prison for something you didn't do, and maybe get killed in the process? I won't lie to you, Mr. Lopez. You are going to have to do some time for the stolen guns, but that's nothing compared to life without parole, or the death penalty is it?" His head was down now, and he was shaking it slightly from side to side trying to decide what to do. Gently I continued, "I want to help you, let me. Tell me about the shotgun, Fernando."

Hearing me gently call him by his first name was finally too much for Lopez. He began blubbering in both Spanish and English, first about not wanting to die in prison, then he began to tell us all he knew. Sanchez had already turned on his pocket recorder. Fernando Lopez talked for the better part of an hour but most of what he had to say was related to his straw-buying program and how the guns were getting across the border. By the time Lopez stopped talking, we still hadn't learned who the shooter was, because Lopez really didn't know the man who had the affinity for shotguns. He'd never done business directly with him. There was obviously a "cut-out" man between Lopez and the shooter. It might be a cartel member, but more likely just a mule, a disposable go-between person. This was common practice meant to protect all parties. Lopez himself used his own version of a cut-out man on occasion between himself and his gun buying cousins.

We were wrapping up our conversation with Lopez. We had learned a lot that the Feds would appreciate, but nothing that really helped the three of us with the death of Lyle James. We were getting

ready to leave Lopez's fate to the ATF and walk out of the interrogation room, when he mumbled something that stunned the three of us.
Fortunately he was looking down at the floor when he said it, thus he
didn't see our reaction.

"I knew I shouldn't have sold those fuckin' Glocks to those Indian
pendejos."

I recovered from my surprise quickly and shot back, "Lyle James
should have been quicker on the draw I guess," I said nonchalantly.

Lopez looked up at me and replied, "Si, or had that redskin mother-
fucker he always pals around with covering his ass like he did when
they ripped off those dead guys."

Whoa! *What are we into here*? Trying again desperately to hide my
surprise, I continued as nonchalantly as I could, "What'd they do, find
a couple dead guys and rob them?"

"Nah, them two dead guys that was found out in the desert," he replied, looking up at me. "It was on the news."

I was wracking my brain trying to think of two recent bodies found
out in the desert, but I was thinking *bodies*, not skeletons. It took me a
minute to make the connection and when I did, I almost jumped out of
my shoes. *Holy shit, can't be*! "Fernando, are you talkin' about the
skeletons that were found a couple days ago?" I asked, now trying to
contain my growing excitement at this new information.

"Yeah, them is the ones."

I was stunned. I looked at him, squinting my eyes. "Let me make
sure I'm clear on this, Fernando. Are you telling me that Lyle and his
buddy were the ones that stole those two skeletons and put them out in
the desert?"

Lopez nodded. "That's what I'm telling' you."

"And just how would you know that?" Sanchez asked him.

"This little puta' I was fuckin' a few days ago told me. She was
fuckin' that Indian, too. Said Lyle was braggin' bout' it one night
when they were goin' at it."

I glanced at Sanchez. His eyes were wide and Olsen's mouth was
agape. I gave them both a stern look which helped them get back their
"poker faces."

"Why would they steal skeletons, Fernando?" I asked Lopez.

"Ask the chick. I wasn't really listening to the bitch. She was telling me all this while she was sucking my dick. I just wanted her to shut
the fuck up and get me off."

This information was mind-blowing and now we knew James had a
partner but we needed a name, *and* I didn't want Lopez to realize we
didn't know it. I gave Sanchez a slight nod, hoping he'd catch on to the
ruse I was going to attempt. As I turned to him I said, "Hey, we turned

up James's buddy's name, what was it again? I can't remember. You still have your notes?"

Sanchez didn't miss a beat. He nodded and started flipping through his notebook as if looking for a specific page. Olsen looked completely lost at this point, wondering if he'd missed something.

Sanchez shook his head at me and said, "I don't have it here. Must be in my notes in my office I guess."

"You talking about Benny?" Lopez asked.

"Yeah, that's it," I replied. "Benny, Benny…" I looked at the ceiling as though I was trying to remember the last name.

"Benny Johnson?" Lopez offered.

"That's it, Benny Johnson." I smiled and winked at the two deputies. "Final question, Fernando. We need to talk to that chick that was screwin' you and Lyle. What's her name?"

Lopez didn't hesitate. "Her name is Debbie Franklin. Can't miss her. Good lookin' black chica with giant titties. Don't know her address but she hangs out in a bar called Whisky Creek in Odessa. You guys gonna tell the DA and the Feds I cooperated, right?"

"Sure thing, Fernando," Sanchez assured him.

We walked out, leaving the corrections deputy to escort Lopez back to his "accommodations" as the three of us stood outside of the interrogation room.

"Well, that sure turned out better than I ever expected," I said.

Olsen turned to me. "Man, you were good in there. You even scared the shit outta me with that whispering routine. Hell, *I* was ready to confess. Where'd you learn how to do that?"

"Just stuff I've picked up over the years. You learn to read people. Some respond to kindness, some like Fernando there, need to be pushed a bit first, though. Keep in mind as soon as he talks to his attorney, he'll claim duress and it'll be up to the judge whether or not to admit the statement we got, but at least the Feds can get their hooks in him now. For us, the more important thing is what we learned from him, and that is that Lyle James has a partner out there somewhere who knows what this is all about."

Sanchez then spoke up. "How do we know Lopez wasn't just jerking us around about all this?"

"Two reasons," I told him. "The first is I never said anything about James's stolen pistol being a Glock."

"And the second?" Sanchez asked.

"I never said Lyle James was an Indian."

Olsen cut in. "So where are we going to find this partner of James?"

I turned to him. "The reservation would be a good place to start, I'm guessing."

"Never happen," Sanchez said. "No one out there will talk to us."

"We won't know until we try," I replied. "Let's go."

"Actually," Sanchez replied, thinking. "The reservation is not that far from the ranch. Why don't you drop your truck off at your trailer and ride with us?"

I nodded my approval at that.

Sanchez took out his cell phone again. "I need to call Lieutenant Davis and let him know what we're doing and about this skeleton crap we just found out. He's gonna shit rubber nickels."

The deputy then stepped over to the wall out of earshot. Olsen and I went to look for the men's room to get rid of some of the coffee we'd been drinking and discovered the break room for the Corrections guys next to the restrooms.

Sanchez joined us there. "Okay, all set. The L-T wasn't too hot on us going out The Res at first, but he got such a hard-on when I told him about the skeletons, he finally agreed. He said *he'll* personally take care of talking to the Franklin woman. He doesn't want us fuckin' up his skeleton deal in the Press, I'm guessing. Said we are to focus on the Lyle murder. One more thing. Out at The Res there's always a jurisdictional issue because it's technically a sovereign nation. We'll respond to an emergency sure, but investigations out there are supposed to be conducted by the Tribal Police, which consists of one cop, by the way, for misdemeanors, minor felonies, and traffic stuff. The Feebees—that's what we call the FBI—do the heavy felony stuff, so we'll have to include the reservation police."

"Feebees, huh?" I said sarcastically. "Spare me."

"You don't like those guys I take it?" Olsen asked.

"I've worked with them over the years, all the way back to when I was an MP. Some of their people are all right," I replied. "But most of 'em are arrogant, egotistical jerk-offs who like to walk around in their dark suits trying to look like Will Smith in *Men in Black*, flashing their credentials. They think getting dirty and doing the mundane work it takes to solve street crime is beneath them. They *are* very good at sitting at their desks crunching numbers and tracking down white collar criminals, terrorist cells, organized crime figures and such, *and* they have fair Hostage Rescue Teams and a great lab, but that's it in my book. "

Being a young SWAT stud himself, Olsen protested, "I thought the FBI's HRT guys were the best in the world?"

"Yeah," I replied, "that's what *they'll* tell you, but if that's so, how is it they have to have their guys trained by other agencies like LAPD,

LASO, and US military snipers like the SEALS? You might want to ask Randy Weaver how good they are."

"Who?" Olsen inquired.

Sanchez shook his head and rolled his eyes at me. "Kids," he said, "they never read any more. Too busy sending pictures of their dicks on their cell phones and playing *Call of Duty* video games."

I chuckled at that one and asked him, "Did Davis tell you whose car Lopez was driving?"

"Yeah," he replied, "Some friend of a friend but, of course, no one can find the guy. He's in the wind. Probably back in Mexico by now. "With that, we left the jail to go find Benny "Two Feathers" Johnson.

"So *who's* Randy Weaver?" Olsen finally asked.

"Google it on one of your gadgets sometime," Sanchez replied.

CHAPTER 16

The Res

A fter we dropped off my truck at the ranch, Sanchez had his dispatch call the Indian reservation's only police officer and advise him we were en route, asking him to meet us in front of the casino. Sonya had met us at the door of the trailer, handing each of us a foil wrapped paper plate with a sandwich and some chips. All three of us were now munching as we drove.

"Nice of your wife to fix this for us," Olsen said. "I didn't realize how hungry I was."

"Yeah, she's always on top of things and she takes pretty good care of me. Not bad lookin' either, eh?" I said, winking at Olsen. Embarrassed, he looked away and I continued, "I can't imagine life without her after all these years together." As an afterthought I added, "Hope I die before her."

Sanchez also looked at Olsen, "She *is* pretty easy on the eyes that's for sure, if you don't mind my saying so. Ya know, I've been divorced twice. How'd you stay married so long? Being in this line of work I mean."

I considered this for a minute before I answered him. "Well, as well as being lovers, we're best friends. I mean she can be a pain-in-the-ass like every woman I've ever known, but I really like her as a person as well as being in love with her and, of course, we all know *men* are never a pain-in-the-ass!"

"That goes without saying," Olsen replied.

Thinking about the hills outside Vista, California, I remembered there had been several Indian casinos built on Rancheria. Some were quite impressive, along the lines of Vegas or Reno casinos. This Indian casino was nothing like I imagined it would be. It consisted of a single tan adobe building, about two-hundred-feet square with a gravel parking lot in front. Several Sinclair gasoline pumps under a canopy were located on one side of the building. A large sign surrounded with flashing Christmas type lights on the front announced *CASSINO – EAT HERE & GET GAS*. An obvious attempt at humor. To its credit though, the building appeared to be well cared for and the grounds were clean. At least 50 cars were parked in the lot. *Gambling and eating business must be okay*. I could also see that new construction was planned for a large area behind the building as grade stakes were stuck in the ground everywhere. A large yellow CAT scraper was parked there as well.

As we pulled into the gravel lot, the reservation police vehicle drove up alongside our SUV and, again, I was surprised. In my imagined stereotype I thought it would be some dirty, rusted, and beat up, hand-me-down patrol car with a single red "bubble-gum" light on the top, driven by a long-haired Indian wearing a plaid western shirt, jeans, boots, and a cowboy hat. *Mmmmm, missed on all counts*. I couldn't have been more wrong. The patrol car was a late-model, dark-blue Chevrolet Tahoe with a large push bar, siren speaker, and Warn winch mounted on the front. The words *RESERVATION POLICE* were boldly printed on the front doors in gold, over a red outline of the reservation's boundary lines. On both rear quarter panels, the same gold lettering, only larger, announced *K-9* with red lettering below it stating *Danger-Keep Back*. The car was clean and freshly waxed, and I could see a state-of-the-art LED light bar on the top. A brindle-colored Belgian Malinois dog stared at us silently through the wire screen behind the rear side window.

The three of us stepped out or our SUV, as did the reservation cop. I could see now he looked more white than Indian. He was tall, in his mid-forties and looked to be in decent shape. His uniform was made up of black tactical pants and shirt, with an embossed, silver, shield-type badge on his left upper chest and a matching name tag announcing *JOHNS* above his right chest pocket. His head was topped by a black baseball cap with *POLICE* across the front in silver lettering. The duty belt he wore was black ballistic nylon and sported all the tools of the trade, which included his leather dog lead, a double-magazine ammo pouch, key fob, hand-set walkie-talkie radio, two handcuff cases, a yellow Taser, and finally a Glock .40-caliber pistol.

As he'd left his front door open, I glanced inside his unit. Both a Remington pump shotgun and a Colt AR-15 semi-automatic rifle were visible in a side-by-side rack between the two front bucket seats. A second shotgun, this one with a yellow colored fore-grip and stock, indicating it was a less lethal weapon, was in an overhead rack just behind the visors. A hard mounted laptop computer was on the console, as well as the usual electronic switch panel for lights and siren.

All in all, a professional and well equipped K-9 officer and his vehicle. *Shouldn't make assumptions*, I reminded myself.

"Michael Johns," he said, introducing himself, sticking out his right hand.

Sanchez greeted him and introduced his partner and myself, then got right down to business. "We're looking for a guy supposed to live here, a Benny Johnson. You know him?"

Officer Johns nodded. "Oh yeah, I know Benny. Local doper rides a black Harley."

Sanchez, Olsen and I all looked at each other.

I spoke up. "Doesn't happen to be a black Dyna Glide does it?"

"Actually," Johns replied. "I think it is now that you mention it. He and his buddy both bought black Dynas at the same time."

"Buddy?" Olsen inquired. The young deputy was getting the hang of it.

"Yeah. Benny has a partner in the dope sales business. Guy named Lyle James."

Bingo!

Sanchez jumped in. "If they sell dope, why don't you bust 'em?"

"Can't." Johns shrugged. "James's grandma has a marijuana card from out of state. And supposedly the growing is for her own use and, since these two assholes don't sell on the reservation here, at least not where I can see it, there's nothing I can do. I've worked those jerk-offs several different times but haven't caught them selling on The Res yet. Nothing I can do off The Res, but I let your guys know about it some time back, and Odessa PD also. So far, nada."

I looked at Johns. "Well, you won't have to worry about Lyle James any more. Got himself shot and killed two days ago."

"No shit?" Johns asked. "I guess there's hope for the world yet. Where'd it happen?"

Sanchez spoke up. "Out at the Rollin's ranch."

"Dope deal gone bad?"

"Possibly," I replied, "but looks more like a professional hit."

Johns whistled. "Wow! Wonder who he pissed off?"

"So is Benny around?" I asked him.

"He was a couple hours ago. Saw him driving around in a pickup truck that belongs to Lyle James's uncle."

"You care if we go pay Benny a visit?" Sanchez asked.

"Follow me," Johns said, climbing into his Tahoe.

"Mind if I ride with you?" I asked him, "I'm tired of sitting on that hard plastic rear seat."

"Not at all," Johns replied. "Hop in."

As we drove along together, curiosity finally got the best of me. "You don't look like an—a Native American."

He laughed. "It's okay, you can say Indian. I'm not all that politically correct and I don't get offended by the term. Might want to draw the line at red-skin, though."

"That would be a misnomer since you look more white than *Indian*," I said, emphasizing the word.

Johns chuckled again. "I'm only half Indian, and not a Lupan at that. I'm half Apache, but don't talk that around. It's a sore subject around here."

Apparently he could see I was confused. "Here's how it works," he explained. "The people here and the reservation belong to the Lupan tribe, so I can't live on The Res. I live down the highway a bit. The only reason I got the reservation police job *here* is because I am Apache, mostly, and I was a K-9 cop with LAPD for 8 years. They didn't have to send anyone to an academy. I still had to go to an abbreviated version at the federal academy down in New Mexico, then to the TSDOPS for several weeks to learn Texas traffic laws, but all in all, the Tribal Counsel here still got a deal."

"Looks like they take care of you pretty well," I said, indicating his Tahoe, his equipment and the dog.

"Yeah, once they opened the casino, they spent quite a bit of money to keep it safe, so I do all right. They spent a ton of money on my dog, Falcon, back there—" He jerked his head toward the rear of the Tahoe. "—what with training, my kennel, food, and all. He was already pretty much a trained police dog when I got him, but I had go to additional handler training with him. We still train together with the state guys all the time. The pay is pretty good for this part of the country, and the counsel built me a brand new office with two holding cells, though I spend most of my time at the casino, showing the colors so to speak. They consider me more of a glorified Security Guard than a cop, but I still do traffic accidents once in a while, and the occasional dope bust. I write a few speeding tickets, recover 'borrowed' cars, and roust the drunks after the casino closes. Once in a great while your buddies the county mounties back there, will call me for the dog. It all keeps a roof over my head and I love working with Falcon. So what's your story?" he asked me.

I proceeded to tell him about retiring and then everything else I'd been involved with to date, from the blown-out tire to the interview with Lopez.

"Wow!" he exclaimed with just a hint of sarcasm—or envy. I couldn't tell which. "Sounds like *real* cop shit! I'd heard about the skeletons out in the desert on TV, but I didn't know one of them was an ancestor of mine. They make anybody on it yet?"

"Officially, I don't know," I told him. "Off the record, we know now it was Benny and Lyle, but I'll deny I told you if asked."

He shot a quick glance at me. "No shit?"

In my best Arnold Schwarzeneggar accent I replied, "No, I am not shitting you."

As we approached the intersection with the reservation road, Johns prepared to make a left turn onto it. We had to wait for an on-coming SUV driving slowly in the opposite direction. After giving it a quick glance, we both shifted our attention to the matters at hand. Neither of us took much notice of the dirty silver Ford Explorer, or the Mexican male driving it.

The black Harley Dyna Glide belonging to Benny Johnson was parked in front of James's grandmother's house.

"He's here," Johns said. He hardly ever goes anywhere without that Harley."

As the Sheriff's SUV came to a stop behind us, I caught movement out of the corner of my eye near the shed on the side of the house.

Benny Johnson had just snapped the padlock on the door of the shed when he saw the two police vehicles parked in front of his house. We spotted each other at the same time. He immediately turned and began sprinting toward the corn field.

Johns yelled, "Benny! *Stop*! We only want to talk to you!"

As the four of us jumped from our cars and ran after him. He didn't stop, of course, and quickly disappeared into the seven-foot-high cornstalks behind the shed. Johns turned and walked back to his Tahoe.

The two deputies and myself were standing at the edge of the corn where Benny had disappeared as Johns pulled his Tahoe up to us. He got out and opened the rear door, hooking his leather lead to his dog's pinch collar. The Malinois had been going totally wild in the back of the unit since seeing us chasing Benny. He was straining at the lead and barking in that high pitched excited bark that dogs have when their predatory instinct has kicked in. Falcon was looking back and forth between us and the corn patch. Johns switched his handset radio from his local dispatch channel which was actually one of the casino's telephone operators, to one of the channels he shared with the Revas County Sheriff's Department. The sheriff's dispatcher was already aware of the foot pursuit as Sanchez had just called it in, but Johns wanted the K-9 warning that he was about to make over his Tahoe's PA system to be logged and recorded, and only the sheriff's dispatcher was capable of that. After talking to the dispatcher for a moment,

Johns turned on his PA system which could be heard through the siren speaker mounted on the front of his Tahoe.

Picking up his hand microphone, Johns announced loudly over the unit's PA system—out into the corn—who he was, who we were, and that if Benny didn't come out, he was going to send the dog in. He made three separate announcements in English, Spanish, and in the native Lupan language. I was impressed with that last one. After five minutes, he repeated his warning. When another five minutes passed without any answer, Johns told us to step behind the dog so the animal wouldn't key on our aggressive posture and bite one of us. This I did gladly. Many times I'd seen up close and personal what kind of damage a ninety-pound police dog can do to human flesh, and I didn't want to be anywhere near the business end of this land shark when he was released.

Johns stepped up, unhooked the lead, and gave a command in Slavic. *That dog is jacked up and looking to bite the shit out of someone,* I thought. *Benny, Benny, Benny, Benny, Benny, you should have come out when you had the chance, but you'll find that out for yourself in a minute.* The dog tore into the corn patch like a brown-and-black heat-seeking missile.

Johns led the way as the four of us slowly moved into the corn. We were following the sounds of the running and sniffing dog. All four of us now had our pistols out, ready to instantly bring them to bear if need be. Thanks to Fernando Lopez, we knew Benny had the second stolen Glock in his possession and we were taking no chances. Scarcely three minutes had passed when we heard crashing off to our right, then a high pitched human scream and a lot of snarling. Johns arrived first.

Benny was on the ground thrashing around and screaming repeatedly, "Get him off!" Falcon's jaws were clamped firmly on Benny's right butt cheek, and the dog was actually pulling him backward along the ground by his ass. I could see that wasn't the only damage. The back of Benny's shirt at the shoulder was also shredded and bloody.

Johns grabbed the dog's collar and began trying to get him off Benny, while again shouting another command to the dog. It wasn't working. Falcon's blood was boiling. He was too jacked up to let go. Olsen looked shocked. He'd never seen a K-9 attack, live and in color before. I could see Johns was having trouble getting the dog under control and we needed Benny in one piece. I shoved my way past Olsen, dropping my Kahr back into my bag. Sanchez was trying to help by pulling the dog's tail, which wasn't doing anything but making the dog bite Benny even harder. I bent over and reaching between the dogs jerking hind legs, I grabbed Falcon by his scrotum and squeezed as hard as I could. It took only two seconds. Falcon let go of Benny's ass and turned on both of his antagonizers.

Throughout their lives, the majority of people never came into face-to-face contact with a dangerous animal, much less got attacked by one. We humans had a tendency to transfer our thought process and emotions to animals, believing they thought like us and felt what we felt, particularly when it came to so-called domesticated dogs. We couldn't have been more wrong. All animals reacted out of pure instinct when the circumstance were right, some quicker than others. When this happened, thousands of years of survival and predatory instincts took over their mind and body. They didn't "think" and they didn't "feel," they just reacted by either running away or attacking. When animals did attack, *really* attack, they were blind to fear, pain, and injury and they could move quicker than the human eye could follow or the brain could process the thought.

There was no way either Sanchez nor myself could let go fast enough to keep from getting shredded by Falcon. Fortunately for both of us, Johns was a big strong guy and had a firm grip on the dog's collar. He was able to jerk Falcon back before the snarling animal's teeth got to either of us, but it was close. The K-9 then turned and tried to bite Johns. It took several hard, open-handed blows to the dog's head, accompanied by shouted commands, before Falcon stopped trying to bite his handler.

Benny lay there groaning. Falcon was starting to settle down now. He was sitting down and switching between panting, growling at everyone, and licking his nuts. Olsen had recovered from his shock and called for an ambulance as I looked over Benny's butt cheek and shoulder. The bite wounds were bloody and at first looked serious, but upon closer examination, I could see they were not *that* bad, relatively speaking of course. *Crap!* *Looks like we will be talking to Benny at the hospital.*

Sanchez walked back through the corn to his SUV and retrieved a first aid kit, but by the time he returned, Benny's wounds had stopped bleeding for the most part. With my help, Olsen stood him up and patted him down. He wasn't armed, though he did have a couple of wadded up and now bloody joints in his shirt pocket. Olsen handcuffed him and all four of us worked our way back through the corn.

As the Indian limped along I asked him, "So, Benny, you gonna give up the life of crime now?"

He looked at me and managed a smile. "Probably not, but I *am* gonna stop running when I'm told to."

Twenty minutes later the ambulance pulled in. The EMS guys placed Benny on the gurney face down, did a preliminary examination of his wounds, put an oxygen mask on his face, and asked Johns a few questions. Johns then turned to Olsen and asked him if he would get his camera and take photos of Benny's injuries. Johns said he carried a camera, but said it wasn't a very good one.

Olsen said, "Sure," and turned toward their SUV.

"You might want to wait on that," I told both of them. They looked at me. "How many bites you got?" I asked Johns, referring to the dog.

"Couple of small ones. No bad skin breakage though. This is the first good one," he replied.

"Some advice from experience?" I asked, motioning all three out of earshot of the EMS guys.

Sanchez was interested now also.

"Of course," Johns replied.

"You want to take your suspect's injury photos *after* his wounds are cleaned up," I told them all. "No current bleeding, no bloody shredded clothing, no dried blood around the wounds, etc. Helps you with the lawsuit later if it comes down to that. But don't wait until he's stitched up either. Sometimes stitches can make the wounds look real bad also, like friggin' *Frankenstein*." As an afterthought I turned to Olsen. "Remember, though, along the lines of what I was showing you about crime scene photos the other day—when you're taking injury photos of a *victim,* you want the photos as gruesome, bloody, bruised, and dramatic as you can get. It'll help get you a conviction. If it's the *suspect*, you want him cleaned up."

Johns looked at me. "Never thought of that. You have been doing this a while haven't you?"

"Too long, brother, and it seems I can't get away from it."

CHAPTER 17

Old Man

The appearance of the two police vehicles on the road near the reservation was a complete surprise. In retrospect, the Mexican man's timing had been lucky. After learning of the arrest of Fernando Lopez, he had decided to immediately drive out to the reservation, kill Benny, and then leave for El Paso. He had lingered in this area far too long. Under normal circumstances, he would have finished his business and been gone by now. Maybe taking Lyle out when he had was a mistake. He probably should have done them both at the same time like he'd originally planned." *Von Moltke again*, he thought. *No battle plan survives first contact. That really is true, isn't it?*

He drove past the two police vehicles, being careful to not to do anything to draw attention to himself. Both were waiting to make a left turn onto the reservation road. There were two men in each. He didn't recognize the cop driving the Tahoe, but noticed it was a reservation Police vehicle. He *did* recognize the man in civilian clothes in the passenger seat as the one he'd seen out at the ranch searching for clues. The two deputies in the second vehicle had also been there. *The sheriff's crime scene unit*, he realized. *Why are they with the reservation police?* he wondered briefly. *Maldicion*! *They must have made the connection between Lyle and Benny.*

The Mexican man needed to know what was going on. He watched in his rearview mirror. As soon as the two SUVs turned left and were out of sight, he made a U-turn back to the reservation road himself and began to follow the two police units. He kept his distance, though he wasn't too concerned about being spotted. The two SUVs threw up a large cloud of dust from the gravel road which would make him hard to spot at best. Moreover, his dirty silver Explorer looked like it belonged on the reservation. As long as he didn't do anything to draw attention to himself, to the cops he might pass as just another Indian in a beat up car.

When he saw the two units pull up in front of a small run-down house with a black Harley parked in front, he began to quickly look for a place to park out of sight, but he didn't get the chance. Stunned, he watched as all of the cops jumped out of their vehicles and ran around the side of the house. It was obvious they were chasing someone toward the corn field behind the house and he was sure that "someone" was Benny. His mind was racing now, wondering if he could work all this to his advantage. Within a minute however, the reservation cop returned to his SUV, got in, and drove it out of sight around the side.

The Mexican man needed to see what was happening. He spotted what looked like an abandoned house just across the street half a block down. The cops were not paying any attention to the road and took no notice of his Explorer as he drove past Benny's place. He pulled around behind the abandoned building and parked. Pulling out his binoculars, he stepped out of his vehicle and moved along the side wall of the house. From here he had a good vantage point. He could see both police vehicles, the shed, and a good portion of the corn field. The cops were nowhere in sight, but he did notice the rear door of the K-9 unit was open. *Shit*! *The dog is out here somewhere.* He looked around warily, until he suddenly heard the snarling and screaming from the center of the corn field. He raised the binoculars. One of the black plastic protective caps was still covering one of the lenses. He flicked it off, intending to stuff it in his pocket, but it slipped out of his grasp and fell to the ground. *Pick it up, later*, he told himself, raising the glasses to his eyes.

He was so focused on the scene unfolding in the corn, he didn't hear the footsteps behind him until they were close. He whirled, reaching under his coat for his revolver, but stopped short of jerking it from its holster.

The old Indian man was staring at him and holding up two fingers in a V. In a crackly voice he asked in English, "Hey, *hombre*, you got any smokeses on you?"

"Any what?"

"Smokeses man, you know, smokeses."

Now realizing this ancient soul was asking for a cigarette, the Mexican man hissed, "No! *Vamanos*! Beat it, old man!"

The old man shuffled away mumbling. The Mexican man turned his attention back to the field just in time to see a bloody, limping, and handcuffed Benny being helped out of the corn by the two deputies. The detective in civilian clothes and the K-9 cop were following right behind. The Mexican man considered the possibilities. How to get at Benny with these cops now in the picture? Up to now, the two deputies and the detective, or whatever he was, had just been an obstacle that he needed to be aware of. Now, however, they were becoming an annoyance. *So they have Benny and must know of his connection to Lyle. How had they found that out? If these cops are any good at all at their jobs, and so far they seem to be, it won't be long before they will be shaking Benny's tree to see what falls out. This will for sure lead them to some of the low-life vatos Benny runs with, which in turn could lead them to the dealer in Pecos that fingered Benny and Lyle to his Zeta bosses. Shit! Another thread that can be picked at.*

Of course he could blow the whole deal off and just head back to El Paso, leaving Benny to the cops, but that really was not an option. The people who hired him were not the type to be understanding if you didn't complete a job they hired you to do, and even if *they* were, his reputation would be shot. As he watched, an ambulance pulled up next to the sheriff's SUV. Paramedics got out and placed Benny on their gurney, then began to work on him. It was time for him to go.

He turned toward his Explorer, his thoughts now on the hospital where they were taking Benny. He also needed to find out more about these cops, in particular this detective. *How good is he? And the two deputies, for that matter? I need more information about all three of them.*

The man got into the Explorer, slowly pulled out onto the road, and headed back the way he had come in.

☙❧☙

The wrinkled old Indian shuffled up to the two deputies and myself then over to the EMS guys, trying to bum "a smokeses."

"What's he want?" Olsen asked me as I watched the old Indian man shuffling away.

"He wanted a cigarette, called it a "smokeses. That cracked me up," I replied. "I gave him one of your Winstons outta the pack on your dash."

"Hey," Olsen shot back. "Those things cost money. I don't pay four bucks a pack to give them away to old Indian moochers."

"Shit, Jim, where's you compassion?" I inquired sarcastically just as Johns walked up with Falcon. He'd heard our exchange.

"You'll be old too someday," he told Olsen. "Besides, those cancer sticks are bad for you, anyway."

"No kidding," I said to Johns. "The old guy told me he tried to bum a cigarette off of the guy who lives over there in that house." I nodded toward the house across and down the street. "But the guy told him to get lost."

Johns looked confused. "He couldn't have meant *that* house." He pointed to the same house. "That house is abandoned. No one's lived there in two years."

"Well that's what he said," I replied. "Said the guy who lived there was out back of the house by a 'Jeep.' He said the guy was looking at us, and told him to '*lagarse*,' whatever that means."

"Beat it," Johns said, looking around for the old Indian. But he was nowhere in sight. Johns walked with his dog down the road to a point where he could see behind the abandoned house. "No car there now," he called to me as he walked back.

Naturally curious, I motioned with a sideways movement of my head for Johns to walk toward the abandoned house with me. It was nothing to behold. Just an old wood-sided, three-room shack, standing back from the road on the small gravel and weed covered lot. There was no real foundation I noticed. Cut off pieces of wood telephone pole had been stuck in the ground as pier posts to support the floor joists. Whatever paint had been on the siding had disappeared long ago, leaving just the bare, weathered, exposed wood beneath. Several windows were broken and those that weren't were covered with a thick layer of dust and grime, making it impossible to see through them. The front door stood ajar. Entering, I could see that all of the rooms were empty, except for trash and some animal droppings. I walked across the front porch to the far front corner of the shack. Johns followed with the dog in tow. *The old Indian probably just* imagined *that he'd seen someone here.* The rough gravel and weeds beneath my feet revealed nothing.

"Ambulance is probably getting ready to leave," Johns said.

"Okay," I replied. "Let's go."

We continued walking down the side of the shack and turned the corner around the back wall in the direction of Benny's house.

Without warning, Falcon suddenly "alerted," whipping his body to the right and pulling so hard on his lead he nearly jerked it out of Johns's hand. Both of us looked that way instantly, Johns' right hand even twitching toward the Glock on his hip, but there was nothing in sight, just more gravel and weeds.

He looked at me. "That's weird."

I shrugged. "Ease your mutt over that way and let's see what he's so interested in," I said, nodding toward the back edge of the gravel lot.

Johns grimaced. "Not nice to call a 10-k dog a mutt."

We walked slowly, Johns watching his dog's actions. "He didn't see anything," Johns told me, observing the dog, "but he smells something on the ground and whatever it is it's a fresh enough scent to grab his attention."

I looked at him. "Maybe the old Indian guy?"

"Maybe, but he's acting more like he smells some*thing*, not some-*one*."

"I didn't know he was an article-search-trained dog," I said.

"He wasn't really at first, but I noticed he seemed to have a knack for it so I started working with him on it," Johns replied. The dog now had his nose to the ground and was working back and forth obviously trying to narrow down a specific spot.

"Hold him up a second," I said.

Johns stopped and gave Falcon the command to sit.

I walked past both to the edge of the gravel. We were starting to lose the light as the sun was setting. I took my little light out of my pocket, using its powerful beam to examine the ground.

"The gravel is disturbed here." I pointed down. "Looks like a car *was* here, just like the old man said."

Just then we heard a loud two-fingered whistle. It was Sanchez across the street. We both turned in his direction and he yelled that the ambulance was getting ready to leave. I shouted back that's we'd only be a few minutes longer. Sanchez turned and walked back the ambulance.

I turned back to Johns and the dog. "Let him sniff around just a bit more, then we'll bail," I said.

It appeared that Falcon was mildly interested in this area of disturbed gravel I'd found, but it was obvious the dog was seeking something else.

Johns eased up on the lead, gave a command, and Falcon again walked forward his nose again to the ground. He passed by my feet giving me a quick sniff accompanied by a disdainful look. I stood very still. *This dog scares the shit out of me. Probably still pissed about me squeezing his sack,* I thought as he looked me up and down then moved on. The dog began working his way toward the back wall of the house, pulling Johns along. Midway toward the wall, the dog stopped. He was sniffing at a small black object on the ground. Johns pulled the dog back and again gave him the command to sit. I walked over and squatted down to examine the object on the ground with my small light.

At first glance, it appeared to be some black plastic piece, maybe off of a car, but it somehow looked familiar. After staring at it for few seconds, I recognized it as a black plastic eye-ring cap.

"What is that?" Johns asked.

"Looks like an eye-ring cap," I told him.

"What, like off a camera?"

"Too small for a camera," I said. "Binoculars." I took out my pocket knife and used the tip to gently flip the cap over. The word *Leica* was embossed on the front flat side.

Johns snorted. "Expensive binoculars."

"Yup," I replied. "Not your run-of-the-mill field glasses that's for sure. Suckers are about twelve to fifteen hundred a pair. No dirt on it or inside it and it's not crushed, so it hasn't been laying here long at all."

"What are you thinking?" Johns asked.

"I'm thinking someone *was* back here watching Benny, or us, or both. You wouldn't happen to have a baggie or some such on you would you?" I asked.

"No baggie but I have some small coin envelopes in my pocket. One of those work?" He produced one of the small two-inch-by-three-inch taupe-colored envelopes from his shirt pocket. "I carry these just for this reason."

"Excellent," I replied. "There'll be a little something extra in your paycheck at Christmas."

"Yeah, that'll be the day," he shot back.

Again using the tip of my knife, I flipped the lens cap into the envelope, then dog-eared the flap so it would stay shut and stuck the thing in my pocket.

"Grab me that BFR right over there by the wall," I told Johns.

"BFR?" he asked.

"Big Fuckin' Rock."

"What's up with this?" he asked as he picked up a large, smooth river rock and brought it back to me.

"I want to mark this spot in case the cap turns out to be something," I said.

"Hell, I have number stands in my Tahoe you can leave here overnight," he offered.

"Nah, don't want one now," I replied. He raised an eyebrow in question. "Couple reasons," I continued. "First we don't know if this really is anything," I said, patting my pocket, "and I don't want to make evidence out of it if it's nothing. Second, a number stand will blow away, or someone like that old Indian will come along and pick it up or kick it or stomp it or something. Not likely anyone will bother this rock. It looks like all the other rocks around here, *and* it won't move or blow away."

Johns nodded pensively as I prepared to place the stone on the ground where the cap had been laying.

"Yeah but how you gonna know *which* rock it is if we don't come back here for a few days? They all look alike around here."

"Watch and learn Grasshopper," I said, and with that I produced a fat black Marks-A-Lot felt pen from my man-purse, as my wife loved to call it, then proceeded to draw a large black X on the bottom side of the rock before setting it down.

"Huh," Johns mumbled. "I never made the connection."

The light was fading fast as the two of us walked back across the road to Benny's house and the two waiting deputies. Sanchez turned his attention from the disappearing tail lights of the ambulance to Johns and myself when he saw us approaching.

"Jeeze—took long enough. You guys goin' down on each other over there or what?" he asked crudely.

"We couldn't, not with my dog watching and all," Johns shot back.

"Yeah," I added, grinning. "Besides, I forgot my Viagra. It's such a bitch getting old."

"Tell me about it," Sanchez replied.

Olsen walked up, overhearing the rude male banter, and commented, "Being young studs, Johns and I get hard when just the wind blows."

I looked at him, smiling. "Yeah, I noticed when you were ogling my ol' lady the other day."

The K-9 officer was bewildered at this comment, looking back and forth between the three of us, not sure what to make of the direction this conversation had taken.

"Private joke," I told him, winking at Sanchez. I then proceeded to fill the two deputies in on our find across the road.

It took the four of us fifteen minutes to wind up our conversation and answer the two deputies' questions. "Hospital, gentlemen?" I asked when we were done.

Getting nods all around, we headed to our vehicles. I opted to again ride with the K-9 officer.

"What? You don't like us anymore?" Olsen asked as I walked toward the Tahoe.

"Being practical," I replied. "The front seat of his Tahoe is much more comfortable than that hard plastic seat in the back of your ride."

We pulled away from Benny's and turned out onto the reservation road. The darkness now enveloped the two police vehicles as we moved over the gravel surface. No moon tonight and the stars were once again magnificent as they commonly were in the night desert sky.

Johns and I were for the most part silent as we drove along, and that was okay. I knew from past experience he was contemplating his dog's performance, Benny's injuries, and how he was going to write his follow-up report. I, on the other hand, was thinking about Benny. *Who had been watching Benny and why? Was it Lyle's killer? Or just someone hoping to rip off Benny for his dope? If it was Lyle's killer, was he there for Benny? Had we actually interrupted him when we showed up?* This was an unnerving thought. If this had indeed been the case, it meant whomever it was had been watching all of us. *Damn! What if he'd actually been right there?* My thoughts shifted. *And what was this deal with Benny and Lyle and the two skeletons in the desert? Why would these two dummies want to steal two sets of old bones?* It all made my head hurt. I needed a bourbon, a cigar, a neck rub. *Speaking of, I wonder what Sonya is doing right now?* I took out my cell phone. *Better let her know what I've been doing all day, lest she starts to worry.*

By the time we all got to the hospital in Pecos, Benny was already having his wounds cleaned. We could tell as soon as we walked into the E.R. by his loud, "Jesus Christ, you bitch! Take it easy with that fuckin' brush will ya!"

The four of us walked around the curtain, partially obscuring Benny's near naked body, and squeezed in on all sides of the bed. An IV had been inserted into the back of Benny's hand. I couldn't tell if it was lactated Ringer's or plasma. *Probably Ringer's*, I thought. *Hasn't bled enough for it to be plasma.*

"Quit whining, Benny," Johns told him. "You brought this on yourself."

"Fuck you!" was Benny's reply.

We could see he'd been "four pointed" in the bed by hospital security upon his arrival.

I looked at Johns and nodded to the straps, raising my eyebrow in question. "Your idea?"

"Yeah," he replied. "Didn't want to take the chance on him runnin'. I called security while you were on the phone to your wife."

I nodded my approval. Olsen was watching the nurse, fascinated by her use of the hard nylon scrub brush and disinfectant on Benny's bite wounds. Olsen had his camera, but the wounds were now bleeding again from being scrubbed and cleaned. Benny was still being vocally abusive to the nurse. *What a dumb-ass. Not smart to piss off the person using the brush on your open lacerations and punctures.*

"Looks like it's gonna be a while boys," I said to them. "Anyone up for some coffee?" We all looked at each other then headed for the hospital cafeteria. "Want anything, Benny?" I asked.

"Fuck you!" was the reply.

We walked away, leaving Benny yowling and cursing. The nurse just scrubbed harder.

The four of us were sitting at a cafeteria table with our coffee in hand, discussing our day's endeavors, when "Mr. Sunshine," aka Lieutenant Davis walked in.

Ignoring Johns, he addressed the three of us in his usual loving manner, "Where's your suspect?"

"They're cleaning him up right now, L-T," Sanchez replied.

Davis finally acknowledged Johns's presence. It was obvious Davis considered Johns an underling since he was only a reservation cop. Again the thought of what a jerk Davis was crossed my mind.

Davis scowled at Johns. "Your dog bit him up pretty bad."

"Looked worse than it was," Johns replied. "Benny was smart enough to just lay there and not pull away, so not much tearing. Mainly puncture wounds, but he's gonna be hurtin' for a while."

"Humph!" Davis looked our way again. "Fill me in on everything all of you have, and I mean from the birth of Christ until now. Don't' leave *anything* out. I particularly want to know what you found out about those bones out in the desert."

Ahhhh, there it is, and just when I was beginning to think he was maybe actually concerned with our entire case. He was consistent, I'd give him that. The four of us were still talking an hour later when Sonya was ushered through the cafeteria door by the ER nurse.

"There you are," my wife said.

After a brief introduction of my wife to Officer Johns and Lieutenant Davis, the E.R. nurse advised us Benny was ready to be photographed. Olsen and Johns excused themselves to accompany the nurse back to Benny's bed. Davis decided he'd heard enough for now, told us to keep him informed, gave a curt nod to Sanchez and myself, then got up to leave.

"Nice meeting you," he told Sonya only as a courtesy. "Your husband is really helping us out on this murder case. He's a lucky man to have such a beautiful wife. You'll have to excuse me now, though, more pressing police matters." With that he turned and walked out.

Jeeze, gag me with a spoon, I thought to myself.

Sonya turned to us. "Is it just my imagination or was that a bit on the insincere side?" she asked, looking after him. "That guy gives me the creeps."

Sanchez and I looked at each other, neither saying a word. Then Sanchez turned to Sonya, removed his hat and bowed. "And to what do we owe the honor of your presence, Ms. Douglas."

"Cut the crap, Sanchez," I told him. "Davis already piled the bullshit on. I called her to pick me up here so you wouldn't have to run me back out to the ranch tonight." I turned to Sonya. "Stay here in the caf-

eteria for a few minutes, hon. Frank and I have to go look in on our
boy. Be right back."

Sanchez and I got up and walked back down the long series of
hallways to the E.R. Johns and Olsen were standing just outside the
curtain surrounding Benny's bed. Benny was quiet for the first time
that night. Johns looked up from his note taking as we approached.

"Benny's whacked out for the night," he advised us. "They gave
him some pain meds and probably a sedative."

"Well, I guess that eliminates question and answer time for tonight," Sanchez replied.

"You get all your injury photos taken?" I asked, looking at Olsen's
camera.

"Yep, all done."

"Guess we might as well call it a night then," I said to no one in
particular.

"I've got paper to write on all this," Johns replied, "so I'm gonna
head back to my office. Gotta let the dog take a dump somewhere also,
if he hasn't already unloaded in the back of my Tahoe."

"Cheery thought," Sanchez said, "and we do as well, not the take a
dump part, paperwork I mean, so we're going to do the same. First
though, I have to arrange for some security for our boy in there since
he's in custody. I'll get our favorite reserve out here to stand by." Once
again he took out his cell phone.

"Well, boys," I said, addressing them all, "nice thing about being in
an 'advisory capacity' as a *retired* investigator, I get to go back and get
some sleep while you all toil away. What time in the morning do you
want to come talk to Mr. Johnson in there?" I asked Sanchez, nodding
toward the curtain.

Sanchez thought for a moment. "I'm thinking about 8:00 a.m. Meet
us at the office?"

"See you then," I replied and turned back toward the cafeteria.
Halfway down the hall I remembered the lens cap in my pocket. I
turned back. Pulling the coin envelope out, I handed it to Olsen. "Put
this in your lab. We'll work on it in the morning."

Sanchez looked surprised. "Shit, the cap. I'd forgotten about it.
Think we can do anything with it?"

I looked down at the envelope. "Might get lucky if what I'm thinking pans out. Talk to you in the a.m." I walked back to the cafeteria.

ℰ⁄ᴐℰ⁄ᴐ

The three cops watched as Douglas walked away. Johns addressed
the two deputies. "That guy seems to know what he's doing."

Sanchez nodded. "Yeah he does. Thought he might just be baggage when we started, but he's sharp and he's already showed us how to do stuff we'd only heard of. He seems like a nice guy. Actually pretty normal for someone from California." All three chuckled.

Olsen chimed in then. "Pretty wife, too."

Sanchez smacked him on the back of his head. "Will you get your mind off your dick for a while, please? That shit gets old." He nodded toward the door. "Let's go."

"What? All I said was his wife was pretty."

"Go!" Sanchez ordered, pointing to the exit. "Out the door horn-dog—walk!" Shaking his head he looked at Johns and rolled his eyes. The problem was, Johns thought Sonya was pretty hot also, but he kept that thought to himself.

As the three lawmen walked out the ambulance entrance to their vehicles, none of them took any special notice of the dirty silver Ford Explorer parked with several other vehicles in the hospital staff parking lot to their right.

☙☙☙

Sonya and I sat in our truck letting the engine warm up a bit while I filled her in on the day's events. Through the years, she had always been a good listener, instinctively knowing when I'd had a stressful day and just needed to collect my thoughts or express my frustrations by telling her my woes. As I prattled on, I absentmindedly noticed both the reservation police and the sheriff's department vehicles pull out of the parking lot and head for the interstate. I put the truck in gear and we slowly drove through the parking lot toward the exit.

"That's weird," I said, thinking out loud.

"What's that?" Sonya asked.

"Oh, there's a car parked back there, I could have sworn I saw earlier this afternoon out by the reservation," I answered, craning my neck around, trying to get a better look.

"Which one?" she asked, looking back.

"Dirty silver Ford SUV parked back there."

"Oh yeah, I see it." She shrugged. "Don't know how you could tell. Looks like all the other dirty cars in the staff lot there."

I could no longer see it in my mirrors. "Can you see anyone in it?"

She looked again. "Nope, empty. Why?

"Not important. Just an employee's car probably." I turned the truck out onto the road and pointed it toward the interstate for our ride back to the ranch. "Man, am I beat."

CHAPTER 18

The Hospital

The Mexican man sat in the E.R. waiting room, a newspaper in his hands as if reading. There were several other people in chairs surrounding him, mostly migrant workers waiting to see the resident doctor for one misery or another. *Peasants,* he thought as he looked at them with distain. It was 2:30 a.m. now and the man was watching the nurses' routines. So far no one had questioned his presence, but he had been prepared should that occur. He had stolen a glance at the Patient Census Board behind the nurses' station. Fortunately, this semi-rural hospital had not fully made the transition to computerized patient tracking as of yet, so the names written on the board in dry-erasable felt pen were there for all to see. He had picked a Hispanic name off the board at random. If asked, he would simply say he was an accompanying relative of that person. It wouldn't hold up under real scrutiny, but no one seemed remotely interested in him at this point. There was one tense moment just as he entered through the E.R. entrance doors and saw the two deputies and the K-9 cop walking out the ambulance entrance down the short hallway, but their paths had not crossed, and they paid him no mind.

The man had deliberately chosen a seat near the nurses' station so he could overhear any conversations that might be advantageous to his getting at Benny. Once again, the census board had come in handy as Benny's name and bed number were posted in bold pink letters. He smiled to himself as he considered how, in so many American television shows and movies, the killer was always depicted dressed in scrubs like a doctor or nurse in order to sneak in and inject some dramatic lethal drug into the victim's IV, or cause an embolism with a syringe full of air. *Ridiculous*, he thought. The Mexican man knew all he needed was fifteen seconds alone with Benny. Nothing fancy. He would push the mute button on monitor, then drive an ice pick into

Benny's skull, upward from the inner corner of his right eye, give it a twist, pull it out, and walk away.

The man didn't carry an actual ice pick, of course. That was too obvious a weapon to be caught with. What he used as an "ice pick" was a new, nine-inch-long, one-quarter-inch-in-diameter, Phillips screwdriver. Being new, the tip was sharp and would easily penetrate the soft flesh of the eye and brain. There would be virtually no blood, and it would take quite a while for the medical staff to figure out why Benny was dead, giving the Mexican man the chance to cleanly make his exit. All he needed was a distraction. As it turned out, luck was with him this morning. That same luck would utterly abandon Benny. The reserve deputy guarding Benny had just stepped into the men's room across the hall from the waiting room when an ambulance with its red and amber lights flashing, pulled up to the double doors of the Emergency Room entrance.

The man could see the EMTs rush out of the cab of the vehicle and around to the rear doors. Simultaneously, the double doors to the patient area in the E.R. burst open with the two nurses and the resident doctor rushing out. All three passed through the ambulance entrance running outside to assist the EMTs with what turned out to be two severely injured, traffic-accident victims.

The Mexican man saw his opportunity. He got up and walked through the men's room door. The reserve deputy was standing at the urinal. The Mexican man stepped up behind him with his revolver in his hand and struck the deputy just above and behind the right ear with the barrel of the weapon. He slumped to the floor, his fingers still grasping his penis, urine dribbling from its tip.

The Mexican man turned swiftly, exiting the men's room, walked right through open doors of the patient area to Benny's bed side, and punched the mute button on the Welch vital-signs monitor. He smiled when he saw that Benny was still in the wrist and ankle restraints. It went just as he planned.

He clamped his gloved hand over Benny's mouth, but it was an unnecessary precaution. The only sounds that were made as he plunged the screwdriver into the corner of Benny's right eye were a single gasp and the stretching of the leather restraints when Benny arched his back up as he died.

The man pulled the screwdriver from Benny's eye. *Excellent. Just as I thought, no bleeding.* The tissue of the eyeball socket had immediately closed over the wound as he withdrew the shaft. Just the slightest trace of blood on the screwdriver itself, which he quickly wiped on Benny's sheet next to the seepage from the dog-bite wounds. It would not be noticed. The man placed the screwdriver in his pocket.

As he walked out from behind the curtain, the vitals monitor screen flat-lined, but the alarm remained silent. It would be some time before one of the nurses noticed it had been muted. He turned left, walking down the hallway, opposite the way he'd entered.

Spotting a green *EXIT* sign on the ceiling, he began heading for it. As he approached the exit doors, he noticed a maintenance tool cart sitting unattended in the hallway near a storage room door. Smiling to himself at his idea, he double checked the screwdriver to be sure no traces of blood or tissue remained on it.

When he was sure there was no one observing him, he placed the screwdriver on the cart in the midst of several others, turned, and walked out the door.

Five minutes later the Mexican man was starting his Explorer in the staff parking lot, pleased with himself. He would allow himself one night to relax a bit and get some well-deserved rest, then tomorrow afternoon he would leave for El Paso.

He reached for the disposable cell phone in his bag and dialed an El Paso phone number.

"Hello?" a male voice answered on the other end.

"Tell my uncle I'll be arriving tomorrow afternoon, but my friends won't be coming with me," the Mexican said.

"That's too bad," replied the voice. "Your uncle and I thought you would be here sooner."

"I had a bit of car trouble which delayed me."

"I hope it was not difficult to repair it," the voice responded.

"No, I was able to repair it myself without assistance."

"Excellent. You are very resourceful as always. I'll inform you uncle of your schedule. Goodbye."

"Goodbye." When the coded exchange was completed, the Mexican man pulled out of the parking lot and drove toward the interstate, his concentration now focused on his trip back to El Paso. He glanced at his watch. 4:00 a.m.

Looking in his side view mirror as he merged from the on-ramp into the southbound lanes of the interstate, he could see no headlights behind him. The lanes in front of him were empty of taillights as well. Satisfied he was temporarily alone on the highway, he rolled down his driver's side window as he accelerated into the darkness of the center lane. Extending his arm outside the open window, he used an overhand toss to launch the disposable cell phone in a high arch, forward and slightly to the left, into the cool early morning air.

His objective was to have the phone strike the concrete with the combined force of both his seventy-five-mile-per-hour speed and its own downward inertia, breaking it into several pieces, all of which would then scatter into the knee-high grass of the median.

Just as the phone left his fingertips, a glint of chrome and the tiniest hint of an amber colored reflector caught his eye near the center of the median as he flashed past.

CHAPTER 19

Interstate

Texas State Trooper Mark Williams had parked his Ford Crown Victoria patrol car in the shallow depression that made up the median between the opposing traffic lanes on the interstate at 3:00 a.m. It was one of his favorite ambush locations. The big block Ford was idling softly, though all of his lights were turned off save for the mobile flat screen computer, which he had switched to the red-colored, night mode. It made the screen harder to read, but saved his night vision. His two-way radio was turned down so as to be barely audible. He was truly in what he liked to refer to as "stealth mode." His unit was now nearly invisible to traffic on the freeway. Mark was a big fan of *Star Trek*, so when he was sitting blacked out like this, he always said to himself, "Cloaking device activated, Captain."

He had been typing on the vehicle's computer keyboard since he'd parked. One of the reasons he liked using the older Ford Crown Victoria as opposed to the new Dodge Chargers, was the room it afforded in the front seat, particularly when using the built-in laptop. He was attempting to finish a traffic accident report he'd started earlier in the evening, but there had been one interruption after another. Traffic was light on the freeway tonight. He had deliberately set his traffic speed radar emitter so as not to alert him unless a vehicle on the interstate was traveling at or over 90 mph. This was being far too lenient, particularly at night, as the posted speed limit was 65 mph after dark, but he really needed to get this report done and did not want to be disturbed until it was completed if at all possible.

Mark was gazing out the front windshield, considering circumstances of his accident investigation, totally lost in thought. A silver SUV crossed his field of vision traveling in the center lane of the highway to his front. In the back of his mind he recognized it as Ford Explorer. Since his radar alert had not activated, he gave it no further attention until he saw the slight reflection of an object being thrown from the open driver's window. With his own window down to allow the cool night air to circulate inside his unit, he actually heard the object hit the pavement just to his front left and heard the scattering of the pieces.

Highway cops nationwide were responsible not only for accident investigations, but also enforcing traffic laws such as speeding, illegal passing, failing to stop at stop signs or red lights, etc. In addition, most of these same traffic officers were also known for having particular pet peeves when it came to the violation of their state's traffic laws. With some it might have been a car having no front license plate, or a pedestrian's right-of-way in a crosswalk, maybe jaywalking violations, or perhaps even driving with just one's parking lights turned on. In the case of Mark Williams, there were two violations for which he had zero tolerance. One was graffiti on *his* highway's signs and overpasses. The other was *littering*.

Sighing at his seeming inability to finish this report tonight, he closed out the report writer program on his computer, then punched the *In Service* button on the home screen. The computer beeped back at him, confirming his status. Turning on his headlights, he dropped the transmission into Drive and, after checking the fast-lane for any oncoming traffic, accelerated out of the swale, his rear tires spinning and throwing dirt and grass clods until they made contact with the concrete. The Explorer was now a mile ahead of him, its tail lights clearly visible.

"One X-ray Twenty Four Eleven," he said into the hand mic.

"One X-ray," replied the female dispatcher's voice.

"I'm eastbound I-20 at mile marker 103. Gonna be making a traffic stop on a light colored Ford Explorer in just few. No plate or description yet, I'm still catching up to him. I'll advise."

"One X-ray 10-4," the dispatcher replied. "Any unit to fill with One X-ray Twenty Four Eleven, eastbound I-20 at mile marker 103?"

A second female voice came upon the air. "One Charles Twenty One Sixty One, I can fill, but I'm about 20 miles out," Trooper Samantha "Sammy" Baker responded.

"Any unit closer than One Charles?" the dispatcher inquired, but she'd already answered her own question by looking at the electronic unit monitor map on one of the three Computer Assisted Dispatch, CAD, screens in front of her. No one else responded to her inquiry. "One Charles Twenty One Sixty One 10-4, fill with One X-ray."

"One Charlie enroute," Baker replied enthusiastically. She loved this job.

The area sergeant had been listening to the conversation on his handset radio as he sat in his office, reviewing the endless piles of pa-

perwork that came with a supervisor's job. Due to the distance involved, he made a quick decision then picked up his radio and spoke
into it. "S-1 to One Charles, code three is authorized," but he flinched
as he said it because he suddenly remembered that Samantha Baker
had a lead foot and loved to drive way too fast. She had been coun-
seled for this on two prior occasions by him personally. He added,
"Take it easy, please, Baker," into the handset mic then tried not to
think about it as he turned back to his stack of officer evaluations.

Sammy grinned as she responded, "10-4."

She *lived* for this shit. Parked on an overpass overlooking I-20, her
engine idling, Sammy now dropped her transmission into Drive and
stomped on the accelerator of her Dodge Charger. The unit's big block
V-8 turbo-charged engine responded like a dog whose tail had just
been stepped on. The rear tires broke contact with the pavement with a
loud, sustained squeal and white smoke poured off the rubber. She
flipped on her powerful overhead LED emergency lights.

The red, blue, and white flashing strobes harshly penetrated the
darkness. Being a clear desert night, the lights could be seen for miles
in every direction. Traffic was light so she left the siren off for now.
Ninety seconds later Sammy's digital speedometer read 138 mph as
she rocketed down the interstate. The Dodge was capable of greater
speed, but it began to get a bit unstable in its handling above 140 mph,
which made even Sammy uncomfortable, not that she wouldn't go
there if she needed to, but she didn't see the need at this point. By her
quick figuring, at 130 mph plus, she would arrive to back-up Mark in
approximately seven minutes, give or take.

"One X-ray Twenty Four Eleven," Mark said into his microphone
as he closed up behind the Explorer and flipped on his emergency
lights.

"One X-ray," the dispatcher replied.

"It's going to be a silver Ford Explorer, Texas license Adam-
Charles-Sam-One-Seven-Eight-Eight, looks like one aboard. The stop
will be eastbound I-20 at Mile Marker 109."

The dispatcher didn't need to be asked to run the license plate for
registration status and any outstanding warrants. She'd done that automatically as soon as Mark had called the plate in. The computerized
response was already back.

"One X-ray, your vehicle is current and clear," the dispatcher replied. "Registered to El Paso Holdings Corporation, 2165 S. Railroad
Avenue in El Paso."

"One X-ray, 10-4."

The Explorer was slowing now, crossing the slow lane toward the
right shoulder of the interstate. Mark switched on his overhead take-

down spotlights, as well as the adjustable spotlight in the windshield support post in front of him. The combination of white lights left no area of the Explorer unexposed, save for the front bumper. The interior and the solo driver were now brightly illuminated. Both vehicles stopped in the emergency lane on the right shoulder of the interstate, with the patrol car behind the Explorer and slightly off-set to the left in order protect Mark from passing traffic, should he decide to walk forward on the driver's side, not that there was much danger from that this particular morning with traffic as light as it was. Still one never knew when a drunk driver—or more likely these days, a text-ing driver—would happen along.

After checking his side view mirror one last time, Williams picked up his Pelican LAPD model flashlight with his left hand and stepped out of his car. With his right hand on his sidearm, he kept his eyes on the driver of the Explorer as he crossed in front of his own car and approached the rear of the SUV from the passenger side.

Sammy, her Dodge just a blue and white blur to the odd car she passed on the freeway, was now less than four minutes from the location of the traffic stop.

CHAPTER 20

Litter Bug

The Mexican man had a decision to make, and make quickly. He had been taken by surprise with the sudden appearance of a vehicle parked in the darkness in the median of the interstate. He had known instinctively it was a cop and chided himself for not being more alert when disposing of the cell phone. He had let his mind wander, thinking of his return to El Paso. *Stupid*, he thought, *but what's done is done*.

When he hadn't seen the patrol car immediately pull out of the depression, there was a moment when he thought the trooper must not have seen him toss the phone, however, as he watched a pair of headlights approach rapidly in his rearview mirror, he knew who it was and cursed his own stupidity and bad luck. When the red and blue lights came on behind him, he quickly considered his options. Had this been a deserted stretch of highway in Mexico, he would probably just have shot the lone cop as he approached the vehicle then driven off. The lack of quick response by Mexican authorities would all but guarantee his escape and would probably be written off as just another drug murder.

This was *not* Mexico however, it was Texas. The trooper, in all probability already had back-up on the way, and certainly his dispatcher had all the information on the Explorer *No, killing this highway cop is not an option, at least at this point*. The man knew his driver's license, registration and proof of insurance were in order, and he had a concealed carry permit for his revolver.

The problem would arise if the officer asked to look through his vehicle for any reason. He couldn't really refuse permission without bringing suspicion on himself. On the other hand, if the cop did search his car, the items in his equipment bag would most certainly be discovered, raising unwanted questions, so that was not an option either. The Mexican man made a decision. He reached slowly up to the dashboard.

No sudden movement, he thought. He pushed the 4WD Hi button with his right index finger. Just as the cop walked up even with the passenger rear door of the Explorer, the Mexican man stepped on the accelerator and took off.

CHAPTER 21

Escape

It all happened so fast. Mark, already alert as he approached the Explorer, jumped both backward and sideways as the Explorer lurched forward. Without conscious effort, he had drawn and aimed his Glock .40-caliber pistol at the driver. He quickly holstered the weapon, however, when he saw the Explorer was accelerating away from him along the shoulder.

Mark was already talking excitedly into his epaulette microphone as he ran to the patrol car's driver's side door. This, of course, stirred up a hornet's nest. Every cop within a reasonable distance dropped what they were doing and headed his way with lights flashing and sirens wailing. For his part, Mark couldn't fathom how the driver of the Explorer could possibly think he could out run Mark's big block Ford patrol car on the open road. *This won't be much of a chase*, he thought as he slid in behind the wheel.

Every day Mark observed all brands and colors of SUVs on his highway. Like most of us, he became conditioned to thinking of them as "cars." He'd forgotten the original reason they had become such a popular vehicle with the soccer moms of the '90s, which was the illusion of power at having four-wheel drive.

Mark dropped his Crown Vic into gear and started after the Explorer. The flashing red and blue lights from Samantha Baker's patrol car caught his attention in his rear view mirror as it approached from his rear, though she was still a mile back. As Mark watched the Explorer accelerate down over the shoulder, he was puzzled as to why the SUV didn't move into the normal traffic lanes of the interstate. It caught him by totally surprise as the Explorer suddenly veered to the right out into the desert, plowed right through a barbwire fence without slowing, and kept going. Instinctively Mark tried to follow. The inertial energy from the patrol car's forward motion carried it out into the desert 150 feet, then the unit's rear wheels bogged down in the loose sand and the patrol car came to a mushy stop, harshly pushing Mark against the shoulder strap of his seat belt.

No matter how hard he tried, Mark could not get his vehicle to move any farther. He opened the door, stepped out onto the dirt, and watched the tail lights of the Explorer disappear into the desert behind a cloud of dust.

"Shit!" he mumbled to himself, just as Trooper Sammy Baker's Dodge slid to a stop up on the shoulder of the highway behind him. Mark reached for his microphone but he could already hear Samantha's voice on her own unit's radio putting the information out over the air. Disgusted, Mark stepped away from his unit, slammed his door shut, and turned toward Baker's Dodge.

She was now standing outside her door and called to him, "You okay, Mark?"

He held up four fingers, a visual designation for Code 4. He could see Baker was smiling now, and he knew he wouldn't be hearing the end of this incident for a while. Brother—and sister—officers could be brutal in their good-natured ribbing about such things. He also knew his sergeant would, in all probability, have a letter of counseling for him to sign for trying to use his patrol car as a "sand rail" off-road. *Dumb*, he chided himself.

Baker teased him singing in a child's voice, "Someone's gonna get a beatin'."

"Blow me, Baker!" Mark told her.

"You wish," she retorted good naturedly.

The two had been close friends for a long time. She smiled to herself as she watched his handsome, lean frame walking toward her through the dirt. *However, if you weren't married, I would seriously consider it.* Rumor was he was getting divorced but she didn't know if that was fact. *If it is, I'm definitely gonna hit on that,* she thought as she watched him walk toward her.

As the Explorer shot out across the desert floor, the Mexican man was pleased to see that the patrol cars could not follow. His gamble had paid off temporarily, but he knew he didn't have much time, considering his situation. It wasn't good. The sky was starting to lighten in the east and, within a very short time, this whole area would be crawling with police.

It might take the TSDPS a while to get their own four wheel drive vehicles here, but most certainly air support in the form of a helicopter or airplane was already on its way, or would be shortly. The sheriff's department and the US Border Patrol used four wheel drive SUVs for regular patrol duties and the man knew they would be on the way, also.

No matter what the petty disputes the different agencies had with each other at the staff level, or even when cops had personal dislikes of other cops, when an "Officer Needs Assistance" call came out, every cop that was close rolled, no matter what agency he or she worked for. *Damn that von Moltke*! Another plan gone wrong.

The Mexican man had two pressing problems now—evasion and escape. He had to get out of this desert then ditch the Explorer where it wouldn't be found for several hours. He suddenly thought of a way he might be able to accomplish both at once with just a bit of luck.

He formulated a plan, which calmed him and allowed him to focus on the mission. As soon as he was sure the two troopers on the interstate could no longer see his taillights, he reached into his equipment bag and put on the night vision goggles. He then turned off all of the vehicle's lights. This done, he pointed the vehicle back in the general direction of the hospital and traveled parallel to the interstate, though he was two miles out into the desert.

The man knew that ditching the Explorer in the desert and leaving on foot was not an option. Both his shoe tracks in the dirt and his scent, should a K-9 cop be present, would ensure his capture in short order. *No,* he thought. *For this plan to work, I need to get back to Pecos, park the Explorer with other cars and mix with people. I must hide in plain sight.*

Two things were in his favor. The first was the darkness. Neither his vehicle, its tracks, nor the dust kicked up by his passing were visible at present. The second was that he was not that far from the edge of town, and particularly the hospital on the outskirts, which of course he had left just an hour before.

The man slowed the Explorer down some. Though the desert here was predominately flat and the brush sparse, he did not want to hit an unseen obstacle, another barbwire fence, or a wash. Any one of these could, and probably would, bring his escape to an abrupt end. Through his night vision goggles he could see the glow from the lights of town growing brighter. Soon the green halos of light would become overpowering in the goggles and he would have to take them off. Another ten minutes of driving brought him to a black ribbon of asphalt roadway crossing his path. There was no cross traffic visible in either direction. He stopped the Explorer in a cloud of dust and got out. He immediately heard multiple sirens. When he lifted the NVG's from his eyes, he could see red and blue lights from several police vehicles on the interstate two miles distant. He smiled as he saw they were all headed away from him, but he was under no illusions. As soon as it was light enough, the authorities would see the Explorer's tracks in the soil and know which direction he'd taken. They would then be all over this and every other nearby road

The Mexican man got back into his SUV, pulled the goggles back over his face, and turned out onto the asphalt surface in the opposite direction of the interstate. After driving two miles in total darkness, he again removed his NVGs and turned on his headlights. Twenty minutes later he pulled into the hospital parking lot. He had considered abandoning the Explorer in a shopping center lot that he'd passed a mile back, but immediately discarded that thought. Being so early in the morning, there were only two other cars there that he could see. The Explorer would stand out and thus draw immediate attention. He knew his SUV would be found eventually, but he needed as good a head start as he could get. This was no time to get in a rush and make a mistake.

The hospital had round-the-clock work shifts as well as walk-in patients and maybe even visitors. The parking lot there would be at least half full, even in these early morning hours. The Mexican man was pleased to see this was the case as he chose a parking stall surrounded by pick-up trucks. The Explorer would be shielded from view from all sides. "*Excellente*," he said to himself under his breath.

The man picked up his bag and took out a cloth rag and plastic ziplock freezer bag containing a spray bottle of Clorox Toilet Bowl Cleaner mixed with paint thinner. It was a noxious solution and the fumes from the two mixed chemicals could even be hazardous in a confined area, but it would serve its purpose of once again destroying any DNA evidence. Looking around to ensure he was not being observed, he stepped out. Working carefully and swiftly, he sprayed the steering wheel, gearshift lever, turn signal lever, dash buttons, armrest, and the interior and exterior driver door handles with the cleaner, then wiped them all down. Having anticipated that this day might come, one in which he had to abandon the Explorer under emergency conditions, he had limited his exposure inside the vehicle to these areas. He was even prepared to go as far as setting fire to the vehicle if it came to that, but that was not an option here as it would certainly draw the authorities This spray solution was just extra insurance as he was certain he'd been careful not to touch or handle any other areas of the Explorer without wearing his black leather gloves. This swift wipe-down would have to suffice.

The Mexican man dropped the rag and bottle back into his equipment bag and locked the Explorer with the remote. He walked to both the front, then the rear of the vehicle, bent down at each with a screwdriver, then stood up. Turning, he walked toward rear of the hospital.

As he approached the rear loading dock, he spotted what he was looking for. An enclosed chain-link fence area with a sign that read

DANGER – HAZRDOUS WASTE –
AUTHORIZED PERSONNEL ONLY.

The man knew that the black plastic garbage cans, with the bright red biohazard insignias embossed on their sides located behind the fence, would contain discarded bloody bandages, contaminated surgical sponges, syringes, linen too bloody to launder, and possibly even human tissue. No one would be looking inside these cans prior to them being hauled to a medical waste disposal incinerator. He walked behind the gate and lifted a lid off one of the cans.

The smell of decomposing human tissue and blood emitting from the can was strong. He removed the zip-locked spray bottle and cloth rag from his equipment bag and dropped both in the garbage can, along with the keys to the Explorer and both license plates he'd just removed from the vehicle. Replacing the lid, he walked back through the chain-link gate and entered the rear *Employees Only* door adjacent to the loading dock. The Mexican man then made his way through several hallways to the hospital lobby where he called a taxi to go back to his motel. He would have to find another way back to El Paso.

e∕ɔe∕ɔ

For hours afterward, police from multiple agencies scoured the surrounding roads, highways, and desert from the ground and in the air, looking for the silver Explorer. It wasn't until nearly noon that hospital security guard John Davidson who was driving through the employee parking lot checking parking permit stickers, discovered the vehicle.

CHAPTER 22

Deoxyribonucleic Acid

Sanchez and Olsen were true to their word and met me at their station the next morning—or I should say, I met them. I walked into their crime lab just as Olsen was preparing to place the lens cover we'd recovered from the old house on the reservation into the Superglue tank.

Sanchez turned and addressed me. "Good morning, Jason. We thought we'd knock out processing this lens cap before we headed over to interview Benny."

"Fine by me," I replied. I was watching Olsen. "Jim, you might want to grab a DNA swab from the *inside* of that cap before you throw it in the tank." I told him.

He frowned. "I already swabbed the outside edges. If our shooter handled it, wouldn't the DNA, or any prints for that matter, be on the outside? This is how you'd grab it to pull it off," he said, demonstrating with his gloved index finger and thumb in a soft pinching motion without actually touching the cap.

I could tell Olsen had already decided in his own mind that whomever had been watching us from behind the old house was the same person that had murdered Lyle and was looking for Benny. While I was leaning that way myself, I didn't want to assume it as fact at this point, nor did I want him to.

"Yeah, that would be the normal way of pulling the cap off binoculars that's true," I told him, "but keep in mind all of the possibilities. We don't *know* for sure that anyone was watching us. Second, if someone was, we don't know for sure that it was our shooter. If, and it's a big *if*, someone was watching us, and *if* it is the same person that killed Lyle, I seriously doubt we'll find anything useful on the outside of the cap. This guy is too good to get caught making an amateur error like not wearing gloves to handle his equipment. The point I'm trying to make is don't make up your mind early in an investigation that things happened a certain way or in a certain order. When you do that, it closes off your thinking and you start trying to force your case to fit your evidence, instead of the other way around. Always try to keep your mind open to *all* possibilities."

Listening to all of this, Sanchez asked," So you think processing the lens cap is just a CYA thing then?"

"Yes and no," I replied. "We have to process it for prints and swab the outside regardless, again, if nothing else just to eliminate some dipshit attorney down the road making a big deal about it, but as far as obtaining any DNA evidence goes, let's get a swab from the inside."

Olsen looked puzzled. "Inside the cap?"

"Absolutely," I told him. "How do you look through binoculars Jim, by putting them up to your face, pressing the rubber eye guards against the skin around your eyes. When you're done, you put the eye-ring caps back on, well, you do if you care about your gear, which this guy seems to." They stared at me, obviously still not grasping the significance, so I continued. "When you put the caps back on, the inside of the cap rubs against the rubber eye guard, possibly leaving transfer DNA onto the inside of the cap."

Sanchez nodded. "I knew that. I was just testing you."

I rolled my eyes. "Granted." Now I was thinking out loud and talking to myself as much as to them. "It's a long shot, and it would just be mitochondrial as opposed to nuclear, but it would still help us."

They both stared at me as if I had two heads.

"Wait, mitochondrial?" Olsen said. "Nuclear? You lost me."

"You might have heard this before, but I'll review it anyway. There are two types of DNA used in forensics, guys: mitochondrial and nuclear. In the simplest of terms, nuclear DNA is from live cells with a nucleus, for instance when you take a swab from the inside of a suspect's cheek, or semen, vaginal fluid, blood, sometimes saliva, etc. Nuclear DNA can be used to positively identify an individual. *Mitochondrial* DNA on the other hand is not as accurate. It can come from dead sloughed skin cells, or hair without a follicle, for instance. You can use Mi-DNA in addition to your other evidence to narrow down to a probable suspect, but it's not necessarily individual specific. It normally can't be used *solely* to positively identify a bad guy like nuclear DNA can, so if we do get something out of the cap it will, in all probability, be mitochondrial DNA and it will undoubtedly help us, but it won't necessarily put our guy on death row." They both looked disappointed. "Hey cheer up, boys. Who knows? We might get lucky." I didn't know how profound this statement would turn out to be.

Olsen retrieved another DNA swab from the sterile container on the shelf. He placed a small drop of distilled water from an adjacent squeeze bottle on the tip of the swab, then gently rubbed the tip of the swab around inside the cap and placed it with the swab he'd previously collected from the outer edge. That done, he finished Supergluing and the dusting of the cap for any partial fingerprints. Not unexpectedly, there were none. The three of us were walking down the hallway to the Property and Evidence section so Olsen could book the lens cap and swabs in, when Davis came through the double doors in front of us. His usual sour look was particularly grave this morning.

Without any greeting he asked, "What time did you three leave the hospital last night?"

The question caught us by surprise, as our train of thought was on the cap and DNA evidence. We looked at each other then back at him. I spoke up first.

"Oh, one thirty, two maybe? Not really sure."

The deputies nodded their agreement.

"Well, you got trouble," Davis replied. "Your Indian is dead. This was *your* deal. Get over to the hospital right-the-fuck now! That half-breed K-9 cop is already over there and I'm sure he's sweating it since it was his dog that did the damage, but he was helping you three out. The sheriff is on my ass because the Feds are on his. They want to know why the hell three of our deputies arrested an Indian on The Res without including them. They backed off a bit when the sheriff told them the reservation cop actually made the arrest and it was a hot-foot-pursuit deal, but let there be no doubt, you three are going to be in the shit right along with him if fuckin' Cochise there died from his dog-bite wounds, now *move i*t!"

Sanchez and I waited for Olsen to drop off his property sheet and evidence envelopes with the Property Technician. He also filled out a *Please Expedite* memo for the DNA analysis, if any was found on the cap swabs, into the state's computerized DNA storage data base. The three of us then quickly headed for the parking lot. All of us were thinking the same thing. *What the hell happened?*

Johns met us in the parking lot. As we approached his parked Tahoe, he got out and greeted us. He was more upbeat than I thought he'd be at this point.

"Hey, guys," he said with a smile.

The three of us greeted him in unison. "Mike."

"WTF?" I blurted out.

He shook his head. "Man, I thought I had *real* problems about an hour ago when I got the call from the 'attending,'" he said. "I was shakin' like a dog shittin' peach pits until I got here and actually talked to the saw-bones about Benny. My career flashed before my eyes, but things have mellowed out a bit since then—well, for me anyway. You're deal just got more complicated, though."

"Really?" Sanchez offered. "How so?"

"I'll let the doc tell you the particulars, but basically he said there's no way the dog-bite injuries were fatal, which lets me off the hook."

"Well, that's somewhat of a relief, I guess." For the first time I noticed five or six TSDPS patrol cars at the other end of the parking lot. "What's all the hub-bub over there in the parking lot?" I asked.

Johns looked that way. "The troopers got to chasin' someone last night and he ditched 'em. The suspect vehicle was found parked here by security, or so I was told anyway."

"Really?" I said. "You mean they got into a foot chase from here?"

"Nah." He shook his head. "It all happened about ten miles up the interstate. Story I got from *my* dispatch was the suspect took off in his car after being stopped. Drove out through the desert and the trooper couldn't follow for some reason."

"Huh." I looked back around at all the patrol cars. *That's weird,* I thought. *Run from the Highway Patrol, then drive back here and ditch your car?* I dismissed it. *Not my problem.*

The four of us turned and walked through the ambulance entrance. A nurse at the station saw us and ushered us into the patient triage area just behind the double doors. The attending physician looked up from reading a patient's chart. "Officers."

Johns nodded his head sideways toward the three of us. "Hey, Doc, tell them what you told me."

The young doctor looked our way. "Mr. Johnson died sometime around 3: a.m. as near as we can figure it. We grabbed the crash cart and did our thing, but it was obvious he was beyond help. At first we thought maybe his heart succumbed to the shock of the fight with you guys and the injuries caused by your dog, then one of the nurses noticed something unusual. As you may or may not know, and you might being in your line of work, the human eyes dilate when death occurs and everything stops working." We all nodded so the doctor continued. "Well, the nurse noticed the pupil of the deceased's right eye was much larger than the left. It's not unusual for there to be a slight difference mind you, but when she called it to my attention, I noticed there was a *big* difference between the two. I grabbed an ophthalmoscope and began checking the retina and pupil, which were blown. Then I noticed some tissue damage in the inside corner of the eye, so I took some forceps and began probing that area a bit. It looks to me like something penetrated the corner of the eye, deeply. With all the rushing around, no one noticed your reserve deputy missing until he stumbled out of the bathroom bleeding from the head. I've got him down the hall. He needed a few stitches and has a headache, but he'll be okay. Of course, the Coroner's Office will be able to tell you more when they do the autopsy, but—"

I stopped him in mid-sentence. "Wait, Doc, are you telling me someone smacked our reserve over the head and then killed Benny?" I was incredulous.

He looked at the floor then back at me. "It looks that way, Deputy."

I looked past the doctor to the curtained area where Benny's had been when we saw him last. "Is the body still here?"

"Yes, we were waiting for you, and the coroner, of course, but we need to get him moved to the morgue as soon as we can. We need the space."

I nodded to the curtain. "May I?"

"Go right ahead," the doc replied. "I have to attend to a patient right over here, but feel free to come get me if you need anything." And he turned and walked to another curtained enclosure.

I turned to Olsen. "Jim, go down and talk to the reserve and see if there's anything he can tell us."

I moved around the curtain and stepped up to Benny's body. His restraints and IV had been removed, as had the finger pad for the vitals monitor. Benny's skin color was that common pallid gray/beige color I'd seen so many times, and we all immediately noticed the area surrounding Benny's hospital bed was beginning to acquire that distinctive combinations of smells that accompany the recently deceased. *Swell, another ghost for my collection.* I bent over and looked at the corner of Benny's eye.

"You don't' think the dog's tooth could have done that?" Sanchez asked referring to the eye wound.

Johns's face took on a concerned look at the question.

"No," I responded. "If Falcon had bitten him in the face and one of his teeth had punctured the corner of the eye here, there would have been bleeding from the wound and punctures elsewhere on the face or head, not to mention massive bruising from the force of the dog's jaws. Malinois bite with several hundred foot-pounds of pressure. Mike?"

Johns nodded. "Yeah, five hundred PSI or so."

"So this was something else," I said as I looked around for something I could maybe see better with, like maybe a magnifying glass. There was nothing on the trays or in the drawers close by.

Olsen retuned, advising that the reserve had seen nothing. "Says one minute he's taking a piss and the next he wakes up on the floor with his dick in his hand and a massive headache."

"Okay then, Jim, do me a favor and go ask the nurse if they have a magnifying glass around here."

Olsen, happy to get away from the smell if even for a few minutes, replied, "Sure," and disappeared through the double doors. He reappeared two minutes later holding what looked like a pair of odd looking reading glasses. "They didn't have a magnifying glass," he advised. "But she did have these," and he held the glasses up for my inspection. "They're like those glasses like you see jewelers use to look at diamonds, with this flip down lens-thing. The nurse told me they use them to do minor crap like pull out small splinters."

"That'll work." I put on the glasses, flipped down the "lens-thing," as Olsen had described it, and bent over Benny's dead face. It didn't take long for me to spot the unique "star" shape on the outer edges of the puncture wound. The doctor would have noticed it also, if he'd seen it before as I had.

I handed the glasses to Sanchez. "Look."

"What am I looking at?" he said as he reluctantly bent over Benny's face. He obviously didn't really like being nose to nose with a dead guy.

"Relax, he ain't gonna bite you. Look close at the front edge of the wound."

"Oh yeah, like four little slices across from each other. What caused that?" he asked as he straightened up.

I looked at Olsen and Johns. "Take a look?"

"I'll pass," Olsen replied.

But Johns accepted the invitation. "I want to see it. Never know when it might come in handy." He put on the glasses and bent over. After a good sixty seconds, he straightened back up also.

All three were now looking at me for an explanation.

"Mid-nineties in Vista, we had a guy who killed some prostitutes. We didn't put it together as a serial killer deal for a while because he killed them in different ways, *and* there were long periods of time between the assaults, but it turned out it was the same guy killing all the girls. One girl he strangled with her own purse strap and two he shot. He cut one's throat with a straight razor. Stabbed two others. It was a real smorgasbord of death. This was spaced out over a period of two years give or take. We had no hard evidence from any of the scenes. Oh, we had a couple of cartridge cases and bullets, but no gun to match them to. He didn't screw any of them so no DNA, not even off of the purse strap. He wore gloves.

"Anyway, one of girls he shot survived and she gave us a pretty fair description. We knew we were looking for a short, chubby white boy in his late twenties or early thirties, etc., etc. We got our first real break about it being the same guy when one of the stabbed girls survived also. She gave us a similar description. She also told us she'd met him at a local truck stop. Bingo! We figured that if he was a trucker, it would explain the time line of the attacks. He was coming through town only intermittently, doing his thing to the girls, then moving on the next day. Sorry, don't mean to be digressing here, boys, and I promise I'll get to the point here in a minute, but it's all part of the explanation.

"The girls that had been stabbed, had not been stabbed with a knife, but with something that had left *that* type of a wound pattern," I said, nodding to Benny. "None of us at the PD had seen anything like it before, nor had the coroner. I sent the close up photos of the stab wounds we'd taken of both girls, over to a friend of mine at CA DOJ, guy named Corey, who was an expert on knife wounds, ice pick wounds, etc. He looked at it briefly and told me what I already knew, that it resembled a small bullet entry wound with no bullet. I ragged on him for that lame explanation, but it had peaked his curiosity and he worked on it for several days on the side. He called me a few days later and told me he thought he knew what had been used.

"When we finally caught this asshole, he actually confessed to all the murders, hated his mommy, and all women were whores, or some crazy-assed shit like that, he told the shrink, but that's not the point. Turned out my buddy at DOJ was right. We found out from the killer's confession that he had used a large Phillips screwdriver from his truck's toolbox to stab those two girls. It left the same wound pattern on the skin of those two hookers that poor old dead Benny has there in his eyeball."

"Fuck!" Olsen blurted out, just coming to grips with what I was implying. Several heads turned our way. He lowered his voice. "You mean someone got in here after we left and stabbed Benny in the eye?"

I nodded. "Looks like it." I told them all. "It will take the autopsy to tell us for sure, but I'd be willing to bet the paycheck I'm not getting that's what has happened. I'm beginning to think that maybe you were right, Jim." I looked at Olsen. "We *were* being watched out there at the reservation, and I think the killer followed us here and killed Benny after we left. If that is the case, we are dealing with a very deliberate and dangerous man here, boys. Not some penny-ante psycho. This guy has *cajones*. Hell, he may have very well been hanging around here watching us and waiting for us to leave."

"Christ on a crutch!" Sanchez said. "You actually think the guy might have been here the same time as us?"

"Very well could have been," I replied. "Could've even been sitting in his car or out in the waiting room, watching us come and go. Think about it. How many people are around here all the time? No one would pay attention to one more person sitting out there. And how many cars in and out? For that matter, how many are just parked out there in the parking lot every day and every night? No one would pay attention to them either."

I paused after this last statement, thinking, *What am I missing here?* Johns and I suddenly looked at each other. His eyes flew open wide as what I'd just said hit us both at the same time.

"Holy shit!" Johns exclaimed. Again, heads turned our way. "You don't think—"

"Could be," I replied.

We both turned and ran for the ambulance entrance. Sanchez and Olsen hadn't made the connection yet and were at a loss at our seemingly crazed actions, but both followed us at a run. The nurses at the station and everyone in the waiting room stared as we barreled through the door in a rush and headed toward the single TSDPS patrol car parked at the other end of the parking lot. It was the only unit still parked near the abandoned Explorer, all the others having returned to their regular duties when the suspect could not be found. A tow truck was parked next to the patrol car, the driver and the trooper talking.

The trooper saw the four of us running toward him. Alarmed, he stepped out of his patrol car looking around for some unseen threat, his right hand on his weapon. When he saw none, he looked back at the four of us as we stopped in front of him, breathing hard.

"What the hell is this all about? You scared the crap outta me! I thought the friggin' boogie-man was creeping up on me," he said, the irritation obvious in his voice.

"Sorry, *amigo*," I replied. "We needed to catch you before you towed that car there." I indicated the Explorer.

"So?" he asked. "Wouldn't the radio have worked?"

I just shrugged. "This was faster."

The trooper recognized Olsen and Sanchez and his irritation with us faded. "Hey, Jim. Hey, Frank."

"Mark, how you been?" Sanchez replied. "Long time, no see,"

Olsen just gave him a nod and a grin

"I was good until two minutes ago when I saw all you guys running at me like that. Damn near shit myself."

"Sorry, *vato*," Sanchez said. The two shook hands. He looked around at all of us, said, "Introductions and explanations all around," and with that introduced the highway patrol officer, to Johns and myself.

"I heard the other day at briefing the SO hired themselves some retired big-time crime scene honcho from California. So you're it, eh?" Williams asked sticking out his hand.

I shook it. "Well, I don't know how big-time I am, and the 'hired' part is a loose term for sure." I glanced at Sanchez disapprovingly as he looked up at the sky. "But I am retired, or was, or will be again when this is over. See? Now even *I'm* confused."

Williams chuckled. "So what can I do for you guys?"

I nodded toward the Explorer. "Tell us the tale."

Cops, *all* cops, love to tell other cops their "war stories." Williams was no exception. He laid it all out for us in detail, from his hiding in his favorite ambush site with his lights out, to sitting here writing up his tow sheet. It was a good story which ate up fifteen minutes in the telling.

"Can you hold up on the tow for a bit, Mark?" Sanchez asked. "I've got to make a call to my lieutenant and then he's probably going to want to talk to your boss before you do anything with it."

Williams looked at the abandoned Explorer, then back at us. "Okay, I guess, but what's up?"

I looked at him. "How much time you got?"

As Sanchez stepped away once again call Lt. Davis, I began to tell Williams what we suspected about his Ford Explorer and, in the briefest fashion possible, how we came to be at this point.

Nothing happens quickly when law enforcement staff from different agencies have to try to solve a problem by mutual decision. This was no exception. It took an hour for Davis to call Sanchez back, and that was only to tell us to stand-by until a decision could be reached. Williams' sergeant was, of course, now with us, as was their Crime Scene Unit van with two technicians. They didn't look happy as they had just left and were now called back, possibly to have to "re-process" the same vehicle. The TSDPS sergeant had already flexed his supervisory muscle and told the four of us not to get near the Explorer until he heard from his lieutenant. That didn't really bother me much at this point, as prior to the arrival of all this state attention, Sanchez had used a "Slim-Jim" to open the door of the Explorer. Williams hadn't been too keen on us doing that, but I assured him my examination would only take a few minutes and we would lock it back up and keep our mouths shut about it. As Sanchez had worked on the door, I walked around the outside.

As soon as the door was opened, the smell of a bleach/paint thinner solution was overwhelming. I gave the interior a quick inspection. Satisfied with the look I'd had at both the inside and the outside of the SUV, I turned to Sanchez. "Call Davis and tell him not to fight with the Highway Patrol over possession of this thing. I'm certain now that our boy *was* using this vehicle, but that we're not going to find anything on it or in it we can use to ID our guy. It's been scrubbed."

"How do you know just by looking at it?" Olsen had asked the question, but they were all listening intently for my answer.

"Let's look at the outside first," I told them. "Walk with me. See the brand new tires? The old ones, I'm sure, are in a tire shop's junk tire heap somewhere." I turned to Sanchez. "I'd bet every penny I have that the tread on those old tires, wherever they are, would match the tire tracks we found out by that embankment at the ranch." I motioned them all over to an un-related Chevrolet sedan parked in the adjacent parking stall. "Look at the layer of dust on this car. Can you see how every fingerprint, smudge, and palm print is visible because of the dust layer?" They all nodded. "Now go back and look at the Explorer." I showed them that, although the Explorer was also covered with a similar layer of dust, not a single smudge or print was visible.

"I didn't realize regular old dust would stick to stuff like that," Johns interjected.

"If the dust is fine enough," I told him, "and if the car is the right color, you can see it just like you can fingerprint powder. Doesn't work as well on light colored paint, particularly in the daylight. Works good in the dark with your flashlight if you hold your light at an angle though." I pointed out other things I'd noticed. "Look how all the reflectors and chrome have been taped over. At first glance it just makes the car look like a junker, but it actually serves a purpose."

"Reflection?" Johns asked.

"Good guess," I told him. "Won't reflect at night. *We* have a thread now, boys. Let's start pulling on it and see what unravels. Right now our guy doesn't have any wheels, that we know of anyway, but that will change quickly."

With our assurances to keep both the Johns and Williams apprised of any new developments, when and if they arose, both walked back to their respective units, Johns to make his arrangements to attend Benny's autopsy and Williams to finish paperwork as he waited for a relief unit to arrive to handle the tow. It had been a long day for him, having worked almost fifteen hours straight by now. The two TSDPS Crime Scene Technicians were applying fingerprint powder to the outside of the Explorer as we drove out of the parking lot.

I was sure their efforts would prove futile, but that really didn't matter. Someone was going to have to process the Explorer for evidence at some point anyway. *Better them than me,* I thought. The state had more people, money, and time to waste.

"I want to make a stop on the way back to your office," I told Sanchez. He looked at me with a raised eyebrow so I added, "The median of the freeway at Williams' ambush site, if you know where it is."

"I do." He nodded. "I always have to watch out for those sneaky bastards when I'm off duty and haulin' down the highway. The professional courtesy thing is not their deal."

CHAPTER 23

The Hunt

D avis wasn't the only one waiting for us when we arrived back at the sheriff's station. Davis, the sheriff himself, and a captain from the TSDPS were all sitting in the conference room, cups of coffee in front of them as the three of us walked in. No one had to ask. We already knew they expected a complete briefing. After the introductions were out of the way, I began, but I was brought up short after two minutes by the sheriff. It was fortunate that the three of us already knew the involvement of Trooper Williams, as the TSDPS Captain either could not, or would not add anything to that part of the conversation.

The sheriff abruptly turned to the Highway Patrol captain, told him that the sheriff's office would keep the TSDPS informed of any new information as it came to light, and thanked him for attending the briefing. They both stood and he unceremoniously ushered the captain to the door.

Interesting, I thought. *The sheriff obviously wants to get rid of this guy before we go on.* The captain curtly offered his thanks. *Oh yeah, he's pissed.* It was obvious the TSDPS official was not happy at being "dismissed."

"Sorry about that fellas," the sheriff said, indicating the uncomfortable moment at the captain's leaving, "but that guy is an insufferable prick. I've known him for fifteen years. He's always been a prick. Information is always a one way street with him. He marched in here today telling me how they would be conducting their own investigation and hinting we should butt out. Well, fuck him! This is *our* homicide investigation, not theirs. He doesn't need to know any more about where we're going with this right now." The sheriff turned to the three of us. "Where *are* we going with this right now?"

Up until now, I had not spent any time talking to the sheriff. We'd always dealt with Davis. I found I liked the sheriff's plain spoken style.

"That's just what we were discussing on our drive back here, boss," Sanchez answered and looked at me to start the ball rolling.

Since when did I get voted spokesman of this club? I briefly wondered. I turned to face the sheriff. "We know, well, we *think*, our guy is temporarily without wheels, but that'll probably change quickly. I suspect he is either staying in, or looking for, a cheap local motel. He'll probably pay cash, use a fake name, etc."

"How'd you figure that?" Davis asked. "What about his car, or an apartment, or safe house of some type?"

I shook my head. "He needed to hang around at least for a few days, so he couldn't sleep in his car every night. Might be rousted by a cop. He'd need some place to organize, rest, and get prepared for each day's activities without being bothered. I figured a cheap motel because just like the hospital, people are coming and going constantly. No one would pay much attention. An apartment wouldn't work. Too many people would be involved. Paperwork, neighbors—definitely not. A safe-house might work if you needed to lay low, but not if you were in and out at all times of the day and night It would need to be remote or it would draw too much attention from the neighbors. And again, he wouldn't go to the trouble to do all the rental bullshit. Of course, he could always be in a house out in the boondocks that belonged to someone he knows, but that would mean a 'commute' to work. It's a possibility for sure, but a lot of exposure. The less time out on the road the better."

Everyone in the room was looking at me and listening intently now, so I continued. "We know which way he was headed when he tossed the cell phone and Williams got on him, so we look out that direction for motels first. You have to remember, he got away clean from the hospital so there was no reason he would be back-tracking or trying to throw off a tail." I was going over it in my head as I spoke. "I think he was probably headed back to his room or whatever, when Williams saw him. Throwing that cell out the window was the first dumb thing our guy has done. We have it, by the way."

"You have what?" the sheriff asked.

"The cell phone," I replied. "Or to be more accurate, pieces of the cell phone."

Davis jumped in. "Where? How?"

"On our way in here," Sanchez said. "We stopped on the interstate where our bad guy tossed it and poked around for a bit. Found most of it right at the edge of the grass in the emergency lane there in the center."

"Olsen's idea to look for it," I said quickly.

The young deputy shot me a questioning glance, as did Sanchez. I winked back at them and shook my head slightly.

The sheriff nodded at Olsen. "Good work, Deputy." He then looked at Davis. "Get a warrant from Judge Hopkins and let's get any information we can from the carrier on that phone."

Davis nodded. "Yes, sir. Where's the phone?"

Olsen spoke up. "It's in the lab on the counter, but we haven't processed it for prints yet."

The sheriff turned to me. "Any chance of getting anything, you think?"

"I seriously doubt it, but we still need to look. If for nothing else, just to cover us, and we need to swab the key pad for any DNA also, again, probably a moot point, but we might get lucky."

The sheriff turned back to Olsen. "Deputy, go take care of that right now so Lieutenant Davis can have that phone, please, and get it to him as soon as you are done. Sanchez and Douglas will catch you up on our conversations here if you miss out on anything."

Olsen got up to leave the room. The sheriff motioned Davis to sit back down. "So tell me more about this eye-ring cap you found."

I looked at both him and Davis. "I think right now it's our best piece of *possible* DNA evidence. Our guy wouldn't have used anything as a barrier on his face, I'm sure. I don't think even he would have thought of that. He might not even know he's lost it yet, but we need to get the swabs analyzed right away."

"I can help with that I think," the sheriff said. "I'm the sheriff of the county so I'll turn the screws." He made a note to himself. "Sounds like you have your work cut out for you, so get to it before this guy gets out of the county, and keep Lieutenant Davis updated with what you're doing."

With that, the meeting was over, Sanchez and I sat down in the conference room to discuss our next move when Johns called my cell phone. The autopsy on Benny Johnson had been completed. He gave me the info. I thanked him and hung up. "Official cause of Benny's death was a long sharp shaft, like that of a screwdriver, shoved through the corner of his eye into the brain."

He got up and walked to the lieutenant's office. Olsen returned within forty-five minutes and, together, we all headed for the first motel on our list.

How could we know that because of our choice of that particular motel, at that particular time, on that particular day, fate would deal the three of us a devastating blow?

CHAPTER 24

Greyhound

The Mexican man made sure the taxi dropped him off a block from his motel. He walked the rest of the way, double checking his surroundings. Confident that his motel hide-out had not been discovered, the man entered his room. His escape through the desert that morning and again at the hospital had been part skill and park luck, and the man did *not* like relying on luck. He knew he needed to get packed and get out of the area as soon as possible. As he gathered his few belongings, he was thinking about how he would get back to El Paso. He could easily steal a car. That, of course, was another tool of the trade at which he'd become adept, but any extra-curricular criminal activity was always a risk.

The man finally decided to take a taxi to the local Greyhound Bus Station and buy a ticket. He loathed the idea of riding a bus with the common rabble that normally used the bus for transportation, but on the up side, it would provide him with a crowd of people he could easily blend in with. With that decision made, he wrapped up all his sheets and towels into one bundle, stepped out of the room and walked down the walkway to an unattended maid's service cart. He dropped the bundle into the hamper, mixing it up with other laundry. When he got back, he wiped down any of the surfaces he thought he might have touched without his gloves, took one last look around the interior, picked up his bag, and put his gloved right hand on the door knob.

As he opened the door for the second time and began to step out of the room, he was surprised to see a sheriff's department SUV pull into the driveway near the office. The Mexican man stepped back into the room and quickly closed the door. Moving to the window, he shifted the shade slightly so he could see outside. He recognized the two deputies and the detective that he had watched out at the ranch, Benny's house, and at the hospital. All three walked toward the office. Just short of the office door, the detective turned to the younger deputy, spoke briefly, then turned again. He and the older deputy entered the office. The younger deputy stayed outside, apparently to watch the parking lot.

How could they know I was here? the man asked himself. *Was this some random event? Doesn't matter. In just a few minutes the clerk will tell them that I was the only one to check in over the past two days. Maldicion! Thirty seconds and I would have been gone!*

He was now trapped in his room, what with the young deputy standing guard over the parking lot. The man needed to lure the deputy away from his position and dispose of him quickly before the other two came back out of the office. He knew instinctively that the younger deputy was probably inexperienced and could be distracted easily. It would need to be something unexpected, yet non-threatening. He opened his motel room door and stepped out. The deputy looked his way. The man walked toward a nearby car, acting as if he were the owner. Fortunately for the man, the car was parked with the driver's side door on the opposite side from the office door and the deputy. Out of his peripheral vision, the man could see the deputy watching him closely now. The Mexican man stopped suddenly, dropped his equipment bag, grabbed his chest with his left hand, and dropped to his knees, letting out a loud groan. As he'd hoped, the young deputy ran to assist him without hesitation and, more importantly, without alerting his companions. The Mexican man was still on his knees with his forehead against the car when the deputy came to a stop next to him.

"Take is easy now, sir. I'll get help right away," the officer said as he put his right hand on the man's shoulder.

The Mexican man suddenly swiveled on his knees and grabbed the officer's gun hand, pinning it. He drove the razor sharp blade from the large folding knife he had been concealing in his right hand in an upward thrust into the deputy's abdomen. As the knife pierced his body underneath the bottom edge of his body armor, the deputy recoiled backward, gasping. He stood up on his tip-toes as if trying to get himself off of the blade.

Having seen the danger at the last second, the officer had turned slightly. It was this slight movement that might end up saving his life. The Mexican man had aimed the blade for the deputy's spleen, kidney, and, if deep enough, the liver. He knew from both his military training and practical experience, that a wound such as this would be instantly debilitating, from the pain and, most certainly, fatal.

Olsen's last-second twist, however, had caused the blade to miss all of these vital organs. The knife penetrated his front left side under the ribcage at a steep angle, with the blade sliding up along the inside of his ribs. The pain was immediate and like nothing the deputy had ever felt before. It was as if someone had poured a bucket of burning coals inside him. He tried to reach for his Glock, but his hand and arm were pinned by the man's iron grip. Olsen's body started shutting down from the shock. His knees buckled and he collapsed to the pavement. His head hit the asphalt hard, but he felt only the pain in his stomach. The last thing he saw as he blacked out was the man standing up and turning away.

୧୬୧୬

Inside the office, Sanchez was standing behind me, listening to my conversation with the clerk. Both of our backs were to the window that looked out into the main parking lot. The clerk told me that the motel's clientele were primarily long term renters, but that he *had* rented a room to a younger Mexican man two days prior. The man paid in cash, day-to-day. He had not come in to pay for today as of yet. Being that it was not check-out time yet, as far as the clerk knew, the man was still in his room. I asked him a few more questions about the man but the clerk didn't really know much more. The man had told him he was here on business. The clerk let me look at the registration sign-in card. The vehicle the man had listed on the card was a Chevrolet pick-up, and the license plate was from Arizona, and no, the clerk had not checked out the vehicle to see if it matched the information on the card.

"We never really do," he admitted.

After obtaining the man's room number, I turned to Sanchez. "Probably be a dead end, but we need to go talk to this guy anyway."

He nodded and we both turned and walked out the door. Both of us caught a glimpse of a Hispanic man carrying a black satchel turning the corner at the far end of the parking lot near the driveway out onto the street.

"Where'd Olsen go?" Sanchez asked.

"Huh, I don't see that boy anywhere," I said, looking around. "Room #119 is right over there." I gestured in that direction with my head. "That's the room this guy is supposed to be staying in."

Movement caught our eye and we watched as a pretty young Mexican girl in a housekeeper's uniform walked around the corner of the motel building from the sidewalk on the street. *Arriving for work most likely,* I thought. It was the same corner the man with the satchel had just gone around in the opposite direction. After walking just a few paces on the walkway in front of the first floor rooms, she stopped suddenly, obviously looking at something on the ground on the far side of a parked car. Her face first took on the look of surprise, then one of shock, and then came a scream of genuine terror. She started backing away, still screaming, "*Madre Dios!*" and crossing herself.

Sanchez started to run, but I yelled, "Slow! Go right! I'll go left!"

Both of us had our weapons out as we rapidly approached the parked car from two different directions. The girl saw this and it was just too much for her. She took off back around the corner of the building at a run, still screaming and crying.

Sanchez and I rounded both ends of the car at the same moment. Olsen lay where he had dropped. His face was ashen. A large pool of blood was still spreading underneath him.

"Shit!" I grabbed his shoulders and rolled him over onto his back. Glancing at Sanchez, I shouted, "Get help right now!" but it wasn't necessary.

He already had his radio in his hand. I tore open Olsen's shirt and could see the one inch slit in his left abdomen pouring blood. Images from the past of wounded buddies I'd treated in the rice paddies of Vietnam came flooding back.

"If we can get the bleeding slowed down he might have a chance!"

"What? What?"

Sanchez was in shock himself. It was understandable. This was not just some injured citizen from a car wreck, or a victim of drive-by shooting. It was *his* partner bleeding out in front of his own eyes.

"Look at the blood from the wound, Frank! It's not bright red and it's not spurting so it's not arterial. There's no froth so it didn't catch the lung, and it's not black so doesn't look like the kidney or liver got penetrated, but this wound has to be plugged right now or he'll bleed out in two minutes tops! Go get your first aid kit from the car!"

As Sanchez took off at a run for his unit, I wiped my thumb off as best I could and stuck it inside Olsen's wound all the way to my hand as a plug. Olsen groaned. I knew it had to hurt, but the bleeding had to be at least slowed down. Sanchez returned with his first-aid kit as we began to hear the first of many distant sirens. He removed a package of blood clotting powder and a compress bandage.

Sanchez was aghast. "Holy shit, man! You stuck your dirty-ass thumb inside him?"

"Frank, listen to me. Infection from my thumb is the least of his worries right now! I have to get this bleeding stopped or he's gonna fucking die right here! Now get ready. When I pull my thumb out you dump that blood-clotting powder on and into the wound, the whole package. Then slap that compress over it and hold it down tight."

The sirens were getting closer now. Lots of them.

CHAPTER 25

Officer Down

W hen Sanchez yelled into his handset that a deputy was down, the air waves came alive. Radio calls from every unit with every agency in the area advised they were responding. It was all that their respective dispatchers could do to keep at least a few units in their assigned patrol areas should some *other* emergency arise. As it was, no less than forty patrol cars from the sheriff's department, TSDPS, the city police, the US Border Patrol, the lone reservation officer, and even the local school authority police pointed the front bumpers of their patrol cars toward the motel and stomped on their gas pedals. Two city police cars, a fire truck with two paramedics, and an ambulance with two emergency medical technicians were the first to arrive, but within minutes the parking lot and adjacent roadway were filled with both marked and un-marked police vehicles. On-lookers were also starting to gather in greater and greater numbers, drawn by the sirens and flashing lights like moths to a flame. The paramedics and the EMTs immediately rushed to Olsen's side with their equipment and took over the medical assistance. The paramedic looked at my bloody hand and thumb then back at Olsen's wound. Figuring out what I had done, he shouted over the racket, "My dad was an Army medic. He told me he did things like that to temporarily plug bullet holes," he said, nodding to my bloody hand, "but I always thought it was just bullshit. He was a combat medic with the 173rd Airborne Brigade in Vietnam in '67."

"Iron Triangle?" I asked.

"Yeah, Operation Cedar Falls."

I nodded, impressed. *Like father like son.*

After their initial triage, the paramedics immediately called for a Life-Flight helicopter. Both agreed that Olsen's chances would be better if they could get him to a larger trauma center than that of the local hospital. An arriving TSDPS sergeant took command of the choked chaos of patrol cars in the roadway, directing officers to clear the area, by moving the on-lookers back, and to block off the street at both ends so the helicopter would have a place to land. Ten minutes later, the heavy thump-thump-thump of rotor blades could be heard.

"That was damn quick," I said to Sanchez.

"It's great!" he replied, starting to regain his wits.

One of the paramedics overheard me and spoke up. "Life-Flight was already on another call. We lucked out though. That's the US Border Patrol's big Sikorsky H-38 rescue bird coming in. He was coming back from a SAR and he was close by and heard the medevac request so he responded."

The helicopter was close now and coming up the street slowly at about three hundred feet. The pilot was looking at the makeshift landing pad. It was a big machine and it would be a tight squeeze, but he was obviously an experienced pilot and he settled the machine onto the roadway without incident, blowing gravel, dust, and everything else not nailed down, in all directions.

As soon as the wheels touched the ground, the Border Patrol agent who doubled as the flight engineer and was also a licensed paramedic, unhooked his umbilical helmet cord, jumped out of the open side cargo door and ran to us, the big machine idling behind him, it's rotors spinning. The paramedics and the Border Patrol agent consulted for a minute, then with the help of the two EMTs, Sanchez and myself, Olsen was rolled onto a backboard with a cervical collar around his neck. They opted not to disturb the compress bandage Sanchez and I had put in place, save to add more bandages to it. Together we picked up the young deputy and hustled him to the side door of the helicopter. After loading him in, the paramedic jumped in also. The rest of us stepped well back. The engine of the big Sikorsky helicopter changed tones as the pilot throttled up. I looked away, knowing what was coming. I didn't think to warn Sanchez who was looking right at the side of the thundering machine.

The pilot "pulled pitch" and the rotor blades bit the surrounding air. The big helicopter rose from the ground. For the second time, everything within a hundred feet that wasn't nailed down sailed away in the man-made dust storm. Sanchez's face caught the full force of sand, grit, and hot air. He turned away, cursing and spitting. The loud racket the machine made faded quickly as it gained altitude and headed off to the East. The two of us stood for a moment then walked toward that corner of the building.

"Frank," I said, "when we first came out of the office—" I paused and thought a moment. "—you know, I think we saw the guy who did this."

"You mean the guy with the satchel?"

I nodded. "We need to get a description out."

Sanchez took out his pocket notebook and together we quickly compiled a fair description of the man we had seen. Hispanic, mid-thirties, maybe six-foot-one and lean. One-hundred-seventy pounds give or take, short cut black hair, and no facial hair. Brown eyes? We had been too far away to call that one and it was just an educated guess so we left that out of the broadcast. Levis, a blue plaid western shirt with the tail out, which meant he was probably carrying a gun. We knew for sure he had a large knife.

After we were comfortable with our combined description of the man, we put it out over the air, along with the added warning about him being armed and extremely dangerous. Almost immediately, many of the units at the motel began to circulate the area. A few were being directed back to their normal duties where needed, but most started hunting for the potential cop killer. All of them now had a target. Maybe we'd get lucky and someone would spot him, but I was very worried that, with the fever for payback raging, some officer would see the guy make a "furtive movement" and blow him away, or worse, hesitate and get blown away himself.

I myself was torn. I now wanted this guy dead in the worst way for what had just happened to my deputy friend, but I also wanted to get to the bottom of the homicides of Benny and Lyle. I knew there had to be some reason a professional killer went after both, and I wanted to know who this guy was. If some cop shot holes in the man without getting *himself* killed, it would do me no good as far as the investigation of the two dead Indians were concerned, or in finding out who had hired it done.

My cell phone rang, breaking my train of thought. It was Sonya. She'd heard the sirens and seen units one after another traverse the interstate which had her worried about me. I briefly filled her in on what had happened. She told me she was going to borrow a car from Juan and go to the hospital. I didn't argue with her. There would have been no point. She had grown fond of Olsen, ever since our first meeting. I told her I would meet her there at some point. I had just hung up when the sheriff and Davis walked up behind us.

The sheriff nodded to both Sanchez and I then came right to the point. "What the hell went wrong here, Deputies?"

"Before we get into all the particulars, Sheriff," I told him, "we need to close off that motel room right there so we can work it. Our guy has been staying in that room."

"Do it," he replied. "And then I want to know how one of my people got gutted like a goddamned fish!"

I retrieved crime scene tape from our SUV and blocked access to both the room and the area of the parking lot where Olsen had been stabbed, including around the car parked there.

The owner of the vehicle now approached Sanchez, saying, "Hey, dude, that's my car. I need to leave."

The older deputy had his wits back about him now, as well as his anger. *Whoops! Critical error, boy-o*, I thought to myself.

Sanchez turned on the man. "What the fuck did you just say to me? Dude? Is that what you called me, you sack of shit? We just had a cop stabbed here! It'll take as long as it takes, so don't come around here again until you see us leave, and if you ever refer to me as dude again, I'm gonna shove my nightstick so far up your ass you'll look like a corn dog. Now fuck off!"

The man slunk away, reminding me of a dog that had just been beaten for pissing on the carpet.

"Take it easy, big guy," I said to Sanchez quietly.

"Yeah? Fuck that asshole!" was the deputy's reply as the sheriff and Davis approached.

Fortunately both had been out of earshot when Sanchez lost his cool with the guy. The four of us gathered just outside the suspect's motel room. For the better part of an hour, Sanchez and I filled the sheriff in on what had happened and why we had made the decision to have Olsen watch the lot.

"What I don't understand," Davis said, echoing the sheriff's thoughts, "is why Olsen was over by that car, when you had him watching from just outside the office."

Sanchez looked perplexed. "We can't figure it either, boss. The only thing we can think of is that he saw something and walked over to check it out."

"Unless he was lured over intentionally," I said pensively. All three looked at me so I continued. "I'm thinking our guy was here in the motel, probably in his room, and he maybe saw us pull in. Maybe we had him boxed in but we just didn't know it. He knows he needs to get out of here but now he's in a fix. He can't bail because Olsen is outside watching the doors to the rooms and the parking lot. We placed him there to observe anyone trying to leave so we could question them. This guy figured out a way to lure Olsen over to the far side of that car. It would have to have been something that Jim wouldn't have suspected was a threat or he would have let us know."

Sanchez spoke up. "Jim's no dummy. He wouldn't have taken on something by himself that he'd seen as a threat."

"That's true," I replied. "But did you notice Jim's weapon was still in the holster. That speaks volumes to the fact that he didn't suspect anything bad was going to happen to him."

"We're going to the hospital," the sheriff interrupted. "You two stay here and process that room."

I saw the unease and disappointment in Sanchez's face. I knew he wanted to be with his partner.

"Sheriff, I can handle the room and the car by myself," I told him. "Sanchez needs to be with his partner."

To my surprise, Davis backed me up on that. "I agree, boss," he told the sheriff.

"All right." The sheriff turned to Sanchez. "Sanchez you ride with us and leave Douglas here your unit."

Sanchez tossed me his keys and mouthed the word "Thanks," at me.

"You need anything else?" Davis asked as the sheriff and Sanchez walked away.

"Yeah, I could use a unit to stand by with me. I don't want to have to be trying to keep the looky-loos off my back while I process this scene, not to mention the shit I'd be in if our guy wanders back by to check out his handy work and I'm here with no one to watch my back. Odds are he wouldn't, but stranger things have happened."

Davis nodded. "Okay, I'll round up a deputy to stand by."

He started to walk away. I glanced across the parking lot and spotted Johns getting in his vehicle to leave.

"Hey L-T," I called to Davis. "See if you can get that K-9 guy to stay." I jerked my chin at Johns's Tahoe parked near the driveway. "I already know him and he's pretty sharp. He's already involved somewhat, and his dog wouldn't be bad to have around either."

Davis paused, thinking about it for a second, then nodded and started walking toward the K-9 unit. After a brief conversation, Johns pulled his Tahoe over near the motel room.

"You gonna be able to hang?" I asked him.

"No sweat. Falcon and I assist the S.O. all the time, so unless there's some major felony on The Res, which by the way only happens about once every two years, I can stay as long as you need me."

"Cool. Listen, Mike, keep your eyes open. I don't think our guy would come back but he could, and we both know how dangerous this guy is, so heads up."

Johns looked around, albeit nervously. "You want me to get Falcon out and walk him around once in a while just for show?"

"That's a good idea, and not just for show," I replied as I walked toward Sanchez's SUV.

Opening the back, I retrieved the camera, number stands, the swab kit, and the fingerprint dusting kit. Juggling all of the items, I set them all down just inside the crime scene tape, where Johns could keep an eye on all of it, yet where none of the items would show up in the scene photos.

I placed my yellow plastic stand number 1 on the asphalt to show the spot where Olsen went down next to the parked car. Although it was plainly visible by the large pool of blood and discarded medical wrappers and tubes on the ground, the number stand would make is easier to describe in the report that I was now going to have to write. *So much for not having to go to court.* Approaching the closed door to Room 119, it dawned on me that no one had been into the room since this whole incident started. *No one thought to clear this room, including you, dummy. We just assumed it was empty.* Setting down the additional number stands, I moved out from directly in front of the door and pulled my small Kahr from its holster on my right hip. Johns, out of his car now and holding Falcon by the lead, saw this and immediately drew his gun from its holster, alarmed. He quickly walked over, staying away from in front of the window and the door, and whispered, "What's up?"

"Probably nothing," I replied. "But the room hasn't been cleared."

Johns raised his weapon. "No shit? Okay, I'll let Falcon go in."

The dog had already sensed the heightened tension level of his handler, and when the gun came out Falcon knew what was happening and let out several high pitched barks.

Johns, still standing back, pounded on the door then loudly stated, "*Police officer*! Open the door or I will send my police dog in!"

After waiting about ten seconds for an answer, he repeated the same thing in Spanish. Another ten seconds went by with no response. Falcon was now going crazy, yapping and barking and straining at the lead. I reached over and tried the door knob with two gloved fingers. It turned and the door opened a crack. Johns took the lead off of Falcon and shoved the door open. All three of us went through, the dog in front, sniffing and turning this way and that. It only took seconds to be sure the room was empty. The dog actually looked disappointed that he hadn't been able to find someone. Johns put Falcon back on his lead and they moved outside. I began a visual inspection of the room.

It was no less than I'd expected from our boy. The room was clean and neat. The trash cans were empty and the bed had been stripped of all of its bedding. *Probably washed by now, or dumped*, I thought. The TV remote lay on top of the TV and I was able to see by the fine layer of dust on it that it had not been used in some time. All of the drawers were empty save for the Gideon's Bible and a telephone book. The motel pen and paper lay untouched on the small end table. The bathroom was no different. The complementary bars of soap, matches, shampoo, and water glasses were all undisturbed. There were no towels. They went the way of the bedding, I was sure. There was no used bar of soap or hair in the tub. The toilet bowl had not been used. The paper *Sanitized For Your Protection* band was still wrapped around the lid and seat.

Didn't think motels even used those any more. Even the toilet paper rolls was still brand new. *Huh! Where'd this guy go to take a crap when he needed to? Probably down the street at the gas station.* It was as if the room hadn't been occupied at all.

I went through all the proper motions. I took photos of the room then collected swabs from the usual places, the door knob and handles of the drawers, the toilet flush handle and the bathtub/shower knobs, the TV remote and the light switches. I liberally spread fingerprint powder around the room, but I already knew this was an exercise in futility, and I was right. I got nothing save for what appeared to be glove smudges.

Having no trace evidence vacuum, I decided to walk over to the office and ask to collect any used bags from any of the motel's vacuums that might have been used in the room. I stepped out of the door of the room and decided to take a short cut across the lot to the office by stepping over a concrete planter and under the branches of a young tree growing in it at the edge of the walkway. I had been looking down lost in thought, and I subsequently drove my forehead straight into the sharp end of a leaf covered branch of the tree which I hadn't noticed was hanging low.

"Shit! That hurt," I blurted out, reaching up to rub my head. I could feel a small gouge at my hairline, though there was no blood.

Johns had seen it happen and chuckled. "That hurt? That *had* to hurt. I saw it," he said, quoting a line from a movie.

"Yeah, yeah, kiss my ass," I shot back. Still rubbing my head, I took two steps, continuing on my way, then stopped again.

Johns saw me stop and he was genuinely concerned this time. "You okay, dude?"

"Bring your flashlight over here, bud," I said. "Mine's outta juice."

He took the lead off of Falcon and put the dog back in the Tahoe, or tried to. As the dog got to the rear door, his head whipped around and he started whining. Johns recognized the dog's alert and instantly looked toward the street and the driveway, but there was nothing there. Falcon had picked up a faint scent but of what Johns didn't know, and it couldn't be too alarming to the dog or he would've been barking furiously. Johns forced the dog to jump into the back seat then walked over to me, carrying his light.

"I can look at your head without my light. It's not like it's dark out here," he said.

"Not my head I'm thinking about. What was up with mutt?"

"Smelled something I guess. He got a whiff of our guy in the room then maybe caught another out here in the lot. No one around though."

"Humph," I said as I walked back to the tree and, using the flashlight, began closely to examine the tree branch that had nailed me. "The tree is in the shadow and my old tired eyes need the extra light so I can look close—right—here." I examined the ends of the tree branches. It didn't take long for me to find the small piece of skin from my forehead along with several of my hairs stuck to the sharp end of the branch.

"What are you looking for?" Johns asked.

"Well, the thought just occurred to me that if *I* ran into this damn thing, someone else might have also." A few seconds later, I spotted what I was looking for. "Son-of-a-bitch! I don't believe it. Check it out."

I held the light close to a nearby parallel branch. Stuck to the end of the second branch were numerous, course, short black hairs, most with their roots still embedded in follicle skin. *Could we be that lucky?*

"We need some tweezers or something," Johns said.

I shook my head, not wanting to risk losing any of the hairs by trying to remove them one at a time. I ran to the SUV, grabbed a large, clean, plastic Ziploc baggie from the rear. Rummaging around in the vehicle's tool box, I hoped to find some hand shears of some type. I came up with some wire cutters. *Dykes are good enough.* I was excited now. *This could be our first real break.* Returning to the tree, I took several photos of the end of the branch and the hairs with Johns holding the light. I then carefully slid the baggie over the entire end of the branch. Once I was sure the hairs were deep inside the baggie, I cut the branch off with the shears.

"How do you know these hairs are from our guy?" Johns asked, nodding to the branch.

"I don't for sure," I said. "But think about it. The only person that would cut across right here in this spot to get to the office would probably be someone staying in this particular room. No other reason for anyone else to walk all the way down here and then walk under this tree."

Johns looked back and forth from the room here to the other rooms, to the office, then back to the tree. "I'll be damned, you might just be right. What are the odds on that?"

Interest in this show had waned with the on-lookers by now and they were all gone. Johns said he wanted to help since he was now just standing around with no one to chase off and nothing else much to do. After I'd collected a few additional swabs from a few strategic locations on the parked car where Olsen had been ambushed, Johns started dusting it for prints. I watched him for a few minutes, but I could see he knew what he was doing.

I still needed to find out about those vacuum bags so I walked to the office to again talk to the desk clerk. Turned out there were none. According to the man behind the counter, the bags were changed out every day. The bags that were currently in the motel's three vacuums were new. The old ones having been tossed out the evening prior. Today had been trash day, of course, so the dumpster had already been emptied, and the housekeepers were presently laundering all the sheets, towels, and bedspreads. *Swell.*

To add insult to injury, the clerk then harangued me for calling his girls "maids" as opposed to "housekeepers." I guess calling them "maids" is not politically correct anymore.

"Well, isn't that special?" I muttered to myself as I walked back to Johns's Tahoe.

By the time the K-9 officer helped me pack up and we had taken down the crime scene tape, four hours had passed. After releasing the car back to the "corn-dog" owner that Sanchez had yelled at, I climbed into the deputies' unit, started it up, and drove toward the hospital. I needed to get those swabs to the Property Evidence Clerk quickly, but I wanted to check on the injured deputy first.

Ten minutes later, and with Johns following out of his own concern for Olsen, the two of us wheeled into the Emergency Room parking lot and parked amongst several marked police and sheriff's units. No less than ten uniformed and plain-clothed officers and deputies were in the ER waiting room, including the sheriff and Davis. I was surprised the sheriff was still here.

Sonya was sitting in a nearby chair reading a magazine. She looked up as Johns and I approached and smiled with both affection and relief.

She stood and kissed me. "I was getting worried,"

"No need," I told her. "I had this wild, howling red-skin to protect me." I nodded at Johns. "I think you guys were introduced the other night right here, but in case you forgot, this is Officer Michael Johns, K-9 cop extraordinaire, from the reservation police. Johns this is my wife Sonya."

Johns smiled and extended his hand. "Nice to meet you *again,* ma'am."

"Oh, yes, I remember. Nice to see you again, Officer."

"Please, call me Mike."

"Only if you'll call me Sonya, and not ma'am. It makes me feel like you're Eddie Haskell and I'm June Cleaver."

Johns looked at her questioningly. "Who?"

Sonya sighed. "Never mind," she said. "You're too young, or I'm too old."

He gave her a close look up and down as men do. "I wouldn't say that at all, ma'am, I mean, Sonya."

She laughed. "Thank you, Mike. That's the first thing I've smiled at all day."

After thinking a few seconds, Johns said, "Hey wait, I know now. *Leave it to Beaver*, right? My grandma said that was her favorite show that TV show."

"Oh, God." Sonya shook her head, looking at me. "His grandma."

The sheriff had seen us walk up to Sonya and he approached our group.

"What's the word boss?" I asked him.

"Olsen's out of surgery and in Recovery. Next twenty-four hours are critical but the doctor says, barring anything out of the ordinary, he should live. Doc also said he was very, *very* lucky. The knife went in more vertical than horizontal and skittered along his ribs on the inside. Clipped the stomach but missed everything else vital. The angle is what saved his ass."

"What about his vest?" Johns asked, referring to Olsen's body armor.

"Went right under it. We'll all be having a talk about that in future briefings, but it looks like your killer knew what he was about. I'm betting he knew just where to stick the knife to avoid the vest."

"Sounds about right," I replied. "Can we talk to him yet?"

"Not for a while. Not until he's moved to ICU anyway. Tomorrow earliest. Sanchez has been in briefly, but now he's pissed because they won't let him stay in there. You need to get him out of here at some point."

"Where is Sanchez?" I asked, looking around.

"He's walked down the hall to take a pi—oops! Sorry, ma'am—use the men's room."

Sonya rolled her eyes then looked at me.

I nodded. "I'll walk him down to the cafeteria for some coffee when he comes back."

Davis had walked up to our group now and was listening. There was a new face with him. It was that of a tall, lean, serious-looking Caucasian man either in his late forties or early fifties, it was hard to tell. Handsome, fit, and tan, he was dressed in an expensive, gray, western-style suit, white shirt, and string tie. He wore polished, gray, ostrich-skin cowboy boots. His salt and pepper hair was partially covered by a pristine, white-straw Stetson cowboy hat. A bulge was obvious under his coat at his right hip, which, of course, made him a cop. There was no badge visible, but I knew in an instant by looking at him that under his suit coat, pinned to the left breast of his shirt would be a small silver star inside a circle with the words *TEXAS RANGER* stamped across the top of it. Evidently, the attack on Olsen drew enough attention to interest the rangers.

The sheriff introduced him. "Folks, this is Captain Edward McBain of the Texas Rangers."

Where have I heard that name before? I wondered. I shook hands with him introducing myself and Sonya. Johns did the same.

The ranger looked back at me. "I've heard some good things about you. You're retired off the job, I heard."

"Thanks and yeah, this year in fact. Just helping these guys out now. Not sure how much help I've been, though."

He smiled. "False modesty is wasted in Texas my friend. The sheriff has already told me how much you've contributed to this investigation."

"I have to admit I was a reluctant recruit at first." I glanced at Davis. "But I'm kind of getting into it now. I *really* want to find this guy and get some answers. You guys are gonna take over the case now, I guess?"

I was fishing and he saw right through it. He held up his hands. "Give it a rest. We're not butting in on your homicide investigation. I'm here because of Trooper Williams' involvement in that little chase out on the highway that might turn out to be the same guy, and since the rangers have a little pull in this state, I can help expedite some things for you."

"A little pull?" I replied, thinking, *That's quite the understatement. Now who's being modest, Mr. Ranger?*

He turned to the sheriff. "I like this guy—well, as much as I can, anyway, considering he's one of those hippie cops from California."

The sheriff regained control of the conversation, asking what we had found at the motel. I gave them all a complete rundown of what I had done and why, with Johns filling in a few details of what he had observed while outside securing the perimeter of the scene. I could see the disappointment starting to creep in on the sheriff's and Davis's faces, but when I reached the part about me hitting my head and finding the additional hair on the branch, everyone's interest level jumped.

"Damn, that was quick thinking on your part," the ranger said. "In fact if you have that hair with you, I'll take it right now when I leave and I'll get our DNA guys to jump on it. Normally it would take ten days to two weeks to get a sample analyzed, but like I said, I have some pull."

"That would be great," I responded. "And since you're feeling so generous, we submitted another set of swabs a couple days ago off of a plastic eye-ring cap. Can you get those bumped up to the front of the line also?"

"Wait," Davis interrupted. "What about all the other swabs you've already booked?"

"Well, L-T, if you're asking for my opinion," I replied. "I think this hair and the cap are our two best bets. The other swabs *might* reveal something, but for some reason, I've just got a hunch about these two items. If we're going to ask for a rush on analysis, let's use The KISS Principle and just do these two right now, the others later."

"Don't sweat it," the ranger advised. "I'll have them all done."

Sanchez returned from his bathroom break and approached the group. "Any word?" he asked.

"Nothing new right now," the sheriff answered. "Douglas here will fill you in later on what he found out at the motel. Since I know you won't go home to rest, I want you to accompany this pretty lady to the cafeteria," he said, nodding to Sonya, "and get something to eat. Then go for a walk and take a break. Give your head a rest." Seeing that Sanchez was about to protest, the sheriff held up his hand. "That's an order, Deputy."

Sonya looked at me for her cue to take Sanchez for a break. I cocked my head sideways, indicating the end of the hallway.

She took Sanchez by the arm, "C'mon, Frank, let's go get something to eat." The two of them ambled off to the cafeteria.

I turned to the ranger. "Captain, shall we?" I nodded toward the door. "I'll get you that hair if you're ready?"

"Okay," he replied. "I'll talk to you later, Sheriff," he said as we moved off.

Where have I heard this ranger's name before? Edward McBain. Ranger Edward McBain. We were halfway across the parking lot walking to Sanchez's SUV when I blurted out, "Ed McBain? *The Comancheros?*"

The ranger laughed out loud. "You picked up on that did you? You *are* pretty observant. I've only run into one other person in all these years that figured it out without having to be told. My mom was a big fan of The Duke, and *The Comancheros* was one of her favorite John Wayne movies so she named me Edward."

I laughed now, too. "So with a name like Ed McBain, you just naturally had to become a Texas Ranger?"

"I was born and raised in Sweetwater and with a name like that, I couldn't do anything else," McBain answered. "My mom would have been crushed. Ten years with TSDPS, then I applied and got accepted to the rangers."

"So do your parents still live around here?"

"No, they passed away several years ago."

"Oh, I'm sorry to hear that. Mine, too."

We reached the SUV and I handed him the evidence envelope. "Here you go. How are we going to maintain the chain of evidence?"

"Just put in your report that you turned it over to me," he replied. "I'll handle the rest."

"You got it, Captain Ed McBain. Nice to meet you."

"Likewise, pilgrim. I'll be in touch."

We shook hands, and he turned and walked away. *Hell, he even walks like The Duke.*

CHAPTER 26

In Plain Sight

Sometimes hiding in plain sight was the easiest way to escape. The Mexican man had always marveled when he watched CNN or FOX news, or the occasional YouTube video as a foot chase developed on camera between a *gambaro* and a police helicopter. The *idiota* always seemed to want to take off on foot through deserted streets and neighborhoods where no one else was around except the police. It was particularly amusing after dark, when the police were able to use the FLIR camera attached to the helicopter. The thug thought he was so smart, hiding in the backyards of houses or in the brush of a field or a park, when in actuality, the heat sensing device made him stand out like a turd in a punchbowl. *It would be much smarter to run to a large crowd of people on a crowded street. Ignorant peasants.* His thoughts made him smile.

After stabbing the young deputy, the Mexican man had walked swiftly around the corner of the motel and down the street two blocks. He spotted an opening into an alley, directly across the street from a Mexican thrift store. *That is very convenient.* The man made an instant decision. Making sure he had not been seen, he entered the alley driveway. Rear walls of buildings lined one side of the narrow, dirty passage, with backyard fences of both wood and chain-link lining the other. A large dumpster and a metal storage container were the only objects in view. Other than that, the alley was empty

The Mexican man stood out of sight behind the large dumpster and removed several clothing items from his equipment bag. He changed his shirt, pants, and shoes. He was not sure if the police had a description of him, but he was taking no chances. Emergency vehicles and police cars were barreling down the street at a rapid pace. It would not be long before the police would be stopping and questioning any single male walking in the area. His black equipment bag had to go also. It was too much of a risk carrying it now.

Rummaging swiftly through the dumpster, he found a discarded FedEx box that could easily be carried under one arm. He removed the goggles, binoculars, and his toiletries from the nylon bag and placed them in the box, folding the cardboard flaps shut. He then shoved the equipment bag into the dumpster, pushing it all the way to the bottom with a stick he found lying nearby. Using the same stick, he covered the bag with unpleasant wet garbage. He kept his revolver on him of course. The previous day in the motel he had substituted his shoulder holster for a concealed carry undershirt, which, while worn like any regular undershirt, was made of sturdy nylon with a sewn-in holster. He even kept the knife. The wounding of the deputy had been too quick for there to be any visible blood residue visible on the blade or grip, but he wiped the knife with some paper trash from the dumpster as a precaution.

The man rolled the clothing and boots he had just removed into a ball and walked back out to the sidewalk. He didn't notice the small slip of paper with a hand written phone number on it fall to the pavement. Waiting until another police car shot by, its lights flashing and siren blaring, he crossed the street to the thrift store. A used-clothing deposit box, similar to the type used by the Salvation Army was located on the sidewalk just outside the store's front door. The Mexican man walked up and dropped the clothing inside. Looking back toward the motel, he noticed a crowd was starting to gather in the street and on both sidewalks, attracted by the emergency vehicles. He hurried to join them and quickly became one of these onlookers, hiding in plain sight. Who knew? He might even pick up some helpful information as he watched the proceedings.

He stood with the others in the crowd, impressed with the flying skills of the helicopter pilot. Obviously the deputy was still alive as he could see paramedics rushing around attending to him. Whether the deputy lived or died didn't matter to the man. His attack on the lawman had served its purpose, allowing him to get away. Soon, many of the police cars began to leave. Most of them repeatedly cruised the area's side streets and alleys.

Mmmm, the police must have some type of a description or they wouldn't be searching the area so thoroughly. But the man knew it wouldn't be a good one. The deputy hadn't really gotten a good look at his face. His attack had been too quick and too brutal, a complete surprise. The two deputies in the office could have only caught a fleeting glimpse of his backside, if that. The man wasn't overly concerned. Still, he needed to find a way out of town quickly now. This situation was becoming much more complicated than it should have been. He searched his memory. *What was that term that he had heard American military pilots use when describing multiple small events that come together leading to disaster? Ah, yes—The shit is piling up.* Well, the shit was piling up here as well. He needed to get on that bus tonight.

The crowd started to thin out but with many of the police units still cruising the area, the man did not want stand out by walking around alone, not just yet anyway. He noticed there was a small grimy taco and beer bar just across the street from the motel. Several Hispanic men were sitting on benches drinking beer, talking, and watching the festivities surrounding the motel. The Mexican man walked over, sat down near them, and ordered a beer. Soon the detective and the reservation police K-9 officer were the only police left at the motel. He was mildly puzzled by the reservation cop's continued presence, and he grew downright concerned when he saw the dog stop and look his way as his handler was trying to get him back in his car. *Could the dog smell me from here?* the man wondered. To his relief, the cop gave only the briefest of glances toward the driveway and street before forcing the dog to jump back in his unit.

The man watched as the reservation cop walked over to the detective. *What are they looking at on that tree?* Alarm suddenly overtook him as he remembered walking into a branch on that same tree two nights ago in the dark. The man ran his index finger over the small scab on his scalp where the branch tip had scraped him. The detective and the K-9 cop took something from the tree. The man longed for his binoculars, but he dared not pull them out here. From where he was sitting, it looked like the two cut off the end of the branch. *Had this detective somehow discovered some of his hair or scalp skin stuck to the branch?* he asked himself. *Damn! If that is so, they will soon have a DNA sample.* Somehow he knew the answer was yes. Why else would they be interested in the tree? This detective, or whoever he was, was clearly becoming a nuisance.

The Mexican man had watched the two cops for several hours by now, and it was obvious they were making preparations to leave the motel, having finished with their crime scene. When three of the beer-drinking men near him got up to leave, the Mexican man got up also. To any observer, he appeared to be one of their group. The three men ambled down the street and around the corner, followed closely by the Mexican man. Five minutes later he was certain he had successfully evaded the few remaining police units cruising the area and was well away from the motel. He turned toward the bus station. It was several blocks, but the walk would do him good and he needed to think. The man wanted to give his employers an updated briefing before leaving. He would call from a payphone at the bus station.

It was a typical Greyhound Bus terminal the man saw as he entered. He took it all in at a glance as a professional in his line of work did, assessing the area for any possible threat. What he saw put him somewhat at ease. A few homeless drunks leaning against the exterior walls near the front doors. Migrant workers sitting on the benches dozing or talking in hushed tones. A few people sitting at the pay-television desks. Two soldiers awaiting their departure, watching a YouTube video on a lap-top computer. A baby crying. Locker doors slamming.

The Mexican man approached the ticket kiosk and read the Arrivals and Departures schedule on the electronic board on the wall. Much to his dismay, the Mexican man discovered there would be no bus to El Paso until 6:00 a.m. the next morning. Looking around, he spotted a bank of pay-phones against the far wall. *The last of a dying breed, thanks to cell phone technology*, he thought to himself.

He walked over, reaching into his pocket for the slip of paper with his contact's phone number on it, as well as some quarters for the phone. He couldn't find the paper, but that didn't matter. He knew the number by heart. The loss of the paper was a small concern, but he was now certain that he'd left it in the pocket of the donated shirt, and it would soon be discarded by the shirts new owner. The man dropped in several quarters and dialed. A disembodied voice answered on the other end of the line. Mixing both English and Spanish and speaking mostly in code, he advised on the success of his "meeting" with Lyle and Benny. He did not go into any of the details, of course. That would have to wait until he briefed his employers in person.

To the Mexican man's surprise, the voice advised him an unforeseen problem had arisen with a local supplier, and could he handle the problem before he left? Additional compensation would, of course, be made plus a generous bonus, both for the trouble of this last minute notification, and for the fact that the supplier was going to be hard to contact. When the reason for this was given, the Mexican man thought for a moment. He advised the voice on the other end of the line that he had already given up his motel room. He *didn't* volunteer that his identity may have been compromised at that same motel. The voice gave him an address and a phone number for a property management company. The address was that of a small "safe-house" in the area for emergencies, which the cartel-owned management company maintained.

Upon hearing this, the Mexican man then agreed to the terms. *It will be a nice challenge*, he thought. He was then given the name of the supplier and his location. The name of the supplier was Fernando Lopez, and the location was the Revas County Jail. The man hung up and immediately dialed the property management company. He told them to leave a key to the door under the front doormat. Walking out the doors of the bus station, he hailed the first taxi parked near the curb.

CHAPTER 27

Ghost

Hospital-waiting-room chairs are high on my list of uncomfortable places to try to catch a few Z's, I thought as I shifted positions and tried to doze. I glanced out from under my baseball cap at the windows. *Humph, dark out now, early evening*? I glanced at my watch. *Wow! 8:00 pm. Guess I did fall asleep after all.*

Sonya sat in the chair next to me reading *Fashion Bride Magazine.* Sanchez had refused Davis's suggestion that he go home and rest, and Davis knew it would do no good to order him to do it. Sanchez was now asleep in a chair across the carpet from me.

I frowned at Sonya. "Fell asleep I guess."

"Yeah." She cocked her head at Sanchez. "You were both snoring as soon as you sat down a couple hours ago."

"Olsen?"

Sonya shook her head. "Nothing new as of yet."

I stood up and stretched. Sanchez opened one eye and looked at me, then shifted, and started snoring again.

"Johns take off?" I asked her.

"Yeah, he said he needed to get a couple hours sleep. Said he'd either come by in the wee hours or call, but he wants you to call him if we hear anything about Olsen. Lieutenant Davis and the sheriff left just an hour ago. I was going to wake you up but they said not to. Said they'd talk to you in the morning, but Davis again wants you to call him if anything develops with Jim."

I stretched again and looked at Sonya. "You want me to take you back out to the ranch?"

Again shaking her head, she answered, "I know the way now. You don't have to drive me, but I do need to go let the dogs out. I'll do that and then come back."

"There's no sense in you coming back tonight," I told her. "Just come on out when you wake up in the morning."

Sonya yawned. "Okay. I'll come out early and bring you guys some coffee and donuts."

I grinned. "Cool! Cop food! Call me when you get there and get inside. I'm sure the Dobermans and the horses will tell Juan you've arrived."

She bent over, kissed me, and wrinkled her nose. "Phew, you both need a shower and a shave."

"Love you too, honey," I replied as she walked away. I pulled at my shirt and smelled it. *Mmmmm, has been a couple days since I last used a bar of soap though. I am getting fairly ripe.*

The mention of coffee and donuts made me hungry. There wasn't anything I could do about food as the cafeteria's buffet line was already closed, but I knew I could at least get some coffee down there. I stood up and saw Sanchez stir. "Coffee? I'm going for some."

"Yeah." He stretched. "I'll walk with you. I need to stretch out, what with these chairs being so comfortable and all."

We were lucky. The coffee in the urn was only an hour old. We sat down at a cafeteria table.

"I want to kill this asshole so bad I can taste it," Sanchez said finally.

"Doesn't sit too well with that badge, does it?" I replied.

"I want him bad, Jason. How are we gonna get him?"

"Well, Frank—" I looked at my coffee cup, thinking. "—we caught a good break with that hair, so—"

"Wait, what hair?" he asked.

"Oh, shit, that's right," I said. "You were down the hall getting into a pissing contest with the doctor about the recovery room when I was briefing the sheriff and Davis." I proceeded to bring the older deputy up to speed about the motel, the skin and hair, and the ranger captain offering to speed things along. "So," I continued, "if the rangers can come up with anything in their CODIS computer, we might have a chance to grab this guy."

Sanchez's eyes were blazing. "Not too concerned about grabbing him. I want to waste the asshole."

"Now, is that the proper attitude for a professional law enforcement officer?" I asked sarcastically.

"Ab—so—fucking—lutely," he replied harshly.

"Well, I have to admit if we do get a chance to shoot holes in this ol' boy, we wouldn't have to worry about getting him into court. You know, you Mexicans are a funny lot. I had a Mexican partner when I worked up in Nor-Cal. That guy hated Mexican crooks way more than he hated black crooks or white crooks. What's up with that?"

Sanchez snorted. "It's a pride and honor thing. You have to be Mexican to understand."

"Well," I told him, "I'm an *honorary* Mexican, that count?"

Sanchez cocked an eyebrow at me. "How do you figure that?"

"Number one, as well as bourbon I like good Anejo tequila. Number two, I've worked on my car up on blocks in the front yard. And number three, my daughter is married to a Mexican guy and so my grandkid is half Mexican."

Sanchez thought about it, then waved his right hand in the sign of the cross and granted me "Honorary Mexican" status. We both chuckled.

"Oh yeah, by the way," I told him, "Sonya says we stink."

"Yeah, I heard her. Nag, nag, nag."

As we sat drinking our second cup of coffee, fantasizing about which weapons we would prefer to use to shoot our bad guy with, a floor nurse walked into the cafeteria.

"There you two are. The attending is looking for you. He's in ICU. It's right down the hall from the Recovery room."

Sanchez was up in an instant with me on his heels. We found the ICU and walked in.

The doctor met us near the doorway. "Deputy Olsen is awake, sort of. Still pretty whacked out from the morphine, but it looks like he's going to live. You can talk to him but keep it simple and brief. He's in cubicle number 8."

We walked through the open bay of the ICU, which had glass-door cubicles on both sides. Spotting the number 8 above the door, the two of us entered.

Olsen lay in the bed, his eyes half open. He was connected to the usual monitor wires, catheter hose, IV line, and oxygen nose piece. The monitor beeped softly every few seconds as the EKG video and other vital signs electronically scrolled across the screen.

"Hey, bud," I said, touching the back of his hand.

His eyes half-focused on us as he tried to smile.

Sanchez was emotional now. He kept wiping his eyes. "Sorry I wasn't there for you man," he said as he, too, grasped Olsen's hand.

Jim raised his fingers, his voice hoarse and scratchy. "How bad is it?"

I tried to look as upbeat as possible as I said, "Looks like you're gonna be with us for a while yet. Doc say you're gonna be okay, but you're gonna have a king size bellyache. The knife didn't catch any of your vitals. Clipped your stomach by a hair and then skidded up the inside of your ribs. You were one lucky SOB."

"Stupid," Olsen said sleepily. "Got suckered in. Guy faked a seizure or heart attack. Saw the blade at the last second and tried to spin away." He grimaced, balling his hands into fists from a pain spasm. "Christ!" he gasped. "Hurts like hell."

Sanchez gripped his hand. "Hey, amigo, don't beat yourself up. Any of us would have done the same thing."

I could see the ICU nurse eyeballing us. She would be kicking us out in a minute.

"Listen Jim," I said. "We don't have much time. Did you see the guy's face?"

"Yeah, saw him good. Looked right at him as he stuck me."

The nurse started for us.

"Okay, don't worry about it right now," I said. "You get some sleep. We'll be back when you're feeling a bit more awake and we'll try to round up an Ident-a-Kit or some such so we can put a description together." I smiled and squeezed his hand again.

"One thing," he said as I began to turn away.

"Yes?"

Olsen grimaced again and spoke softly. "Guy had black eyes. Dead eyes, like a doll's eyes. No emotion, no remorse, just—dead—eyes." He began to drift off.

Nurse was on us now. "You two need to leave now, the deputy needs rest."

As we walked out, I saw her press the morphine pump three times. Olsen's eyes were already closed.

"*Hijo de puta*," Sanchez mumbled under his breath. "You are so fucking dead," he growled, as if speaking directly to Olsen's attacker. "You're gonna pay for this in spades."

The two of us made the appropriate cell phone calls about Olsen's updated condition. Sanchez called our bosses, while I called Johns and Sonya to let both of them know.

"Thank God," was Sonya's reply.

"No need for you to come back here now. Nothing more we can do until tomorrow. Jim's doped up and sleeping," I told her. "I'll get Frank to drop me off at the ranch in a while." We said our goodbyes and I turned to Sanchez. "We both need some sleep. Drop me off at the trailer, will you?"

He nodded. We walked out to the SUV.

"You guys have an Ident-a-Kit?" I asked as we climbed in.

"No, we've never had to use one before. There's never been a need since I've been working here because the state has one of those fancy computer ID programs. Can't remember the name of it. Think we should call that ranger and ask?"

"Yeah, sounds like Jim got a good look at the guy."

As Sanchez and I laid our heads on pillows that night for some badly needed rest, Technicians at the state's crime lab worked overtime to identify the suspect.

The ranger captain had been true to his word. As soon as we had parted company the previous day, he had personally driven the hair and skin sample to the state lab. He also tracked down the sample swabs from the eye-ring cap. They had been delivered to the lab in the daily evidence run the day before, but were still in the storage refrigerator together with all the other samples we had collected. The ranger took custody of them. The next morning, the supervising state geneticist was in the lab, working his magic on both sets of samples. Under normal circumstances, DNA analysis would take up to two weeks, but with the captain's authorization and prodding, this time it took mere hours. The first analysis indicated that the two samples were identical. It was now clear that DNA from both the eye-ring cap and the tree were from the same *male* individual.

Upon completion of the sample analysis and comparison, the DNA results were entered into the Texas CODIS. Within hours the computer had churned out its results. *NO KNOWN RECORD ON FILE.*

Captain McBain called my cell phone as I was driving to meet Sanchez at the sheriff's office and gave me the word. He advised that our combined cases would still have the highest priority should we find anything else, and that all of the other DNA samples would be tested as soon as possible. I advised him of Olsen's improved status and then inquired about a facial recognition or sketch program.

"Oh yeah, we've got a good one," he replied.

Of course you do, I thought. *The state always has deepest pockets.* The ranger advised that he would see to it that a technician went to the hospital as soon as the doctor would allow. Thanking him, I hung up as I pulled into the S.O. parking lot. Sanchez was already sitting in the SUV waiting for me.

"Good news—bad news deal," I told him as I climbed in.

"Let's have it."

"Good news is both the DNA from the cap and the DNA from the tree are the same, and it's a male."

Sanchez was annoyed. "BFD, we already knew it was a guy."

"Bad news is there is no match in CODIS."

Sanchez looked away, clearly disappointed. "Shit, this guy is like a fucking ghost! Every time we get close, he just vaporizes into thin air. Now we're back to square one."

"Well, not quite," I offered. "We have Olsen's pending description, and we have some DNA now. We also know for sure now it *was* our guy watching us out at the reservation when we hooked up Benny."

Sanchez was despondent. "If you say so."

I studied him. "We'll catch this guy, Frank. We just have to keep working it. Big pictures come together a little piece at a time. Now, do we need to go check in with the bosses?"

Sanchez nodded. "They're both visiting Olsen this morning. We can touch bases with them there but they are going to want something." He started the SUV and once again pointed it toward the hospital.

The sheriff and Davis were standing next to the deputy's bed when we walked in. Olsen was obviously still in a great deal of pain, but he was more alert and greeted both of us with a weak smile. After a short conversation, the four of us were once again ushered out. This time by two nurses. They advised that Jim needed his morning poking and prodding which included his blood draw, bandage changes, and attendance to his urine and drainage tube bags. *Damn lucky he isn't going to need a colostomy bag,* I thought to myself, moving into the hallway. *Nasty chore for someone emptying those friggin' things.*

As we moved away from his doorway, I repeated the conversation I'd had with the ranger captain to the sheriff and Davis. I could tell the sheriff was not real comfortable with handing over so much of the technical part of the investigation to the state, but what other choice did he have. None really. The state had more money, people, and high-tech gizmos than his office had.

As we stood there in the hallway, I recognized the surgeon who had operated on Jim, walking out of another room, reading a patient's chart. "Hey, doc!" I called after him. Turning to the three men I was standing with I said, "Excuse me, guys, I want to ask the surgeon something."

"If it involves Jim or this case, I want to hear it also," the sheriff said. "And that's not a request."

I glanced at the Sheriff. *He's a bit testy this morning.*

The doctor approached our group. "Yes?"

"Doc, the rangers want to send a sketch artist out here to talk to our deputy. I was wondering if it could be done today?"

"How long would it take?" the doctor asked.

"Well, I'm not certain, but I would think an hour or so."

The doctor shook his head. "I would not recommend that today for sure, and maybe not even by tomorrow. Mr. Olsen is too weak and on too much pain medication for him to try to stay awake and alert for more than fifteen minutes or so at a time today. He is handling the pain pretty well and we're going to try to reduce the amount we're giving him this evening. Check with me tomorrow."

"Look, Doc," I implored, "it's critical that we get started on a likeness of the suspect. How about if we kept it to fifteen or twenty minutes? Would that be ok?"

The doctor hesitated then nodded his approval. "But only fifteen minutes, no longer."

"You got it, Doc."

I shook his hand and reached for my cell phone to call the ranger captain.

As the surgeon walked away, the sheriff turned to both of us. "So? Where do you two go from here?"

Good question, I thought. For lack of any better answer, I told him we needed to go back over all the information and evidence we'd compiled so far and see if we'd missed anything. I wanted to talk to Trooper Williams again, and I wanted to follow-up on any other DNA that may have turned up.

It was a lame answer. I knew it and he knew it. I was stalling and hoping for an ID from the sketch. You don't get to be sheriff without being able to know bullshit when you see it or, in this case, hear it.

He gave me the *Don't-blow-smoke-up-my-ass* look, but nodded, and turned to Davis. "I want these two on this every minute. Don't let anyone or anything bother or interrupt them. Give them everything they ask for. Overtime is approved, and so is paying a reserve deputy to help out if they need one." He turned back to both of us but he was looking directly at me. "I want answers, gentlemen, and I want them sooner rather than later. We clear?"

Before either of us could answer, he turned and strode down the hall with the lieutenant in tow.

Sanchez stared at me. "Go back over all our evidence? That's the best you could come up with?"

"Hey, cut me some slack, dude. It was the best I could do on short notice."

Sanchez rolled his eyes. "So where *do* we go from here?"

"Good question."

CHAPTER 28

Preparation

It was a small house just outside the city limits, more the size of a flat. One small bedroom, a single small bathroom with only a shower and no tub, and a small living room which also housed a kitchenette at one end. Its main redeeming value was that it sat on a full acre of desert away from the main roadway, surrounded by a barbwire, livestock fence. There were no other houses nearby, though it was hooked into the city's utility systems.

The Mexican man stood on the porch and cast his expert, tactical eye over his surroundings. The un-gated gravel driveway and the open land around the house was a two-edged sword. No one could approach without being seen, but he could not slip out, or flee in an emergency without the same being said. He walked around the rear of the house. There was no garage, but just as he'd been told, an older model Dodge Power Wagon 4-WD pickup truck was parked there, covered with a tarp. He unhooked the black-rubber bungee straps holding the tarp in place against the desert winds then slid the tarp off. The truck was dusty but appeared to be in reasonably good condition. The tires were all inflated at least. The driver's side door was unlocked and the keys were above the visor just as he'd been advised they would be.

He opened the hood and made a brief check of all the engine fluids. They were all at their proper levels. Slamming the hood shut, he climbed into the driver's seat and turned the ignition key. It took three attempts, but the truck started and once it warmed up, the engine ran smoothly. The fuel gauge read two-thirds full.

After letting the engine idle for a good five minutes, he put the transmission in gear and pulled out onto the main road, driving a mile in one direction, then he turned around and drove past the house for a mile in the other. The V-8 engine seemed to have good power, though he knew it wouldn't win any races. Next, he switched the transmission into four wheel drive and deliberately drove the truck off the asphalt roadway and into the soft sand and dirt of the desert. If the truck's four-wheel-drive system did not work, he wanted to find out now. He needn't have been concerned. Like all Dodge 4-WD Power Wagons, what it lacked in passenger compartment amenities and ride, it made up for in toughness and torque.

Twenty minutes of off-road workout later, the man pulled the truck behind the house and parked it. One last item to check. The registration and insurance card, in the name of the Mexican man's "uncle" who lived in Dallas, were in the glove compartment, and there was a current registration sticker on the windshield, as was normal in Texas. Should the police have any reason to contact the registered owner, they would find that there indeed was such a real person living in Dallas and that he had loaned his "nephew" his truck. The story would hold up, if only for a short time.

The Mexican man placed his FedEx box and three large plastic Wal*Mart shopping bags on the couch. When the cab pulled away from the bus terminal, he'd instructed the cab driver to take him to a local Super Wal*Mart and to keep the meter running while he did some shopping for food, clothing, some additional sundries, a box of Remington 12 gauge 00-buckshot shotgun shells, and a cheap rifle sling. He handed the cabbie a hundred dollar bill just to make sure the guy hung around, and reinforced it with a promise of a large tip. The next stop was Radio Shack for another disposable cell phone. Returning to the cab, the Mexican man gave the driver the address to the house. He wasn't comfortable with it and would have preferred to have the cab driver drop him a block from the house as was his habit, but the practicality of the situation negated that. He had too much merchandise to carry that far, and it would have seemed very unusual to the cabbie to have dropped him off on a deserted stretch of roadway. The driver would undoubtedly mention the "weird fare" to someone. The Mexican man briefly entertained the thought of disposing of the cab driver, but just as quickly dismissed it. Too many complications. Instead he took a different tact.

After paying for the $23 cab ride and telling the driver to keep the change, he held both his hands out to the cab driver. In his left hand were two new one hundred dollar bills. Laying in the palm of his right hand was a live shotgun shell. "Which will it be?"

The driver looked at the items in both the Mexican man's hands, immediately understanding. He nodded, accepted the money, then replied, "I took some old lady to her doctor's appointment then dropped her at the old folk's home over on Fourth Street for her Bingo game."

The Mexican man nodded. "Seems we have reached an accord."

He stepped away and the cab drove off. It was now time to get down to the business of killing Fernando Lopez. This would have to be simple and quick. He couldn't spend all the prep time he usually did. After putting his groceries and other items away, he set up his cell phone and made a call. When he was finished, the man walked out to the truck and drove back into town. *A Big 5 Sporting Goods will do nicely*, he thought. He spotted one and pulled into the parking lot.

Entering the store, he headed straight for the gun department. He knew what he wanted but he needed to make a show of being a shopper choosing just the right shotgun for "home defense." He finally settled on a Mossberg 500 pump-action in 12-gauge. It was the perfect choice actually. It held seven shells, and it came with an additional pistol grip which, when installed, would make the weapon short and it would be easily concealable under a long coat with the sling over one shoulder. He would have to provide good identification to make the purchase, but after its use, he would permanently dispose of it, then report it stolen. Since he was a Texas resident, the background check for a shotgun or rifle took only about 15 minutes by phone or fax. After filling out the proper form and presenting one of his falsified driver's licenses, the man walked next door to the Starbucks for a coffee. By the time he walked back, everything was complete and he left the sporting goods store with the new shotgun in its box.

It took the Mexican man but a few minutes to change the configuration of the shotgun once he got it back to the safe-house. He installed the sling, loaded the weapon and hung it over his right shoulder, with the barrel pointed down. After practicing bringing it up into a hip-firing position several times, he was satisfied. It wouldn't be the easiest to use or walk around with, but it would be deadly effective if the man could get into position with it and, of course, he still had his revolver and his knife should the need arise for either. The man was still practicing with the sling arrangement when the cell phone rang. "Yes?"

The male voice on the other end of the line replied, "It has been handled. The bail will be posted by the end of the day and he will walk." The line went dead.

The Mexican man loaded everything he needed into the truck then headed to the Revas County Jail to keep his deadly appointment with Mr. Lopez.

CHAPTER 29

The Jail

*W*e need a break. Something. Anything, I thought.

Sanchez and I both sat somewhat dejectedly in the sheriff's office crime lab. We had just arrived back from again talking to Trooper Williams. He couldn't shed any more light on the case than he had already, though he did tell us that the technicians who processed the Explorer had come up empty. This was no surprise to me. The VIN on the Ford had been traced back to a company in El Paso who owned the vehicle as part of their fleet, and at the ranger's request, El Paso PD had contacted the owner of the company. He told them that he was not even aware the vehicle was missing from their parking garage.

An El Paso HEAT detective had called Williams back and advised him that the company was suspected of having some illicit ties to Mexico so their explanation might be true or it might not. There was no way to prove or disprove it. The rangers had finally gotten a sketch artist out to Olsen so at some point we would at least have a description of his attacker. But for right now, we were at a standstill. I was not happy and neither was the sheriff.

As if that weren't enough, Davis walked through the door. "Got some bad news."

I glared at him. "Today's the day for it."

Davis dropped the bomb on us, "Fernando Lopez just made bail."

Sanchez now looked up at Davis. "How the hell did that happen? I thought you couldn't bail on a federal gun charge until you went before a magistrate."

Davis shrugged. "Feds never filed. Something to do with that bullshit Fast and Furious information they're trying to cover up. They left all the charges to the state and Lopez's prelim was yesterday. Judge set bail at 250 K."

"Where'd that grimy little fuck come up with ten percent of that?" Sanchez asked. "No way he's got twenty five thousand dollars in his savings account."

Davis shrugged. "Some high priced attorney showed up with the bond and we have to let him walk. He'll be released sometime today after all the paperwork is done." He turned and walked out.

I looked at Sanchez, "Well, how did *that* feel?"

"If I'm gonna get screwed, I'd like to be kissed first, or at least given a reach-around," Sanchez replied.

The mirth of the sexual connotation relieved our frustration, if only for a moment. The phone in the lab rang and I picked it up.

"Your wife is on 2156," a dispatcher told me.

"Really?"

"Really, and could you tell her to call on 2147 when she needs to. The 2156 line is a semi-emergency line."

"Okay, sorry and thanks," I told her as I punched the proper button.

"Sorry to call you there," Sonya said when I answered, "but I dropped my phone in the sink when I was doing dishes this morning. You think it's ruined?"

I once again shook my head. "Yeah, it's probably fragged. You can try to dry it out and see." I then told her how to take it apart and use her hair dryer on it.

She asked how the investigation was going and I let all my frustration out telling her about it. She listened through it all. She'd always been good about that.

When I'd finished ranting, she said, "Maybe you're asking the wrong question about the bail money."

I paused. "What do you mean?"

"Maybe this Lopez guy didn't have the money and someone else wanted him out of there, so they put up the money. I mean, no one other than you guys knows you already got information out of him, right?"

"Yeah, so?" I was getting irritated at our dead end and was taking it out on her.

"So, maybe someone wants him out *before* he can be persuaded to talk to the police."

Of course! I was stunned. It was so obvious and none of us had seen it.

"Sonya, you're not just a pretty girl, you're a genius as well! I gotta go. Dry out your phone and I'll try to call it later."

"No wait!" she said. "Juan loaned me an extra phone he had at the house," and she gave me the number.

"Oh, okay, good thing because the sheriff's dispatcher got all bitchy about you calling in on this line. I'll call you later at that cell number. Gotta go."

Sanchez was looking at me like I'd gone crazy. "What was *that* all about?"

"My beautiful wife just pointed out how stupid we've been."

"Huh?"

I had put it together now. "Look, Frank, why were Lyle and Benny killed?"

"We don't know, crossed someone maybe?"

I nodded. "For sure, but despite what we see in the movies, there's only a few organizations that are really capable of sending a professional assassin after someone. The mob, or what's left of it, but they're not much of a threat anymore since the RICO laws have all but wiped them out. The Mossad, the CIA or some other government's intelligence service, but they are not interested in killing two small time dope peddlers. Ragheads like Hamas maybe, but again, why? Nope, there's only one that has absolutely no qualms at all about killing anyone, publicly and brutally, if they see them as a threat to their business interests."

Sanchez nodded his understanding. "Has to be one of the Mexican cartels," he said, looking away pensively then back at me. "So let me get this straight. You think Benny and Lyle were slinging dope where they shouldn't, or maybe they were about to expand their business where it wasn't wanted, or they owed money which they had no intention of paying it back, and one of the cartels decided to whack them?"

"Yes to any or all of the above," I replied. "Don't forget they had just acquired all that new growing property of Grandma's. I'm thinking the cartel got a case of the ass at them. The why really doesn't matter. What matters is the connection to the bikers and to Lopez."

Sanchez saw it then. "Holy shit! Lopez had contact with both the Indians, and our shooter, and he's a weapons buyer for the cartel. Lopez is a common link because of the weapons. The cartel has somehow found out about it and now wants Lopez dead too!"

"It would be almost impossible to get at Lopez in county lock-up," I mused, thinking out loud now. "They could get to him in prison, but they won't wait that long. The jails here are too small and too well guarded.

Sanchez nodded. "For sure, they're not gonna want to wait for two years for him to get prosecuted, sentenced, and shuffled off to prison. You think *they* posted his bail?"

"I do. It's a good investment. Twenty-five thousand dollars to them is pocket change. I think our guy is going to hang around and whack

Lopez. Probably going to be waiting for him. He'll know by now Lopez is getting out today, but he won't know the exact time. If we're right about all of this, he's sitting somewhere close by watching the jail right now."

We both got up and headed into Davis' office rejuvenated. We needed both his approval and the help it would bring. It would take more than the two of us to canvas the area. After listening to our hypothesis and our reasoning leading up to it, Davis pondered it for a few minutes in silence, then picked up the phone and made two phone calls. The first was to the sergeant in charge of the prisoner booking area of the jail. The sergeant came on the line and, after checking his paperwork and the computer system, advised that Lopez was still in custody, though he was already going through out-processing. Davis told the sergeant that there was a threat to Lopez and that he was to be kept in one of the isolation cells by himself at the jail for his own protection, at least for now.

"I know, I know, Sergeant," Davis said into the phone. "If his attorney shows up, which he probably will, you tell him the computers are down, and it'll be tomorrow morning at the earliest before his client can be freed."

The second phone call Davis made was to the dispatch supervisor. He briefly explained what was going on then told her he wanted all four patrol units brought out of the field. "I want this sent to their computers," he said to her. "Don't broadcast it over the air. Tell the units to start toward the jail, but to find a place to park at least two blocks away on all four sides. I also want a dispatcher set up on a separate channel with only these four units on it. You can advise all the city and TSDPS patrol units to monitor that channel on their scanners. They will, anyway, I'm sure, but make it clear to stay off that channel unless they somehow are directly involved with this surveillance, and I don't want anyone going near the jail."

I waved at Davis.

"Hold on a minute," he told the supervisor. Covering the mouthpiece he looked at me, annoyed at the interruption. "What?"

"L-T, you don't want to make it look like something out of the ordinary is going on. If our guy is watching and no units are coming and going as usual, he'll know something is up."

Davis thought about it for a moment then returned to the phone. "Okay, I'm revising that last order. I don't want anyone near the jail unless they have a prisoner to book. If that's the case, it's business as usual. Are we completely clear on that?"

The Dispatch Supervisor asked a few questions which Davis answered. He then hung up and buzzed the sheriff's secretary to make sure the big guy was in his office.

The three of us walked down the hall to see the boss. Once seated, Sanchez and I repeated what we had just told the lieutenant, with Davis adding the procedures he had just put in place.

"That's more like it, gentleman," the sheriff said to us, "but we still don't know who we're looking for, do we?"

"No, sir, not yet," I replied, "but we do know *what* we're looking for, I think."

"Must I wait for it?" the sheriff asked.

"Sorry," I replied. "We know he'll need to hang around for some time watching the jail, but he'll need to do so without attracting suspicion so he's not going to be sitting in a car with binoculars to his eyes. He could try a rooftop, but our boy is smarter than that."

"How's that?" Davis asked. "Would seem like a good place to watch from."

"No good way to egress," I said. "It looks good when Jason Bourne does it in the movies, but in real life, rooftops are a trap with only one way out." He nodded, obviously seeing my point so I continued "No, our boy will be doing something that we might see every day, but not notice."

"Give me an example," the sheriff said.

Sanchez looked up from his coffee. "Like maybe a gardener or something?"

"Something along those lines," I replied.

The sheriff stood up, ending the meeting. "Then get out of my office and go catch this guy."

Davis walked out with the two of us. "I'll be coordinating the units. We'll all be on channel six. It'll be dedicated, with our own dispatcher. You two grab an unmarked car and start working the area around the jail. I'll keep the marked units out of sight but close by. You see anything suspicious, I don't care if it's a dog pissing on a lamppost, I want to know about it, you got it?"

I added one last comment. "L-T, we know this guy is a pro and will rock-n-roll at the drop of a hat if he thinks he's cornered. We have to assume he's armed, or re-armed as the case may be. The units need to be aware of that, and maybe even call out your SWAT guys to gather up their gear."

"I know how to do my job, Deputy," Davis retorted. "Go to work."

We both nodded and headed to the parking lot for an unmarked car.

"Way to piss Davis off, *vato*," Sanchez said.

"Jeeze Louise, what kind of a burr does he have up his ass about SWAT being around?" I asked.

"It's not the team itself. It's one of our other lieutenants who's now the current SWAT commander. Guy named Allen Corn. What a name, eh? Davis hates his ass from something that happened long time ago. Rumor has it that back in the day when they were both sergeants, and friends I might add, Corn was screwing Davis's now ex-wife. Would have been hard not to if she gave you the nod. She was quite the looker and still is. I see her around once in a while. Pretty woman with a body that just won't quit. Shit, if I'd have been Corn…" Sanchez winked and grinned, apparently pondering the thought before continuing. "It's a nice fantasy but not me, brother. My wife is old school Mexican. She'd cut my nuts off while I was sleeping and the rest of her family would use them to make ball-sack burritos or some shit. Anyway, the way I heard it, she chased poor old Al Corn around for months, trying to get at that wood. Flirting with him at all the official functions and rubbing those huge boobs of hers against him at every S.O. dinner, dance, and picnic. Oh, he tried to be good for a while, but that little 'Choncha' kept it up and that boy finally succumbed to her womanly charms. Way I heard it, they never actually got caught at it, but Davis somehow found out Corn was layin' the pipe to her and he's hated him ever since, even though it was *his* wife that started the whole thing. Davis went to the sheriff about it and I.A. took a brief look into it, but nothing the boss could do. Consenting adults, off duty and all that crap. Oh, and get this. To add insult to injury, Corn marries the broad not long after she and Davis were divorced. Davis wouldn't ask Corn for squat, or SWAT I should say, if Al Qaeda showed up on the sheriff's front lawn."

I snorted and shook my head. "Same old 'Police Olympics.' Cops and extra-marital sex is an age-old story. The only new wrinkle is that now some of them exchanged bodily fluids with the *same* sex. Guess that gives a whole new meaning to the term 'double unit,'" I told Sanchez, chuckling at my own joke.

"Yeah," he shot back. "Never leave your buddy's behind."

The water I was drinking shot out of my nose at that one.

We had our choice of unmarked vehicles in the parking lot. Two Ford Crown Vics that looked very much like unmarked police cars, a "narc" van that looked like it drove straight off the set of a *Cheech & Chong* movie to this parking lot, and two older-model white Chevy pickup trucks with the Revas County logo on the doors. "One of the trucks," I said simply.

As we climbed in, I nodded over at the tie-dyed van. "You guys really use that thing for narc buys and surveillance?"

"I never have," Sanchez replied. "Hideous, isn't it?"

"More like hilarious," I retorted. "Right out of 1975. What kind of a pseudo-hippie van has black tinted windows, a spotlight, and a trailer hitch? That thing screams 'NARC.' You might as well paint a big sign on the side that says 'WE'RE COPS!'"

Sanchez started the truck and together we drove out of the parking lot and began to circle the two block area that surrounded the sheriff's office and the jail.

The jail itself was a fairly new multi-storied structure located in the downtown area, across the street and a block south of the sheriff's office. As jails go, it was a fairly attractive structure with its southwest design and desert-sand-colored exterior walls.

The building took up the better part of an entire city block. The property it sat on had been donated to the county by a local rancher, who's family could trace its roots back to the war of independence with Mexico, and had at one time or another owned most of the land in and around the city. The only provision for the donation was that the rancher's name be featured prominently on the building plaque inlaid in the concrete wall which bore a likeness of the donating rancher and read: *This Building is Dedicated to Robert C. Blassingame Who Helped Settle the Great State of Texas.* Of course, it also didn't hurt that the rancher's descendants received a sizable tax break the year the donation was made. The jail could comfortably house two-hundred-and-fifty prisoners, but unlike some other jails in the state, it normally only had a rotating population of around one-hundred-fifty or so. The county employed twenty seven correctional officers to run the jail, one nurse, and a cooking staff of four. Four sheriff's sergeants and one lieutenant comprised the supervisory staff.

Directly across the street from the jail's main entrance was a small park, around which were built several additional county buildings. These included the offices of the county engineer and the public library. Sanchez parked the truck in the parking lot of these county offices. I was hoping we would blend in here, appearing to anyone looking that we were just two more county workers in a county pickup truck.

"We are going to have to get out and walk around. We can't see anything from here," I said.

Sanchez agreed. "How we going to do that and not look obvious?"

I thought for a moment, looking around. "We need some props," I told him as I stepped out of the truck and started walking toward the county engineer's office behind us.

We entered the office, both of us showing our badges to the receptionist behind the main counter.

"How may I help you, Deputies," she said, looking at me.

"Is the county engineer in?" I asked.

"Yes, but he's getting ready to leave on an inspection. One of his assistants could probably help you."

"No, I need to see the boss. Tell him we will be brief and tell him I can have the sheriff call him with our bona fides if need be."

She looked at me, annoyed a bit now. "Hold on just a minute," she said, picking up her phone. When she hung up, she directed us down the hall. "Third door on the right."

Sanchez grinned at me. "You do have a way with the ladies," he said sarcastically, but I knew she was just doing her job and looking out for her boss.

"Thank you, and sorry for the trouble, miss." I hoped addressing her as "miss" instead of "ma'am" would ease her tension toward us a bit. It did and she smiled back at me. *And women say men are predictable,* I thought as Sanchez and I walked into the engineer's office.

"I'm kind of busy right now, Deputies. Can this wait a couple hours?" the engineer asked.

"No, sir," Sanchez replied.

"Sorry to bother you, but this will only take a minute," I said and briefly explained what we were doing and what we needed. He stood up and called across the hallway to the number two man in the office, a deputy engineer,

"Ross? Take care of these two sheriff's deputies. Whatever they need give it to them. Gentlemen, sorry to rush off but I'm already late," he said and moved past another man just entering the room.

We accompanied the deputy engineer to an equipment room and a few minutes later walked out the back door, both of us wearing orange safety vests and bright yellow hard hats. I was carrying a Meridian level on a tripod and Sanchez was carrying an accompanying aluminum grade rod.

"I get it," he said. "We can walk all over the place acting like county surveyor types. Excellent idea, *vato.*"

I looked at him. "White man clever like fox, eh? *And* the scope on the level is 22x power. Voila, instant spotting scope. No time like the present to try it out. Let's start down at the end of the street."

We placed the gear in the bed of the truck and drove to the end of the block. Parking in the middle of the street so as to be of the greatest annoyance to the most motorists trying to get past us, we turned on the four-way flashers and overhead amber light bar. While I got the equipment out of the truck, Sanchez made a quick call to Davis on his cell phone, explaining what we were about to attempt. Davis advised he would be at the jail himself and would have the other units ready to roll our way should we need them.

"I'll stay here by the truck and set up the scope so I can swing it to cover both sides of the street all the way down," I told Sanchez. "You walk down there." I gestured down the street. "And watch back this way. With me looking that way and you back this way, it gives us 360 degrees of coverage."

Sanchez glanced down the street. "How far down you want me to go?"

"Not too far. You might need to get back here quickly. No more than 300 feet or so. Make sure you keep the gradient side of the rod facing toward me. If our guy is around he might pick up on it if there are no marks for me to be looking at."

"You think he'd notice something like that?"

"I wouldn't be surprised. So far this guy has shown himself to be pretty good at what he does. Another thing. Don't' stay in that spot too long. I'll wave at you once in a while and when I do, move to another spot somewhere."

Sanchez nodded and started walking to his chosen spot near the curb of the sidewalk across the street from the jail. I set up and adjusted the tripod, grabbed a clipboard out of the truck so it would seem I was making notes, then settled my eye to the rubber eyepiece and focused the lens. *Always wondered about these things when you see guys using them. They're not quite as powerful as the Leopold 40x spotting scope I used at the rifle range, but it has good clarity.* I could see very well. To my surprise, it had a zoom feature to adjust the magnification setting. I watched Sanchez for a minute. At this range I could see every wrinkle in his face.

When I was sure he was in his chosen position, I slowly swung the scope and began studying the street, breaking it down into sections, scanning every parked car, every face that lingered more than a few seconds in one spot, and every window and doorway. We would perform this same ritual for the remainder of today, and again tomorrow if necessary. I wasn't concerned with observation at night, as prisoners were not released back into the world after 5:00 pm. This information was readily available to the public, so I was sure our man would know this. The real problem would come if Lopez was not released either today *or* tomorrow. The killer would then know something was wrong, but that was out of my control so I decided not to worry about it for now. Besides, I didn't think Lopez could be held any longer than that, anyway. His attorney would throw a fit and Davis would be forced to release him.

As I looked through the scope, I briefly entertained thoughts of trying to pressure Lopez into helping us, acting as bait as it were by making him aware of the danger he was in, but he was not stupid. He played daily in a dangerous sandbox, so I was certain he wouldn't go for it. Nothing short of dropping *all* the charges would entice him into it. He sure wasn't going to do it out of a sense of civic duty, and I didn't think the district attorney would go for dropping the charges, especially now that the Feds had bowed out.

My mind was wandering and I chastised myself. *Another problem for another time. Get back to the business at hand.*

CHAPTER 30

Books

After his second pass, circling the jail and the surrounding two city blocks in the Dodge pickup, the Mexican man had seen what he needed to. Instinct kept him from making a third pass. He pulled into the rear parking lot of the Revas County Public Library and got out of his truck. He was dressed in gray slacks and a light blue polo shirt which he had purchased just that morning. He carried a brown leather briefcase. Picking up the briefcase off the seat and leaving the truck unlocked should he need to access it quickly, he walked around the library building to the front entrance. Upon entering through the double glass doors, he visually examined his surroundings. He took note of the rows of shelved books. Several people were sitting at long mahogany reading tables with books, periodicals, or newspapers in their hands. Three people were standing at the index card file cabinet near the back of the room. The library was quiet, and he attracted no attention from anyone.

The man approached the middle-aged female librarian behind the front counter who was sorting books. "Pardon me, do you have any private reading areas?" he asked her. "I have some confidential business papers I need to go through," he said and held up his briefcase.

"Why yes," the woman replied. "Go upstairs to the second floor. There are several computer cubicles and you can use one of those."

The man smiled at her. "Thank you so much."

The woman smiled back and returned to her books. The Mexican man climbed the stairs and was pleased with what he found. The second floor was empty save for one college-aged boy sitting in one of the private cubicles using an older Apple Macintosh computer. The boy paid no attention to the man as he walked by. No doubt the boy was supposed to be studying, but with earphones in his ears, he was much more interested in the Xhamster group sex porn video he was watching. In his haste to view the bare breasts and genitalia of the on-screen sex action, the boy hadn't bothered to pull the privacy curtain completely shut behind him.

The Mexican man smiled to himself and shook his head as he passed behind the boy. *Pornography is hastening America's downfall.* He walked to the very last cubicle, located directly in front of the front tinted glass wall of the building. *This is perfect.* He was blocked from being seen from the rear by the curtain and, if he stood up, he could see over the half-wall of the cubicle and get a clear view of the park, the street, and the front entrance to the jail. The man closed the curtain behind him then opened his briefcase. His binoculars were there, along with his revolver. Somehow, his employer had obtained a photograph of Lopez which had been waiting for him at the safe house. He didn't question how this had been accomplished. It was best not to ask too many questions and just appreciate the help. He took out the photo and the binoculars. This was the first he'd noticed that one of the eyepiece caps was missing. *Mmmm, unusual.* He checked the briefcase. *Probably in my equipment bag.* He gave it no more thought for now. Lifting the 10x30 binoculars to his eyes, he examined the scene below him. Families, obviously waiting for the release of prisoners, were gathered in small groups in the park. Workers came and went from the county offices next door. Cars, trucks, and pedestrians traversed the streets and sidewalks. A two-man county surveying crew was working in the roadway. Even an occasional police car would pass by, turning at the corner bringing in a prisoner for booking to the sally port at the rear of the jail. The Mexican man settled in and began watching the front entrance to the jail for Fernando Lopez to come walking down the front steps.

Two hours passed without event. Several times the Mexican man stood and stretched. Things had pretty much remained the same on the street, however, something was nagging at him. There was something about the scene on the street before him that bothered him, but he just couldn't quite put his finger on what it was. He decided to scrutinize the surrounding area again through his binoculars, while keeping an eye on the jail steps for Lopez. He began looking at every detail. The people's faces and clothing, the cars, the doors, and windows. *What was it that was alerting him to danger? What was it?*

The survey crew still in the street came to his attention next. He could see only the side of the man's face that was holding the gradient rod. *Nothing unusual about him.* The rod holder, a stout looking Hispanic male, had moved back and forth across the street several times, communicating with the surveyor behind the scope using both hand signals and a two-way radio. The Mexican man thought something looked familiar about the surveyor himself, but his face was mostly hidden behind the scope and tripod so he hadn't been able to get a good look at the man. He switched his observation back to the rod holder. *Why is he constantly looking around and not at the surveyor?* As he watched, the rod holder squatted down briefly, apparently to relieve the stress on his back from standing so long. A black object protruded from the small of the man's back and the Mexican man immediately recognized its shape.

A pistol! Why would the man have a pistol in the small of his back? Although it was perfectly legal in the state of Texas to carry a concealed firearm without a permit, and *lots* of people in Texas carried guns, the Mexican man knew that in all probability the county would not allow its non-law enforcement employees to carry a gun while on the job and using a county vehicle. There were liability issues. The rod-holding man stood back up now and the pistol disappeared out of sight under his orange safety vest.

The Mexican man swung the binoculars back to the surveyor. It took a few seconds for him to realize what he was seeing. The surveyor behind the tripod had his eye to the leveling scope, but the scope was not pointed at the rod holder. It was pointed right at the library window behind which the Mexican man now stood. *He is looking at me!*

The surveyor took his face away from the scope and looked at the library window with his naked eye, then went back to the scope. Next he reached for the two-way radio on his belt. In that instant, the Mexican man recognized the face and realized that the "surveyor" was a cop, and not just any cop, it was that cursed detective, who along with the other two deputies that had been on his trail. *Of course! That's what is wrong. The survey crew has been surveying the same areas of the street and sidewalk over and over!* He chided himself for missing that detail. *Huevonada! The smallest things!*

It was clearly a stake-out and he had now been spotted. He tossed the binoculars and the photo of Lopez into the briefcase, slammed it shut, and walked swiftly down the stairs and out through the rear door of the library. As he started his pickup, he looked around to see if he was under observation. Confident that he had moved swiftly enough in his escape from the building that no one had spotted him outside yet, he still was cautious. Satisfied, the man shifted the transmission of his truck into drive and pulled out of the parking lot, driving to the end of the block. He had to stop at the traffic light with the other traffic and, in doing so, he was able to look down the street and see the front of the jail. A man in a suit followed by two uniformed deputies was already running across the grass of the park to the library. All had their weapons drawn. The survey crew was nowhere to be seen. Now the Mexican man could hear sirens approaching from two different directions. The traffic light turned green and he turned at the intersection, driving his truck in the opposite direction from the commotion now behind him. It had been a fairly well-laid trap, and it was only by chance that he had spotted it and escaped. *How did they know I would be here?*

The Mexican man was becoming angry with this detective. It appeared that this cop was pretty good at figuring things out. The Mexican man decided that before he could complete his assignment, these two remaining deputies needed to be removed from the equation, but he would need permission for such an action.

CHAPTER 31

Close

I see him!" I shouted into the handset radio. "Second floor library window, far left!"

Forgetting my own rule, I started running toward the front of the building. Sanchez, startled for a second when he heard my excited broadcast, now saw me running and dropped the rod. He also began running toward the library, drawing his pistol from its holster. Behind us, Davis and two of the deputies he had pulled from their jail duties were pounding down the steps of the jail and crossing the street. Sanchez was up even with me now.

"Go around back, but be careful, man!" I huffed at him.

He changed direction and headed for the side of the building. One of the deputies running with Davis followed him. With our weapons out, the remaining three of us barged through the front doors, scaring the poor librarian and the people inside out of ten years of their lives. We ran across the floor and up the stairs, stopping just short of exposing ourselves to anyone on the upper floor. I peeked around the corner, my weapon held close to my waist. The only occupant was a young college-aged kid. With his earphones in, he hadn't heard us coming up the stairs behind him. We were now joined by Sanchez and the other deputy.

"Nothing out back. Only three cars in the rear lot, all cold," Sanchez said, referring to any residual engine heat. At Davis's nod, we topped the stairs and spread out across the room, each of us covering a different sector with the muzzles of our pistols. It took only seconds to see that the man was gone.

"Shit, shit, shit, shit! *Shit*!" I said loudly and disgustedly. "We had that asshole!"

The kid heard *that*, turned in his seat, and instantly went pale. Seeing five cops standing behind him with guns drawn scared him badly.

He stammered, "I—I—ummm."

Davis looked at him and shouted, "Hey, dumb-ass. Do you know it's against the law to be watching porn on a country library computer?"

"I—I—" the kid stammered.

"Yeah, you already said that," Davis said. "Did you just see a guy run outta here?" The youth shook his head. "Then get lost dip-shit!"

The kid scooped up his books and ran for the stairs.

Davis walked over to the computer, watched the action on the screen for five seconds, then hit the power button, shutting it off. Turning to us, he shrugged. "I've already seen it. It's called *Shaving Ryan's Privates.*"

That made all of us chuckle, relieving some of the tension and shelving the adrenaline. *Damn, Davis is almost human today*, I thought as I walked toward the cubicle where the Mexican man had been standing. "Any need to keep these men here?" Davis asked me, referring to the extra deputies.

"No. Our guy, if it indeed *was* our guy, and I'm sure it was, is long gone."

With a sour face, Davis released the two deputies, as well as the two outside in their cars, to go back to their regular duties.

"So?" he asked me. "Any use processing this cubicle or computer and keyboard?"

"Yes and no," I replied.

Davis stared at me. "Huh?"

"I'm sure our guy didn't touch it, or was gloved up, both, but we wouldn't get anything off of this type of plastic anyway." I nodded at the computer on the table.

"What do you mean?" Sanchez asked.

"The long version?" Davis nodded so I began. "There are all types of plastics in the world, you know? Toys, guns, medical supplies, cars, computers. The list is endless." He nodded again so I continued. "Different plastic compounds react differently to being touched by people, probably because of the type and amount of petroleum used to make it, or so I've been told. A few plastics, and even some types of rubber, will hold a print really well and when you dust it with fingerprint powder, it will lift easy with your tape, and everything is all good. Other types of plastics will hold a print, you can see it good and all, but it won't lift, no matter how many times you try, so you have to photograph it. *Then* there are the types of plastics that just absorb your dusting powder turning the entire surface black, or gray, or whatever color powder you're using. On occasion, with this type of plastic, you can use a small amount, and I'm talking *very* small amount, of a super-fine fluorescent dusting powder like Red-Wop, in conjunction with a UV black light and you might—notice I said *might*—get a print worth photographing, but the odds are not good. Unfortunately, this computer keyboard and monitor are not only made from that type of plastic, it's also textured. Rough to the touch. We won't get shit off of that, but we still need to throw dust on it anyway."

Sanchez raised an eyebrow. "Another CYA for the lawyers?"

I nodded

Davis spoke up. "What about the glass screen?"

I turned back to him. "Look at it from an angle L-T."

He did. "Looks clean."

"Yeah, the librarian probably cleans them every morning," I replied. "This one hasn't been touched by anyone today." Davis looked unhappy with my analysis. "Look Lieutenant," I said trying to soothe him. "We can drag this whole thing down to the office, Superglue it if you want, and collect a hundred DNA swabs to send to the state, but you know what they'll do with them."

He nodded. "Would Superglue produce any prints?"

I shrugged, looking back at the machine. "I can't say 'no' for certain, but probably not," I replied. "I've been doing this for a long time and I've never gotten a decent print off of this type of rough plastic finish. *If* the plastic was smooth then maybe, but it's like they say, '*If* Mama Cass had given Karen Carpenter the other half of that sandwich, they would both be alive today.'"

Sanchez snorted. Davis didn't get it. "Would Superglue fuck the computer up?" he asked.

"Might," I replied.

He thought a moment, no doubt about having to pay for a new computer out of the sheriff's department's budget, then said, "All right, just dust it here then and let the library keep it. Dusting won't ruin it will it?"

"Nah. It'll just be a big mess to clean up."

Davis nodded again. "Do it. It'll give the librarian something to tell her sewing circle on Saturday. Come by my office when you're done." With that he holstered his Glock, turned, and walked down the stairs.

Sanchez looked my way. "Why don't you stay here and I'll go get the dusting kit. It'll be a few. Gotta drive back to the unit to get it."

He turned and followed Davis. As I waited for the deputy to return, I sat on a stool looking out the front window of the library wondering how we could have done things any differently. The sheriff would want explanations, but there really weren't any. It was just bad luck that both the killer and myself chose the very same moment in time to look each other's way. Had he been looking a different direction, I would have seen him first, and the same could be said about me. While

I knew the man was cautious and would be carefully examining his surroundings for trouble, there were several buildings in the immediate area that offered the same view and the same public access. There was no way for us to have predicted he would choose the library for an OP. *Just too much ground for us to have to watch, with too few people. Sounds familiar,* I thought.

Sanchez returned and we scattered fingerprint powder liberally on the computer and inside the surrounding cubicle. The results were as I predicted. By the time we left, the beige colored computer and keyboard were a black mess, and the librarian was pissed off.

She had just come upstairs to see why the computer room was still closed.

"We're all done now," I told her. "You can have your room back."

"You're going to clean that mess up I hope," she said.

Sanchez looked at her and simply replied, "No, ma'am. Sorry but it's not what we do. A good commercial de-greaser will get the dust off, just so you know." She glared at us as we walked out of the room and down the stairs. The deputy whispered to me, "Think that dusting powder will come off?"

"Yeah, well, most of it, but that beige plastic is now permanently stained gray."

"Well then, let's get the hell out of here." Sanchez picked up his pace. "She looks like she's meaner 'n' hell."

We hastened out the back door and had just hit the grass of the park when my cell phone rang and I answered. It was one of the sheriff's dispatchers.

"There's a call for you, a Harry Bennings," she advised. "He says he's the manager of the motel where Deputy Olsen got injured."

This was a surprise. "He's on the line now?"

"Yes, I can transfer it if you'd like."

"Do so, please," I told her and there was a "click" in my ear. "Hello? Mr. Bennings?

"Yeah," he replied. "You the plain clothes dick that was out here the other day when that cop got hurt?"

Dick? Oh, detective. Haven't heard that term in a while. "Yes sir, Jason Douglas."

"Well listen," the man continued. "I don't know if this is important or not, but the next morning after that all happened, a friend of mine that owns a business two blocks down, he comes by for coffee before he opens up sometimes and we shoot the shit. So he comes by and we're talkin' about that deputy getting stabbed and all, and my friend, he tells me he was in his storage shed out behind his business in the alley getting some product out when he hears all them cops cars com-

min' down the street. He's got one of them long steel containers like
they use for railroad haulin' that he uses as a storage shed. Anyway,
when he hears all the sirens, he starts to come out of the shed but then
he sees this Mexican dude 'snoopin' and poopin' down that alley and
comin' toward him like he's lookin' for something to steal or some
shit, so my buddy, he's an ex-Marine like me and nobody's fool, he
pulls the shed door shut so he can just barely see this guy. Figures he'll
surprise the guy see, and fuck him up if he *is* stealin' shit you know?"

The manager was rambling on and I was losing interest in his story.

"Sir, if you don't mind, I'm kind of busy right now," I began.

"Hold on. I'm getting there," he said. "So while my friend is
watching, this Mexican dude goes behind this dumpster and changes
clothes. Then he takes some stuff out of a canvas bag he's carrying—"

"Wait!" I interrupted him. Sanchez was watching me now with a
puzzled look. "Did you say a canvas bag?"

"Yeah, a black canvas bag, like a sports equipment bag."

Oh, shit! I thought. *The guy we saw bailing from the motel had a
black canvas bag in his hand*! I was suddenly very interested in what
Harry Bennings had to say next. "Go on sir," I told him.

"Well anyway, this Mexican dude changes clothes right there behind the dumpster and then digs a box out of the trash and puts in it
what looks like some binoculars and maybe a pistol, along with some
other shit. Then he rolls up his old clothes and leaves the alley the way
he came in. My buddy thought the whole thing was weird, but at the
time he figured the guy was just another homeless jerk-off that we see
around all the time so he didn't say anything about it, until he was talking to me that is."

"Sir, now this is important. Could your friend see this guy? Like,
see his face good?" I asked him?

"Hell, yeah! He was only like 30 feet away."

"Okay, Mr. Bennings, I need to come talk to your friend right
away. Can you give me his name and the name of his business?"

"Yeah, it's Aldo, Aldo Martinez. Don't know the exact address of
his business but it's the only cigar shop on the block. Cigarettes and
cigars."

"Thank you very much, sir," I told him.

"You can call me Harry," he said, "but wait, I didn't tell you the
most important part. As this dude is walking back down the alley, a
piece of paper fell out of his rolled up clothes. My buddy picked it up
off the ground after the guy is gone. He showed it to me. It looks like it
has a number printed on it, but it's a weird kind of paper, like crepe
paper or something."

Holy shit! *That sounds like it might be flash-paper,* I thought as I asked him, "Does your buddy still have the paper?"

"Nope!"

My heart sank, but only briefly.

"I have it," he said. "I told him to leave it with me and I would call you and see if you wanted it. He doesn't like cops all that much. Neither do I, come to think of it, but I felt bad that the deputy got hurt at my motel so I figured what the hell, I'd call and try to help out."

I couldn't believe what I was hearing. "Listen, Harry, that might be the kind of paper that burns very easily, in fact if it is, it's made to do just that."

"You mean like flash-paper?" He was pretty sharp.

"Exactly, Harry. Keep it away from *any* heat source or flame and out of direct sunlight, okay? Oh, and try not to handle it any more. We'll be right there."

He said he'd be waiting for us. I looked at Sanchez, barely able to contain my excitement as I hung up. I was jogging toward our county truck as I told Sanchez, "C'mon man, we gotta go! I'll explain on the way."

I had just turned the ignition key when Davis called on Sanchez's phone. Davis had been standing on the steps of the jail talking to one of the sergeants and had seen us run to the truck.

"I don't know L-T," Sanchez said into the phone. "Someone called Douglas's phone and now he has a major woody about something, so we're haulin' ass somewhere. Here, talk to him," he said, handing me the phone.

I quickly recounted my conversation with the motel manager for both their benefit.

"You need anything?" Davis inquired. "Want another unit out there or anything?"

"No need," I replied. "It'll just be a grab and run. If the paper turns out to be anything, we can go back and take photos of the alley and all that stuff later. Wait, on second thought, get a unit to go stand-by the dumpster and hold the alley until we can check it out."

"All right. I'll be in with the boss. He's already on my ass wanting to know what's going on, and I was about to tell him about your library fuck-up, but I'll hold off for now."

"We'll be in touch," I told him, then added, "Asshole," after I hung up.

Sanchez looked at me. "You two have quite the love affair going." He held up his hand as I started to reiterate. "I heard it all."

With nothing except amber lights on the top of our county truck, we were stuck driving like any other motorist in the early evening traffic and we were both growing impatient. It took thirty minutes to reach the motel driveway. We parked the truck and walked into the office. An attractive female desk clerk was standing behind the customer service counter and greeted us.

"Good evening gentlemen, you must be the detectives Harry has been waiting for?" We both nodded and showed her our identification. Smiling, she said, "Just a minute. I'll let him know you're here."

As she walked away, both of us took in her shapely behind and I thought to myself, *I hate to see you leave, but I love to watch you go.* Sanchez must have been thinking something similar, because he leaned over to me and whispered, "Nice. Think ol' Harry here hired her for her filing skills?"

"All you men are pigs," I replied.

The manager's voice cut short our private fantasies. "Deputies? C'mon back," he called from his office.

Smiling sweetly, the girl squeezed by us in the narrow hallway returning to her duties at the counter. Her ample left breast inadvertently brushed my arm as she passed. *Damn, she even smells good! I've been so caught up in this case I didn't realize how much I missed Sonya's affections. It's way past time for some one-on-one.*

We shook hands with Harry Bennings as we introduced ourselves. The manager called out, "Debbie? Bring in some coffee, please."

A moment later the girl appeared with a tray with three cups of coffee, some sugar and cream. "Deputies, this is my daughter Debbie."

Oops! Sanchez glanced at me and rolled his eyes then looked at his shoes. The manager must've been a mind reader.

After she walked out, he said "I know, I know. Everyone smirks and thinks she's my 'personal secretary' at first glance. I know she's a 'looker.' Unfortunately for many of the men in this town, so does she."

The ice was broken but even so, both of us were a bit embarrassed at our first assumption. I quickly got down to business.

"Where is that paper, sir?"

The manager pulled a standard white paper envelope from his desk drawer and handed it to me. Inside was a piece of paper approximately two inches wide and three inches long. Holding the envelope open, I used a pencil from the manager's desk to flip the paper back and forth so I could see both sides. One side was blank, but on the other side were two sets of hand printed numbers. There was a ten digit number with no spaces or dashes, but it was definitely a phone number. Several numbers were written below. I didn't recognize these. I showed it to Sanchez.

"It's a Mexico area code. The numbers beneath are the international dialing code," he said, recognizing it instantly.

We talked with Harry Bennings for a few moments longer, jotting down some notes that would later comprise his written statement. We then excused ourselves, thanked him, and said goodbye. Ten minutes later we walked into Aldo Martinez's tobacco shop. Martinez recounted his story for us, but there wasn't much he could add that the motel manager hadn't already told us. He showed us around the alley behind the store, including the dumpster and the shipping container where he'd concealed himself to watch the Mexican man, telling us there was nothing in the dumpster now. It had been emptied that morning. *Of course, it has. Man, we just can't catch a break.* We released the deputy that had been sent by Davis to stand by in the alley.

The motel manager's description of the distance between the container and the dumpster had been fairly accurate. Only about thirty feet separated both. After advising Martinez we would need to come back at some point in the future and document the area of the alley, we obtained both his written statement and his assurances that he would be willing to testify in court about the incident should it come to that. After a cursory look inside the empty dumpster, we walked back to the truck. We were now anxious to get the slip of paper back to the lab.

We had just climbed into the cab when a sheriff's patrol car pulled up next to us in the street. It was the area sergeant. I rolled down my window.

"Sheriff wants to see you two as soon as you get back," he told us.

"What's up," I asked.

"I didn't ask, he didn't say."

"Ok, thanks," I replied.

"Heard you guys got something?"

"Yeah. Well, maybe. We got a piece of paper, but don't know where it will lead yet," Sanchez replied.

"How'd you hear about it?" I asked him.

"Heard Davis talking to the sheriff."

Mmmmm, might need to discuss confidentiality with this group, I thought. *Never know about people anymore.* We both gave the sergeant a "SWAT nod," as we pulled away.

Sanchez looked at his watch. "Gettin' late. You want to mess with the note tonight or wait till in the morning to start on it?"

I blew out a breath, thinking about his question. "Depends on what the boss says. I don't want to rush it." We parked the county truck back in the sheriff's office lot and walked through the rear doors. Davis saw us come in and ushered us into the sheriff's outer office where his secretary waved us through.

She smiled. "He's expecting you, go on in."

"Thanks, Sylvia," Davis offered.

The sheriff looked up from his desk as we entered. "Tell me you've got some good news for me, gentlemen, especially after this library fiasco." It was more a command than a question.

"We do, boss-man," I said and began to recount all of the events of the day, starting with our decision to portray surveyors and ending with our walking into this office. I even threw in the part about our ogling the motel manager's daughter, less a few details, just in case the guy decided to complain. The sheriff wasn't too happy about that, but was less concerned after we told him we never did *say* anything directly to the manager about the girl.

"We were just thinking it, boss," Sanchez added.

"Watch that shit, Deputy," the sheriff warned. "I know that boys will be boys, but you would be wise to keep your thoughts and opinions about the opposite sex to yourselves. I don't need any harassment grief, and I'll land on *both* of you with my size-13s if I get any. We clear?"

"Yes, sir," we both said in unison.

"Smart thinking using the surveyor ploy, though," he said. "So tell me what you think about the note."

I pulled the envelope out, but then paused. "One thing I'd like to bring up before we go any further, if I could, Sheriff?" He nodded for me to continue. "I think it's critical that we keep a tight lid on all this, and not mention anything we find to anyone else beyond this point."

"Has someone been talking out of turn?"

He looked at each of us closely, Davis particularly. *Careful,* I cautioned myself. *This has to be handled delicately.* I decided not to bring up the area sergeant's admonition. "Just gossip in general that I'm aware of, sir, but I was just thinking that our guy is a pro and we think he's connected to one of the cartels."

"Go on." The sheriff was studying me, his eyes hard. He obviously knew where I was going with this.

"Well, sir, this close to the border and with the amount of money that a cartel has at its disposal to buy information, I was just thinking they could, and probably would, pay handsomely for any info about a critical investigation such as this one. Someone might be tempted to say something for some extra pocket money."

"Special Deputy Douglas, I don't like what you are inferring about anyone in this agency." *Uh oh, now I've done it.* "That being said, I do respect you for having the balls to bring it up. As much as I'd hate to think someone working here might be some type of lowly traitorous scum who would do that, I have to face the fact that it is not an impossibility." He paused for a moment. "All right, nothing gets talked about outside this group, nor does any information get put out." He pointedly looked at Davis again. "Unless *I* personally ok it, and I mean nothing. I even want us all to be cautious who's standing near us when we're discussing this case in person or on our phones. Sorry, but that includes wives and sweethearts." He let that thought hang for a moment. "Now, tell me about the note."

I took the envelope out of my note binder and held it open for the Sheriff to inspect.

"You think the phone number will help us?" he asked.

"I doubt it," I replied. "It's probably a "dead-drop."

"What's a dead-drop?" Sanchez asked.

I turned to him. "It's a phone number listed to a false name and address. It can be shit-canned in an instant. In the old days, it was usually a vacant office or apartment rented under an assumed name, but these days with all this tech stuff, it's probably not even a *real* physical location. Might just be a disposable cell phone routed through several different IPs or URLs or whatever you call all that techno-jargon bullshit that I don't understand. Let's just say it can't be traced back to anyone." I turned back to the sheriff. "I'm hoping for a fingerprint off the paper. I'm sure he didn't expect to lose it and maybe, just maybe, if we're really lucky, he doesn't know yet that he *has* lost it."

The sheriff thought a moment. "When are you going to start on it?"

I looked at Sanchez, "We're beat, boss. I thought we'd tackle it first thing in the morning if that's okay with you."

"It's not going anywhere I guess. Although, I'd like to see it done tonight, you two look like hell. Go get some sleep. See you tomorrow. Make it early," he said, ending the meeting.

"Your wife took your truck so I guess I'm dropping you, eh?"

"Eh? What are you, fucking Canadian?"

Sanchez grinned. "Sheeet, *mano*, us Mes-ee-cans were saying 'eh' long before Bob and Doug McKenzie were ever seen on *Second City TV.*

I looked at him with a surprised expression. "I'm impressed you know of The McKenzie Brothers, Frank. You truly are a man of the world."

We both chuckled. Checking my watch as we walked to the SUV, I told Sanchez, "Let's swing by and see Olsen before you drop me."

"Sounds good," he said as he pointed the SUV toward the hospital.

Olsen cheered right up when he saw us walk into his hospital room. As anyone knows who's had an extended hospital stay, one can only take so much hospital food and TV before you start going crazy. Unfortunately for Olsen, though, he would be here at least another week. There were drain tubes to contend with and infections to monitor, not to mention bandage changes and bedpan duties. He *hated* that last one most of all and had already been in trouble from the nurse for trying to walk to the bathroom when he should not have been.

"That's the bad news," he told us. "The good news is that a second surgery has been dropped from the agenda and the nurses are going to try to get me out of bed tomorrow morning for an 'official' trip to the can."

We spent the next thirty minutes catching him up on our investigation. He told us the rangers had sent a "Computerized Facial Recognition Technician" around today.

"Just a fancy name for a sketch artist," I said.

Olsen had tried to put a face on our killer using the latest in computer software, but he wasn't really sure how accurate it was. He told us that while he could see the guy's face in his mind's eye well enough, the problem was with the Post Traumatic Stress Disorder he had suffered as a result of the attack—at least that's what the hospital shrink had told him after the ranger left—he couldn't quite get the face in his head to match the face on the ranger's computer, but Olsen thought it was close anyway. We spent over an hour with him before "Nurse Ratchet" showed up again to run us off, but that was okay. I could see Jim was getting tired so it was time to go.

It was late when Sanchez pulled through the ranch gate and stopped at the RV. I was surprised that Sonya was still up. The lights were still on, anyway.

"I'll drive myself in tomorrow morning, bud," I told him. "That way you won't have to come out again so early."

"Appreciate it," he said. "See you in the a.m."

He dropped the SUV into gear and pulled away. Sonya was still awake and reading in bed I saw as I closed the door behind me. The little mutts were ecstatic to see me, jumping up and whining. After showing them the attention they demanded, I poured myself a bourbon and water and sat down in one of the two small recliners in the RV. *What a day*, I mused.

"So?" Sonya inquired. I began filling her in on the events or this afternoon, hoping to "fill her in" in another way also, but it was not in the cards. I fell asleep with a half-filled drink still in my hand. When she realized I was no longer talking, she got up and ushered me to bed. She was disappointed in my lack of stamina for tonight also, but she took it in stride, stuck me in the sheets, and set the alarm for 5:00 a.m.

CHAPTER 32

Tools

The Mexican man had made a decision. He would finish his business with Lopez as his bosses wished him to do, but first this troublesome detective had to go. Until he was out of the way, the path to Lopez and to his eventually being able to leave this shitty little town and get back to El Paso was blocked. This last encounter at the library had been too close a call to ignore. He still wasn't sure how the detective had figured out he would be watching the jail. Maybe it was just dumb luck, but he doubted it. It was never good to underestimate an opponent. *Something led the two deputies there.*

Either way, these two cops were like a rock stuck in his shoe. A constant annoyance. He began to plan the demise of the one for sure, and preferably both. It would be difficult as they were almost always together, partners, and now both were hunting him. That Mexican deputy surely would not let the stabbing of the younger deputy go unavenged, if at all possible. So now both of these two cops had to go. If they were together when it happened, so much the better.

Tomorrow he would follow the two and find a weakness. An unguarded moment perhaps, or possibly a loved one or relative that could be used against them. People, no matter how hard they tried not to be, were creatures of habit. He would find the weak spot. Then it would just take the right time and place to kill them both, but first he needed to seek permission. He would not take on the killing of two American law enforcement officers without his employers giving the go-ahead. The man used the second disposable cell phone he had just purchased today to call the number again.

"Yes?" the voice on the other end asked.

"There is a secondary problem with the scheduled work."

"Go on."

"The two individuals we've previously discussed are competing for the job. If management wishes me to continue, I will need to address

this new competition problem *before* I can complete the work as originally planned. If such is the case, I will need some additional equipment. There has been storm damage to mine and several items are no
longer serviceable."

"Heavy equipment?"

"No. Hand tools only."

"Will you require additional funds or personnel?"

"No. I should think the amount already on deposit will suffice, and
I am capable on my own."

"Very well, I will consult with management. Call back in fifteen
minutes."

The line went dead. Fifteen minutes later, to the minute, the Mexican man re-dialed.

"Management wishes to convey their concern over this new development, however, you are the one on the job site so you know best.
Make your best decision, but be aware, management wants there to be
no problems, and more importantly, no repercussions from the leaders
of the competition, is that clear?" The veiled threat behind that statement was obvious.

"There will be none."

"Very well, then you may proceed. What tools do you require?" the
voice asked.

The Mexican man continued to use predestinated code for several
additional weapons and ammunition he would need that could not be
traced back to him.

"The tools will be delivered to you tomorrow." The voice did not
say how or where, but the man was not concerned. He knew the weapons would show up as promised. "Is that all?" the voice asked.

"One additional item," the Mexican man said. "If you come by any
information concerning the original job specifications, please notify
me immediately, no matter the time or day."

"Very well. Continue to check in daily. Use the other office number. We have been having trouble with this line and we are going to
have it changed." The line went dead.

What the hell did that mean? the Mexican man wondered. He took
off his shirt and lay down, leaving his pants on. He was immediately
asleep.

☙❧

Just before daylight, an ever-so-slight scraping noise near the front
door brought him instantly alert, revolver in his hand. He quickly
slipped on the night vision goggles and switched them on. In total

darkness, he noiselessly made his way in stocking feet through the house, his revolver at the ready in one hand, carrying his shoes in the other. Standing back and to one side of the window that overlooked the front of the house, he knew he was virtually invisible to anyone outside, yet he could see the front yard and porch clearly. Nothing moved. There was a three quarter moon tonight. The entire front yard area, all the way to the road, was bathed in pale blue moonlight, which of course was pale green due to the NVGs.

The man stood motionless, watching for thirty minutes. All was quiet and nothing moved. In the distance a rooster crowed, and the man could feel the rumbling of a freight train on the tracks over a mile away. Finally, he made his way to the back of the house, slid his feet into his shoes, then slipped silently out the back door, and stood for a moment. Since it was near dawn, the moon was in the lower quadrant of the sky, thus the rear and one side of the house were heavily shadowed. *Nothing out here either,* he decided.

He crept in near-total silence, pausing every few seconds to listen. Making his way around the side of the house, he stayed in the shadow's black cloak. As he reached the front corner of the structure, he moved his head away from the wall just enough to see the porch and yard. He could now make out the dark shape of what looked like a duffle bag, laying on the front porch near the front door. By now, the sky was beginning to lighten in the east, so the man took off the goggles. Confident that there was no one lurking on the property, he stepped up onto the porch. It was indeed a duffle bag. His "tools" had been delivered. He smiled to himself, took the single door key out of his pants pocket, and unlocked the front door. The bag was quite heavy, he noticed, picking it up. He stepped through the door and into the living room.

After closing the heavy drapes, the Mexican man turned on a small lamp and carefully removed the items from the duffle bag, laying each out on the couch. Everything he had asked for was there. Several additional weapons, ammunition, a back-up set of both binoculars and NVGs, along with some clothing and a police scanner.

When it was full daylight, he loaded weaponry and ammunition into his truck and drove several miles down the road from the safe house. He needed to check out the function ability of all of the new weapons. Parking on a gravel road, which ran along the remote edge of the Indian reservation, he was certain there was no one around for miles. He had scouted this entire area days ago. Here he would not be interrupted as he test fired all of the weapons.

The Mexican man walked out into the desert 50 feet. Here amongst the brush and cactus there would be no need to pick up his spent brass casings. First came sub-machine pistol. It was a 9mm caliber Heckler & Koch MP5. It functioned flawlessly, even with the large "drum" type magazine. Then came his revolver and a small Colt .380 caliber "pocket pistol." All went well until the second pistol sent to him, a Colt M1911 .45 auto, had ammunition feed problems. Every third or fourth round would hang up sliding into the chamber, causing the weapon to jam.

The Mexican man removed the magazine from the weapon, dissembled it, and examined it. He could see nothing obviously wrong with it. It appeared to be fairly new and in perfect condition, save for the fact that just like all of his other weapons, the serial number had been ground off. The magazine lips looked okay, but after reassembling the pistol, he tried it again, with the same results. The man had no use for a weapon that might malfunction at a critical moment. When he'd finished shooting the smaller pocket pistol, he walked out into the desert 500 feet from the road. Bending down, he dug a foot deep hole in the sandy soil with his hands. He then removed the magazine and shells from the .45 Colt, placed it in the hole, and covered it up with dirt. Using a broken branch from some nearby brush, he smoothed over the hole, making it impossible to see the ground had been disturbed. Buried as it was in this vast desert, the malfunctioning .45 would lay undiscovered until the end of time, or so he thought. Satisfied that all of the other weapons functioned perfectly, the man got in the truck and drove back to the safe house. He was ready.

CHAPTER 33

Identified

S o, what are we going to use on it? Ninhydrin?" Sanchez asked me as we walked into the lab.

"Depends," I told him. "I have to look at the paper first. There'll be some issues if it's flash paper. Can't use anything on it that will generate heat."

I put on a pair of gloves and a surgical mask then walked to the evidence lockers against the back wall. Opening the locker near the center in which we'd secured the slip of paper the evening prior, I removed the small paper sack which contained the slip.

"I've been meaning to ask you." He nodded to stacks of several size new brown paper bags stacked below the counter. "I notice you put everything we've collected into these paper bags, and not into these plastic evidence bags we buy special for that purpose. Why is that?"

I replied to him as I continued working, "Some of it is old habit, I guess, but there are things that you just can't put in plastic, even though every forensic supply company is more than happy to sell you fancy plastic bags that say *EVIDENCE* on them, at a much higher price than the price of the paper bags, of course."

"What things can't you put in plastic bags?"

"Maybe, I should rephrase that," I said. "Plastic bags can be used to *transport* just about anything back to your lab. The problem arises because of human nature. Unfortunately, all of us human-type creatures are born with a lazy streak. Someone sticks an item of evidence in a plastic evidence bag, then when they get it back to the lab, if it's something they don't have to process, they look at it and say to themselves 'Screw it, I'll just seal it up and book it as is.' That's the lazy part. Unfortunately, if the evidence item has even the slightest trace of moisture in it and you seal that bag off from the air, well, what happens to old cheese or bread?"

"Mold?"

"Yup. Mold, or mildew if you'd prefer, is guaranteed to destroy just about any type of organic trace evidence like paper or cardboard or blood. It turns human semen into gross green slime and will rust and corrode steel if it sits long enough. That's why I just stay with paper bags. Besides the paper bags are much easier on the budget."

I opened the bag and took out the slip of paper. It looked like any heat sensitive paper, similar to that dispensed from modern cash registers and gas pumps. The phone number—if that was indeed what it was—was the only printing visible.

Sanchez, after slipping on his own latex gloves, slid the paper slip into a clear plastic sleeve and walked across the hall to the photocopier. After making a copy of both sides, he removed the paper from the sleeve and laid it on the examination table in the center of the lab. Handing me a medical scalpel, he watched while I sliced a tiny sliver of the paper from one corner. I moved the paper sliver into a small foil cup, struck a match, and briefly held it to the small sliver of paper.

"Well, we know it's not flash paper," I said as we both watched the paper sliver start to scorch as opposed to instantly disappearing in a puff of smoke.

"Looks like regular old heat-sensitive paper. So, Ninhydrin?" Sanchez asked.

I shook my head. "Not yet. Ninhydrin will turn heat-sensitive paper totally black. The chemical reaction creates heat. The black will eventually go away if you let it set for several days, but we don't have the time. We're going to try something else first."

Looking through some of the drawers in the lab, I found some iodine fuming pipettes. Plastic tubes about ten inches long with the diameter of a pencil. I took two out of the plastic envelope. Sanchez looked at the two translucent white tubes.

"I always wondered what we were supposed to do with those things," he said.

"Look close and you'll see a glass crush capsule near the center of the inside of the tube." I held it up for him to see.

"Oh yeah, I see it."

"The capsule is full of iodine, so what you do is you crush the capsule inside the tube, kind of like an ammonia inhaler, but you sure don't want to inhale this crap. You hold the one end of the tube close to the paper, and blow hard on the mouthpiece on the other end. Your breath forces the iodine vapor through the tube and onto the paper. If there's a print there, the iodine will react with the secretions from the pores and develop the print. The advantage is the iodine won't turn the paper black. It works quickly and you can use other techniques after using iodine, with some provisions. The disadvantage is the print is only visible for a short time. No more than an hour usually, but it starts to fade in about ten minutes. You can bring it back but you have to keep doing it over and over."

"So how do we preserve the print?" he asked.

"That's one of the provisions. You can make the print permanently visible by 'fixing' it with a couple other chemicals, but if you treat it with another chemical, there's always a risk you might screw it up. It's best just to photograph it. Go ahead and try it. Like this." I demonstrated to Sanchez how to use the tube. "One thing," I reminded him. Get your breathing right and be sure to blow. Don't suck," I winked at him and he smiled at the double connotation. "Inhaling that iodine vapor in your lungs would be most…unpleasant."

"Good thing to know," Sanchez said as he bent over the paper with the tube, took a breath, and began to blow on the end of the tube.

The vapor was invisible, and after 20 seconds of working the bottom end of the tube back and forth across the blank side of the paper, there was nothing visible. I turned the paper over to the printed side. Sanchez crushed the capsule in the second pipette. He lowered the lower tip over the paper, took another breath, and placed his mouth on the mouthpiece. No more than five seconds of his breath passed over the iodine crystals and out onto the slip of paper, when a pale yellow shape began to take form near one edge.

"Well, kiss my sister's black cat's ass!" I exclaimed. "Work the end of the tube around just that area, Frank. Take another breath if you need to."

He needed to. Then he concentrated the lower end of the tube on and around the yellow stain. It was changing color now, turning first a deeper yellow then almost a brown. He finally ran out of air and pulled his head away.

We both stood there shocked by the image that had developed. There near the edge of the paper was an almost perfect yellowish/brown colored image of a partial fingerprint. I quickly grabbed a magnifying loupe from the shelf behind me, placed it over the print, placing my eye over the lens. I was dumbfounded by what I saw. *Would our guy have made a mistake like this*? There on the slip of paper beneath my eyes was a near perfect image of a thumbprint. I could tell by the rounded outer edges that it was a thumb. *Probably a right thumb. The pattern is a double loop whorl. All of the ridges, furrows, bifurcations, core, and both deltas are clearly visible.* "Shit, the only part of the print that isn't there is the lowest portion near the distal 'Phalanx' crease."

"The what?" Sanchez asked.

I hadn't realized I was mumbling out loud. "Oh, sorry. Didn't realize I was thinking out loud. That's the first crease just beneath the pad of your thumb."

Sanchez was looking at his thumb. I smiled. Everyone does that. "This print is so good, I don't want to risk messing with anything else. Look in that chemical locker and see if you've got a bottle of anything that is labeled Benzoflavone."

Sanchez rummaged through the locker, moving brown bottles of liquid and dry crystal compounds, and finally came out with a small bottle labeled "Fingerprint Stabilizer." He handed it to me. There was nothing on the label listing it as "Benzoflavone."

I walked over to the lab wall bulletin board, on which hung a clip-board with all of the Manufacture Safety Data Sheets, printouts for all of the chemicals stored in the lab. I quickly flipped through the pages until I found the one I was looking for. *Yes!* This bottle of stabilizer was indeed Benzoflavone. I unlocked the spray plunger on the top of the bottle, shook the contents gently.

Sanchez looked at me questioningly. "I thought you weren't going to hit it with anything else?"

"This is for *after* we photograph it, wait, on second thought, I think we'll have your AFIS operator just enter it direct from this paper, *then* we'll photo it and treat it."

The two of us were both wary and ecstatic. This was as close as we could get to identifying our shooter, *if* it was our shooter's print, but I still couldn't quite accept the fact that our killer would make a mistake like this. As soon as the print was dry, it again went between the clear sheets of plastic and we practically ran it down the hall to the AFIS room. The female technician sitting at the entry scanner was a sour-faced woman in her mid-fifties whom I had not met before. Her name was Janice.

Sanchez winced when he saw who it was. He was plainly hoping it would again be someone else, hell, anyone else.

Janice as it turned out, was a most unpleasant woman. Sanchez introduced us, but she paid me scant attention. I could immediately tell she was one of those people whose emotional switch was constantly hardwired to the "pissed-off" position. She was *not* happy at having us request she change her morning routine and enter our print ahead of her other work, and she made that perfectly clear with the rolling of her eyes, her disgusted sigh, and then her response of, "You've got to be fucking kidding me."

Sanchez tried to be civil. "Look, Janice, this is important. We need to know who this guy is right away."

"Yeah, yeah, they're all important. I'll get to it in a bit," she said dryly and snatched the print from Sanchez's hand. "You haven't even made up your paperwork and latent envelope!" she snapped. "I'm not doing shit until you get all of your paperwork done."

Sanchez again looked at me, shaking his head. I didn't quite know what to make of all of this, but since I really had no dog in this hunt with this woman, I leaned over the back of her chair and whispered in her ear. When I'd finished, she spun around, glaring at me, then turned right back around, grabbed the print up from the counter, slammed it down on the glass bed of the scanner, and went to work on it.

I smiled at her sweetly, thanked her, and said, "Give us a call as soon as you get anything. We'll be in Lieutenant Davis's office."

"Whatever," was her only reply.

When we were out of earshot and walking down the hallway, I turned to Sanchez. "Holy shit, man, what a bitch. What's her friggin' problem?"

"No one really knows. She's been that way as long as I've known her, some fifteen years now."

"I feel sorry for her husband," I said.

"Not married," he replied. "And no boyfriend that I know of. Folks around here figured maybe she batted for the other team, but no girlfriends have ever turned up either."

I looked back down the hall toward the AFIS room. "She's probably too fuckin' mean for man, woman, or beast."

Sanchez laughed. "Yeah, unfortunately for all of us, she's a hard worker and one of the best AFIS people we've ever had, so the sheriff puts up with her crap. By the way, what did you say to her?"

"Nothing much, really. I told her that if she didn't put that print in for us right now, we would drive over and have the rangers do it, and if it turned out to be a big deal, that her name would figure prominently in our report, accompanied by words like 'uncooperative, unprofessional, and inept.'"

"Oh shit, man! You have made an enemy for life!" Sanchez warned.

Maybe, maybe not." He looked at me with a raised eyebrow so I continued. "You'd be surprised about people like that. Lots of times they continue acting that way because no one stands up to them. Don't forget, I'm retired. I don't have to put up with bullshit like that anymore. Now let's go see Davis."

Thirty minutes had passed with the two of us sitting in Davis's office, telling him about our print and how we came by it, when his phone rang. It was "Miss Happy-Face" from the AFIS room. Davis listened for several minutes, then waved us out of his office. We walked to the break room where we sat drinking coffee for an hour before the sheriff summoned us to *his* office where he and Davis both sat.

The sheriff looked at me. "Our AFIS operator said you two threatened her."

"Actually, boss, it was just me," I confessed. "Sanchez had nothing to do with it. She didn't want to help us out right away. I just had a little 'come to Jesus' talk with her."

"Well, she says you threatened her. If you *really* worked for me, I'd have your ass for whatever you said, however effective it might have been, but you don't work here and we do, so don't do it again. Janice is a major pain in the ass and she files complaints with both Internal Affairs and her union constantly which I have to deal with on a regular basis, but she's good at what she does. When she found out you were provisional and nothing could be done about you, she went off like a friggin' skyrocket. You need to try to get along with her. We clear?"

I was getting pissed now, and the respect was edging out of my voice. "I'll make a small effort, but I'm not going to kiss that bitch's ass either. I'm too old and too *retired* to put up with crap from people like her. This isn't my first rodeo, so you just say the word and I'll pack up my saddle and ropes, load my horse, and head on down the road. I'll be just a distant fucking memory and you guys can continue on without me!"

The sheriff closed his eyes, rubbed his forehead, and said, "Take is easy. Just try to avoid trouble with her, okay?"

"I'll try, but you keep her on her leash."

"Now, on to more pressing matters," the sheriff said and nodded to Davis.

The lieutenant turned to us. "Janice didn't get any hits from the state's data base, however, she did get a hit from the FBI's data base. Funny thing, though. It wasn't from the criminal data base. It was from the *applicant* data base. You guys hit the jackpot. Turns out your thumbprint belongs to the right thumb of a Mexican Special Forces soldier that trained with the US Army at Fort Bragg." He handed me the print-out.

I looked at it. "Well, well. Fort Bragg, eh? That means he was training with the "Green Beanies." Sanchez looked puzzled, so I added, "Green Berets. US Army Special Forces. They train the troops of other countries, sometimes here or abroad as 'advisors.'"

Sanchez nodded his understanding. He already knew of the military's "advisory" capacity.

Davis continued. "The Feebees say your boy mustered out of the Mexican Military eighteen months ago. Seems he got a better offer. They think he's working for the Zeta Cartel now."

"That makes sense," I said. "I knew this guy had to have had some professional training. Do we have a name and address?"

"We have a name but not an address. Oh, and we also have a two-year-old military ID photograph." He handed it over. "His name is Miguel Rocha, or Michael Rocha, if you prefer. Seems he's used both. Here's his photograph, and this is interesting." Davis paused. "Look at the composite put together by the rangers from Olsen's description. Put it next to the military photo."

The similarities were obvious.

"Same guy, go figure," I said dryly.

"Now we just have to figure out how to catch him," Sanchez said.

"If he's still around," Davis replied.

"I'm sure he is," I said.

"What makes you think so after you two got so close to him yesterday?" the sheriff asked.

I looked out the window as I answered. "Several reasons. He thinks he's beat us at every turn so far, which is actually close to the mark, so he's not worried about any threat from what he surely considers two hick cops."

"Hey!" Sanchez said playfully. "I'm no hick like you, I'm Mexican."

Davis gave him a look that said, "Don't interrupt again."

I continued. "He can't know yet, about our having found the paper with the number on it, much less the thumbprint on it, and I'm assuming now that the print is his. With any luck he may not even realize the paper is missing—yet. Finally, he won't quit trying to get to Lopez unless his employers tell him to quit. Bailing out on a job wouldn't be good for his reputation or his health. Those aren't the kind of people that take it well when you take their money and don't finish sawing your end of the log."

Sanchez again spoke up. "Maybe we can follow Lopez and use him to smoke our guy out—"

Davis interrupted. "That reminds me and I meant to tell you this earlier, but then you went and pissed off Janice and I forgot about it. It seems Fernando Lopez heard through the 'jail mail' that our mysterious Mexican man is waiting for him on the outside. He has suddenly, and prudently I might add, lost interest in being released on bail. He had his attorney withdraw the bail petition."

I was contemplating this most recent development, when Davis again broke my chain of thought.

Changing subjects, he turned to Sanchez. "The Armorer tells me you haven't qualified with your weapon for this quarter yet?"

"Not yet," Sanchez replied.

"Do it today, in fact, now." He looked at me. "You, too."

"Why me?" I asked him.

"You're carrying a gun, aren't you?" I nodded. "You're a sworn deputy, albeit provisional, so you need to qualify. It's *not* a request. Go now, both of you."

As the two of us stood up, the sheriff said, "When you get back, have a plan in mind to catch this S.O.B. before he gets to Lopez."

As we walked together down the hall toward the parking lot, I turned to Sanchez. "I'm not a hick, I'm Meseecan? What does being a Mexican have to do with *not* being a hick? You tellin' me there's no Mexican equivalent of a hick?"

"Oh, mano." Sanchez shook his head. "Everyone knows you have to be a gringo to be a hick or a red neck, 'specially one who lives in a trailer like you."

I thought about that for a moment. "So in the great tradition of mixed race lawmen partners, like the Lone Ranger and Tonto, Cisco and Pancho, Freebie and the Bean, and…what were their names?…the *I Sp*y guys? Oh yeah, Kelly Robinson and Alexander Scott, I guess we could call ourselves, wait for it—" I paused for effect. "The Hick and the Spic!" I laughed out loud at my own joke.

Sanchez tried hard to stifle a laugh. "You know what? Blow me, gringo trailer-trash *pendejo*!"

I was laughing hard now. "You gotta admit that's some funny shit right there." I was still laughing as we climbed into our SUV.

CHAPTER 34

Punching Paper

A ny thoughts?" Sanchez asked me as we stood at the cleaning station scrubbing the powder and lead residue from our weapons.

"Well, I shot as well as you did today," I answered knowing that was not shooting he was referring to.

"No dummy," he replied. "About catching this guy."

"Working on it," I replied.

"The guy could be anywhere, and we know Lopez isn't going to willingly act as bait, that's for sure."

"That's a given," I replied, a bit despondent from the lack of ideas.

"We're gonna need to tell the sheriff *something* when we get back."

"I know, so what say we won't go back, at least for a while," I suggested. "Let's drive around and kick this can a while."

"Okay, where you want to go?"

"Let's start out at the ranch so I can check in with the Sonya, then we'll go see how Olsen's doing."

Sanchez nodded but added, "Davis is going to call, wondering where we are. Range qualification doesn't take all day you know."

"Yeah." I thought a moment. "Okay, let's call him and throw him a bone. Dial him up and gimme your phone."

Sanchez handed me his phone, punching "auto-dial" in the process. "Good luck," he said.

"Davis," the lieutenant said when he answered.

"Hey L-T, your two fair haired boys here. Just wanted to let you know we're going back by the library to ask around a bit and see if anyone saw anything yesterday, before we head back to the office."

There was a pause. "Don't bullshit me. You're stalling for time?"

Shit, this guy is nobody's fool.

"Maybe a bit," I admitted. "We are going back to the library to ask around some more, but I need to check in with the wife and we're gonna go see Jim, also.

Another pause. "Did you guys get qual'd?"

"A—firm—a—tory. We're both dead-eye shots, just like Wild Bill Hickok," I told him.

"Hickok's dead," Davis replied dryly, then continued. "All right but don't screw around long. Listen up, one more thing, and this is serious. Friend of mine is a state narc lieutenant. Something came across his desk this morning that he thought I should know about. Guess he got word about all this shit goin' on with your case from that ranger captain. Anyway, the ranger narcs guys work with DEA a lot down by the border. Evidently a well-placed DEA 'snitch' dropped a dime to his handler that the Zetas sent a guy up here to whack a couple of small time dealers that were planning on expanding their business down El Paso way."

I looked at Sanchez and winked. "So our hunch was correct, eh? Benny and Lyle did piss someone off."

Davis continued. "Looks like it, but hold on, there's more. Evidently this guy is supposed to take care of another set of problems while he's here. The key word there being 'set.'"

"A *set* of problems, huh?"

"That's a direct quote according to my lieutenant friend."

"Lopez could hardly be called a 'set,' if indeed he's only one of the problems this guy's going to take care of."

"My thoughts also," Davis replied. "Supposedly a duffle bag of clothing and other supplies including several guns and ammunition was delivered to the guy up here a couple nights ago."

I bolted upright in my seat. "Holy shit, L-T! Do we know where they were delivered to?"

I could imagine Davis shaking his head on the other end of the line as he said, "Don't get your dick hard yet. The snitch didn't know where the stuff was delivered, only that it *was*. But I just thought I'd pass it along to you two. *If* this is your shooter, we already know how dangerous he is, and now apparently he's armed or, as you said, re-armed, and he's probably packing heavy. You two might want to be a tad careful."

No shit, Sherlock. "Okay, L-T. Thanks for the heads up. We'll see you later this afternoon."

The connection terminated without him bothering with a goodbye.

Sonya was helping Juan with the horses in the stables when the Dobermans announced our arrival with their barking and ran to the

SUV. Sanchez cast a wary eye on the two dogs as he shut off the ignition.

"Those dogs scare the shit out of me just looking at them."

"I know." I nodded and cast an eye their way also. "But they're not really a threat if they know you."

Brave talk, I thought as I climbed out of my side of the SUV with both dogs sniffing my legs and crotch. Having the toothy end of those land sharks that close to my balls was not something I wanted to think about. Sonya and Juan came to the stables door to see who it was. Juan waved and called the dogs then turned and went back in.

"S'up sweetie?" I kissed her.

"What are you guys doing here? Hi, Frank!" She waved at Sanchez who waved back and greeted her.

"We're on our way to see Jim," I said. "But I just wanted to come by and catch you up and see how you were."

"Oh, I'm fine. We're just currying and feeding. These horses are so cool. Gonna go riding later today." She looked back toward the open stables door.

"Listen to me." I became serious. "I want you to keep an eye out around here." I proceeded to fill her in on my conversation with Davis. When I was done, I took out my little Kahr and handed it to her. "I want you to keep this thing close at all times, and when I say close, I mean on you. It's small enough to fit in the pocket of your jeans, or if you want when you go riding you can stick it in my fanny pack and take that, but either way keep it with you, okay?"

She looked at the small pistol with some distain. "Okay, I guess."

"No," I said sternly. "No 'I guess.' Promise me you'll keep it handy."

She looked at me for a moment, then said, "Okay, I promise, but I've only shot it that once and it's kind of hard for me to pull the trigger. Can't I keep the Taurus? I like that one."

"I know you do and you shoot it well, but it's big and I know you won't keep it with you. This one is small so you're more apt to carry it."

She thought about it for a minute. "Okie-dokie,"

"So, anything else going on?" I asked.

"Nope. Some guy stopped by early in an old pickup and Juan talked to him up by the gate. I thought maybe they knew each other 'cause I could hear them speaking Spanish, but Juan said the guy was looking for directions to a harvesting job a couple miles from here."

I was instantly suspicious. "You think he was legit?"

She shrugged. "Juan seemed to think so. The Dobermans sure didn't like him, though."

I pondered this information for a moment before responding. "Mmmmm, okay. You still got that same phone that Juan let you use, right?"

"Yep, right here in my pocket." She turned around and the outline of the small phone was visible in the back pocket of her tight Daisy Dukes. *Always did like those shorts,* I thought to myself as I checked out her backside. She paid no attention to my attention. "How come Frank won't get out of the car?" she asked

"He's scared of the dogs."

"Oh, they're big and loveable," she said, grinning.

"Mmm-hmm, just like a Great White Shark," I replied. "I'll call later and check in. Love you." I kissed her again.

"Back at 'cha," she said.

Before I climbed back into the SUV, I retrieved my S&W .45 and two extra magazines from the RV. With this accomplished, we drove out the gate. Something was bugging me. I was quiet, staring through the front windshield.

"What's wrong?" Sanchez asked.

We are becoming partners, I thought. *He's starting to be able to read me and I him.*

"Nothing wrong, per se. Just thinking about this asshole and kind of worrying about Sonya being out here by herself."

"She's not by herself. Don't forget Juan and his Mini-14, not to mention those two goddamn dogs. And she's a pretty good shot, so you tell me."

"Yeah, you're right, I guess. I hadn't even thought about it until something she said just now."

"What's that?" he asked.

"Said some Mexican dude who was looking for an ag job, picking or some such a couple miles away was lost and stopped at the gate to ask directions. Juan pointed him in the right direction, I guess. Just started me thinking."

Sanchez was suddenly all business. "Wait, did this guy say 'ag job,' or 'picking job'?"

"'Picking,' Sonya said."

Sanchez looked at me then back to the road. "Uh, *vato*?"

"Yeah?" I replied.

"Look around you and tell me what you see?"

I looked around the outside of the SUV. The sun was reflecting off the desert floor. The rising heat made vertical waves in the air. "Why?"

"Just humor me," he said.

I blew out my breath, looking around as we traveled down the road. "I don't know, desert, I guess. Couple gravel roads. Some barbwire fence. Sand, brush, dirt, and dust."

Sanchez put his chin down and looked at me over the top of his glasses. "Really? That's all you see?"

I looked again. It took a minute, but finally I blurted. "Son-of-a-bitch! There's no agriculture anywhere in sight."

Sanchez nodded. "Very good. Except for alfalfa grown on Rollins' ranch, for which they don't hire migrant workers, by the way, there's no ag for miles in any direction. There's no water for irrigation out here, so nothing grown and—"

I finished the sentence for him. "Not a goddamn thing to pick." I snatched up my phone and dialed Sonya's new number. She answered on the fourth ring.

"Hey, it's me."

"Miss me that much already?" she asked.

"I need to talk to Juan right now."

She heard the urgency in my voice. "What's wrong?"

"What color was that pickup truck this morning? The lost guy."

She thought for a moment. "Blue I think. I'm not sure. I didn't pay that much attention, I guess."

"Did the guy for sure say he was looking for a 'picking job'?"

"That's what Juan told me," she answered. "Why?"

"I think that guy was bullshitting Juan about the job. Put Juan on the phone. Please, hon."

I handed the phone to Sanchez who had pulled to the shoulder of the road now.

"Here, Juan speaks better Spanish than English," I said. "You can get to everything quicker since you *habla* and I don't—well, not very well, anyway."

Sanchez put the phone to his face just as Juan got on the other end. They spoke back and forth in their native tongues in that rapid-fire exchange that is Spanish.

Soon, Sanchez looked at me, put his hand over the bottom of the phone, and asked, "Anything else?"

This made me snort. "How the hell should I know? I can't understand you two at all. I can only hope *you've* got everything we need."

Sanchez nodded, spoke a few more words to Juan, then hung up. "Okay. Juan said he didn't recognize the guy or the truck from being around here. Said the guy was somewhere shy of forty, dressed like a farm worker, and was properly cordial and contrite. Spoke good Spanish, almost too good. None of the slang used around this area. Juan kind of grilled him since people don't usually come down the ranch road. The guy had all the right answers. Dropped the name of a local rancher about fifteen miles from here who *does* hire workers on occasion. Juan said the guy seemed legit. Oh yeah, said the truck was an older blue and silver Dodge Power Wagon. He was sure of it. He didn't think to look at the plates. Guy turned around and left and didn't come back. I told him to call if anything like that happens again. He said he'll tell Sonya the same thing. I told him to keep his Ruger and the dogs close. That there may be skullduggery afoot."

I rolled my eyes. "Skullduggery afoot? Great, now I'm riding with the Mexican Sherlock Holmes. Okay. Sounds like it's under control for now *and,* it might have even been a legit coincidence, but just so you know?"

"Yeah?"

"I don't like coincidences. Not at all, and we've had several. Don't believe in them one bit. Skullduggery afoot," I mumbled. "Jeeze Louise."

CHAPTER 35

Shots Fired

Olsen was on the mend. We caught him shuffling out of the bathroom with the help of a better-than-average-looking nurse "Hi, guys," he said cheerfully when he saw us.

"Waddup, homie," I shot back. "Looks like you're healin'."

"Yee-ahh," he said as he eased into the bed. "Still sore as hell but the doc says I'm doin' good. Said they might release me day after tomorrow to go home, but only if I swear on my honor's honor that I'll do what he tells me and stay in bed. Of course, I'll have these drain bag-tube things in for another ten days or so."

I nodded at the nurse as she walked away. "She's easy on the eyes."

"Yeah, nice, huh? Day-shift chick. I been asking her to go out with me when I'm all healed up. All she'll say is 'Don't you have a girlfriend?'"

"Well, I hope you get laid soon by *someone*," I told him. "I'm tired of Sonya having dreams about you."

He changed the subject quickly, embarrassed again. "So what's up with my computer sketch deal."

Sanchez grinned. "*Vato*, do we have a lot to tell you since yesterday."

Then Sanchez and I tag teamed him with all of the events over the past three days.

"Wow!" he said when we were done. "So you think he's still around, huh?"

"That's what we've heard," I said. "He wants to get to Lopez, but we don't really know what this other 'set of problems' might be, though we suspect—"

Sanchez held up a finger interrupting me, then cocked his head to listen to his epaulette microphone. He spoke into it briefly then looked at me with a surprised expression. "We gotta continue this later. Come on, man, we gotta go! Talk to you later, Jimmy!" he said as he ran out the door.

I followed at a jog. *Now what?*

We ran to the parking lot. To my bewilderment, Sanchez opened the back hatch and threw me a ballistic vest, which I slipped on and fastened as we jumped into the SUV. Sanchez flipped on the overhead lights and the siren and stomped on the gas, squealing the tires as we headed for the hospital parking lot exit.

"Armed robbery right down the road here!" he shouted over the siren. "We're the closest unit!"

"I thought we weren't supposed to get involved in this stuff," I shouted back. "I know I'm not!"

"We're still cops remember? And we're the only ones close! You still remember how to do this, right?"

"Yeah, I remember, but I didn't sign on for this shit!" I shouted back reluctantly, though the adrenaline was flowing now and old habits were returning in a flood. I added as an afterthought, "Shit, don't tell Sonya, she'll have a cow and I'll never hear the end of it."

Sanchez shut off the siren after a half mile. *We must be close,* I thought. *Be just my luck to make it to retirement and then get shot playing cop in a hold-up in Texas.*

Sanchez had the accelerator pressed to the floor and I could see the speedometer needle pegged at 120 mph. We were barreling down a straight stretch of frontage road parallel to the interstate. Shit, shit, shit, *shit!*

Sanchez didn't have to shout to be heard now. "It's this mini-mart up here on the left about a mile and a half! Bad place to have a robbery, for us, anyway. No cover at all. Big parking lot in front with open desert all around. No place to sneak up. We'll have pull in fast and use the unit for cover.

The radio, turned up in volume now, blasted our call sign. "One Henry 43, TSDPS has two troopers en route also! ETA two!"

Sanchez answered, "10-4!"

"I didn't sign up for this shit you know," I again shouted at Sanchez.

"I know. Want me to let you out?"

"Screw you!"

He grinned at me. "Hey, we're 'The Spic and the Hick, remember?"

We both rolled down our windows and I released the Remington Model 870 12-gauge, pump-action shotgun from its mount between the seats.

"Bullshit! I want first billing if I'm gonna maybe get shot for free!" I said.

"All right, we'll put 'Hick' first," he said as we arrived.

The front of the mini-mart was in view when a mid-eighties brown and white Chevrolet Monte Carlo came tearing out from between the gas pumps and lurched to a stop near the front doors. Our Explorer bounced across the driveway and fishtailed into the parking lot, Sanchez trying to rein it in like a runaway horse. The scene before us then unfolded in that surreal slow motion, as often happened when stress and adrenaline took over the human nervous system. Two black men ran out the front doors and were trying to get into the Monte Carlo when a third brown-skinned man, obviously a clerk or perhaps the owner, ran out the door behind them, aiming and firing a revolver at both, almost at point blank range.

Clerk is ballsy, or stupid. Maybe both. It's funny the things that can go through your mind when time is measured in "nanoseconds" *Morons, using a two-door car for a getaway when there's three of you.*

The man climbing into the passenger side of the Monte Carlo jerked as the clerk fired and I knew he was hit. In my fifty-nine years on this earth, I'd seen both men and animals shot, having done some of that shooting myself. I'd seen how bodies react to bullet penetration. The man jerked then tried to turn on the clerk and raise his own weapon, but his body wouldn't respond. It was shutting down and he began to collapse half in and half out of the vehicle. This was good luck for the clerk, since the weapon that guy was trying to raise was a short barreled shotgun.

The man on the driver's side stopped trying to climb in over the driver. He stood up and raised his pistol over the top of the car and returned fire at the clerk. Glass shattered the windows of the store, but the clerk didn't seem to be affected and he continued firing until his revolver was empty. He just kept pulling the trigger over and over, the hammer clicking on the spent casings in the cylinder. The stress of the engagement would not let the clerk's brain understand that the gun was empty—again, a *very* common occurrence in firefights.

As we slid to a stop, I could hear Sanchez's voice faintly, as if he were a long distance away, yet he was sitting right next to me. He was shouting into the unit's hand mic. "One Henry 43! Shots fired! Shots fired!"

The Explorer was stopped now in front of the Monte Carlo, facing it. We both flung open our doors, rolled out, and crouched down behind them. I extended the shotgun through the open window. I heard Sanchez curse and I briefly wondered if he was hit, but couldn't look his way right then. I tried to take a bead on the man on the driver's side but my shot was blocked by the hood of our own unit. I would have had to stand straight up to take the shot and that was *not* going to happen.

I aimed at the right front tire of the Monte Carlo and fired, hoping to disable the vehicle. Holes from the BB-sized buckshot appeared in the front fender of the car and the tire went flat. I pumped the shotgun and fired again, this time at the grill. Steam and green anti-freeze began to spew from the buckshot holes now in the radiator. I heard Sanchez's pistol bark twice so I knew he was at least still in the fight.

I raised up just long enough to put another shotgun blast into the front windshield of the Chevy trying for the driver, but the angle was bad and all I accomplished was to shatter the windshield. I calculated quickly. *Three rounds gone, three left.* I knew the shotgun only held six shells. *I'll have to transition to my pistol in a few more seconds.*

Suddenly there were sirens and flashing lights seemingly everywhere. Two TSDPS cars blew into the parking lot, followed by our old buddy Michael Johns, the reservation K-9 copper. The State Troopers bailed out with their AR-15 rifles and were plainly getting ready to "hose down" the car and the occupants. I could hear Johns's dog Falcon going totally wild, barking and yelping hysterically in the back of the Tahoe. Johns was out now with his 12-gauge Benelli M-2, a nine shot auto-loading shotgun.

Things were going to get terminal for these crooks very quickly. The same thought must have occurred to at least one of the dummies because the next thing I heard was the guy standing on the driver's side of the Monte Carlo shouting, "Hey! Hey! We had enough! Don't be killin' us! We ain't hosticle to you law enfocements no mo!"

Both the man standing and driver had their hands raised. I exhaled loudly. It was over. It had only been a minute and a half since we bounced into the parking lot. Sanchez and I both stood as the troopers moved to the Monte Carlo, knocked the two suspects to the ground, and handcuffed them. Other troopers moved to the downed suspect and the clerk just as additional sheriff's units arrived.

I leaned against the SUV, knowing what was coming next. *Yup, right on time.* My hands began to shake violently, as did my knees. Bile started to rise to the back of my throat. Those who have experienced it know it's not fear. The fear and apprehension actually comes beforehand. The shaking and nausea is the body's way of trying to shed the sudden and massive infusion of adrenalin that has blasted through your muscles, nerves, and brain tissue. I glanced over at Sanchez. He was still kneeling behind the door. He, too, was shaking like a dog shittin' peach pits.

Johns jogged over to us. "You okay?"

"I'm good," I replied and looked at Sanchez. "You good, partner? Thought you might've been hit when I heard you cuss."

"I'm okay. I threw my gun."

Johns looked at him. "Said what?"

"Don't tell no one, either of you. When I brought my pistol up to aim, I was so jacked up and my hands were so sweaty, it flew right out of my hand. It's laying right over there." He nodded at his Glock, laying on the concrete between the two gas islands. "Had to pull my back-up."

This struck me as incredibly funny for some reason and I started laughing hard. He and Johns then joined in. Another stress release.

We walked over together to get his pistol. Sanchez looked at it on both sides. "A few scratches but no worse for wear. Guess it's true what they say about Glocks."

After a few moments, one of the troopers walked over. It turned out to be Mark Williams.

"Nice to see a familiar face," I said to him, smiling. "I thought you were working Mids?"

"Day off, working extra for someone," he replied. He'd seen us laughing and thought we'd gone crazy. "What's up with you guys? You okay?"

Sanchez had already retrieved his weapon by this time. "Yeah, it's all good. Just relieving some stress."

"I hear that," the trooper responded.

We all turned as we heard one of the suspects loudly complain, "Hey, these cuffs are givin' me edemas!"

I shook my head. "Hosticle? Law enfocements? Edemas? God bless the American education system."

"Yeah," Johns agreed. "I have a feeling these assholes spent more time slinging dope, stealin', and chasing ho's than they did in school learning the King's English."

Williams took his cell phone away from his ear. Engaged in our banter as we had been, the three of us hadn't even noticed he made a call. "Just got off the phone with my captain. Looks like this is your lucky day. I've got two pieces of good news for you."

"How so?" Sanchez inquired. Both us had finally stopped shaking.

"Well first." Williams looked around the property. "This little piece of paradise is built on a state easement for the interstate. It seems there's gonna be an on-ramp here someday, so it's officially state property. We'll be taking the paper on your little Wild West show here, instead of your people. Our homicide guys are on the way as I speak."

"And the second piece of good news?" I asked.

"That one asshole on the other side of the car is dead." Williams jerked his chin in the direction of the Monte Carlo. The clerk shot the shit out of him from about three feet, but the only thing either of you 'dead-eyes' hit was the Monte Carlo, so you're interviews with Internal Affairs, the DA investigators, *and* our Homicide guys should be fairly brief."

"How's the clerk?" I asked.

"Owner, I should have said," Williams corrected. "He's okay. One lucky motherfucker, though. Bullets went all around him just like in *Pulp Fiction*. He doesn't quite understand why he's sitting in handcuffs in the back of my car, but he'll come out of it okay. By later today it'll be ruled a 'justifiable homicide' and the Homicide guys will kick him loose after he's interviewed. After all, this *is* Texas and we have the 'stand your ground law' here."

"Justifiable? Most excellent," I said. We all walked over to the Monte Carlo to look at our handy work.

"Who was on the shotgun?" Williams asked.

"*Moi*," I answered.

"Quick thinking disabling the vehicle like that."

"Well, I'd love to tell you it was a well-thought-out tactical decision, but the truth is I couldn't see shit from over there—" I nodded at passenger side of the Explorer. "—without sticking my head up above the hood, so I just figured I'd better just start blasting away at something. The car seemed like the largest target."

"Now why do I not believe that? I'm thinking you put a bit more thought than that into it."

Sanchez and Johns were looking at the two .40-caliber holes in the driver side windshield support post. Both holes were within three inches of each other about halfway up the post. The bullets were still lodged in the sheet metal, the copper end of one bullet clearly visible.

"Good shooting," Johns said seriously.

"Not that good," Sanchez replied. "I didn't hit the guy."

Johns looked back and forth between the Explorer and the Chevy. "Yeah, but looking at the angle, he was right behind the post and that's the only thing that saved his sorry black ass. You'd have center punched him otherwise."

Sanchez and I sat back down in the Explorer to await the arrival of the State Homicide Detectives. We both laid our heads back, closed our eyes, and let the remainder of the stress bleed off as additional police and sheriff's units arrived. Following soon were all the clowns and jugglers that normally accompany this type of circus. Local news vans, the throng of spectators, and, of course, the staff weenies from every agency who want to be seen on the news as contributing something important, but which normally only amounted to contaminating the crime scene. There was such a side-show in progress, no one paid much attention to the blue and gray Dodge pickup with its sole Mexican occupant as it cruised slowly by then parked on the shoulder of the frontage road one-quarter mile away.

By the time Sanchez and I were finished with all of the investigative interviews and our Explorer had been released from the scene it was 2:00 a.m. We had both called our wives but only told them we'd be working late, both of us holding back the details as to why. When we were done at the local TSDPS office, a trooper we'd not met previously gave us a ride back to the mini-mart for our SUV.

"Turns out these three assholes are wanted by Dallas PD for a string of robberies up there, one of which went south and a customer was shot and killed. You guys done good," he told us.

The state CSI guys were still at the scene when we arrived back at the mini-mart, but they were getting ready to wrap up. A tow truck was hooking up to the Monte Carlo. The Coroner had picked up the body two hours ago, though there was still a large pool of his blood on the concrete. I walked over to one of the Crime Scene guys. The embroidered name on his shirt read "S. Weston." I asked him, "You guys are done with the Explorer I heard."

"Yeah. You're good to go."

"How many times did the clerk hit the guy?" I inquired.

"Couldn't tell for sure but it looked like three. Two in the back and one in the side with this." He opened an evidence bag and I took a peek inside.

"Well, well. A Colt Python. He have magnums in it?" I asked.

Weston nodded, adding, "Jacketed hollow-points."

I smiled to myself. *So .357's JHPs, eh? That'll ruin your whole fucking day.*

He then asked me "Which one of you had the shotgun?"

"That would be me, why?"

"Did they tell you that you hit the driver?"

"I did? No, the Homicide guys didn't say anything about it."

"Probably waiting for our report and the hospital's, I guess. Yeah, the crook behind the wheel ended up with a face and neck full of glass and even a couple of BBs from the blast you put through the windshield." Weston chuckled. "I heard hospital's still picking shit out of him. I'm sure that's taking some of the glamour out of being the getaway driver."

"That makes me feel better. At least I did some damage. Thanks, man," I said to him as I climbed into the Explorer for what seemed like the hundredth time.

This sheriff's SUV was starting to feel like my second home. Sanchez drove me out to the ranch. He and I barely made it. We were both exhausted.

"Hey, mano," I said to him as I climbed out of the SUV, "why don't you just sleep here tonight? I'm beat and I know you are, too. Been one hell-of-a-day today."

Sanchez smiled. "I *am* staying, but not with you guys in your little trailer, unless you're inviting me in for a 'ménage a trois.' Hell, on second thought, I'm even too tired for that! Seriously, though, thanks anyway, but Juan offered me a room up at the house, and I'm going to take him up on it. Already called my wife."

I looked in at him. "You tell your wife about our shoot-em up yet?"

"Didn't have to. She saw us on TV. We're all over the news."

Shit, I thought. *That means Sonya probably saw it, too. If she did, there'll be hell to pay.*

"All right bud, pick me up in the morning and we'll try to get back to the business at hand." And with that I turned toward the RV door. "Night, spic," I called to him.

"Night, hick," he shot back over his shoulder.

I noticed that a light was on in the bedroom. *That's not good.* She was waiting up, reading.

"Saw you on the news," she said matter-of-factly. I was expecting an onslaught, but to my surprise, all I got from her was, "This isn't an episode of *CSI*. You're not supposed to be kicking down doors and getting in car chases, *or* going to armed robberies. You're retired, re-member?"

"Not much I could do," I replied. "We were the closest unit and I couldn't let Sanchez very well go alone."

She thought about that for a moment and simply said, "You okay?"

"Yeah, just beat, and still scared shitless," I said as I climbed into bed beside her.

She reached up and turned off the light. She kissed me then rolled over, saying, "You get yourself killed and I will *never* forgive you."

So our Mexican man now has a name, Michael Rocha. It was my last conscious thought as sleep washed over me.

එආආ

It seemed like I had just closed my eyes when my cell phone rang, waking me from the dreamless sleep I was enjoying. I moved the shade and looked out. The sun was starting to make its appearance in the east. It looked like it was going to be another beautiful warm Texas day. My cell phone rang again, but it was in the other room and I just wasn't ready to jump to its demand quite yet. A few minutes later Sanchez was pounding on the RV door, telling me to wake up because everyone in the world wanted us back at the sheriff's office.

Coffee, need coffee. Thirty minutes later we turned off the gravel ranch road onto the asphalt county road toward town.

"So, you okay?" he asked me.

"Think so," I answered in a short, clipped sentence. "Stiff. Not near enough sleep. Need coffee. Let's try to avoid such excitement again today, please. As my wife pointed out to me last night, I'm retired. I'm not supposed to be doing that kind of cop crap."

We rode in silence for a few minutes. There was no one on the road this early, I noticed. I was staring vacantly out into the surrounding desert, daydreaming. We'd just topped a slight rise when Sanchez's slowing of the Explorer brought my attention back to the present. There was a blue and gray Dodge pickup truck parked on the shoulder of the road with its hood up.

"Someone broke down maybe?" I asked.

"Looks like," Sanchez replied and he slowed the SUV to a crawl as we neared it. He stopped the Explorer in the traffic lane next to the pickup, and I rolled my window down. The truck had no rear license plate. There didn't seem to be anyone around. I opened my door and stepped out just enough to make sure no one was lying slumped over in the seat.

"Humph. Guess whoever it was got a ride. No one inside sleeping, or dead. No plates," I said taking one last look around.

Suddenly a white Ford sedan blew past us on Sanchez's side. As I sat back down in my seat, a red pickup truck also passed. It was followed by a semi-truck, the driver laying on his horn. *What is this, a fucking parade? Where'd all these vehicles come from?* I wondered, irritated at the loud noise of the air horn.

"We gotta get outta here before we get our asses run over," Sanchez said as he accelerated away. "Whoever owns that pickup probably hoofed it to town or got a ride."

I nodded looking at the Dodge in my side view mirror. "I've always liked the look of those older four-wheel drive Dodge Power Wagons. Beefy looking."

"We had several at VPD. They were supposed to be used for the area out by the river. There's a river valley and bluffs that run along the north edge of town. Anyway, some of the guys really liked driving them instead of a patrol car because they had so much room for all your crap. Knew this guy, last name of Quint. He drove one of those Power Wagons every shift. Used to blast music from his cassette player through the PA speaker. He was a good guy. A joker though. Always in trouble for pranks and jokes. That Dodge back there kind of reminded me of my '92 Silverado."

"How so?" Sanchez asked. "That's a Dodge, not a Chevy."

"Just the color," I answered. "That one is blue and silver or gray or whatever. Mine was blue and silver. Similar look."

ℰↄℰↄ

As the sheriff's SUV cleared the next small rise and disappeared from sight, there was movement on the opposite side of the road from the Dodge pickup. The Mexican man, Michael Rocha, stepped out from behind a large Cholla cactus. In his hands was his H&K MP5 9mm sub-machine gun with a muzzle suppressor, a "silencer" some errantly called it. Disappointed at the missed opportunity, Rocha watched the SUV disappear down the black ribbon of the county road.

CHAPTER 36

Hunted

It was somewhat amateurish for his first attempt, but Rocha, thought he should give it a try. After all, sometimes the simplest approach was the best. He had known the two deputies, or detectives as it were, would pass this way after having followed them out here to the ranch road last night. After hearing about the robbery and shooting at the mini-mart on his police radio scanner, Rocha had parked down the frontage road and kept close watch on their Explorer in the mini-mart lot, figuring correctly that one or both would eventually return for the vehicle when the crime scene was vacated. Of course, it wasn't a sure thing. Someone *else* could always show up to retrieve the SUV. He'd had to change locations several times so as not to draw attention to himself by parking in one location too long, however, he was never far off. Using his binocular, he'd been able to keep the Explorer under constant observation. As he'd anticipated, both deputies had finally returned for it well after midnight.

When the deputies drove away from the robbery scene, Rocha followed. At first he'd been able to blend in with other traffic, but as the detectives continued down the lesser traveled county roads, he'd turned off his headlights and again donned his NVGs. Rocha's previous trips to the ranch, eliminating Lyle and then scouting the ranch posing as an errant farm worker, had told him two things. The horses and dogs were easily alerted, and the single lane gravel road had no other outlet.

He was now certain he could not approach the ranch's gated entrance down this single lane gravel road in a vehicle without being detected and challenged. He decided on a new simple and impromptu plan after only a few minutes reflection on the possibilities of an early morning ambush along this county road. *It can be done if the conditions are right. It's reasonably deserted and the sound will not carry any more than a few hundred yards.*

Rocha knew the detectives' day would start early, and although there was another route into town, it was longer and out of their way. Rocha was confident the two would pass by this spot on the road. He smiled. *Creatures of habit, yes indeed.* When the taillights of the Explorer make the turn down the ranch road in the darkness, Rocha turned the truck around, turned on his headlights, and drove back along the county road until he found a particular spot his trained eye had noticed the day before when scouting the ranch. It was a straight stretch of asphalt between two slight rises.

There was a wide enough shoulder to park the truck, and several large Cholla cactus were close to the road on both sides. He could only hope the two detectives would be curious enough in the morning to stop and aid a stranded motorist, or at least check out the truck, thus presenting themselves as stationary targets.

Climbing out of the truck, Rocha first removed the rear license plate and tossed it under the seat. He then opened the hood. Carrying his duffle bag, he walked to the far side of one of the large Cholla directly across the road from his truck. From here he had both a clear view of the roadway and clear field of fire on three sides of his truck. After donning a tan, camouflage-colored sweatshirt against the cool night air of the desert, he spread a small brown canvas tarp on the sand in an attempt to avoid some of the more unpleasant desert residents. Rocha then lay down on it and readied his weapon. He flipped the rate-of-fire selector switch to III. The MP5 would now only fire three-shot bursts with each pull of the trigger. Although Hollywood and TV directors love to depict otherwise, full-auto fire, even from an easy to handle weapon like the MP5, can be unpredictable in its results from any distance over ten yards. Rocha was a good twenty five yards from the Dodge. It would be an easy shot for aimed and controlled fire, but not necessarily so from a weapon firing on full auto. Rocha was not here to shoot up the cars like some thug gangster in a drive-by, not to mention that shooting lots of holes in one's own truck was *not* conducive to remaining undetected by the authorities. When he was confident that all was ready, Rocha closed his eyes and listened to the desert. He heard the not-so-distant hooting of a Ferruginous Pigmy Owl. Then there was the howl of several coyotes, followed by the distant braying of a wild burrow.

Just after daybreak, the alarm on Rocha's Rolex wrist chronometer reminded him of the time. He hadn't been asleep, in normal terms, anyway. He had been in that light dozing state of those who know combat. Rocha now sat up and stretched his muscles as best he could without exposing himself. A high pitched squeal in the distance behind him told him a desert rodent or rabbit had met it's end in the jaws of a predator's ambush. He smiled at the thought. He urinated while lying on his side, then began his vigil. He didn't have to wait long. Fifty minutes after the sun made its appearance over the first rise, the sheriff's department Ford Explorer slowed to a stop right next to his truck. *So far so good*, Rocha thought. No other cars had passed by in either direction.

The deputy that was driving stayed in the SUV, while the detective in the passenger seat stepped out. Rocha decided he would shoot the passenger detective first, as it would be the farthest shot and he didn't want him taking cover on the other side of the vehicle. Rocha could then kill the driver before he could recover from the shock of seeing his partner shot. He raised the MP5 and was applying slight pressure to the trigger when a white Ford sedan suddenly burst over the rise to his right at high speed. It passed the Explorer, swerving into the opposite lane. Rocha took aim again but within seconds the white Ford was followed by a red Ford pickup. Then a semi-truck blew past, blasting its air horn at the deputies.

By the time the semi had passed, so had Rocha's opportunity. Both of those meddling cops were back in the Explorer and it was accelerating away from the Dodge pickup. Rocha sighed and stood up slowly after checking to see if there was any other traffic visible in either direction. There wasn't. He stepped out of his concealment, picked up his tarp, bag, and weapon, and walked to his truck. In retrospect, had it not been for the unexpected traffic this time of the morning, his simple plan would probably have worked. Fate had stepped in and granted the deputies a temporary reprieve.

Rocha shrugged. *Ni modo, asi es la vida.* He put the license plate back on the truck, started it, then drove off at a leisurely pace toward town. There was no rush. He was certain the detectives' first stop would be the sheriff's office.

℘⅋℘

Unknown to Rocha, fate was soon to deal him another surprise. No sooner had his truck had vanished over the top of the second rise, when one of the desert bushes on that very same hill seemed to come to life. The bush stood up, and it was holding a scoped rifle.

CHAPTER 37

The Bush

H oly screamin' snake-shit!" the "bush" blurted out to no one in particular. *Did I really just see that? Did I really almost blow that guy away?*

These two questions raced through the mind of the man under the mesh and burlap fabric of the ghillie suit. The suit made him closely resemble a typical clump of desert brush. The man stood on the rise trying to process what had just taken place below, and what he had almost done.

The man was a pilot. An experienced commercial airline pilot with twenty-five years under his belt. As such, he was no stranger to sudden, and sometimes unpleasant, changes to his immediate environment, but what had just happened was unlike any situation he had faced before. Hell, it was unlike any situation he'd ever *heard of* before. The man's name was Daryl Jackson.

Jackson had been sitting in his chosen coyote hunting stand on the desert rise since 4:00 a.m. He had ridden across the desert on a Yamaha Rhino ATV almost seven miles from the dirt road where he'd parked his truck and trailer. As a last minute thought, he had entered his truck's location into his hand-held Etrex GPS device. It was a good thing he did. He had ridden much farther across the darkened sand than he'd originally planned, and he wasn't quite sure he could find his way back.

It had been difficult to pick out a suitable location in the dark however. He had come across several areas that had interested him, but he really wanted to find some higher ground. When he spotted the rise ahead of him in his ATV headlights, he turned the Rhino around and found a place to park it. Jackson then hiked back to the small hill, setting up the speaker and the decoy for the caller as he walked. He placed both together in the wash between the rise and the Rhino, then piled up a few rocks to conceal the speaker.

After climbing to the top of the rise and finding what looked like a spot without too many rocks or thorns, he comfortably positioned his butt on a stadium cushion he'd brought with him and tried out the call one time to make sure it was working. He could not see the furry rabbit decoy jerking in the darkness, of course, but the caller was working fine. The high pitched squeal of a "dying rabbit" that emitted from the speaker was a terrifying sound to those unaccustomed to it. Jackson then sat silently, waiting for the disturbance of his passage to be forgotten by the creatures of the desert.

Checking his watch, Jackson decided to wait until the breaking dawn provided shooting light before using the call again. While he did have a powerful spotlight that was designed to be attached to the rifle's scope, he wasn't sure it was legal to do so in Texas, and besides, ambient daylight was always better for shooting. Dawn would be here soon enough. When the sun finally made its appearance, allowing him to see fairly well, Jackson switched on the caller for a few seconds, making the decoy jerk and twitch at the same time.

He swiveled his head slowly, scanning the surrounding desert with his eyes. *There*! He thought he saw movement down behind a large Cholla below him. He raised the rifle to his shoulder, placing his eye behind the scope. *Oh, man, is that a road?* He swung the rifle past the Cholla. *Crap! Yeah it is, but I should be far enough away from it to be legal for shooting. No cars anyway.*

Moving the scope reticle crosshairs back to the Cholla, he placed his right index finger on the trigger and thumb on the safety lever on the left side of the bolt in anticipation of seeing a coyote working his way toward the decoy. What he saw next made him move his finger off the trigger instantly. Cranking the scope up to 20x, he could clearly see the shape of a Hispanic man lying on a small tarp at the base of the cactus.

Jackson's heart began to race. His first thought was that the man was an illegal, sleeping or possibly trying to hide from the Border Patrol, but as he watched, the man stretched, sat up, and placed something across his lap. *What the hell is that? Shit that looks like a submachine gun.* Jackson couldn't get a clear look at the weapon. His view was blocked by the man's body, but he knew guns and he thought it looked like either an Uzi or maybe an MP5. *What are you up to?*

Jackson watched the man, considering briefly that maybe he'd encountered another hunter. He immediately dismissed that thought. No one hunted with a sub-machine gun, at least not a normal person anyway. His next thought was maybe it was a drug smuggler. If it was, Jackson wanted to get out of here. He didn't need that kind of trouble. The sun was full up now and he could clearly see the man's weapon. It was indeed an MP5. *Expensive weapon for a rag-tag smuggler to carry.*

Jackson was now fascinated. He was concerned yes, but not to the point of worry. As long as he didn't move or draw attention to himself, the ghillie suit would keep his presence completely unknown to the other man. Should the stranger, by some miracle, become aware of Jackson's presence and became hostile, the short range sub-machine gun was no match for Jackson's bolt-action Savage at this distance. It was a good 250 yards. He thought a moment about having to defend himself in such a manner. There was no question in his mind that he could and would shoot to defend himself if it came to that, but he did not want any confrontation with a drug smuggler if he could avoid it. They usually did not travel alone, or so he'd read in news stories.

As a precaution, he kept his scope's reticle centered on the man's back as he watched. Jackson was still contemplating the man's intentions when he caught movement out of his peripheral vision. A vehicle topped the far rise to his right. Jackson saw that it was a sheriff's department Ford Explorer. As it approached, it slowed. For the first time Jackson noticed the Dodge pickup truck parked on the far shoulder of the road with its hood up. He had been so intent on the armed stranger, the Dodge had gone unnoticed. As the sheriff's vehicle came to a stop, Jack saw the stranger raise the MP5 and take aim at the two deputies inside. Now it suddenly made sense.

This is a set-up! *He's going to ambush those two cops!* Jackson was watching it all unfold right in front of him like some bazaar YouTube video. He realized that if he did not intervene somehow, the two cops were probably going to die. Thoughts raced through his mind now. *But what if it's not what it seems? Should I at least fire a round off to alert them?* Jackson stared through the scope which was still centered between the Hispanic man's shoulder blades. *No time! He's gonna kill those cops. Shoot this asshole. Pull the trigger. Pull the trigger. Pull the trigger!* his mind screamed at him.

His finger applied the necessary three pounds of pressure to move the trigger rearward. Nothing happened. The scope twitched, but the rifle didn't fire. Jackson was dumbfounded. He then quickly realized that in his excitement he had forgotten to flip the safety off. In the few seconds it took his mind to process the problem, come up with a solution, and command his thumb to move the safety lever forward, the situation below him changed. Several vehicles were now passing by the sheriff's unit on the road, and the armed man had lowered his weapon. Several seconds later, the sheriff's SUV itself sped away. Soon the man carrying the MP5 stood up, collected the tarp he'd been laying on and a duffle bag that Jackson hadn't noticed, then walked across the road.

As Jackson watched, the man closed the hood, climbed into the driver's seat, and started the truck, then he, too, drove away. Jackson lowered his rifle and sat stunned, and shaking, his mouth agape. Finally, when the Dodge had disappeared over the next rise and his nerves had steadied a bit, Jackson, stood up, his unused rifle gripped in his hand. *I've gotta tell someone about this*, he decided. He hurriedly hiked back to the Rhino, collecting his speaker and decoy along the way. After stowing everything in the small bed of the ATV, Jackson punched the location coordinates of his truck into the GPS and tore off across the desert floor, throwing up a cloud of dust behind him. He found that he really didn't need the GPS now in the daylight. The Rhino's tracks from the drive out were clearly visible. Within the hour Jackson had the ATV loaded on the trailer and was driving toward town. He would contact the first cop he came across about what he'd seen.

He decided he would, however, leave out the part about nearly shooting the man. As Jackson approached the on-ramp to the interstate, he spotted a TSDPS unit parked on the shoulder, the state trooper watching the flow of traffic on the four lanes of concrete in front of him. Jackson pulled in behind the patrol car. The female trooper was already watching him in her rear view mirror.

CHAPTER 38

Near Thing

Trooper Samantha Baker was tired and agitated. She did not feel good. Near the end of her ten hour night shift, Sammy didn't' really want to get involved with any speeders. Not only did she have several reports to finish, but her period had started right before work and now she was cramping up. On top of that she had a headache the size of Texas. She decided to park her blue and white patrol car where everyone coming *and* going on the interstate this morning would see it. *In fact*, she thought, *they'd have to be blind not to see it. That should slow them down a bit.*

Sammy set her laser speed-detecting radar to a minimum speed of 85 mph, popped a couple of Midol, and had just begun to type on her unit's laptop when she heard the gravel crunch on the shoulder of the on-ramp behind her under the weight of a vehicle. She looked up and into her rearview mirror. *Well that's just great*, she thought when she saw the Caucasian man, driving a Chevrolet pickup and pulling an ATV on a trailer, stop behind her. *A friggin' tourist with an "Excuse me, Officer, how do I get to bum-fuck nowhere?" question no doubt.*

She was irritated at the sight, as only women can get when they are interrupted doing something they consider important. Sammy quickly jotted down the front license plate number on the notepad attached to her console.

Unlike some women in law enforcement, Sammy was very attractive. In her bare feet she stood five-feet-six-inches tall and at one-hundred-thirty-five pounds she had a nice shape—muscular and firm, yet not so much that she looked like a female body builder. Her dark brown, short cut hair combined with her bright green eyes were striking. She kept her 36-C-sized breasts, twenty-six-inch waist, and thirty-eight-inch hips and butt looking good by watching what she ate and altering her weight training and running five days a week.

Sammy liked to show off all that effort by wrapping it up in nice packaging. She always paid extra to have her uniforms tailored to fit her body well, and she *never* left the house without her hair fixed and her lightly applied make-up on. As well as being attractive, Sammy was also blatantly *heterosexual*. She liked working with men, most of them anyway, and she liked sleeping with men when it suited her. Sammy just didn't like being *bothered* by men, especially when she was tired, busy, and had menstrual cramps. *Men are so lame, but they do come in handy once in a great while.* She smiled as she thought about the fact that men should be stored in locked glass cases like fire extinguishers, with signs attached that read *Break Glass When Horny*.

Sammy sighed watching her rear view mirror, waiting for the guy to get out of his truck. What she was not prepared for at all was to see something that looked like Chewbacca get out and start toward her. Sammy quickly hopped out of her driver's seat and put her hand on her weapon. "Whoa! Stay right there please, sir!" she commanded him and held up her left palm up.

Jackson stopped, not realizing at first why the female trooper was so overtly aggressive, hand on her gun and all, then he realized he was still wearing the ghillie suit.

"Oh, sorry, I forgot I was still wearing this thing. I've been out hunting this morning. I need to tell you something." *Damn, she is good looking for a cop.*

"Hunting?" Sammy asked. "Are you armed?"

"Rifle in my truck but it's unloaded," Jackson replied. "No hand-gun on me."

"Okay, take that camo suit off and let's see some ID," she said.

As he unzipped the front of his ghillie suit and began to slip it off, Sammy got on her radio and gave the dispatcher all of the information she had at this point, keeping a wary eye on the man the entire time. Another trooper was immediately dispatched to assist her. Jackson now stood before her in a flannel shirt, jeans, and hunting boots, the ghillie suit at his feet.

"Okay, sir, keep your hands where I can see them. Please turn around slowly and let me see the back of your belt." As Jackson turned, Sammy looked for any tell-tale bulges in his waist band or pockets, or even a pistol in the small of his back. Just a wallet in the back pocket of his jeans stood out. "Step over here by the rear of my car please, and again, keep your hands where I can see them," she directed.

When Jackson had complied, she walked to the driver side of his truck and glanced in. Sure enough there was the rifle he spoke of.

"If you want to check, my other hunting gear and varmint caller in the rear of the Rhino back there." Jackson gestured at the ATV. "I really have been out coyote hunting this morning. I saw something I need to tell you about, it's important."

"In a minute," she replied rather curtly, then went on, "Break out your ID and your hunting license."

Both then heard a powerful engine accelerate behind them. Jackson looked that way, but Sammy recognized the sound of the big V-8 and knew it would be her back-up arriving so she kept her eyes on the hunter. The second TSDPS patrol car came to a stop behind Jackson's trailer. Trooper Mark Williams held up four fingers with a questioning look on his face as he exited his car.

"I'm good," Samantha answered. She moved to him so she could talk in hushed tones. Still keeping an eye on Jackson, she asked Williams, "Can you run the plates for me please? And then have a look around through his gear and his truck. He said he's been out coyote hunting."

He nodded, looking at the truck and trailer. "Why'd you stop him?"

"I didn't. He just pulled up behind me and jumped out wearing that," she waved a hand at the ghillie suit laying on the ground. "Scared the shit outta me. Looked like a giant walking bush or fucking Bigfoot or something." Williams chuckled. "It's not funny Mark!" she growled, still irritated at this whole situation "I nearly pissed myself."

"Ooooh, kinky," he replied.

Sammy gave him "the look." She was not in any mood to be playful this morning.

Williams realized it, nodded, and turned to walk between the truck and trailer quietly saying to himself, "Alllll-righty then."

He began talking into his epaulette microphone. It took almost fifteen minutes for Jackson, his vehicles, his gear, and his rifle to be checked out.

When both troopers were finally convinced that Jackson was who and what he said he was, Sammy turned to him. "Now, sir, you said you have something to tell me?"

Jackson began to relate for both troopers every detail of his early morning encounter, starting with his arrival in the desert before daylight, and ending with his pulling up behind the patrol car, leaving out only the part about almost blowing the armed stranger's heart and lungs all over the desert floor with his .308.

Both troopers listened a bit disinterestedly at first, but that suddenly changed when Jackson got to the stranger with the MP5. Now their attention was riveted. When Jackson had finished, the troopers looked at each other, stunned.

"Why didn't you say something about this earlier?" Sammy demanded of him.

"Earlier? When earlier?" Jackson replied.

"When you first pulled up and got out!" Sammy exclaimed more heatedly than she meant to.

Jackson groaned. *Jeeze, isn't that just like a chick or what? Now it's on me?* Now it was Jackson's turn to get mad. He'd flown with many pushy female co-pilots over the years and he'd never allowed himself to be pushed around by the opposite sex, nor was he going to start allowing it now, cop or not.

"Hey listen, sweetheart, if you'll recall, I tried to tell you twice but you were too busy doing the 'cops and robbers' routine with me to let me get a word in, and why are you yelling at me? What is it, you're time of the month or what?"

Oh shit, Williams thought. *This is not going to end well.*

Although quite accurate, that last comment lit Sammy off like a sky rocket. She took a step toward Jackson her fists and teeth clenched. Williams quickly stepped between the two, facing the hunter.

"I apologize for all the hoops we made you jump through, sir, but it's not every day we encounter someone in a ghillie suit with what looks like a sniper rifle. I'm sure you understand."

Jackson looked at Sammy for a few seconds then nodded. Williams had already starting to put two and two together, knowing a lot about the case details that Sanchez and that retired CSI guy Douglas were working on.

"You said the two deputies were in a Ford Explorer?" Williams asked. Jackson nodded. "Were they in uniform or plain clothes?"

"One in uniform, one was in plain clothes," Jackson replied.

That answer clenched it in Williams' mind. It had to have been Sanchez and Douglas in the Explorer.

Williams turned to Baker. "Sammy, I've got to get this information to the sheriff's office right away."

Sammy was bewildered, her anger at Jackson forgotten. "Why don't you just call the S.O. on the phone?" she asked Williams. "And what's this all about Mark?"

"Too much information for a phone call and too much to go into with you right now, but I promise I'll catch you up when there is time. I'll call our sergeant and tell him what I'm doing. Mr. Jackson, I need you to follow me a few miles to the sheriff's office and repeat to them what you told us. Will you do that?"

"Sure."

Jackson started walking to his truck. Sammy turned back to her patrol car shaking her head. *I gotta get away from both of these two jerk-*

offs. I need some food, a shower, a fresh tampon, another half bottle of Midol and I need to sleep for two friggin' days straight. Then she remembered the two un-finished reports that still needed to be completed, which pissed her off all over again.

Five minutes later, Jackson's pickup and trailer were following Williams' patrol car, their small convoy hurrying down the interstate. Williams' overhead lights were still on, much to Daryl Jackson's amusement. *Cool,* he thought, *a police escort just like on TV.*

CHAPTER 39

War

I don't care if you were the closest unit!" Davis's face was red with anger, his voice two octaves higher than usual. Sanchez and I were sitting in his office chairs, receiving the tongue lashing for our decision to get involved in the robbery at the mini-mart. "Right now you're supposed to be solving a murder," Davis continued. "Not go tearing around the countryside chasing two-bit thugs robbing a liquor store!"

Sanchez tried to interject, "Actually L-T it was my fault. I'm the one who made the decision since we were closest."

"Not entirely true," I interjected before Davis could respond. "It may have been Frank's decision, Lieutenant, but I agreed with it."

Sanchez and I both knew it wasn't quite accurate, but he was now my de facto partner as well as my friend and I wasn't about to throw him under the bus. My mind wandered. *Benjamin Franklin said it best,* "*We must hang together, or we will most assuredly hang separately.*"

Davis's raised voice re-focused me on the conversation at hand. "Special Deputy Douglas, while I appreciate your loyalty to your partner here, I don't appreciate either of you disobeying my orders!" He studied me. "Now I know why your old boss told me you were such a pain in the ass! He warned me you did things as you saw fit without much regard for rules. I should have listened to him and sent you on your way. You are here as a consultant. Not a *real* deputy. I only gave you 'provisional deputy' status and that badge to help open some doors in the investigation, not for you to go out and play cop. Do you have any idea the mess it would have made if you'd gotten yourself killed out there? Do you? The sheriff is threatening to have my balls for breakfast over this. He says if I can't control you—" He looked at Sanchez then back at me. "—*both* of you, he'll stick me over at the jail for the rest of my career. Not to mention the lawsuit some shit-bird attorney would file on your wife's behalf against our office, who would gladly burn the county, the sheriff, me, your silly little friend here." He nodded at Sanchez. "And every other fucking person he could think of!"

Spit was actually flying out of Davis's mouth now he was so mad. His face wasn't red with anger anymore. Now it was actually a shade of purple. *Jeeze, he's gonna have a stroke right here*, I thought.

"Hey L-T, calm down," Sanchez interrupted. "Without Douglas here, we probably wouldn't have found out who this shooter is, or figured out what he's doing here, and don't forget we *did* catch those assholes robbing the mini-mart."

"No," Davis spat back. "You didn't catch shit. Two gave up and the owner shot the other one dead. Now I've got to figure out how to keep you both on the clock for the murder investigation when I'm supposed to put you on administrative shooting leave for three days and send you to the departmental shrink!" He looked back and forth between us, his face color fading back to semi-normal. "Neither of you are to get involved in anything, and I mean *anything,* that is not related to this murder investigation of these two Indian dopers unless myself or the sheriff personally tell you to do so. Are we perfectly clear?" We both nodded. "I want to hear you say it, Goddamn it!"

"Clear," we both replied.

"Now get out of my office and go do whatever it is you have to do to catch this guy, and if anyone asks, you don't say shit about what you're doing. Refer them to me. You're both officially on administrative leave. I want results and I want it yesterday!"

"Wow." Sanchez looked at me as we walked away from Davis's office. "He was not a happy man."

"No shit. I thought he was going to vapor-lock right there."

That brought a snort from Sanchez. "Shhhh—he'll hear us."

We hurried to the crime lab door, both stifling laughter like school boys making fun of the principle.

The sheriff's office crime lab had become our solitary sanctuary. A place to which we could retreat, think and talk without being bothered. It was the place to be out of sight, if not out of mind. Today, however, it was occupied by a familiar face. Michael Johns, the reservation K-9 cop was standing at the center counter, looking down at a .45 handgun laying on the counter top. I immediately spotted the white residue from superglue fumes on the weapon so I knew Johns had fingerprinted it for some reason. He looked up as we walked it, then smiled and greeted us. "Hey, guys, didn't expect to see you here."

"Nor we you, noble savage," Sanchez replied. "How's it hangin'?"

"A little to the left and halfway to my knees," Johns shot back quickly.

"Sheeeit, that's not what your ol' lady tells me," I said, completing a typical male banter that guys know so well.

"That'd be funny except I ain't got an ol' lady. You guys okay after your gunfight at the 'OK Corral' yesterday?"

Sanchez nodded. "Yeah, other than getting our asses chewed for being there at all." He related to Davis's sixty-minute tirade.

When he was finished, Johns simply replied, "What a dick. You guys are genuine heroes of the Republic of Texas."

I looked from him to the pistol. "What's with the shootin' iron?"

He followed my gaze downward. "Oh, I let Falcon out to take a dump out in the desert this morning over by a far corner of the reservation. About the only place I can let him run wild since he's cooped up in the back seat a lot. There's no one ever out there for him to accidently chew on and—"

Sanchez interrupted him. "Oh you mean like the time he ate the homeless guy in the box?"

Johns gestured for quiet with his hand. "Shhhhh, we don't speak of such things."

Seeing the quizzical look on my face, Sanchez turned to me. "I was still on nights then. I get this call to respond to 'Sam's Club,' you know, as in 'Wal*Mart?'" I nodded and he continued. "Well this particular store is built on a county island. It's about four in the morning, and the call is to investigate a man screaming. Turns out Officer Johns here, on his way back from dropping some ass-wipe off at the jail, had pulled into the parking lot to let that land shark he calls a dog out of his Tahoe to go take a leak. While Johns is talking dirty to his girlfriend on his cell, the dog starts sniffing around behind the building, finds a homeless guy in a box, and decides in his own simple doggie brain that he should go all 'Marv Albert' on the guy. I get there, the homeless guy is screaming and the dog is barking and snarling and still wants a piece of the guy even after Johns here pulled him off." He grinned at Johns. "How much did you end up paying that guy to keep shut about it? Five hundred bucks wasn't it?"

"No it wasn't *five* hundred. It was three hundred from the fund," Johns replied with feigned insult. Then he added good naturedly, "And I wasn't talking dirty to *my* girlfriend. I was talking dirty to *your* ol' lady. Now, may I please go on with my gun story?"

Without missing a beat Sanchez shot back, "Shit, you wish. My hot little Mexican wife would break your young balls, but by all means, please do." He nodded at the gun.

"So anyway, as I was saying before I was so *rudely* interrupted, I'm texting and waiting for the dog to finish his business this morning, when I see Falcon coming back with this pistol in his mouth."

"Wait," Sanchez interrupted. "The mutt is carrying the gun in his teeth?"

Johns nodded. "Oh yeah. that's not so unusual for a dog that's been trained to do article searches. They often come back with guns, or sometimes even gun *parts*, clenched in their jaws."

"No shit? I didn't know that." Sanchez looked at me, "Did you know that?"

"Yeah," I replied "We had a cop in Vista, Shawn I-forget-his-name. He was up fishing at a local lake on his days off and he loses his duty weapon. It fell out of his daypack or some horseshit, so he comes to briefing that night and tells his sergeant, who of course has to inform the lieutenant."

"Ouch," Johns said.

"Oh, yeah. Anyway, the lieutenant grabs one of our K-9 guys and his dog Coco. The L-T, the sergeant, the K-9 guy, and the cop who lost his gun *all* drive back up to the lake at one o'clock in the morning. It's like forty miles away, and they look for this gun in the rocks in the middle of the night with flashlights. Can't find it and they're just about to leave when here comes the dog with that big ol' Beretta in his mouth. Pretty amazing stuff. Gives you an idea how good dogs' noses really are. Sorry, Mike, go on with your gun story," I said to Johns.

"Yeah, well, anyway, this thing was unloaded, no mag in it, nothing. When Falcon drops it at my feet, I can see his snoot and front paws are covered with dirt. It was obvious he dug it up. I followed his tracks back out and sure enough there's a hole about a foot deep several hundred feet off the road with cowboy boot prints all around. Nice gun." We all looked down at it as Johns continued. "Dirty, but a fairly new Springfield Armory M1911 style .45, which aren't cheap. I figured it had been ditched for a reason, maybe a murder weapon? No one would deliberately just bury a new high dollar .45 without a reason, right? So I took it back to my office and I'm wanting to run the serial number on it but guess what?"

"Serial number ground off," I said.

"You guessed it, which means it's stolen, or been used for something wicked, or both. I was able to print it at my office. Didn't get anything, though. My problem now is I don't know how to try to restore the serial number. I knew you guys had some stuff here, but no one seems to know how to do it. One of your guys across the hall says he always just sends it over to the state lab, but you know how that goes. I'll be lucky if I hear anything back in three months, if ever."

I adopted my best Australian accent, which wasn't very good, and said, "No worries, mate." I began looking through drawers and cabinets and soon found just what I needed to help Johns out. Turning to

Sanchez, I said, "Over in the chemical locker you'll find a small bottle labeled Fry's Reagent. Grab it for me, will you?"

He turned toward the locker as I walked over to the shelf and took down a package of long stemmed swabs, then retrieved a roll of emery type sandpaper from another drawer. All of these items I placed on the counter near the weapon, along with an unusual looking electrical box. The box had a volt meter on the front along with an off/on switch and an adjustable dial. A cord with a plug for 11-volt AC wall outlet was attached to the rear of the box, with two thinner cords, one red and one black, protruding from the sides. Both had alligator-type clips on the ends.

"What is that thing?" Johns inquired.

"It's a 12-volt power source, a transformer basically," I told him. "It converts 110-volt electricity from a wall outlet into low voltage DC current. You can control the output with the dial on the front."

"How'd you know that they had this stuff here?" Johns asked.

"Oh, I've been rummaging around in here for days," I replied.

With that, I put on a pair of gloves and picked up the weapon, placing it in a vise attached to the counter. After gathering all my supplies near the gun, I began to demonstrate how to use them. I first attached the black alligator clip to the trigger guard of the pistol then plugged in the transformer. Taking the emery paper, I sanded on the damaged serial number of the pistol until it was smooth. Picking up a swab, I dipped it into the small jar of reagent, soaking the head of the swab in the green liquid, then clipped the red alligator clip to the head of the same swab so that the metal of the clip was in contact with the liquid on the swab tip. I explained to Sanchez and Johns that the current needed to pass through the green liquid and onto the steel when I touched the swab to the weapon.

"Turn on the vent fan over there will you?" I said to Johns, nodding to a switch on the wall. "This stuff smells foul when you get started."

Flipping the transformer switch to 'on" and adjusting the current using the knob and the volt meter, I began to rub the green tipped liquid on the swab tip lightly back and forth across the sanded area of the serial number. The reagent on the swab immediately bubbled and crackled, giving off smoke and turning black. I repeated this procedure ten times, changing out the swabs and re-sanding the metal with the emery paper each time. On the eleventh pass of sanding and swabbing, a number briefly appeared then disappeared again after a few seconds.

"Get me a fingerprint loupe or a magnifying glass, please, someone, and a pen and paper," I said.

Sanchez grabbed a loupe off of the shelf, and took out his pen and notebook.

"I'm going to hit this again," I said. "But when I do the number will only be visible for a few seconds. I need to use the loupe to look at it and I'll call off the number to you. Ready? Okay, here we go." I repeated the procedure once again and immediately placed the loupe over the serial number. Just as I'd told them, the faint number came into view briefly. "S205689," I called off to Sanchez. Johns was writing it down also.

"Hey, that's a pretty good trick," Johns said.

"Yeah," I replied. "But don't get too excited about it. We got lucky. It only works about a third of the time, if that. Depends on how bad the damage is to the weapon and how hard the serial number was stamped on there by the manufacturer in the first place."

"Still, at least I've got somewhere to start now," Johns said. "Thanks much."

I had just taken off my gloves when Davis walked in. He ignored Johns' presence entirely.

"There you two are. Dispatch is looking for you. Said there's a TSDPS Trooper, Williams I think is his name, outback in the lot waiting for you. What's that about?"

I looked at Sanchez who just shrugged his shoulders. "I don't know, Lieutenant, but we'll go see."

"Thanks again, guys," Johns said as we walked out the door.

"No sweat," I replied, "let me know if anything comes of it."

Davis gave me a sideways glance. "Thanks for what?" he asked suspiciously.

"Nothing really. I just told the guy how to process some evidence."

Davis scowled. "Just remember what I said about getting involved with other stuff."

I winked at Sanchez. "Will do, L-T." With that Davis walked off. *Yup, Johns was right. What a dick.* "Well, let's go see what Mark wants."

Williams was standing next to his patrol car with an older man. We greeted each other with handshakes as Williams introduced the retired pilot Daryl Jackson to us, then asked, "Were you guys out on county road 3658 this morning early?"

"Yeah," Sanchez replied. "That's the way we come in from Rollins' ranch. We stayed out there last night."

"Thought it had to be you. You need to hear this."

He nodded at Jackson, who started recalling the morning's events as he had witnessed them. When it was done, Sanchez and I just stood there in silence trying to process what we'd just heard. Although we had discussed it at length, it was still shocking for both of us to come to grips with being told that not only were we the targets of a professional killer, but that we had been mere seconds away from being shot and probably killed. It was only by the hand of fate that we hadn't been.

"Excuse us for a moment, Mr. Jackson." I motioned for Williams and Sanchez to walk away a few paces with me. "Have you told anyone else about this?" I asked Williams.

"Well, my sergeant knows I was bringing Mr. Jackson here over to see you, but all I told him was that Jackson was a possible witness to a crime that involved the S.O. I didn't tell him what the crime was. Sammy Baker knows, though."

"Who's Sammy Baker?" I asked.

"She's the trooper that Jackson first saw when he was looking for a cop to tell his story to."

"Shit. I was hoping no one else knew about this," I said. "I don't want it to get out that we know about our killer's intentions, or he might skip and we'll never catch up to him. We already know he's got an 'ear' at the jail. The less people that know about this the better."

Williams thought a minute then said, "Look, Sammy and I are pretty tight. If I tell her to keep it zipped, she will."

"Really? You think so?" I asked. "I know women hate to be told this and they all deny it, but chicks aren't known for their propensity to keep secrets for very long, if at all. It's like in their genetic code to gossip."

Williams snorted. "Yeah that's true, but Sammy's different than most. She hangs with men more than women. The only woman friend she has is my ex-wife. I don't think they speak much nowadays, though. I think I can keep that end of the pipe plugged up, no pun intended."

I thought a moment. "All right. Go talk to Sammy and tell her mum's the word until I can figure out what to do about this."

I turned, looking for Daryl Jackson. He had walked back over to his truck. Williams and Sanchez continued the conversation without me as I returned to Jackson.

"Anything else you can think of, Mr. Jackson, that we need to know?"

"Not really, no," he replied.

I glanced in his truck and saw the Savage rifle. He had not had the time to put it back in the case yet.

"Wow, that is a nice rifle," I said.

"Want to see it?" he asked, opening the driver's side door.

Jackson picked it up and handed it to me. I opened the bolt confirming the weapon was unloaded. I looked around to make sure there were no bystanders then held the rifle's scope up to my eye. The rifle was heavy and it would not be comfortable to hold it to one's shoulder for a long time, but the view through the scope was amazing. The clarity was the best I'd ever seen, and when I cranked the power ring to the maximum position of 20x power, even the smallest details hundreds of yards down the street were visible. Of course on that setting the reticle jumped all over the place as I could not hold the rifle steady, but if I'd been laying prone and using the attached bi-pod, it would be bad news for whatever I decided to shoot at. As I looked though the scope, it brought back memories of all the hunting trips I'd been on through the years, and my own days on the rifle range.

"This is sweet," I told him as I handed the rifle back.

"You know iron?" he asked.

"Oh, yeah. I've got a pre-'64 Winchester Model 70 .270 with a Leopold three by nine that I deer hunt with. But like you, I used to do a lot of varmint hunting, coyote calling, and target shooting. For that I had a custom Sako Deluxe .243."

"Pre-Garcia?" he asked

I nodded. "Yeah. Had a nice four by twelve Leopold on it. Worked up my own loads for it and all that. It was a great rifle but nothing like this."

Jackson was interested now. "A pre-Garcia Sako is nothing to sneeze at and neither is a pre-'64 Model 70. How do they shoot?"

I thought about it a moment. "The Winchester will shoot MOA or close to it with factory Federal Premium ammo and that's fine for any kind of larger game. On a good day, the Sako with my hand loads and shooting from a bench rest, *and* when I hadn't drunk too much coffee that morning, would shoot five shot groups with all five rounds cutting each other, so, call it three eights to half inch group at 100 yards."

Jackson looked skeptical, but I told him it was the God's truth and that, when conditions had been good, such as little or no wind and no heat coming off the ground in the mornings, it had been common for me to regularly vaporize ground squirrels at 300 yards, give or take. I'd once even shot a perched crow out of a tree at somewhere in the vicinity of 400 yards. "That rifle was one great shooting piece of steel and wood," I told him.

"Damn," he said. "If that's no bullshit, then that was a hell-of-a-shot. Crow is a small target at 100 yards, much less 400. Listen, Deputy, I'll tell you something shooter to shooter that I didn't tell the trooper. I almost blew that guy apart this morning when he took aim at you two."

I was surprised at this admission. "Why didn't you?"

"Well…" He thought about it for close to thirty seconds before answering. He looked distressed. "Buck fever, I guess. I pulled the trigger but I was so jacked up I'd left the safety on. By the time I got it flipped off, everything changed. Those cars came by and then you guys were gone. I just choked. It took me too long to react. It's been too many years since I've been in a situation like that and everything happened so fast."

I looked at him closely for the first time. I could see the seriousness in his eyes, and I recognized the look of a man who has seen combat in one form or another. "You were in the military, I take it?"

He nodded." Army helicopter pilot back in the day, reserve. AH-64s. Seen some shit in Grenada and the Balkans."

Sanchez walked up as we were talking. "Williams jumped on the phone and is trying to head that Sammy Baker chick off before she talks to anyone," he said. "We all done here now?"

"I guess so," I replied, "unless Mr. Jackson has anything else?"

Jackson leaned close and said quietly to us both. "Listen, you guys. I'm a pretty good shot with this thing at very long ranges. If you should need me for anything—anything at all, and I'm sure you know what I mean, here's my cell phone number." He handed me a slip of paper.

I took the slip of paper and put it in my pocket. "We'll call you if we have any more questions. In the meantime, you might want to stay clear of that part of the desert when you hunt, the place you were this morning, I mean. We travel around out there and this guy might come back. If you think of anything else, you let us know, okay?"

Jackson nodded. "So I'm free to go?"

"Yes, sir, and umm, thanks for the heads up and the uh…effort."

He nodded again as he climbed into his truck.

Sanchez looked at me as Jackson drove out or the lot. "You would think a guy like that might have done something to warn us this morning when he saw what was about to happen."

I gestured at the retreating truck and trailer. "He was going to do more than warn us." And I told Sanchez what Jackson had tried to do.

"No shit?"

"No shit."

Sanchez frowned. "You think he was being straight with you or just trying to be a big talker?"

"He was being straight. I could see it in his eyes. I think he had only a few seconds to make a decision and he made the right one. It was the mechanics of the decision that let him down. I'm amazed he actually pulled, or rather *tried* to pull the trigger."

Sanchez shook his head. "Guy has balls, I'll give him that, but forgetting to flip his safety off? I mean, come on."

"Been many years since he's seen any action. Hunting isn't combat. He doesn't train all the time like cops and soldiers do. He gets credit in my book for even being *willing* to drop the hammer, and I don't doubt he'd do it again."

The deputy shrugged. "If you say so I guess."

After dwelling on the situation in silence for a moment, I turned to Sanchez. "This cartel guy is dangerous. He's a professional, motivated, apparently fairly well equipped, and for whatever reason he's after us now, as well as Lopez."

"Yeah…so?"

"So we're now at war my friend. I want to ask you something and I want you to think carefully before you answer this. How far are you willing to go to get this guy? I mean, from a cop's point of view about being a cop."

Sanchez looked away and thought a moment then he looked back at me. "What do you have in mind?"

"Look, Frank, I don't think we have the time to dick around with normal investigative tools, protocols, and procedures while we ourselves are being hunted. When you're investigating a 'who-done-it' murder, a lot of the time you're like a blind man in a dark room, stumbling around groping for clues. And yes, we have found quite a few, but it's too slow a process for us. This guy doesn't need any clues. He knows who we are, what we look like, where we work, and what we're doing. He's undoubtedly following us at least part of the time. Hell, he probably knows where you and Olsen live. We know he knows where I'm staying." This last thought unnerved the deputy a bit. "This guy has all the advantages. Frank."

Sanchez thought about it for several moments. When he answered it was obvious he was talking to himself as much as me. "This asshole stabbed my partner. He's murdered two people in cold blood that we know of for sure. I mean, even if those Indians were no real loss, it shows what he's capable of. He's undoubtedly murdered others and he will again. He is planning on killing us and, apparently, has already tried. I say we do *whatever* we have to do to put an end to it. Put an end to him."

I was again looking at the spot where Jackson's truck had disappeared and quietly said to him. "I was hoping to hear you say that. Because we really only have two choices. We can try to kill him, or we can wait around for him to kill us. We do have one thing going for us now, though."

His eyebrow went up. "What's that?"

"Our killer doesn't know that *we* know what he's driving now. A blue and silver Dodge pickup truck."

Williams had walked up behind us and overheard the last of our conversation. "Did I just hear you say your guy is driving a blue and silver pickup truck? I didn't get that from Jackson."

"Yeah, we're pretty sure," I replied. "A Dodge pickup truck. Why?"

"See, now that's funny," he said. "At your robbery and shooting at the mini-mart, after you guys had gone back to HQ to talk to the homicide guys, I saw a blue and silver Dodge truck drive by a couple times. It even parked down the street for a bit. Didn't think anything of it at the time. Thought it was just another nosy bystander. Of course, that was before this Daryl Jackson thing."

"Can't be coincidence," I said. "Listen, again I need you to keep this to yourself. It's our only edge right now and if it turns out to be the right vehicle description, I don't want this guy knowing that we know what his ride looks like."

"Okay," Williams said. "But what do you want me to do if I just happen to see a truck matching the description rolling down the road somewhere? For that matter, we could probably spot it pretty damn quick if *all* of our people were looking out for it. Want me to put a BOL on it?"

"No!" Sanchez and I answered in unison.

I scowled at him. "We don't want every cop in the county looking for it, at least not now. You know how that would go. Someone would get a wild hair up his ass and pull a traffic stop on it, and that would not be good for the cop. Remember this guy will rock-n-roll at the drop of a hat if he thinks he's cornered. If you yourself see it, just call us right away, but don't stop it, follow it."

Williams argued the point for a bit, but eventually agreed and nodded.

"Did you get hold of Samantha Baker by the way?" I asked him.

"Yeah. She's on board with it, but she's a woman *and* a good cop, which makes her just curious as hell. She's wanting some type of explanation in exchange for her silence."

I thought about this for a moment. "Can you really trust her?"

"Known her for years. We've become…close since my wife and I separated." *Shit, sleeping with her I'll bet, or at least wants to,* I thought as he continued. "And she's never given me reason not to. She's a close friend, and another set of eyes looking for the truck might come in handy."

"All right," I said. "It's against my better judgment, but she's already involved so fill her in on what we know so far, but for God's sake, tell her to keep her pie hole shut about it. No other cops. No pillow talk with a bang-buddy, nothing."

Williams flinched at my last comment but nodded. "I'll tell her."

I looked at him sideways, catching his reaction. "You sleeping with her?" I asked bluntly. He didn't answer. "Never mind, not my business, just keep it under control, please."

Williams was uncomfortable talking about Sammy Baker I could tell. *Must not just be friends with benefits. Maybe he's in love with the girl*, I suddenly realized.

He changed the subject. "Listen, guys, you're not going to do anything stupid, I hope?" he said, referring to a portion of our conversation he's overheard.

"The less you know Trooper Williams—" I smiled wryly at him, "—the less you'll have to testify to later."

He walked back to his patrol car shaking his head and mumbling. He turned. "If you need anything…"

I waved my hand at him.

Sanchez spoke up while still looking at Williams. "So what are we going to do now?"

I turned to him. "We're gonna do what soldiers in war do. We're going to hunt this fucker down and kill him before he does the same to us."

CHAPTER 40

The Six-P Principle

Rocha laid his cell phone down on the small table in the kitchen of the safe house. He was contemplating his next move. The Dodge truck was parked and covered at the rear of the house. Rocha was disappointed with his first attempt to eliminate the two deputies. It was little consolation that his ad-hoc plan had *almost* worked. The timing of the traffic on the road could not have been worse for him, or better for the two deputies. They had no way of knowing how close to them the dark shadow of death had passed. It also bothered him to know that he had exposed his truck to their inspection, no matter how brief, but they gained nothing from it. Now he would have to switch vehicles again. *Damn,* Rocha chastised himself. *I should have remembered the Six-P Principle.*

Rocha had just hung up the phone. He'd been talking to his employer. Again the voice had stressed the need to silence Lopez, and again, he had advised them that the two investigating deputies needed to be dealt with first. They did not agree and they were becoming impatient. The longer this job continued, the more risk there was of exposure.

The law might or might not suspect the cartel's complicity in the murders of the two Indians, but if it were publicly exposed that there had been cartel sponsored murders within the borders of the United States, the American press would grab the "Native American" angle and run with it, particularly in light of the recent story of the stolen Native American skeleton found in the desert. That story had yet to die down. *Wonder what is the deal with that, anyway.*

Rocha quickly dismissed this random thought as unimportant. He knew that the public pressure that would be brought to bear, by yet another story involving the death of Indians, could, and probably would, trigger a hard federal response by the US Government, and *that* could seriously interrupt business, not to mention exposing and possibly losing a valuable asset like Rocha himself.

His bosses had decided to order him to leave. They would have one or more of the gang members now behind the jail's bars kill Lopez. Rocha argued against it. He explained to them that there were two problems with this approach. The first was that a jail stabbing was not a sure thing. An unsuccessful "shiv" attack or a beating that Lopez survived would almost guarantee he would talk to investigators.

The second problem was even more daunting. Lopez had been moved to solitary confinement for his own protection.

It appeared now as if no one would have a chance to silence him until such time as he made bail and was on the street. None of their contacts inside the jail knew whether Lopez had given the police any information or not, though word had been received he had been interviewed at least once. If Lopez had indeed talked, then the deaths of both detectives *and* Lopez were now a necessity, as it would effectively end the investigation. There would be no sure way to tie any of this to the cartel. It was this last fact that finally swayed the argument to kill the two detectives in Rocha's favor.

When asked about the third wounded deputy in the hospital, Rocha had advised that he was not all that concerned with him. He was convinced the investigation could not have been far along when he had stabbed the young deputy and taken him out of the equation. While silencing him might factor into the equation at some point in the future, he doubted it would be necessary. One, young, inexperienced deputy was not near the threat the two older and more experienced investigators were.

Rocha's bosses finally conceded to his persistence in the matter, albeit reluctantly, and re-affirmed their permission to kill the two deputies before ending Lopez's existence. Rocha of course didn't mention the fact that he had already made one attempt on the deputies' lives on his own accord. His bosses would *not* have been happy about that. *Time for a new plan*, as he sat and thought about the Six P's. He would now have to start the hunt all over again. It shouldn't be too difficult, though. Cops had rules, regulations, and laws they had to follow. Michael Rocha did not.

He had never hunted grizzly or polar bear in the wilds of Alaska or rutting moose in Canada. He had never been on safari hunting lion, elephant, or cape buffalo on the Serengeti, nor had he hunted tiger in India. He was a hunter of men, still he did know that all of those dangerous animals had one thing in common. They were truly the masters of their environment. Smart, cunning, and all were *extremely* deadly when they themselves were hunting, or defending their territory.

Over the years, many were the hunters of the world's most dangerous game who discovered far too late, that the animals they were hunting were instead hunting them. Rocha would soon discover that some men could be the same.

CHAPTER 41

Hard Heart

The living room of Olsen's home was comfortable. The four bedroom house was well decorated in a southwest motif, which I found unusual for a single guy living alone. Most guys, including me, usually weren't nearly as creative or imaginative. In the living room were two large, swivel reclining chairs and a matching and comfortable-looking sectional couch. A sixty inch flat screen TV was attached to one wall, complete with a Bose Surround Sound system.

Olsen was resting on that same couch now, propped up on pillows, having been released from the hospital the day before. A tray of necessities had been placed near him by his girlfriend, Tammy, who at present was doting on him hand and foot. Tammy was a pleasant girl as well as easy on the eyes. She was close to Olsen's age, from what I could tell. Nicely tanned with a slim, yet muscular figure. In typical guy fashion, I gave her the once over. *Nice butt. Not much in the way of boobs, though. Probably why Sonya's rack intrigued him so much at our first meeting.*

I smiled remembering his embarrassment at being caught staring at Sonya's chest. Tammy cared for Olsen a lot it appeared, bringing him anything he asked for with a smile. A five-year-old female black German Sheppard named Tootsie lay near the edge of the couch. Sanchez and I sat in the two recliners. We had swiveled to face Olsen and the dog. The dog knew Sanchez but didn't know me, thus she kept a watchful eye on me every time I shifted position.

"How you feeling?" I asked him.

"Not bad really, considering the alternative. Sore when I twist, but I can actually get up and down, with Tammy's help, of course. Doc says it's because the damage was linear, whatever the fuck that means."

"It means the knife went in and came out on a straight up and down axis. No cross cutting of the muscles or tissue."

"Doc said it was wicked sharp too, and maybe even double edged," Olsen continued.

"Good thing for you the guy stuck you and didn't slash you," I told him. "That would have spilled your guts and you'd be taking a dirt nap in a pine box now."

Sanchez looked at me. "Nobody gets buried in pine boxes any more, you know, like back in the 1800s when *you* were a cop."

"Screw you," I shot back. "You're no spring chicken either, *mano*."

Olsen laughed "That's a fact, pops. Oooh, laughing hurts."

Sanchez flipped both of us the middle finger.

I changed position in the chair and the dog's head came up. "I don't think that mutt likes me."

Olsen reached down a scratched her ears. "She's a sweetheart. She was a drug dog at one time for TSDPS. Got a leg injury during training and couldn't work anymore. Handler is a good friend of mine and he was pretty broke up about losing his partner here. He lives in an apartment now and couldn't have her there, so I took her home to save her from 'the long walk.' Once she accepts you, you'll be part of her pack for life."

"Listen, Jim," I said quietly. "We need to talk—alone." I nodded at Tammy who was now in the kitchen.

"She's in the kitchen. She can't hear us," he replied.

Sanchez spoke up. "This is going to take a while and we can't take the chance on *anyone* overhearing our conversation, bro."

Olsen looked back and forth between the two of us pensively then called to her. "Tammy?" The girl walked in. "The saw-bones gave me a couple of 'scrips. Can you go get them filled down at Wal*Mart for me please?"

The girl looked at Jim, then at both of us. She was no dummy. "Okay," she said knowingly. "I have a couple errands I need to run, anyway. I'll call you before I head back."

"That's my girl." Olsen gave her a kiss and playfully patted her butt cheek. "Take my truck. Keys are on the hook."

"Bye, guys," she said and turned toward the door. "Don't let him get up by himself."

Olsen watched her as she walked away. "Hate to see you leave, baby, but I love to watch you go."

She turned, flipped him the bird.

"Hey, that's my line, Olsen," I said. "Bye, Tammy. Sorry, cop stuff." She smiled and closed the door behind her. "Doesn't she have to go back to work at some point?" I asked.

"Nah. She's going to school up in Austin. You know, 'Hook 'em Horns?'" He raised the thumb and little fingers on his right hand. "She's on a break right now."

"Oh? What's her major?"

"She's wants to be a corporate attorney."

Sanchez snorted. "Just what the world needs."

I looked at the door she'd just walked through. "Well, you know what they say, you don't need an attorney until you need one."

Olsen looked at us both. "What's with the extra hardware?" He waved at hand at both of our shirt tails. "Correct me if I'm wrong, but it looks like both you guys are carrying *extra* magazines and back-up guns. I miss something?"

It took an hour for me to explain everything we now knew. When I was done, Olsen whistled softly.

"So this guy is after you two for sure and maybe me as well. If so, why didn't he finish me off when he cut me?"

"I've been trying to figure that out myself," I said. "The only thing I can think of is that he wasn't after any of us specifically right then. He was just trying to get away. He must not have reached a decision about us until later. Maybe after we just missed him at the library, who knows."

"So? What are we going to do?" Olsen asked.

"*You* are not going to do anything," Sanchez said. "Except keep a gun handy, lay low, and heal up."

"Bullshit!" Olsen blurted. "For all we know, this guy is after me too, so again I ask, what are *we* going to do?"

Sanchez looked at me for support, but all I could do was shrug. "He might just be right, Frank. We don't know that Rocha won't come after Jim, particularly when he's sure we're out of the way."

"Rocha?" the young deputy asked, puzzled.

I thought for a moment. "Oh, man, that's right. I didn't tell you we now have a name to go with the face." I explained how we had come to find the identity of the Mexican man, then told them, "Look, Jim, Frank and I have been over this, and I have a couple ideas swirling around in my head concerning Mr. Rocha, but first things first. We all know this guy is a pro, and if he doesn't already know where we live, which I'm sure he does, he will soon. He'll find out about our wives and your girlfriend soon enough also, again if he doesn't already know. It's only a matter of time before he uses them against us. We've got to get the girls someplace safe before we can do anything about him. Jim, when Tammy gets back, keep her here. I'm going to go collect Sonya. Frank, you get your wife. Shit, I never asked about kids. You have any kids at home?"

"Fortunately no. They're visiting Chi-Chi's sister down in Yuma for the summer."

"Chi-Chi?" I asked.

"That's my wife's first name," Sanchez said then made a face.

I paused and smiled at him. "No shit? Your wife's real name is Chi-Chi? It's not like a nickname or something?" I asked, unable to contain my grinning.

"Go ahead. I've heard them all," he said. "Yes, Jason, her real name is Chi-Chi and to answer the second question which I know is killing you, yes she's well endowed."

I didn't know what to say to that.

Olsen laughed out loud. "You never told him?" he asked Sanchez.

"It never came up till now, asshole!" Sanchez replied testily. "And for your information, that whole Chi-Chi meaning tits is totally a gringo thing. Lots of Mexican girls, and even some Italian women are named Chi-Chi."

Olsen snorted. "Don't feel bad, Jason. I laughed all day when he told me for the first time."

"Fuck you, Jim," Sanchez said.

"All right, all right. We've had our morning laugh. boys." I turned serious again. "Let's get back to the business at hand. Jim, keep Tammy here. Frank, get your wife over here." I smiled. *Chi-Chi, holy shit, I hope I can keep a straight face when I meet her and say her name for the first time.* "I'll go round up Sonya and we'll meet back here in a couple hours. Jim, what do you think about your dog and my little dogs getting along?"

"Tootsie's a lover, not a fighter. She loves other dogs. They'll be fine. She'll probably adopt them as her own. It's *people* she doesn't like."

I looked at my watch. "We'll make Jim's place here our primary A.O. The odds of Rocha knowing where Jim lives are pretty slim, at least at this point. Since Jim's not real mobile, that makes him perfect for providing security for the women here, plus there's the dogs. Mine are good noise makers and Tootsie is pretty intimidating. Frank, tell your wife to bring whatever personal stuff you guys need for say, oh, three or four days, and bring any extra hardware and ammo you have."

Olsen spoke up. "You won't need to bring anything except your personal stuff."

"Why's that?" I asked.

Olsen grinned. "Go to my bedroom and open my gun safe in the closet. The combo is 37-66-78-94. It's digital so no need to clear it first."

I got up and walked to his bedroom's walk-in closet, except there was no closet and it was not a gun safe The closet doors were a cosmetic addition to what only can be described as a gun vault. I was in awe. *His entire closet is a fucking gun vault.* A Rhinovault to be precise, and it was huge. I recognized it as the type that was large enough to be used as an emergency panic room or an emergency tornado/storm room for two, or maybe even three people.

I punched in the four digit combination and the heavy steel door unlocked. With some effort, I pulled it open. What I saw inside astounded me. Lined up in many of the fifty-four velvet-covered racks were seven M-4 and AR-15 type tactical assault rifles, all of different makes, with different scope, laser, and flashlight configurations. There were three sniper type rifles, one of which was a near duplicate of Daryl Jackson's Savage. It even had the same Nightforce scope mounted on it. The second was a Barrett semi-auto in .50 BMG caliber. The third was an older US Marine Corps M-14, of the type used in Vietnam circa 1968.

There were six bolt action and lever action hunting rifles in calibers ranging from a .458 Win magnum elephant gun to 30.06. Three very expensive 12-gauge hunting shotguns were present, an auto-loading Browning, a pump Perazzi skeet and trap gun, and an over/under Charles Daley. Also included in the shotgun collection were two 12-gauge Benelli short barreled tactical defense shotguns, an older Spaz 12 assault shotgun, and two side by side Bonehill 10-gauge double-barrel coach guns. *Wow, those are old collectables.*

My eyes were wide with surprise and envy. As if the long-guns *and* the accompanying array of 20 revolvers and semi-auto handguns, spanning a spectrum of calibers, weren't enough to give any gun lover a woody, I then spotted the cases of ammunition and hi-capacity magazines for all of these weapons stacked against the back wall of the vault. The amount of ammo was staggering. Also amongst the crated ammunition were flash-bang, smoke, and CS gas grenades, several M17A2 gas masks, and two pair of Russian NVGs. I whistled softly. *Holy Mary mother of Christ! Olsen was not been kidding. We really don't need to bring anything. He's got enough here to go to war.* Leaving the vault door open, I walked back out to the living room. The look on my face was probably somewhere between shock and post-sex bliss.

Sanchez looked up. His eyes darted from me to the bedroom then to Olsen then back to me. "You look like you've just humped the cat."

"You know about Olsen's, umm, collection?" I asked him.

His raised eyebrows told me he didn't. I jerked my head toward the room. Sanchez stood up and walked into Olsen's bedroom. "Holy shit!

What the hell is all this, Jimmy?" Sanchez walked back into the living room. "Where the hell did you get all that stuff, man?"

Olsen looked toward the bedroom. "I just accumulated it over the past few years. The hunting rifles and shotguns are mostly family stuff. My dad's and grand-pa's hand-me-downs, well, except for the .458. All the other stuff is just a hobby, I guess you'd call it. You know that being on SWAT, I shoot a lot. And I just like to collect guns. I'm single so right now I have the money to do it. All the ammo and stuff I got mainly from gun shows—well, I should say *did* get from guns shows until Obama and his cronies dried up the ammo supply. Guess it's finally going to come in handy, eh?"

Sanchez shook his head. "I thought I knew you, man. I never knew you were into all that gun stuff."

"Guess you didn't know him as well at you thought," I replied sarcastically as I started toward the front door. "I'm going to go get Sonya. When we all get back, we'll try to—" I paused mid-sentence looking at a pair of Jim's dusty cowboy boots sitting on the floor by the front door, then I looked at Sanchez. The wheels were turning in my head jogged by the sight of the boots. "Frank, what was it Johns said about finding that .45 he was processing in the lab when we saw him?"

Sanchez didn't seem sure where I was going with this and he thought a moment. "Umm, said his dog found it and brought it to him."

"No, no, I mean about where the dog found it."

"Said his dog dug it out of a hole. He back-tracked the dog and found the hole."

My mind was working overtime now. "That's right, but he said the hole was surrounded by—"

Sanchez snapped his fingers and finished the sentence for me. "Cowboy boot tracks! There were cowboy boot tracks out where poor ol' Lenny got blown away. You think it's possible?"

"I don't know," I replied. "But it's another coincidence, don't you think? We need to get those photos, and I need to get hold of Johns and look at the tracks out by that hole."

Sanchez shook his head again. "The track film we took out there went over to the state photo lab and the photos are now either booked into Property or Davis has them."

Once again Olsen came to the rescue. "Umm, guys?" We turned to him. "Just after we took those boot track photos out there near Lenny, and then you moved on, I took several shots of the tracks with my little digital camera, also, just for my own future reference about what to put in the frame. I looked at them later and they actually looked pretty good. I downloaded them onto my computer. I can hook it up to my TV while you're gone."

Sanchez and I were once again surprised at Olsen's resourcefulness.

"Damn, you sure are coming in handy today," I told him with a smile. "But wait till we get back and I'll do it. You're not supposed to be moving around. I'll get hold of Johns and arrange a meet."

The door closed behind us and soon after, Sanchez dropped me off at the ranch and drove away. It took much longer than I'd thought it would to get Sonya and the little dogs out of the RV. The dogs weren't the problem. It was my wife. Even though I'd called and given her a heads-up, she took what seemed like forever before she was ready to go. I shouldn't have been surprised. She'd always been like molasses in January when it came to actually walking out the door to go anywhere. There was hair to fix and make-up to put on. That I didn't mind so much. It goes with being a chick and Sonya always wanted to look good, which I was actually grateful for.

"You never know when a rich, good-looking sugar-daddy will come along to check you out," she once told me.

No, her getting dolled up wasn't the problem. What drove me nuts was her putting on the final lip balm, putting dishes away, straightening pillows, shuffling papers from counter to counter, straightening pictures, looking for sunglasses, fiddling with her purse, and the fifteen other things she always did before she hit the steps. I'd always told her if the RV ever caught fire, she'd burn up because she just couldn't leave without performing at least ten unnecessary tasks.

This ritual aggravated the hell out of me but what could I do? They were women, and women lived and loved in their own world. John Gray really had it right when he wrote *Men are from Mars and Women are from Venus.*

Sonya's dallying today, though, did give me a chance to inform Juan of our plans and ask him to keep an eye out for strangers. Finally with Sonya and the dogs loaded in the truck, we drove out the ranch gate. As we were driving, I called Johns on his cell phone. He advised me to call again when we were on our way out to the reservation and he'd give me directions to the north boundary road and meet us there.

Everyone had gathered at Olsen's house by the time Sonya and I arrived. Sanchez greeted us at the front door and I had to laugh. He was dressed in Levis and a white wife-beater undershirt. His Glock was stuck loosely in his front waistband. "Man, I was just about to come looking for you."

"I know," I replied. I jerked my head sideways toward Sonya and rolled my eyes. Sanchez raised his chin knowingly. "By the way

Frank," I said as I looked him up and down again, "you look like some kind of old cholo gangster in that get-up. All you need is a Pendleton shirt, a bandana around your head, and a tattoo on your neck."

He clucked his tongue. "Man, no one uses the term cholo any more you old red neck," he shot back. "But that *does* give me an idea for my next Halloween party though. Come on, Jim's got those photos up on his screen."

Introductions were made all around. Sonya, Tammy and Chi-Chi immediately bonded and headed toward the bedrooms to organize their personal belongings, all jabbering at once. I stared after them.

To no one in particular, I said, "You ever notice that when you get two or more women together, they can all talk at the same time and they all understand each other?"

I turned back to the men in the room. They both nodded. It was then I noticed the Spaz-12 assault shotgun leaning against the end of the couch, within easy reach of Olsen's right hand.

"If you have to fire that thing, isn't that going to be a little hard on you? Not to mention your furnishings?" I asked him.

"Probably, but you know, no pain, no gain. Nine rounds semi-auto as fast as you can pull the trigger. You'd have to use a spatula to pick up the remains."

I nodded. "Not to change the subject, boys, but we also have to think about Lieutenant Davis and the sheriff. It won't be too long before they start wondering what we're doing."

Sanchez spoke up. "I've already taken care of that, at least for a couple days. I called the L-T, and without giving him any of the particulars about Daryl Jackson's story, told him that we'd learned our guy might be considering targeting us as well as Lopez. I made up a cock and bull story about how we'd heard that the office was possibly being watched, and that we needed to be off the grid for a few days so we could work unhindered, blah, blah."

Olsen looked at him. "And he bought that? From what you told me he went into orbit the last time you made a decision on your own."

Sanchez turned to him. "Whether he did or didn't, I didn't give him much choice. I told him *we* were the ones in deep shit and we were gonna do it our way. He finally calmed down some and agreed to let us off the chain for a couple days, but he's definitely not happy about it. I knew he'd be curious as hell about what Trooper Williams wanted to talk to us about out in the parking lot, so I told him that one of Williams' reliable CIs was the source of the info we got."

Olsen smiled. "So you lied to him?"

"*Lie* is such an ugly word," Sanchez replied. "I prefer to think of it as I just led him where he already wanted to go."

"So you lied to him," I repeated, grinning.

"In the words of my father, '*Si*.'" Sanchez shrugged. "It accomplished what I wanted. Davis said he would clear it with the boss and then officially put us on the usual three days paid administrative leave for the shooting, with two provisos. The first is that we tell no one we're still working when we're supposed to be off."

I nodded. "And the second?"

"At some point in the near future, we all have to go talk to the Department's shrink for real, just to cover Davis's ass."

"Great," I said sarcastically.

"Hey, it's a small price to pay for a few days on our own," Sanchez replied.

I turned to Olsen. "We need to look at your boot photos and then Frank and I will go meet with Johns to check out those tracks and see if they look like they might be the same."

Olsen nodded toward the flat screen TV on the wall. One of the images from his digital camera was displayed on the large screen.

"Wow, I wasn't expecting them to look this clear on your TV."

"Yeah, it's all HD," Olsen replied. "This is one of those new TV's that can do it all, Netflix, internet access, all that crap. I just downloaded the track photos directly to the TV."

"You were supposed to wait till we got back," I said as I stepped a bit closer studying the image. *Nothing much unusual. Left boot with a smooth boot sole. Standard riding heel with a serrated surface. Call it thirteen inches long which means about men's size 11. Damn, no unusual wear pattern on either the sole or the heel.*" Got any more?" I asked Olsen.

Nodding, he punched a button on the remote. The image on the screen changed to that of the right boot and I immediately noticed the heel. *That's what I was looking for*!

I pointed to the heel on the right boot. "Remember what I was telling you guys about individual characteristics as opposed to class characteristics?" Olsen nodded. "Look at the heel on the right boot," I continued. "It has been clearly worn down on the outside rear edge. Our guy has an unusual gate when he walks. Maybe an old injury, or even a mild birth defect."

"Or maybe he just walks weird like you do, honey," Sonya said behind me.

Unbeknownst to me, the women had walked back up the hall. All three women were standing at the edge of the living room, their gaze moving from the image on the screen to the three of us.

"Could be," I offered.

"You walk weird?" Sanchez asked.

"Yeah," I replied. "My johnson is so big it makes me lean to one side when I walk." This comment made everyone roll their eyes.

"Jason, you are so crude," Sonya exclaimed. "Please to excuse my husband ladies."

"Aye," Chi-Chi agreed. "What is it with all you men? Frank is the same. You all talk like you are hung like a caballos. Do you think women brag to each other about the size of our breasts?"

"Maybe you should," Frank said, reaching for Chi-Chi's chest.

She slapped his hand away saying, "Keep that up hombre, and you will never touch one of mine again."

I turned to Olsen who was still shaking his head at my comment. "Jim, hold the fort. We'll be back in a while. Frank and I are going to go meet with Johns. Hopefully those tracks will still be out there and in some kind of shape."

Olsen patted the stock of the Spaz 12. I kissed Sonya, and once again Sanchez and I walked out to the sheriff's SUV.

When we were rolling, I dialed Johns's number. The K-9 officer gave us directions to the semi-remote boundary road. An hour later the three of us were standing together at the edge of the gravel road. Johns was pointing out the area and we began to re-trace his dogs wanderings. There had been no weather to speak of, the wind being my main concern. In the deserts of Arizona, Nevada, and Texas, the winds can change the landscape easily, but it had been calm for several days now. It wasn't long before we located Johns and Falcon's tracks. Several of the cowboy book tracks were visible also, but only faintly. The ground here, having been baked hard by the west Texas sun for months, had no trace of moisture in it that would hold a track. After fifteen minutes of walking slowly and examining every disturbance in the soil, we came upon the hole that had produced the pistol. The outline of several partial boot tracks were visible here also, but these tracks near the hole had been all but destroyed by a combination of Falcon's feet, Johns's duty boots, and a plethora of the small feet of roadrunners, rabbits, coyotes, insects, and lizards.

Seeing the disappointment etched on my face at the overlapping track chaos, Johns said, "Sorry, Jason. It looks like the tracks of our mysterious hole digger are pretty much gone thanks to Falcon, me, and the critter highway through here. Damn, I was so concerned about the pistol, I never even thought of preserving the tracks."

"Don't sweat it, Mike. Unless you're in the habit of doing crime scenes on a regular basis, tracks are an easy thing to forget. Hell, even in a big city like Vista, only the most experienced patrol guys would think to look for and preserve shoe tracks. The paramedics and ambulance EMS guys *never* thought of it and were constantly walking over tracks and cutting clothing off of victims right through bullet hole or knife cuts in the cloth. Not to mention if there was something big that went down and the department's staff weenies would arrive and stomp around on everything, wiping out tracks, kicking shell casings under cars, stepping in blood, and tracking it all around, picking things up to look at, and then putting them back down. All kinds of dumb-ass crap."

"The Clown and Juggler Show, staff weenies," Sanchez mused, "I need to remember all these terms you use."

"We used to call the whole bunch the EET, Evidence Eradication Team," I told them both. "There's no way to tell how much physical evidence was lost just so that those guys could be seen by the TV cameras trying to look like indispensable cogs in the wheels of justice."

"Just like Davis and the Indian skeleton deal," Sanchez said.

"Exactly," I replied, turning my attention back to the tracks and the surrounding soil.

"What exactly are you looking for?" Johns asked me.

I explained what I'd noticed about the worn heel. Johns and Sanchez began to search in an ever widening circle also.

Two minutes later, Johns called out. "Got something here!"

Sanchez and I walked over to the spot where Johns stood. There in a small area of softer dirt near a small Cholla cactus, were two near perfect boot tracks, parallel and even with each other. Near the base of the Cholla was the outline of a spot of moisture that had long since dried.

"Guy stood here and took a piss," Sanchez observed.

"Yep," I replied. "And look at the track of the right boot." The small circles and wave patter in the heel were plainly visible. "The boot that made this track is brand new." I took a quick measurement with a small tape measure I'd pulled from the SUV's tool box. "Length is the same," I told them both. "Or as close as you can get, anyway. This is our guy."

"How can you be sure?" Johns asked. "This boot is new."

"It all adds up," I answered. "Might be intuition but I just feel it."

Johns looked skeptical, but Sanchez stared at me for a moment then spoke to Johns. "I've heard long-time hunters say the same thing about game. They just *know* their quarry is in a certain spot on a ridge or down in some canyon. Almost like they know there's a mind working on the other end."

"So why come out here to bury a nice gun?" Johns asked.

"You didn't test fire that thing did you?" I asked him.

Johns shook his head. "No, why?"

I was thinking out loud again now. "There's some reason he didn't want it. Could be there's something wrong with it, or might be traceable, or maybe he just didn't like it. Who knows? He couldn't just throw it away in some dumpster, someone might find it and turn it in. There's no big body of water to toss it in either, so I'm guessing he figured no one is going to find it buried out here, right? 'Course he didn't figure on Falcon's nose."

Sanchez looked across the expanse of desert. "But why here in this spot?"

I glanced around. "Random, maybe, or trying out new hardware. Who knows?"

Sanchez stared down at the tracks. "Guess we don't need to do anything about these tracks, huh? I mean, since we're not going to worry about—"

I cut Sanchez off mid-sentence. "Let's go back now."

He was surprised at first by my rude interruption then winced as he realized he'd forgotten that Johns was not privy to our recent decision regarding our own self-preservation.

Johns was at a loss. "Not going to worry about what? You don't want photos of these tracks?"

"No need," I told him. "All we have is an unidentified guy with a new boot heel taking a leak in the desert. No crime in that. Can't prove this guy had anything to do with your gun. C'mon. We need to get back." I nodded toward the cars where we bid Johns goodbye.

"Listen, guys," he said to us. "If you need anything, anything at all, call me. There's lots of open range out here."

It was just the way he said it that made me wonder if he suspected what we might have in mind. It was nearly dark by the time Sanchez and I got back to Olsen's apartment. Everyone there was growing concerned as I had not called, and after being properly chastised by the women for not doing so, it was time to eat. The three women had prepared a good supper. All of us sat around Olsen's couch with our plates on our laps and made casual small talk, but there was an underlying concern over our situation.

When the eating was done, Sanchez and I helped Jim to a lounge on the patio. The warm Texas summer night was a pleasant, if temporary, distraction. Brandy was poured and the three of us lit cigars.

"I'm not supposed to be doing any of this according to my doctor," Olsen said as he raised his brandy snifter and cigar. "But what the hell? As I almost found out, life is short so why not enjoy it while we can? So, boys, what's our next move?"

He stared at me and I looked seriously back at both of them. "As I see it," I began, "and don't be shy about telling me if you disagree, not one of us nor our wives, or kids in your case, Frank, are going to be safe while this guy is still walking this earth. I don't think he's the type to stop coming after us. Even if we can get enough on him to arrest him, his employers will have some high-priced attorney spring him in a matter of hours and we're back to where we are now." Sanchez looked like he was about to speak, but I held up my hand. "Hold on, Frank. This is something that needs to be thought through and talked through."

"We're law officers, for Christ's sake," Olsen growled. "You sayin' we're just gonna ice this guy like common murderers?"

"Murder is not the right word, Jim," I said. "I've thought this through and here's my opinion. This is just like war. You don't *murder* people in war, you kill them, and just like in war, there's only two ways for this to end. Either we kill him or he kills us, and maybe our families. Personally, I'd prefer it to be him. You both need to think about this carefully and, I mean, *really* think about it. This will be a life changing event for all of us, so this needs to be a unanimous decision without reservation. I wish we had more time to discuss it, but we don't." I glanced back and forth between them. "Like Jim says, you're cops, and providing that, by some miracle, we survive this, and we don't all go to prison when it's over, you two are going to have to live with it for the rest of your lives. You'll sure never be able to share any guilt feelings with anyone, or probably even talk to a shrink about it."

"What about telling the women?" Sanchez interjected. "It affects them also."

"Yes it does," I replied, "but how much you tell them is a decision you're going to have to make yourself. I've decided I'm going to tell Sonya, but only you know your women. Couple things for you to consider when deciding, though. First, can she handle it, emotionally, I mean? The second, the big one, of course, is can she keep her mouth shut? Some women have problems with that. No one, and I mean *no one*, can ever know anything about this. Remember, there's no statute of limitations on murder, which is what they'll call it. No one will ever give a shit that it's preemptive self-defense."

The three of us sat silently thinking about what I'd said through four sips of brandy and as many puffs on our cigars.

Sanchez spoke without hesitation. "You already know where I stand. Fuck this guy *and* the horse he rode in on."

Olsen looked up at me and asked, "There's no other way?"

I shook my head. "Jim, if I thought for a moment there was, we would not be talking about this now. Barring this guy just suddenly deciding to go away, which I think is highly unlikely, I'm convinced this is our only course of action to protect ourselves and our loved ones."

After another five minutes passed silently, Olsen said, "This is against everything I've ever been taught, but I don't see any other way either. We need to kill the evil son-of-a-bitch."

Sanchez looked at me with a grim expression and simply nodded.

I sat my cigar in the ashtray. "Okay, now that we've reached a consensus, we need to find this guy and take him out. We want to get him away from town, if at all possible. There's too much of a chance for innocents to get hurt, or for him to get away, or for us to get accused of murdering the guy, and we for sure don't want to get into any situation that would put us in confrontation with any other cops."

They both nodded, then Sanchez said, "What about his handlers? Don't you think they'd send someone to avenge him?"

"Maybe, but I don't think so if we do this right," I replied. "You have to remember, it's not like this guy is family to them. He's an employee. A contract killer. If he just disappears without a trace, they'll suspect foul play, of course, but without a body or any other information, who would they retaliate against? They'll figure that's the cost of doing business, or that he fell prey to one of his misadventures and they'll move on. No, we need to kill him and bury him out there in the desert where he'll never be found. Like I said, he'll just disappear, *if* we do it right and everybody dummies-up."

Frank was staring at me. "Not a side of you I've seen ,Jason. You can be a cold bastard."

"The Central Highlands of Vietnam taught me that it's not your weapons, or your training, or your reactions, or even your physical strength and ability that enables you to kill. Those skills help you kill, for sure, but they're just tools. No—" I looked at my cigar. "It's the *hard heart* that kills. You both need to harden your hearts, because this is going to be cold bastard work. Always keep it in your mind that this guy will do the same to you and your family without hesitation or remorse."

I nodded to Olsen reclining on the couch. "Never forget what he did to Jim at the drop of a hat, not to mention both the Indians. One more thing to consider. As police officers you have a certain mind set. You are trained and prepared to shoot to defend your life or the life of another. Oh, we've all made jokes about blowing some scrote away, and we for sure don't shed any tears when a bad guy dies as a result of a confrontation with a cop, but that's not the same as *planning* to deliberately kill without warning. If your hearts are not hard or if you don't accept beforehand what we are going to do and mentally prepare for it, you will hesitate when the time comes to pull the trigger, and if you hesitate even for an instant, this guy will kill you, because he won't hesitate. He might get *all* of us because one of us isn't ready. Hell, he might get all of us anyway."

"Damn, man, you're a cheery soul," Olsen said morosely.

"Just telling it like it is, Jim," I said as I stood. "On that note, I'm turning in, boys. We're going hunting early tomorrow."

CHAPTER 42

It Begins

Twenty seven miles from the pillow on which Jason's head lay, flames fueled by gasoline, rubber, plastic and vinyl were shooting high into the desert night. The flames immediately drew the attention of a U.S. Border Patrol Silverfox prototype observation drone, circling in an oval racetrack pattern seven miles away. The USBP pilot of the drone, sitting in a chair at a computer console in a covert building at the United States Marine Air Station in Yuma, Arizona, quickly told his observer to check with their own ground radar operator, the control tower in El Paso, and the FAA to see if there were any conflicts with any other aircraft in the in area.

The observer, who was sitting next to the pilot monitoring the images relayed by the drone's camera, did so. When told there were not any other aircraft in the immediate vicinity, the agent pilot notified his duty officer and requested permission to investigate the fire. Permission was granted and the pilot guided the drone toward the flames from its normal patrol quadrant above the interstate.

The Silverfox descended from its height of ten thousand feet down to just below five thousand, circling the fire. Adjusting the angle of the powerful telescopic high resolution camera protruding from the nose of the drone, the observer could easily see that the source of the flames was a burning vehicle, a pickup truck to be precise. The observer switched to the FLIR camera and scanned the surrounding desert floor. He couldn't point it at the fire, of course, as the optics would be overloaded by the light from the flames. No, he wanted to see the surrounding, darkened desert floor. Finding no other signs of life save for three concealed jack-rabbits and a pair of prowling coyotes, the observer advised the pilot who shrugged and returned the drone to its normal patrol area and height. The observer notified one of the USBP ground units in the area, and then called the Revas County Sheriff's Department.

Thirty minutes later, the midnight sheriff's deputy assigned to that particular area of desert, rolled up to the still smoking and foul smelling remains of the truck. A USBP 4wd SUV was already on the scene. The Border Patrol agent conversed with the deputy briefly before departing.

"No one around. Our drone checked out the area." The agent waved his hand at the dessert. "No bodies inside. Looks like a torch job. Maybe stolen, or an insurance scam. Anyway, it's your deal now, I'm outta here."

The deputy waved at the agent as the man drove away. After making sure there were no bodies inside as the agent had said, the deputy mused, *Well, no need to have county fire keep rolling this way. It's all over now. Nothing left to burn.* He called dispatch and cancelled the fire response, but did request a flat-bed tow truck. Looking at his watch, he smiled. *If I'm lucky and can waste enough time out here, this will be my going home call. I can sit out here waiting for the tow, finish my reports, and after doing the tow sheet, catch some sleep while the tow driver dicks around with the pickup.*

It was perfect. No one around for miles. Of course he'd have to turn his radio up loud so if dispatch called him he'd wake up, but this time of the morning, there wasn't much radio traffic. Listening for his call sign would be a small price to pay to get some extra shuteye.

The deputy walked around the smoking, stinking mess that had once been a pickup truck. It was still too hot to touch. Maybe he could get a VIN number off of the dash plate. As he passed the front end, he recognized the off-set double grill and the blackened Ram's head icon. "So you were once a Dodge pickup, huh?" he asked the truck. "Too bad. You look like you were once a pretty nice truck."

The deputy started back to his own vehicle. As he passed by the right rear wheel, he pointed his flashlight at the deformed tire. This tire didn't get as hot as the other three, which were now nothing more than lumps of black goo on the sand. He was curious about that, so he walked closer, illuminating the tire and wheel. *Fire is funny*, he thought. *Melt three tires but not the fourth.*

It was then he noticed that some of the paint inside the fender well had survived also. "Aha! You were a blue Dodge truck, eh?"

A thought suddenly struck him. *Wait. What was it I heard Lieutenant Davis talking about in the hallway yesterday? Oh yeah, Frank Sanchez was looking for a blue and silver Dodge pick-up. I think that's what he said.* The deputy got on his radio and asked dispatch for Sanchez's cell number.

e/ɔe/ɔ

As so often happens in my dreams, the dark-haired, green-eyed Victoria's Secret swim suit model was slowly walking toward me. Now she was reaching behind her back with both hands, about to undo her swimsuit top so that I could see, and hopefully fondle, those beautiful breasts.

She looked into my eyes and her perfect lips puckered as she spoke my name. "Jason!"

What the hell is this? Why is Sanchez's voice coming out of those beautiful lips?

"Jason, wake up, bud."

The knocking on the bedroom door destroyed what was left of the image of my midnight fantasy as I awoke and scowled. I was temporarily disoriented by not being in my own bed, but it passed instantly.

"Jason, you awake? I just got a call from one of my buddies. Another deputy. He's out on a call in the desert and may have found our pickup."

That brought me instantly alert. "Five minutes."

℮↗℈℮↗℈

We turned onto the sandy OHV trail off of the gravel access road. This land all belonged to the US Bureau of Land Management. After a fifteen-minute drive over sandy, rocky ground, we spotted the red and blue lights of the deputy's vehicle and the yellow flashing lights of the tow truck.

As we pulled up behind him, the deputy stepped out and greeted us. Introductions were made, and we walked to the charred remains of the truck.

"I finally got to the VIN. Last known registration was—" the deputy started to say,

"Hold it," Frank interrupted him. "Let me guess. A company which doesn't exist from another city?"

The deputy looked at him, shaking his head. "Actually, we don't know. The VIN doesn't match this truck. We're trying to run it down now."

"Doesn't really matter," I told them. "If it's the truck we think it is, you won't be able to trace it back to its source anyway. Mind if I have a look around?"

"Be my guest," the deputy replied. "You're the retired hot-shit crime scene guy I been hearin' 'bout, huh?"

"Well, I'm retired, or so I thought." I glanced at Frank with disdain. "And I was a crime scene guy. As far as how hot-shit I am, so far

I haven't caught anyone yet. By the way, how did you know to call Frank? This is supposed to be on the down-low."

He didn't look up from his clipboard as he said, "I overheard Lieutenant Davis talking about it back at the office."

I rolled my eyes at Sanchez. "So much for secrecy."

I left Frank and the deputy to exchange pleasantries between themselves and walked around the truck. There wasn't much left. The entire truck, save for the right tire, had been destroyed by the flames. I walked the desert floor in an ever widening spiral with the truck as the center. About thirty yards from it, I found something that concerned me.

Frank walked up behind me. "What?" he asked.

I pointed to the tracks in front of me. "Cowboy boots, eh? Looks like this is our truck. Wait. Are those quad tracks or something?" There were knobby tire tracks next to the boot tracks. I knelt down to examine them.

"Think he had it in the back of the truck?" Sanchez asked "Used it to split, maybe?"

"Not likely," I replied. "No tracks back by the bed of the truck or between there and here, and these tracks were left by a two-seater, not a quad. Two-seaters won't fit in the back of the truck."

Sanchez frowned. "You think our guy has a partner?"

I stared off into the desert, thinking out loud. "Shit, I hope not. That'll change the whole equation. Anything is possible, I guess, but it doesn't really fit his M.O. Our guy seems to prefer to work alone. Less chance of someone else fucking up his work or talking out of turn."

Sanchez pursed his lips. "You're saying it was some random encounter with an OHV rider out here? Maybe, our guy talked him into a ride."

I looked back at the tracks then at Sanchez. "Or jacked someone's OHV at gunpoint. Either way, this just got a whole lot more complicated, I'm thinking."

The other deputy yelled over at us, "Frank, you guys find something over there?" he asked.

I quickly told Sanchez to not say anything about the tracks we'd found.

"Nah, just takin' a leak," he yelled back.

"Can I let the tow guy get this thing outta here now?" he yelled.

Frank told him it was good to go.

As we walked back toward the other deputy, another thought occurred to me. "Frank, since we're out of touch with the office for a few days, ask your buddy there to call you if any missing persons reports come in over the next couple days, or if any bodies show up unexpectedly."

"Okay, but why?" he asked.

"Think about it," I replied. "If some poor, unlucky schmo just happened to be recreating out here and came along and gave our guy a ride..." I let the thought sink in.

"Oh, shit!"

"Exactly."

CHAPTER 43

Razor

The Polaris Razor 800-S was an impressive machine, Rocha thought. It tore across the desert landscape at almost 60 miles per hour. With an 800-cc engine, nineteen inch wheels, and only Rocha's weight as cargo, it handled the desert terrain with ease as its power-to-weight ratio was excellent. This machine's engine apparently had been altered by the owner, and it felt like it could go much faster, but even over this fairly even ground, one never knew what was just out of the reach of the headlights.

Rocha didn't want to wreck the machine as it might come in handy later, or even worse, injure himself. He reminded himself that he was not wearing the helmet. The Arai motocross helmet that the driver of the Razor had been wearing had been too small for Rocha.

Just after the truck had begun to burn, a set of small headlights had come toward him across the sand, taking Rocha by surprise. The Razor stopped just short of where he had been standing, away from the heat of the flames. Rocha had originally been prepared to hike the seven miles cross country back to the safe house. It would not have been a problem for him. He was in excellent shape, the terrain was reasonably flat, and he had his hand-held GPS. The appearance of the Razor was an unexpected annoyance, but then he recognized it as a real convenience. Of course, the driver would have to be disposed of.

The man driving the Razor pulled up and asked Rocha if he could be of assistance, obviously thinking there had been a mishap. He accepted the offered ride, telling the driver of the Razor his truck had caught fire when the transmission had become too hot as he was four-wheeling through the sand. The driver of the Razor wasn't suspicious about the late hour, as he himself was out on his OHV after dark. He invited Rocha to climb in.

After traveling a mile from the truck, Rocha asked the driver to pull over so he could relieve himself. The man agreed, saying that it would be a good idea for himself to do the same. Rocha climbed out, turned his back as if unzipping his fly. He waited for the driver of the Razor to dismount and unzip also. As the driver stood with his back turned to Rocha, holding his penis, Rocha shot him three times between the shoulder blades with his .357 magnum revolver. The three 124-grain, semi-jacketed hollow point bullets didn't lose much of their 1,527-feet-per-second velocity, nor did the hollow cavity in the tips of the bullets have time to expand any great amount as they entered the center of the man's back in a three-inch triangle.

The driver was a slightly built man. Had he had more muscle mass or been of a fatter build, the bullets might have been able to perform as they had been designed to do, not that it mattered. All three bullets passed completely through the driver's body. The ballistic energy from the magnum loads shattered his spine, ruptured both lungs, then exploded his heart before exiting his chest.

The man collapsed like a deflated balloon, though his brain continued to function for almost thirty seconds after his body hit the ground. His legs and arms twitched and jerked several times then went still. Rocha had noticed a shovel strapped to the rear of the roll cage of the Razor. He stepped over the driver's body and retrieved the spade from its rack. Rocha then dug a hole, six feet long and three deep, next to the spot where the man lay. It was not hard work as the desert was mostly sand here. He could have just left the body where it lay, but desert scavengers, particularly vultures, might attract attention to the corpse.

Removing the driver's helmet, wallet, and jewelry, he rolled the man's body into the grave. He then scooped up the coagulated blood and sand mixture, where the man had gone down, as best he could and tossed it into the hole. Rocha filled in the shallow grave, replacing the shovel in the rack. After tossing the driver's personal effects into the passenger seat, Rocha climbed behind the steering wheel of the Razor and drove back and forth over the area, eliminating any remaining trace of blood or the grave site. When this was complete, he took the small hand held GPS from his shirt pocket and checked his course back through the desert to the safe house. Giving the dead man no more thought, Rocha stepped on the gas and the Razor took off like a shot. He found driving the small buggy over the open ground quite exhilarating and decided he would keep the machine at the safe house for now. Later, when he needed it no longer he would burn it just like he did the truck.

It was dawn when he stopped in the desert just short of the road that fronted the safe house. He had judged it pretty close and was a mile south of the house. After making sure there was no traffic in sight, he drove the machine to the house, then up the gravel driveway, and around the back. Rocha covered it with the same tarp he'd used to cover the truck.

He was tired. The night's events had taken a toll. He would worry about obtaining another means of transportation after some well-deserved sleep. Rocha took one last look around the property. Satisfied that his privacy was complete, he entered the house, went into the bedroom, reloaded the revolver, and placed it under the pillow. The MP5 he leaned against the wall, within easy reach, then he disrobed and lay down.

His last thoughts, as he closed his eyes, were of a new plan to eliminate the two deputies. *Perhaps it is time to try a different tactic. The deputies probably have families, or at least wives, or girlfriends maybe? Family is always a cop's main weakness.*

It was decided. Rocha would go for the families to draw the men out. He smiled just as the blackness of sleep overtook him.

CHAPTER 44

Tracks

The tumblers on the Schlage dead bolt clicked into alignment as Sanchez inserted the key Olsen had given him into the front door lock. We didn't just walk in, however. We stood to one side of the door as Sanchez called out through the three inch open door. "Emerson."

"Biggins," Olsen called back from the couch.

It was a coded sign and countersign we had worked out in case the worst should happen and the killer showed up at the house. The juvenile reference to large breasts had, again, been Olsen's.

As we walked inside, I saw the Spaz 12 shotgun laying across Olsen's lap. The menacing snout of the weapon slightly angled toward the front door, obviously having been pointed our way as he'd heard us approach.

"Be careful where you point that thing," I told him.

Tammy walked in in her pajamas. "That's what I tell him all the time." She smiled coyly, glancing at the fly of Olsen's pajama bottoms which had popped open. "Oh, you mean the shotgun. Jim sweetie, you might want to close the barn door. Everyone can see your *other* gun."

Olsen shifted position and re-buttoned his fly.

"Holy crap, you guys stink," Sonya exclaimed as she greeted Sanchez and myself with hot coffee.

"Stink?" I asked.

"Yeah, as in fire and smoke stink."

"Oh." I sniffed myself and nodded.

Chi-Chi was still asleep, but the other two girls joined us as we related the night's events.

"So you don't know who was in the dune-buggy thing?" Tammy asked.

"Nope," Sanchez told her. "I think maybe the guy has an accomplice, but who knows? Jason here doesn't think so."

I shook my head. "No, that's not quite what I said. I just said our guy didn't bring the OHV with him in the back of the truck, but no matter, either way our guy left in some type of OHV."

"So why didn't you follow the tracks?" Sonya asked.

"It was too dark. There's so many tire tracks out there we wouldn't have been able to tell one from another," I replied. "That's pretty much it as far as our night went."

With the end of the night's events described, both women got up and headed into the kitchen.

"You guys want breakfast?" Tammy called back through the door.

"Wow, that sounds good," Sanchez replied.

"And some sleep," I added just as Sanchez's cell phone buzzed and vibrated.

It was the deputy from the truck fire. The two men conversed on the phone for a good ten minutes. When he hung up, Sanchez turned to Olsen and myself.

"That was Daniel Johnson, the deputy we met out at the truck. His wife is one of our day-shift dispatchers. I guess he clued her in to be listening for any missing persons called in."

I perked up a bit. "Yeah?"

"Well, seems that a call just now came in from a group of guys who are all hanging out for a week together in their RVs riding their quads and such, saying one of their crew is missing."

"Nothing else? What happened to 'where' or 'when'?" I asked.

"Daniel didn't have all the details. He's going to call me back if she can get any other info about it."

One hour later we were just cleaning up the breakfast dishes and contemplating naps when Sanchez's cell phone again summoned him. A second extended conversation with Johnson took place, after which Sanchez said, "Jim, can you pull up a BLM map of this area on the internet?"

"No need," Olsen replied. "I have a topo map CD of this whole sector that I ordered last year when that little kid went missing, remember? Hey, Tammy, can you hand me my CD binder, please?"

The girl retrieved a thick black CD binder case from the bedroom. Olsen flipped through several pages of the binder until he found what he was looking for. He inserted it into the CD drive on his laptop, and several seconds later we were looking at a map of the desert displayed on the flat-screen TV on the wall.

Sanchez got up and walked toward the TV. "Apparently, this guy went missing on a night ride with several of his buddies when they got separated. According to them, they were right...here," Sanchez said, pointing to a spot on the screen, "when they lost sight of his headlights.

They went back to search for him but couldn't find him in the dark. They said they weren't too worried at the time because the terrain wasn't steep or hazardous and the guy was experienced. He had all his safety gear, water, and snacks and had a GPS. It wasn't until late morning when the guy didn't show up, that they started to become concerned."

I looked at the map on the screen lost in thought

Olsen spoke up. "You thinking he might have run into Rocha?" He looked at the TV. "The spot where they think he went missing is about ten miles from where you said the truck was burning. Pretty far away to be connected, don't you think?"

"Not really," I replied. "On open ground like that, when you're on a quad or a two-seater, ten miles is nothing, as long as you've got the gas, of course. Frank, did Johnson say what kind of OHV this guy was driving?"

Sanchez looked at me. "An orange, white, and black Razor 800-S. So far, the TSDPS's air search hasn't turned up anything. Tracks from hundreds of OHVs go every-which-way out there. My buddy told me the highway patrol is going to search until they get low on fuel, proba- bly only two or three more hours. Some sheriff's posse SAR volun- teers on OHVs and horses are going to go out also."

I was looking back at the map and both Sanchez and Olsen were studying me.

"You think he ran into Rocha out there and is probably dead, don't you?" Olsen asked.

I turned to him and nodded. "I'd bet next month's retirement check on it."

¢⁄つ¢⁄つ

The search plane was joined by a USBP helicopter at mid-day, and together they searched the area until dusk. We were all surprised by the extent of this air effort, that is until we heard later that day that the group of men sharing their passion for four wheeling were all high-rent doctor buddies from the Dallas/Fort Worth area. The missing man was a prominent and well-respected surgeon. His family was big money in Dallas, which explained all the attention this search was getting. The man's money and social standing were now doing the talking.

Both aircraft landed just before dark, but the OHV search lasted well into the night. Nothing was found of the missing Razor or it's renowned-surgeon driver. Since the search area was relatively small and the ground for the most part flat and open, the search was discon- tinued at midnight, all possibilities exhausted. The posse and the aircraft were out again at first light, but another day of searching proved just as fruitless. Sheriff's deputies, the TSDPS, and the USBP would, of course, continue to keep an eye out for the missing man and vehicle over the next few weeks as they pursued their normal duties, but until any new leads or information were uncovered, the formal search was officially ended in the early evening hours of the second day.

"Who knows?" said one of the local posse volunteers to his partner as they unsaddled their horses and loaded them back into their horse trailer. "Maybe he's down in some Mexican whore house with five women and a donkey, or trying to score some coke."

"I doubt that, this guy being who he is," replied the other man. "But if he was stupid enough to do something like that, his body is probably laying in a Mexican ditch about now and his head is on a stick being used as a fuckin' Tiki Torch at some cartel member's back yard patio barbeque."

Looking south toward the distant border, the first man replied, "Yeah, lots of folks just disappear in that shit-hole of a country. We'll probably never know what happened to him. Just goes to show, you can be highly educated and still be a friggin' dumb-ass."

"Hey, just like our president."

"Absolutely. I'm hungry. Let's go eat."

CHAPTER 45

Concerns

The sound of the engine of the light plane operated by the TSDPS woke Rocha from his nap. He looked out the kitchen window just in time to see the blue-and-white, high-wing Cessna 206 fly over the safe house. The words *HIGHWAY PATROL* were plainly visible on the side, and the plane was unusually low as it passed over.

Rocha stepped out as the plane banked left and circled the house, the pilot obviously looking over the house and the surrounding desert. Rocha waved at the pilot, who was plainly visible in the left hand seat. Rocha was concerned, but not overly so. He knew the plane might be searching for the missing Razor and it's driver, but the OHV was well covered under the tan-colored tarp, the tarp matching the color of the desert soil very closely. Rocha had even placed several small bushes he'd pulled from the ground near the house, on top of the tarp. He knew from his own experiences that from a moving plane, even as low as five-hundred feet, the Razor would be impossible to distinguish.

The Cessna made one more pass, then the pilot waggled its wings in answer to Rocha's wave, and flew off. Of more concern was the distinctive whop, whop, whop of the rotor blades of a Bell 412 helicopter, a slimmed down and newer version of the vaunted Huey UH-1 of Vietnam fame. He'd heard the chopper in the distance thirty minutes later.

Rocha picked up his binoculars, this time stepping out onto the front porch. The green-and-white helicopter was about a mile away, moving slowly at low altitude, north to south. Through his binoculars, he could clearly see the gold U.S. Border Patrol emblem painted on the side. This *did* worry him. Whether they were looking for the Razor or just searching for a *mojado*, the low altitude combined with the substantial rotor wash beneath the main rotor blades of the helicopter could easily destroy his camouflage-tarp-arrangement covering the

Razor. He let out a sigh of relief as the chopper turned its tail toward the house and moved slowly away.

Still, a helicopter so close to the ground was not something he had planned on. He needed to re-think the hiding location and the covering of the Razor just in case the helicopter should return, but with this search in progress, he would have to wait until darkness to move the machine.

Over the next few hours, Rocha kept a sharp lookout for the two aircraft, particularly the helicopter, but neither returned. When darkness fell, he walked around the house to the dilapidated shed in the rear yard. Rummaging around inside with a flashlight, he found an old ball-peen hammer and a coffee can half full of rusted nails. He uncovered the Razor, started it up and pulled it up within inches of the side wall of the house, facing it toward the back yard. Recovering it with the tarp, he spent the next thirty minutes, nailing the tarp to the wall. When Rocha was confident the tarp was secure, he carried over two large rocks, some scrap lumber, and even two old rusted car wheels that had been laying near the shed, placing all on the opposite edge of the tarp, pinning it to the ground. The last wheel he moved had come with a surprise. A surprise in the form of a two foot long Western Diamond-back Rattlesnake which had taken up residence beneath the underside of the wheel.

When Rocha lifted the wheel, the snake's tale immediately started its tell-tail buzzing and the snake coiled into its S-shaped. cocked position ready to strike. Rocha was no stranger to these desert vipers, however. He just backed away slowly, knowing that in a few minutes the reptile would calm itself and slither away to find a warmer spot. Still, Rocha decided he would start being a little more careful around the shed. A trip to the local hospital with a snake bite was not on his schedule.

When he'd finished, he stood back and examined his efforts. The tarp covered almost everything. It came all the way to the ground on the rear and sides of the Razor shielding it completely from view from both the front and side of the house. The front rail bumper of the machine was slightly visible from the back yard area as the tarp didn't quite reach the ground on that side, but he was confident that the machine was far enough back into its make-shift garage, and enough of the tarp hung over the front that he didn't *think* it could be spotted from the air.

The open end of the tarp might actually be a good thing. With that end slightly open, he could quickly climb in and drive it out without removing the tarp, if it came to that. He completed his task by placing pieces of the scrap lumber strategically on top of the tarp, both to help hold it in place and to make the whole mess look like a junk pile to the casual observer. Rocha walked back into the house, retrieved extra ammunition for the MP5 and his revolver, along with bottles of water and some canned stew, placing it all in the Razor just as an added precaution.

Finally satisfied with his efforts, he sat down to think, rest, and drink some well-deserved and badly needed water. He was sure his employers were growing impatient, as was he. He needed to wrap this thing up. It had turned from a simple mission of whacking two small-time drug dealers, into something much more complex than he'd wanted. But he was into it now and he would finish it.

He decided he would walk into town and steal a car. It would have to be a vehicle that no one would miss for a few days. He remembered passing by a tow company's storage and impound lot on this edge of town as he'd driven out to the safe house for the first time. It was perfect, he thought. *It's fairly close, and there will be only a chain link fence and maybe a guard dog to deal with.* He selected two items from his equipment bag then walked out the front door.

The evening was very pleasant. Warm, but not uncomfortably so, with an ever-so-slight breeze bringing the smells of the desert to Rocha's nose as he walked along the shoulder of the road. There was only a sliver of a moon showing, just enough to see the black outline of the asphalt. An hour's brisk walk brought him to a point where the lights of the town were visible. There were no lights in the tow yard, however, though Rocha could see it was full of cars and trucks. Many of them were wrecked junkers, but several looked drivable. He noticed that even the office and the metal building that served as a shop were dark.

This pleased Rocha. He examined the fence. At one time it had made a formidable barrier, but time and neglect had taken its toll. Entire sections of the duel strands of razor wire along the top edge were missing and the fence was rusting away in several locations.

Walking the rear perimeter, he came across a spot where the fence had been severely pushed outward. It was obvious that someone had struck the fence with a vehicle from the inside, probably while parking it. The fence being pushed outward left a two foot gap between the bottom of the steel mesh and the ground, creating a convenient, if somewhat dirty, entry point. Rocha whistled softly and shook the fence, hoping to attract the guard dog, if indeed there was one. He then readied the .22 caliber Ruger Mark II pistol he had retrieved from his equipment bag, along with the suppressor. He smiled as he again thought how most people commonly and mistakenly call a suppressor a silencer and screwed it onto the end of the barrel. *Americans watch far too much TV. It will contribute to their downfall one day soon.*

The Ruger was a favorite of Rocha's, and he used it frequently. He'd had an unscrupulous gunsmith remove the front sight and it's support band, in the process bobbing the barrel three-quarters of an inch. The gunsmith then re-crowned the end of the barrel and threaded it so it would accept the one-inch-diameter-by six-inch-long suppressor. It was highly illegal, of course, *But then, so was killing people with it.*

With the suppressor installed and no sights, it was strictly a short range weapon, but it was deadly. When loaded with sub-sonic .22 hollow point ammunition, the only audible sound of the weapon's firing was a soft pfffft and the clicking of the bolt as it cycled open and shut, neither of which could be heard from more than several feet away. The only drawback to the weapon was its overall length. With the suppressor screwed on, the pistol was somewhat long for comfortable concealed carry. He whistled a bit louder this time and shook the fence harder. Still, there was no response from a dog. After he'd seen the gap at the bottom of the fence, he really didn't think there would be. No self-respecting guard dog would hang around inside the fence when he could easily pass through this gap to freedom. Sliding the weapon back into his waistband, Rocha slid under the fence, then stood up, brushed himself off, and began his car shopping. Soon he found a late model Crown Victoria that would fit his needs perfectly. It was a nondescript, white-painted vehicle, dirty with nothing special about it. It looked like just another car on the road. The only problem was the registration sticker on the windshield was expired. Nothing he could do about that now.

He decided he would cover it with dirt from the outside and chance that it wouldn't be seen for the short time he would need the car. The man removed the rear plate with his Leatherman multi-tool and re-placed it with a license plate from a late model Ford pickup parked near the office. His first inclination was to break the steering column and hot-wire the ignition but, as an afterthought, he walked over and looked through the office window with his small flashlight. He could see rows of keys hanging on a hook-board behind the counter. He needed to get to those keys without leaving any sign of a break-in.

Rocha quietly began checking the windows of the office, hoping to find one unlocked. What he found was just as good. On the far side, he discovered a large evaporation-type swamp-cooler mounted on a wooden platform. The cooler's output vent was loosely stuck into an open window of the office. He slid the cooler away from the window just enough to slip past it and, once inside, pulled it back into place. He spent the next several minutes searching the hook-board for the keys to the Ford, finally locating them by the small, attached tag bearing the license plate number. As a bonus, he spotted a key labeled *Front Gate* hanging at the bottom of the board. *My lucky night*, he thought. *The damaged fence, no dog, the swamp cooler, and now the gate. Too bad I'm not in Vegas.*

The Ford's engine did nothing but crank over and over the first four times he turned the key in the ignition, but finally on his fifth attempt the engine caught and it started. Rocha let it warm up until it idled smoothly. Looking under the dash, he found the fuse block and, again using his small light and multi-tool, removed the fuses that allowed electrical power to flow to both the brake lights, tail lights, and the back-up lights. Totally blacked out now, the vehicle slowly rolled toward the gate. Making sure there were no other headlights visible on the road in front of the business, he unlocked the gate and pulled the Ford into the outer parking lot. He knew he had to move quickly now.

Leaving the Ford idling unattended lest it not start again, was a risk. Rocha swiftly retraced his steps. Walking back inside the lot, he closed and locked the gate and re-entered the office. He hung the gate key back on its hook on the board, however, just before he locked the office door by pulling it shut from the outside, he spotted several pairs of work overalls on hangars in an open closet. The words *Desert Action Tow* were stenciled on the backs of each. Hoping to avoid crawling through the dirt again in his own clothing, he retrieved a pair that looked to be his size and slipped into them. Rocha then exited the tow yard the same way he'd come in. After sliding under the fence for the second time, he jogged around the perimeter to the front parking lot where his newly acquired ride sat idling a bit more smoothly than when he left it minutes earlier. He climbed in and slowly drove away.

After he'd put a mile between the towing yard and himself, Rocha pulled over to the shoulder and replaced the two fuses, restoring his brake and back-up lights. Fifteen minutes later, he pulled the Ford around behind the safe house, where it would not be visible from the road, and parked it. Rocha entered the kitchen pulling off the overalls just as his cell phone rang. He recognized the number.

"Yes?"

"Mr. Lopez will be available at 9:00 a.m. tomorrow. Please conclude your business there and return as soon as possible."

The line went dead. *So Fernando Lopez will finally bail out of jail at 9:00 a.m. This will change things.* Rocha looked at his watch. *Good. Time enough for a short nap, a shower, and a shave.* An idea suddenly came to him. There would be no need to clean up, after all. Not for what he now had in mind.

He looked down at the half removed overalls and smiled. Within minutes, still clad in the rumpled and dirty overalls, he was asleep on the couch. To Rocha, it seemed as if he'd just closed his eyes when the alarm on his cell phone woke him three hours later. After a cup of bitter coffee left over in the pot from two days hence, he gathered a few necessary items and walked to the Ford. He let it warm up, then shifted into Drive, and pulled out of the driveway, turning the car toward town.

It was 9:20 a.m. when Rocha, looking through his binoculars, saw Lopez exit the front double doors of the jail, accompanied by his attorney. Rocha was parked in the parking lot of the county offices, along with the other dirty white county cars, directly across the street from the jail. The two men shook hands, then the attorney walked one way on the sidewalk and Lopez the other. Rocha could easily determine the path Lopez was going to follow. Road construction at the end of the street would make it necessary for Lopez to turn the corner and walk a full block on an adjoining side street.

Rocha started the car and pulled out of the lot, turning the opposite direction Lopez was walking. While he could have just pulled up next to Lopez and shot him as he walked, of course, a drive-by was not Rocha's style. He looked upon such tactics with disdain. These were the techniques of street thugs and gangs, and he considered them cowardly and un-professional, not to mention the fact that the outcome was always unpredictable. Many times there was collateral damage, with innocent people nearby getting hit by stray bullets, and *that* drew cops like flies to cow shit. It also whipped the public into a frenzy. Besides, even if he were so inclined, he was not armed with the proper weapon for such a task.

Rocha hurriedly circled the block and parked near the curb on the side street Lopez was rapidly approaching. Leaving the engine running, Rocha got out, still wearing the tow yard coveralls, and opened the hood of the Ford. He positioned himself under the hood so as to be able to see Lopez approaching the back end of the Crown Victoria. He placed the suppressed .22 just inside the engine compartment within easy reach. To the casual observer, Rocha was simply a mechanic trying to fix someone's car. Rocha hoped no one would notice the lack of a tow truck close-by. He began to tinker under the hood, hoping he had Lopez's route and timing figured right. He didn't have to wait long for his answer. Lopez turned the corner and walked toward him.

CHAPTER 46

Sunshine

The term "perfect weather" was used often in the spring. In Southwest Texas in the summer, the term wasn't bantered about nearly as much, but this morning was an exception.

Lopez was a happy man as he walked along the sidewalk in the warm morning sun. After all, it was a beautiful day, he was free on bail, and he was on his way to get the money he had stashed in a locker in the Greyhound Bus Station for just such an emergency as this. And then, of course, he was getting the hell out of here.

He had no intention of hanging around for his court date. By the time that rolled around, he would be back in Guadalajara, living with his brother. He shrugged. After a few years he would sneak back across the border and do it all over again. *Who knows?* He smiled. *By that time this black American President, in his quest to keep himself and his party in power by buying the votes of minorities and, in particular, Hispanics, might do away with the border all together and allow everyone, even known criminals, to cross freely back and forth at will.*

Lopez laughed out loud at that one. Americans were such fools. He *was* mildly concerned that word of his talking to the police might have leaked, and he'd have to lay low for some time, but so far all seemed well. The rumors that a gunman was after him apparently had been false.

He enjoyed the morning as he walked. With the exception of a few parked cars, the street was quiet and deserted. The sky was crystal clear, the sun warm with an ever-so-slight breeze blowing, making for the perfect temperature. The moving air was also spreading the fragrance of the freshly cut grass from a park back around the corner. As he walked past the rear bumper of a car parked at the curb with its hood up, he noticed a Mexican mechanic, wearing a set of overalls with the words *Desert Action Tow* on the back, working on the exposed engine. When he passed the front of the car, the mechanic stood up and smiled at him, then appeared to offer what, at first, appeared to be some kind of tool. Too late he saw the ugly snout of the suppressor, suddenly recognizing it for what it was.

Pffft-click. Pffft-click.

Lopez felt like two wasps had stung him in the chest. He looked down, surprised to see blood spreading across the front of his shirt. He reached for his wounds but his hands would not respond. *That's weird*, he thought. Suddenly his right leg wobbled and gave out, then his left did the same. He was falling. He could taste blood in his mouth. Lopez crumpled to the pavement. His mind still could not accept what was happening. He'd been shot and was dying.

He tried to speak. Maybe to ask why, or maybe to offer a penance, but no words came out, only a gagging, gargling sound and frothy bright red arterial blood. He saw the mechanic look both ways up and down the street, then step over to stand above him. The mechanic pointed the black snout of the suppressor at his forehead. The last impressions registering in Lopez mind were the tiny flash at the end of the suppressor's muzzle and the hammering of the 40 grain hollow-point bullet as it impacted his skull just above the right eye. Pffft-click.

Rocha looked around one last time. The street was still deserted. Rocha closed the hood, got into the Ford, and pulled away from the curb, leaving Lopez's body sprawled on the sidewalk, a pool of blood spreading on the concrete under him. *That worked out extremely well*, Rocha thought as he approached the end of the block. Better than he could have hoped. With Lopez presenting himself so handily for the slaughter, there would be no need to go after the two deputies now, after all, though it chaffed him that he had made the plan to hunt and kill them and would now abandon it.

The risk was not worth the gain just for personal satisfaction, he decided. Rocha was tempted to just drive to the nearest interstate on-ramp and point the Ford toward El Paso and, subsequently, Juarez, but he knew that would leave ends untied. He had weapons and other items at the safe house that he needed to either retrieve or dispose of, as well as destroying the Razor OHV. He would keep the Ford for transportation to El Paso, then abandon it near the border. It would be found, of course, but the authorities would write it off as just another car theft.

Rocha was pleased with himself. *By tonight I will be well on my way south, leaving this useless piece of desert behind me.*

CHAPTER 47

Flight

The red-and-white Cessna 182A Skylane sat near the hanger, it's propeller spinning as the engine idled, warming up. The pilot, sitting in the left hand seat adjusting the fuel/air mixture, was Daryl Jackson. The plane belonged to a friend of Jackson's. He shut down the engine as we approached.

Sanchez and I had been prepared to hire a pilot and rent a plane in an attempt to get a bird's-eye view of the area surrounding the spot where the Dodge truck had been found. I figured Davis would throw a fit over the expenditure, but we'd tell him after the fact, not before.

It was then I remembered how eagerly Jackson had been to help out should we "need anything." When I called him and explained what we wanted to do, Jackson jumped at the chance. He told us he would fly us for nothing, and that there was no need to rent a plane. He had a close friend that lived in Pecos who was also a retired pilot. The man owned a flying service out at the airport and Jackson was sure his friend would loan him a plane, in this case the Cessna. Jackson made the call and his buddy agreed, as long as we paid the insurance and fuel. As an afterthought, I called Michael Johns on the off chance he might want to go up with us. He knew that particular area of the desert better than anyone, it being so close to the reservation boundary.

As it turned out he was on his day off and he also jumped at that chance to go flying. I told him to meet us at the flying service hangar. Johns was waiting for us when the two of us drove in.

Seeing him standing by his Tahoe, I was confused and nodded at the marked police unit. "I thought you said you were on a day off?"

"Oh, the Tahoe," he said. "I get to drive it around all the time now, as long as I don't do anything stupid with it, *and* I'm willing to re-spond to an emergency. It's a perk."

"Sweet," I said. "I bet that saves you some coin on gas."

"Yeah, but like I said, even if I'm off-duty and something goes down at The Res, I have to respond no matter what I'm doing, but it's a good trade-off. I get the better end of the deal. If I leave town, I can't take it, of course."

The three of us found Jackson doing his pre-flight on the small plane as we approached the hangar. As he loaded two nylon equipment bags on the floorboard behind his seat, I explained to him that we wanted to fly over the area of the burned out pick-up truck, and that there were just too many vehicle tracks in the sand to make any sense of it from the ground. Maybe it would look different from the air.

"What's in the bags?" I asked him.

"Nothing exciting," he replied. "Some personal gear in one and two gallons of water and some MREs in the other. I always carry both bags when I fly the desert. You just never know where you might end up sometime."

When Jackson was satisfied that all was in order with the aircraft, he climbed in, motioned us all toward the tail of the plane, and re-started the machine. He then yelled at us over the engine noise, asking us if we were ready. We all nodded.

Not knowing if any of us were experienced in the art of climbing into a small plane with the engine running, he waved us to the door on the right side, yelling "Watch the prop. Walk around the tail and come up from the rear."

I needed no such warning. Several years before I had retired, I had been called upon to photograph an "industrial accident," one of the more gruesome tasks of the Crime Scene Bureau, at a local regional airport. In the dark, the pilot of a small plane, much like this one as a matter of fact, had landed to perform some task which escapes me now, maybe to take a leak. The man left the engine running for some reason. He climbed out of the cockpit and, in the dark, walked right into his own spinning propeller. The engine of the plane was only idling but that fact made no difference. The whirling aluminum prop caught the man on top of his right shoulder, one blade slicing all the way down through the middle of his torso to his belt line before the engine stalled. Surprisingly, the man was still alive when the patrol officer arrived, but only for about two minutes. Another ghost for the collection.

Johns climbed in the rear seat and Sanchez prepared to do the same when his cell phone rang. He stepped away from the plane to listen and talk. When he hung up he motioned me over away from the noise of the engine. "That was Davis. Fernando Lopez is dead."

"What? You've got to be *shittin'* me," I blurted out. "What the hell happened?"

He shrugged. "No one seems to know. No one saw anything or heard anything after his attorney walked him out of the jail. They found him dead on a sidewalk on that side street by the construction near the jail. He was shot three times, apparently at close range with a small caliber. Twice to the chest, once in the forehead. It's a jurisdictional mess, I guess. City police are there and they're arguing over the scene with the State CSB guys, who are doing the scene as a favor for the Feds. Davis is having to oversee it all since Lopez was technically still in the county's custody. The L-T says it looks like a professional hit. Our guy?"

"You really need to ask?" I responded, shaking my head and thinking that while Lopez was no loss to society, he still might have been useful. "I'll bet the Feds are shitting a brick. He was their whole gun case."

"Davis wants to know what the hell we're doing going up in an airplane." Sanchez said. "He wants us to come back to the office. Actually, I think he wants *me* to come back to the office and *you* to go away."

"So what'd you tell him?" I asked.

"I told him we had a lead we were following up on and we'd check in with him later."

"I'll bet that pissed him off," I said.

Sanchez shook his head. "I thought it would, too, but he's so distracted by all the crap with the missing surgeon and now this Lopez killing, he doesn't know whether to shit or wind his wristwatch. All he said was, 'Okay' and to get back as soon as possible."

I shrugged and jerked my head at the waiting plane. "Let's go."

Sanchez and I boarded the Cessna. The seats in the plane's interior were configured with a single seat in the far back where Johns settled himself, a double seat in the center, where Sanchez placed himself, joking, "I don't like the front seat, the mountains are always up there."

Jackson piloted from the left front seat and I sat in the right front. It was a tight squeeze for me, with the second set of controls taking up much of the space. As I was seated right there, I shut and latched the right side door. Jackson reached across me and checked it. Nodding, he then told us all to put on headset/microphone combinations similar to the one he already had on, that hung on hooks near each seat. After making sure the headsets were all working properly and we could hear each other, Jackson taxied the Cessna away from the hangar, making contact with the tower as the plane rolled along. "Pecos, Cessna 182 Alpha requesting departure southwest at 0800 hours."

The tower answered him. "Cessna 182 Alpha, Pecos, cleared for immediate departure runway 3 Romeo. Squawk 230.3. Winds southwest at 5 knots. Visibility 20 miles. Be advised, United Express 737 inbound to the northeast at the outer marker at 10 miles, descending from ten thousand. Have a good flight."

"Pecos, Cessna 182 Alpha roger and thanks. See you in a couple hours."

Jackson turned onto the designated runway and throttled up. Two minutes later we were airborne, climbing to three thousand feet.

"Did you have to file any kind of flight plan?" I asked Jackson.

"No," he replied, his voice a bit tinny through the headphones. "We're not required to if you're just out recreational flying over an unpopulated area and not close to some airport or other restricted area."

"Do we have any minimum altitude that we have to abide by?" I continued.

"Same answer," he replied. "But it's not a good idea to go much below a thousand feet. Doesn't give you much space to work with in case a problem develops. That whole airflow-over-the-wing thing can be kind of important."

I snorted.

"You fly?" he asked me.

"Not really," I replied. "Oh, I've taken the controls from friends who've taken me up in *their* planes, but never landed or taken off or anything. I did get to try my hand in a Huey once. What a joke. Army W-3 I knew was the pilot and he took me up in his bird on a Sunday. He needed to log some hours. His co-pilot moved out of the way for a few minutes. Hardest thing I've ever tried. It really *is* like trying to ride a unicycle while perched on top of a basketball. I was all over the sky, but my buddy said I didn't do too bad for my first time. I think he was just being nice, though, since he kept his hands very close to the cyclic stick and the collective and never took his feet off the pedals."

Jackson chuckled at that one and banked the plane southwest toward the area where the Dodge truck had been found.

I continued the conversation as we flew. "Is this the only plane your friend owns?"

"No. He's got a couple 'tail-draggers' and a twin Beech. He wanted to loan us that one. Said it's much roomier inside, but I told him we needed the high-wing configuration of this Cessna since we're doing the low and slow observation thing."

I nodded my agreement with his decision. "What else did you fly in the military?"

"Nothing glamorous," Jackson replied. "Before I made the jump to Army helicopters I was an ash-and-trash hauler in a C-130 Hercules."

I knew he was being modest. I'd already done a little homework and found that Daryl Jackson had actually flown in the Air Force, piloting an AC-130 "Spooky" gunship, with multiple tours in Grenada, Panama, and Desert Storm. *Why he wants to keep that to himself is his business,* I thought. I myself had flown as a passenger and soldier in many different aircraft over the years, planes both large and small, helicopters both military and civilian, and a hot air balloon. Hell, I'd even been up in the Goodyear Blimp once. It never ceased to amaze me how different the ground looked from the air at low altitude.

I was looking down at tracks from every kind of quad, two-seater, three-wheeler, Jeep, and 4WD pickup truck. Tracks could be seen crisscrossing the sand and dirt in every direction for miles. Fifteen minutes of flight time brought us to the black charred spot of desert sand where the truck had been. Jackson began circling.

"I don't know how we'll sort anything out of that mess down there." Sanchez's voice came through my headset. He was referring to the mish-mash of tracks beneath us.

"Hard, I know," I answered. "But you see how they all seem to generally follow the same OHV trails or sand washes? There's a few that go cross country, sure, but eventually even those end up circling back in the same general direction of the designated trails." I turned to Jackson. "I'd like to fly an expanding spiral search pattern with the burned spot as the center and see if anything stands out."

"You got it," he replied.

Johns, Sanchez, and I all had brought binoculars with us. The three of us began to "glass" the surrounding landscape. It was on the ninth circular pass, a good two miles from the center of the search, that Johns spotted something out of the ordinary.

"Hey, look out at four o'clock, no wait—shit! I lost it now. Daryl, can you circle back the other way?"

Jackson banked the plane right and began a slow circle.

Johns appeared to be speaking mostly to himself. "Where is it? Where is it? There! Three o'clock."

All of us then spotted the solo set of OHV tracks leading off into the desert, heading east, away from all of the others.

"Can you get lower?" I asked Jackson.

"Yeah, I guess," he replied a bit reluctantly. "I'll drop it down to a thousand for one pass, then we'll climb back up, turn around, and do it again if we have to."

At a mere thousand feet off the ground, the brush seemed close enough to touch. Two coyotes, spooked by the plane's engine noise, bolted from a brush-choked sand wash as we passed over.

"Damn! See that?" Daryl Jackson exclaimed as we passed over the running animals. "I should have had my pistol out."

"Can you shoot from a plane like this?" I asked him.

He laughed. "You can, but it's illegal as hell. I've done it once just to see what it was like. I was flying over a patch of desert even more desolate than this one, long ways from anywhere, so I knew no one would know. Fun as hell, but damn loud in the cockpit. The hot brass went everywhere. I had to spend an hour after I landed making sure there were no casings left in the plane."

Without diverting his attention from flying so low, he reached down around and into one of the equipment bags and shook out a Calico Liberty III .9mm assault pistol. I whistled softly. Although officially classified as a pistol, it functioned more like a sub-machine gun. With its odd looking 50-round cylindrical drum mounted on top of the receiver, it looked more like a science-fiction ray-gun than a firearm. I took it from him and looked it over.

"You ever see one of these before?" Jackson asked, adding, "Careful the mag is full but there's not one in the pipe." I pointed the muzzle at the floor and eased the bolt part way back to check the empty chamber. He looked at me with a raised eyebrow. "Don't trust me, eh?"

"Nothing personal," I replied. "I just want to make sure I don't accidentally shoot my dick off. Yeah, I've seen one once before, but it's been a long time. Believe it or not, we had a mass murder committed at a Mexican bar in Vista with one. Eight people shot, seven of them died. It was a drug rip-off gone bad. Crazy-assed son-of-a-bitch named Johnny Mionke and two of his thug buddies. Twin brothers, last name of Van-something. They walked inside right at closing time and just started shooting everyone that was still in the bar. Mionke used one of these. We recovered it two weeks later in the trunk of a car he'd been using."

Intrigued by the conversation, Sanchez and Johns were staring at me now as Jackson asked, "So I take it you caught these guys?"

"Yeah—well, sort of. Mionke is doing multiple life sentences now. One of those brothers is in Federal prison for fifty years. VanHeffel, that was it, on weapons trafficking charges. If he ever gets out, which will never happen, he'll also be tried on the state murder charges. The other brother died in prison as I recall. Not sure what from but, no matter, he's smoking a turd in hell now, the evil son-of-a-bitch. Mionke's sister Lynn is also doing 25-to-life for a murder *she* committed. Johnny and his crazy bitch-of-a-sister robbed an old man who'd given them a ride, then *she* shoots him in the back of the head with a derringer when he pulls up to let them out at a stop sign."

Sanchez's mouth was agape. "Jesus, no bullshit?"

"Gospel truth," I replied.

"Nice family," Johns added.

Everyone was fascinated so I continued with the story. "Johnny boy actually got caught by the Oklahoma cops. Several weeks after the bar killings, he shot one of our guys in the face. It was at *that* scene that I found the Calico in the car trunk. Wasn't his car though, so we couldn't link him to it."

"No prints?" Sanchez asked.

"Nope, and that was when DNA analysis was in its infancy so nothing there either. Anyway, after shooting our Vista cop, Mionke, his sister, and their co-girlfriend fled to Oklahoma to his grandfather's house. The Okie cops were all set up on a country road, after they got a tip he'd walked to a nearby fishing hole. They were going to go all Bonnie and Clyde on his ass, but they didn't know his grandfather was with him until they both came diddy-bopping down the road. They had to just arrest him instead of shooting the crazy fuck full of holes like they should have. He still had the revolver on him that he shot our cop with. On top of *that*, we liked the asshole for several *other* murders we were never able to prove. The guy just liked killing people."

Jackson glanced at me. "Your cop die? The one shot in the face?"

"Almost, but no. Messed him up, though," I replied. "He was a friend of mine. Blew out all his teeth on the left side of his jaw. Bullet frags lodged all around his spine. His teeth are actually what saved him. They broke the bullet into fragments."

Johns frowned. "Wait, what did you mean by 'co-girlfriend'?"

I smiled at him. "Caught that, huh? Johnny and his sister both liked screwing this nineteen-year-old chick. She was pretty good looking as I recall. Johnny and Lynn also liked screwing each other. Nothing like incest to keep you close, you know? We recovered several Polaroid shots of their group sex action there at the house where our cop got shot. The co-girlfriend is actually the one who ratted Johnny and Lynn out. She got scared of all their crazy antics on the way to Oklahoma and called her mother. The mom tipped us off. We tipped the Oklahoma cops and put a bug in their ear about how bad this guy was." Jackson shook his head as I handed the weapon back to him. "Funny the things that stick with you, though," I told them as I looked through my binoculars. "When I first walked into that bar that night, I can remember seeing some of the victims piled up under the pool table. They must've been trying to all hide from the gunfire and that's where they died. The one woman that survived was under there, too, on the bottom of the pile. The other bodies saved her from being shot again."

Jackson frowned. "What do you mean 'shot again'?"

"Oh yeah, I left that part out, didn't I? After using the Calico on everyone, Mionke went around administering a 'coupe-de-grace' with his .22 magnum revolver to each. Missed her for some reason though.

It was the same gun he later shot our guy with. The same gun he had on him in Oklahoma."

"The shit you've seen." Jackson shook his head. "I don't know how you sleep at night."

I stared absently through the front windscreen and snorted. "I don't talk much about the things I've seen. People mostly think it's bullshit, anyway, when I do, and besides, I've found out that sleep is way over-rated. We'll get enough sleep when we're dead." Changing the subject to the OHV tracks as we circled back, I spoke into my mike to anyone who was listening. "Now what do you suppose a two-seater would be doing out here all by itself?"

"How can you tell it's a two-seater?" Jackson asked.

"Look." I pointed. "When the tracks cross the right kind of dirt, you can see the lugs on the tires are much bigger than those on most quads. It could be a quad with an oversize tire/wheel kit, but the wheel base looks too long for a quad. Hard to tell from up here for sure, but it looks like a two-seater, to me anyway. Let's keep following the tracks and see where they go."

Jackson pulled back on the yoke and the Cessna climbed enough to make another turn back across the tracks. He then dropped it back down to about 800 feet as we followed their path No more than three miles had passed under us when Jackson again began to circle. It was plain to see the OHV had stopped here, then had driven back and forth over a small area, after which the set of tire tracks continued their journey east. I made a circular motion with my finger to Jackson and continued to examine the ground through my binoculars. He nodded and kept the plane in a tight right bank.

Sanchez spoke up. "What the hell do you make of that?"

He was looking at the same spot, as was Johns, who added, "Looks like whoever it was stopped and got out. See the foot prints in the sand? Two sets. Now we know for sure it was a two-seater."

I pulled my eyes away from my binoculars for a moment, thinking, then looked through them again, just to confirm what I was seeing. The plane climbed again and circled back.

"What I also see is two sets of foot prints walking away from the OHV and only one set of tracks returning to it."

Johns looked hard through his binoculars. "Yeah, you're right. That *can't* be good."

Once again I pulled out my little Garmin GPS from my pocket and after making sure it was receiving satellite signal, I punched the *Mark Waypoint* button.

Sanchez watched what I was doing. "You carry that thing every-where you go?"

I nodded. "Every time I'm out and about in strange country. You never know when it's going to come in handy, like now," I replied. Looking at Jackson, I asked, "Any chance we could set this thing down somewhere close?"

"No way, man," he quickly returned. "It may look smooth from up here, but that ground is way too uneven and rough. Don't forget this little baby is borrowed, not that I'd try it even if it was mine."

"No problem, just thought I'd ask."

I jerked my chin upward indicating we should continue to follow the tracks, just as Sanchez's phone vibrated. He pulled off the head set and yelled, "Hello!" over the noise of the engine.

For the second time that day it was Davis. Sanchez and he conversed, or tried to, for a short five minutes, with Sanchez pretty much yelling every word. Sanchez tugged his headphones back on. "From what I could get from the L-T over this noise, apparently someone near the Lopez scene this morning saw a full size white car leaving the area. There was no other description, no plate, no make, no suspect info, nothing. Just a big white car. Davis isn't sure it was even involved, but wanted us to know. He also said the three .22 casings found at the scene are some brand called Lapua. Ever hear of that brand before?"

I nodded. "Yeah. It's subsonic ammo. Low power and slow speed. Made to be fired out of a suppressed pistol or even a suppressed rifle, but up close. There would be almost no sound at all, just the click of the bolt. No wonder no one heard anything. Definitely not your run-of-the-mill drive-by ammo for sure." We followed the OHV track another four miles, where they abruptly ended at an asphalt road. "Nothing on the other side," I told Jackson. "He must've used the road."

Jackson banked the plane left and circled back. "Now what?" he asked.

I shook my head. "I don't know. Head back, I guess. We'll have to grab a four wheel drive or some such and go back out to that spot where the two-seater stopped, where those foot prints were."

Johns was looking at the only nearby house through his binoculars. "Hey, Daryl, make a pass over by that house."

Jackson climbed back to fifteen hundred feet so as not to draw a complaint from some unseen desert resident. He banked the plane sharply, flying right over the house.

"Now see, that's odd," Johns told us all. "I know this area pretty damn good. No one has lived in that house for as long and I've been working at the reservation, and now there's a car parked out back."

"Maybe someone bought the place," Sanchez offered.

Jackson banked the plane for another pass over the structure and as he lined the plane up parallel to the back yard, and I, too, now noticed the car parked behind the house. It was a dirty white Ford Crown Victoria.

Sanchez said absentmindedly, "You don't see too many full size Crown Vics that aren't cop cars since they don't make them anymore. That one looks like an unmarked cop car."

"Nope, not a cop car, look at the plate," I replied as I examined it through my binoculars. You know what else?" I pulled my eyes away from my binoculars and glanced over my shoulder at him. "It's a big car, it's white, *and* it's parked behind a supposedly deserted house out in the middle of nowhere."

Johns lifted his binoculars back to his eyes. "Check out that pile of junk next to the house. There's something kind of weird-looking about it. Right there, see it? That weird scrap pile or whatever it is."

I motioned with my hand to Jackson. "Daryl, drop down lower and fly parallel to the back yard. Let's try to get a good look at the car and whatever Johns is seeing. It kind of does look like a tarp covering something."

Jackson climbed, turned, then lowered the nose of the plane. We leveled out at five hundred feet. My Nikon image-stabilized binoculars that I wore around my neck were made for this. When the stabilizer button on the top of the binoculars was pushed down and held, the image became instantly stable and clear. As we passed the rear of the house and the end of the tarp shelter, the stabilized and clear image that presented itself through the lenses was indisputable. The orange and black color scheme, along with the front rail bumper and front tires of a small OHV were plainly visible.

As we flashed by, Sanchez started yelling, "Oh shit! Go around! Go around! Did you see that? That's gotta be the missing Razor everyone is looking for."

Jackson jerked the yoke of the Cessna toward his stomach and throttled up. At this low altitude in the dense cool morning air, the prop bit hard as did the flaps and ailerons. The Cessna rocketed skyward. Jackson turned the wheel and kicked the pedals hard and, again, the plane responded instantly, dipping it's left wing over in a tight left turn and we were again in a dive. It was like being on a carnival ride at the fair. *This guy is a good stick*, I thought as we dived toward the house once more. This time we would pass no more than fifty yards from the house and no higher than 300 feet. As we approached the rear of the house again, we were so low I could have sworn I could hear brush hitting the bottom of the fuselage. I was looking intently at the opening to the tarp enclosure when motion near the back porch landing of the house caught my eye. I shifted my binoculars. It took only a second for me to realize I was looking at a man standing on the dirt just off the porch, and that he was holding something in both his hands and point-ing it at the plane. My eyes went wide.

I turned to Jackson and shouted into my microphone, "Gun! Break left!" just as I saw orange flame leap from the muzzle of the weapon in the hands of the man on the ground.

Being a former combat pilot, the shouted warning was one that Jackson knew well. He didn't hesitate or think about it. He just reacted instantly. In seemingly one motion, he jerked the yoke to his belly, slammed the throttle open, turned the wheel, and kicked the pedals trying desperately to climb and twist the little Cessna out of range. I had to give him credit. Jackson was quick, but the laws of physics and the design and power of the small plane were not our friends that morning. A hail of 115 grain .9mm hollow-point bullets hammered the fuselage of the little plane punching jagged holes in the aluminum and plastic, stitching it from the nose to the tail.

The rate of fire from an HK MP5 .9mm sub-machine gun varies from between 700 and 900 rounds per minute, depending on the par-ticular series of weapon. The difference however, is purely academic when you are on the receiving end of that fire. No less than five bullets slammed into the right side of the engine nacelle, severing oil lines and blowing off large chunks of the aluminum engine block.

The power plant immediately began to smoke and cough. Several bullets smashed their way through the instrument panel in front of Jackson, shattering gauges and dials. One bullet passed in front of both my shins and tore a hole through Jackson's lower right thigh as it passed through the cockpit on its ballistic trajectory out the left side of the aircraft. The Plexiglas windows all along the right side exploded inward, sending razor sharp shards of clear plastic flying. Sanchez grunted as he was stuck by two bullets, one tearing into his left shoul-der and the second shattering his left wrist as he held his binoculars. The only thing that saved *me* from taking one or more bullets to my face was my turning to warn Jackson about the gun.

As it was, one of the small deadly projectiles tore off my head set, blowing the right earpiece apart and slicing the top of my ear away from my scalp. My lower lip was split as the microphone was ripped from in front of my mouth. A second bullet shattered my binoculars, stripping them from my grasp and lacerating both of my hands with shattered lens glass. Just as suddenly as it had begun, the gunfire stopped as we swiftly climbed up and away from the house, but the damage had already been done.

I looked at the damaged interior of the plane, stunned by what I saw. There were bullet holes everywhere. All the windows were shat-tered. The control panel was smashed, and the amount of blood covering the seats and floor of the plane was not only alarming, it was spreading. Wind howled through every hole in the fuselage and the engine was smoking badly, coughing, and running rough.

"Mayday! Mayday! Mayday!" Jackson shouted into his mic, but he was getting no response.

He repeated the mayday call several times. The results were the same. Blood was now flowing around my feet and I suddenly thought of Johns. I spun in my seat and my heart sank. Michael Johns was dead. I knew he was dead at first glance, but I unhooked my belt and climbed over Sanchez to check his pulse just to be sure. It was his blood that now covered the rear seat and floor of the aircraft. From what I could see, he had been struck multiple times, probably dying instantly. Ironically, it was his death that had probably saved the rest of us, for as the plane had made its climbing turn, Johns's body had shielded Sanchez, Jackson, and myself from additional gunfire from the rear, several bullets striking his back. There was nothing I could do for him, so I turned my attention to Jackson. Sanchez was seriously injured also, but none of us would survive if Jackson passed out and turned our little plane into a smoking hole in the ground.

To my surprise, Jackson was already giving all of his attention to keeping the plane in the air long enough to find a place to set it down. I bent down as best I could in the cramped space and sliced his right pants leg open with my knife, from the knee to the crotch. He squirmed as he felt my knife blade approach his testicles.

"Be careful with that blade," he yelled over the wind and engine noise. We all had to yell now to be heard. "I'd still like to have use of my manhood for a few more years, providing by some miracle we get out of this and my dick is actually still there. Is my dick still there? My crotch hurts like hell!"

Wiping away the blood, I examined his upper thigh, penis, and scrotum. "You lucked out," I told him. "The bullet passed clean through your lower thigh just in front of your butt cheek. Didn't hit bone or your femoral artery, your dick, or your balls. The wound is already closing up and just seeping."

"Thank God," he replied. "Feels like I got kicked in the balls by a mule. I was sure my dick was shot off. There's a big towel under your seat. I saw it when I was doing my pre-flight. First aid kit is back there on the bulkhead next to Johns's seat! How's Sanchez and Johns?"

I pulled the towel out and cut a large strip off. As I was tying it around Jackson's thigh, I told him, "Sanchez is shot in the shoulder and wrist. I'm gonna go help him next. Johns is dead."

"Mother-fuck!" he exclaimed then winced.

"We gonna be able to stay in the air until you can land this thing somewhere?"

He shook his head. "I'm trying, but I just don't know. The good news is the engine is still running, though I don't know how, and we're not on fire. The rest I'll let you know shortly, but one way or the other this crate is not going to stay in the air much longer!"

I nodded, plugging up the two holes in his thigh as best I could with strips cut from the Towel, then turned my attention to Sanchez. Frank had already retrieved the first aid kit and was trying to treat his own shoulder wound but was struggling due to his injured wrist. As it turned out, the wrist wound was the worst.

"Mike is dead," he shouted.

"I know," I replied.

The adrenalin was starting to wear off and we were all going into shock. Sanchez was starting to shake, as was I. My hands shook so badly I could hardly hold the compress bandage. I examined his shoulder and was surprised to see the copper end of a bullet protruding from the furrow it had dug in the tissue. Sanchez was starting to stare vacantly at me.

"Stay with me, Frank!" His eyes re-focused. "This bullet must have hit something else before it hit you. It had just enough energy left to pierce your skin but not much else."

I flipped open my knife for the second time. This worried Sanchez as my hands were shaking, but I managed to flip the bloody bullet out of his flesh and into my hand. Sure enough, the nose of the projectile was jagged and deformed. It had indeed struck something hard before glancing off and into Sanchez. *Probably the airframe*, I mused.

I handed the bullet to Sanchez. "You need to hang onto that. It's your lucky charm now." I placed a compress bandage from the kit over his shoulder wound and had him hold it while I taped it in place.

There wasn't much I could do with his wrist except to wrap some gauze around the entry and exit holes the bullet had made as it passed through. The hollow tipped projectile had not found enough tissue in the wrist to start it's designed expansion, thus both holes were small, but the energy of the bullet strike had broken both the ulnar and radial bones. His wrist was swollen and discolored badly. I bandaged it as best I could, with him gasping in pain. I then retrieved the sling from the first-aid kit. Once his arm was settled in the sling, I gave him four aspirin.

He chewed them up and swallowed them dry, making a face. "Ugh, that's almost as bad as being shot. You're a mess, Jason," he told me as he looked me over. "Your ear is half off and you're cut everywhere. Your face, your hands, and your lip are split wide open. The bleeding has stopped for now but you sure look like hell." He glanced back over his shoulder at the dead K-9 officer. "Shit, man. We lost Johns."

I nodded. "We'll mourn later, Frank. We need to help Daryl land this thing or we're all in deep shit!"

As if to underscore my point, Jackson yelled at us, "Uh, boys—we may have a problem here!"

"Ya think?" Sanchez asked sarcastically.

"No, I mean *another* problem," Jackson yelled, pointing out his side window at the rearview mirror mounted on the wing strut. "There's a small dust cloud behind us on the ground. Someone is coming!"

"Daryl," I said with alarm in my voice. "We need to get this thing pointed back toward civilization!"

"Um, yeah, well we have a bit of a problem there too," Jackson replied. "Neither the rudder nor the ailerons are responding. Flaps and throttle are still working for now thank God, but I've only got limited control!"

Sanchez, looked confused, not understanding the problem. He grimaced in pain and shouted, "I don't understand!"

Jackson shouted back, "It's like screwing a fat chick on a water bed. We can go up and down and we can go faster and slower, but we can't turn her around!"

Interesting metaphor, I thought. *A pilot's sense of humor, I guess.* Jackson then tried to force the plane to maneuver. He was able to turn the plane just enough that I could see behind us. I removed Johns's bloody binoculars from around his neck and put them to my eyes. Sure enough, about three miles behind us was a cloud of dust being raised by a vehicle traveling at high speed. I couldn't make it out well at this distance, but I could see that it was small and I caught a flash of orange in the afternoon sunlight. It was also gaining on us. There was no doubt in my mind it was the Polaris Razor, and I knew the man driving it was following to ensure we were finished.

I turned to Jackson. "Radio?"

"Dead," he replied. "First thing I checked when I saw how bad we were hit. Must've happened when the panel got all shot to shit. You think it's him coming for us?"

I nodded. "I'm sure of it. What about cell phone?" I asked as I dug mine out of my pocket.

"No service," he shouted. "I just checked that, too!"

I looked at my phone. No bars. "Okay," I told him. "Just put as much distance between him and us as possible for now."

"I've been trying," he replied, "but that thing is fast and I'm down to like sixty-five knots. Barely enough to keep us in the air. I don't dare do anything rash or we'll stall. How fast will those damn things go?"

Damn, we are in serious trouble here! "I don't know for sure," I replied. "I'm assuming that if they're stock, probably sixty, give or take."

Jackson looked at his airspeed indicator. It was one of the few dials still working. He again checked the mirror. "Well," he said, "the one chasing us must *not* be stock because he's gaining on us."

Sanchez yelled again. "Won't this thing go faster?"

Jackson nodded. "Normally yes, but look at the smoke coming off the engine." He nodded at the whitish brown smoke being caught and whipped away in the prop blast. "We're losing oil. I'm surprised it hasn't seized already."

"Just do the best you can," I shouted at him, "and hand me that Calico."

Keeping one hand on the yoke and his eyes on the desert, Jackson dug into his bag with one hand and handed over the ugly .9mm assault pistol, but then as an afterthought, he asked, "What about me?"

I turned to Sanchez. "Grab Johns's pistol and mags and hand 'em up!"

He nodded, handing the bloody weapon and both magazines to Jackson, who dropped it all in his bag. He then advanced the throttle a fraction. Our airspeed climbed to seventy knots, but it didn't last long. Less than ten minutes later the engine let off a shriek and spewed out a large puff of white smoke.

"We're done!" Jackson shouted and immediately cut the ignition and feathered the prop.

The Cessna's nose jerked up. The little plane then went into a shallow, gliding dive toward the desert floor. With only fifteen hundred feet of air under the wheels, it didn't take long to get there.

I pointed out the shattered front windscreen. "There's a jeep trail or whatever right there," I exclaimed. "See it?"

"Yeah, I see it," Jackson yelled back. "I'll try for it, but help me push the pedals and turn the wheel." With both of us pushing the controls, Jackson was able to get the small plane turned just enough to line up with the cut in the brush. "Hang on! This is going to be harsh," he yelled as he guided the nose of the aircraft between two large Saguaro cactus.

The tops of both cacti were sheared off as the wings struck them. The tricycle landing gear made contact with the desert floor and the small plane bounced hard, leaping into the air. I was certain the plane would flip over, but Jackson somehow managed to keep it upright. The plane slammed the desert floor again and shook violently. Dirt, sand, rocks, and brush pounded and grabbed at the landing gear and fuse-lage. The little plane shimmied back and forth across the trail and fi-nally shuttered to a sudden stop, skewing sideways at the last second and snapping off the nose wheel. The crash-landing threw us hard against our harnesses, making us all groan in pain.

As the dust settled around us, we looked at each other in disbelief. We were still alive. *But for how long?* I wondered. The three of us were all injured and we were on foot in desolate country. No one knew where we'd gone, *and* we had a professional killer coming for us. The odds of our surviving this day were not good. On the up side, the plane had not caught fire on impact, we were fairly well armed, and we had some rations and water that would last us a few days, *and,* we weren't that far from civilization. At some point, a search would be organized when we didn't return the plane. I silently wondered if the search and rescue folks would find the three of us alive. Or would our bones be found covered with desert sand, much like the Apache warrior and the Cavalry Soldier with which this all had begun?

CHAPTER 48

Speed

Sand and dust spewed out from behind the rear wheels of the Razor 800S as it sped across the desert at almost 100 miles per hour. Rocha kept the accelerator pressed to the floorboard. He was pleased the machine's previous owner had made the expensive modifications to the engine so that it would go much faster than any stock model. There was even a NOS bottle attached to the rear roll bar should he want to flip the dash switch and inject the engine with nitrous oxide for additional speed and power, but so far there had been no need. The Razor could easily reach 100 miles per hour with no such help. True, it was a gamble to traverse this unpredictable terrain at such speeds, but it was fairly flat here and Rocha risked it.

He needed to find the downed plane and its occupants and make sure they would pose no more threat before any search was organized. *Funny how things work out*, he thought with a smile. *I am going to kill them now, when I'd already decided not to.* The plane was crippled. It's slow speed and the smoke trail it left in the sky made it easy to follow and he'd been gaining on it steadily. Suddenly he saw it pitch up and nose over out of sight a mile and a half or so ahead of him. It was down now, he was sure, and he was reasonably close, but he hadn't been able to pinpoint its *exact* location.

What he couldn't figure out is why the plane had continued its path out into the desert instead of turning back toward town. *Flight controls damaged maybe*? Rocha had hoped to get closer before the plane fell from the sky as he suspected it would, but just as in golf, he'd have to "play it where it lay." He brought the Razor to a sliding stop, unhooked his four-point harness, and stood up in the seat, trying to see any indication of where the plane had gone down. Of course, there was always a chance the machine had crashed killing all aboard, but so far his luck had not been running that way.

He saw nothing from his vantage point, nothing at all, no dust cloud or column of smoke to mark its location. "*Maldicion*!" he cursed under his breath.

He was confident he would eventually find it, but it would take time and time was not a luxury he had. *Had they made radio contact with the authorities*? he asked himself. He didn't think so. Highway Patrol or Border Patrol aircraft would already have been in the area searching. He swiveled his head and searched the sky just to make sure. He was pleased to see that the sky remained empty.

Rocha's decision to shoot the plane down had seemed sound at the time, but now he wasn't so sure. He recounted it in his mind. He had heard the plane's approach from the kitchen of the house and had stepped out on the front porch. At first he'd thought it was just another search plane looking for the missing owner of the Razor As he had watched, the red-and-white Cessna passed over the asphalt road a mile from the house. Suddenly it banked and flew straight at him and right over the house. It had been a deliberate maneuver. Something had drawn their attention to the house. Rocha stepped inside as it passed over. Reaching into his duffle bag, he had taken out a large set of 10x50 power Russian military binoculars. He'd then picked up the MP5 sub-machine gun and exchanged the thirty-round, stick magazine in the weapon with a Beta C-mag one-hundred-round drum, which he'd also pulled from the duffle bag. Stepping out onto the rear landing, Rocha had kept out of sight just as the plane made a second pass over the rear of the house. He'd known instantly they had seen the Razor parked under the tarp just feet from where he stood.

Looking through the powerful binoculars as the plane came abreast of him, he'd seen four people in the aircraft. The pilot he could not make out well, nor the person in the rear, but the plane had passed close enough that he'd immediately recognized two of the occupants of the plane, even with binoculars to their eyes and their headsets on.

Rocha had stared in disbelief. It was the two deputies that had been dogging his every move. *How could they have known*? Rocha began to breathe quickly. *Something had drawn their attention to the house. The car? It had to be. Someone must've seen the car when I left Lopez.*

The plane had climbed and circled, then dived again at the house. This time Rocha could see it would pass very low to the ground and mere yards from the house. It had been too good an opportunity to pass up. As the plane approached, he had stepped off the porch and taken a bead on the engine cowling. At this range, with this weapon and the abundance of ammunition it now held, he'd been certain he could destroy the engine and knock the plane out of the sky right then and there, hopefully killing all the occupants in the process. If they weren't killed on impact, he would finish them off himself and burn the plane with the bodies inside.

Helmuth von Moltke picked that moment to again pay Rocha a visit, for just as he squeezed the trigger, the plane lurched up and away in a climbing turn. Of the fifty or so bullets that were meant for the small plane's engine, only a handful found their mark. Several others stitched their way along the side and into the tail of the aircraft, but the majority pierced only empty air below and behind the climbing plane.

Rocha cursed. The Cessna had limped away trailing smoke. Without another thought, Rocha had thrown the MP5 into the Razor, strapped in and sped off after the damaged plane and its occupants.

He shook himself from his thoughts now, sat down and strapped himself back into the seat. He then stomped on the accelerator. Speed was what he needed now. He was close to the downed aircraft of that he was sure, and time was of the essence. He had to finish it now.

CHAPTER 49

Wait

Sonya, Chi-Chi, and Olsen with Tammy by his side, all sat in Davis's office. Olson was still weak but he'd needed to get out of the house and be here, so with Tammy's help he had accompanied the wives to the sheriff's office. As he gingerly walked the halls, using a cane in one hand for support and with Tammy holding onto the same elbow, he was greeted by smiling co-workers with handshakes and even a few hugs, which when given with too much enthusiasm, made him grimace and grunt with the soreness of his injury.

Olsen really didn't want all the attention but he endured it, smiling and exchanging greetings with all as he guided the wives to Davis's office. Sonya and Chi-Chi were worried sick, and even Davis now considered something might be wrong at this point. No one had heard from any of the deputies since Davis's last phone call. No one even knew where they had gotten hold of the plane, though Sonya did know that Daryl Jackson had offered to fly them around.

Jason told her before he left that they were going out to look at some tracks in the desert, but he hadn't told her *where*. To his credit, Davis was doing his best to organize some type of search, while still juggling the Lopez shooting investigation. He had unsuccessfully been trying to call both deputies' cell phones for the past hour. He told their wives he was in the process of trying to find someone to start calling the flying services at the airport and the tower, and see what he could find out about whose plane it was and get a description, and if anyone knew the plane's destination, but thought he wasn't hopeful about that last one. The news about Jackson being the pilot was news to Davis and he was *not* happy to hear that.

"L-T, I can start making those calls for you," Olsen said.

"You're off work, injured," Davis replied.

"I know," Olsen shot back. "But I can't just sit around the house while these guys are missing, and I'd like to help if I can."

Davis looked at him for a moment. "All right start making calls, but if anyone asks, you're *not* working."

It didn't take long for Olsen to find the owner of the aircraft. His second phone call produced results. The owner of the flying service that had loaned Jackson the plane gave Olsen the description of the Cessna, as well as the tail registration number. He also advised Olsen that he would take off immediately and begin searching for the plane and the occupants. Olsen passed along the information to Davis, then dialed the TSDPS air support office.

Upon hearing about the missing aircraft and the two deputies, the captain in charge of the air unit advised that he'd pass along to his pilot and observer the description of the Cessna and would break them from their interstate traffic duties and have them start looking. Two more similar calls were made. The first was to the US Border Patrol for any search support they could give, and the second was to the commander of the local chapter of the Civil Air Patrol or CAP. The US Border Patrol Air Commander advised he could not officially break his helicopter from its regular patrol duties, but he could arrange to have the bird "do some additional training and observation" in the area in question as it transited to and from its assigned patrol area. Both Olsen and the air-commander understood what that meant, and Olsen thanked him. The Commandant of the CAP advised they only had two pilots available, just himself and one other, but they would begin searching as soon as they could get to the airport and get their planes prepped and in the air.

When the phone calls were all done, Davis called dispatch and told them to have the two deputies assigned to the remote desert area west of the interstate start looking down every four-wheel drive road they could think of. He had no sooner completed that task when the lieutenant in charge of the volunteer sheriff's posse called and offered his group's assistance also. He had heard the radio call go out to the desert deputies on the scanner he kept at his business. Davis thanked him and gave him all the information they had on the missing Cessna. For the second time in a week, the posse members got phone calls and instructions to trailer up their horses, quads, and jeeps and head out for a desert search.

Davis told Sonya and Chi-Chi, "This is going to be an all-out effort by everyone involved. I'm sure we'll find your husbands."

He said it with conviction because he knew the statement was true. The missing deputies and the plane *would* be found quickly, he was sure of it. After all, the weather was good with unlimited visibility, the plane was brightly colored, and the terrain open and fairly flat. What he didn't say was what he was thinking. *We'll probably find them in several hundred pieces scattered across the sand.*

No one said it out loud, but all of them were hoping this would not be the case.

"Now if you'll excuse me ladies," he said, "I need to go brief the sheriff on all this, and you need to get Deputy Olsen home so he can rest. I'll call you the minute I hear anything, I promise."

Realizing there was nothing more they could do here, Sonya and Chi-Chi thanked Davis and, with Tammy's help, ushered Olsen out the door. There was nothing they could do now but wait.

CHAPTER 50

Nowhere to Run

Small eddies of dust picked up by the breeze swirled around the broken plane. No one felt like moving, injured as we were, but I knew it was imperative that we do so. A flood of old memories came rushing back in that instant, a true *deja-vu* experience for me. I'd been through this all before as a passenger in a helicopter crash in Vietnam while transporting a prisoner. Then as now, we needed to scramble to get out of the machine, though for very different reasons. Back then the main danger had been fire. Now it was a very capable killer coming for us.

"We need to get the hell out of here, guys," I told them as I put my shoulder to the door and forced it open. "Let me take a quick look around, then I'll help you get out."

Picking up the Calico assault pistol, I climbed out and quickly assessed the plane's condition. It was a mess. I was no expert on airframe repair, but it looked like a total loss to me. There were bullet holes all along the right side and all the windows were either completely gone or badly holed. The nose wheel and the right side landing gear were both crushed, causing the right wing tip to nearly touch the ground. The propeller blades were bent like pretzels and the leading edges of both wings were damaged where they'd hit the cactus. Looking at the broken plane, I figured I wasn't going to hurt it any more than it already was, so I clamored up and stood on top of the askew wing where its root joined the fuselage.

I needed to survey the surrounding desert. We had come to a stop where the trail widened into a small clearing surrounded by cactus, brush, and Mesquite trees. As I glassed the surrounding terrain from my position atop the wing, I could hear Jackson and Sanchez jabbering at each other, talking a mile a minute, their voices loud. The tension of the last thirty minutes was rushing out of both their bodies in the form of excited conversation.

"Shhhh. Quiet, *quiet*!" I hushed them both. "I hear something."

They both fell silent and I cupped my hands behind my ears and opened my mouth a bit. This was an old hunter's trick that allowed me to hear better. Turning my head back and forth so that my cupped hands acted as sound scoops, I heard the sound of an engine. It was a vehicle on the ground. It was still some distance away and seemed to be traversing the desert back and forth instead of directly approaching us, but I already knew it was the engine of the Razor.

The killer didn't know our exact location. He was driving back and forth in the machine, but moving in our direction as well. The volume of the sound was growing slightly louder with each pass. He was slow- ly getting closer to us, and I knew it was only a matter of time before he found the plane, and us. I climbed down and informed Sanchez and Jackson of our situation. The cabin of the Cessna was not conducive to getting in and out of easily, even under normal conditions. It was much more difficult now with the plane being damaged as it was, not to men- tion the injuries we had all sustained. We were all hurting, but Sanchez and Jackson were worse off than I, since they were the ones with bullet holes in their flesh.

Jackson grunted in pain as I helped him from his seat. He leaned against the plane, supporting himself on his good leg. I went back for Sanchez, helping him around to the shade cast by the higher left wing where Jackson waited.

"I guess we need to get as far away from the plane as we can," Jackson offered.

It was as much a question as a statement.

I shook my head. "No. We're on foot and we're all injured, you two are shot. This guy's got a vehicle and he's healthy. I'm sure he's probably got some decent tracking skills, considering his military training," I mused. "He'd be all over us like white on rice before we made it two miles."

"So what do you want to do?" Sanchez said angrily. "We can't just sit around doing nothing, waiting to be slaughtered like sheep!"

I was examining our surroundings. "I have a plan, but we need to hurry. He'll find us soon, I think."

As if to underscore what I'd just said, the sound of the distant en- gine returned. It was louder this time, and I wondered if we'd run out of time, but the sound soon faded again as the machine again turned away.

"We need to lure him into an ambush and kill him," I told them both.

Sanchez looked skeptical. "Won't be easy. According to his file the guy is ex-Mexican army soldier with US Spec-ops training."

"I remember, but it's fifty-fifty chance the guy will be that good," I replied. "Unlike American green beanies, some of these Mexican military guys are good, and some are total clowns."

Jackson supported himself against the plane. "So which one is he?"

I shrugged. "Guess we're about to find out. Let's move. Daryl, you're gimped up and you can't move all that well, so you're going to be our security guy here for a few minutes while I do a couple things."

I helped him hobble over into the shade of a Mesquite tree at the edge of the trail. It offered some concealment near its base. From here he could watch both the plane and our back trail. I helped him lay down and piled up a few rocks to break up his outline.

"Glad to see you wore something in earth tones," I told him as I looked at his blood stained khaki shirt. Sanchez was watching us and trying to hear what I was saying. "Wait here just a minute," I told Jackson.

I walked back to Sanchez and helped him limp over to where Jackson lay partially concealed. I wanted them both to hear what I had to say. I handed Jackson the Calico temporarily, as it was by far our deadliest weapon and would be of better use out here in the open.

"Here," I said to him. "You cover us with this for now and give me Johns's pistol." He'd dragged his bag out with him so we traded weapons. "If this guy shows up while I'm working over there—" I waved at the plane. "—wait until you have a decent shot if you can, then don't hesitate and, for God's sake, don't miss."

Jackson checked the weapon. "You want me to just shoot him in cold blood? You guys don't want to try to arrest him or something?"

I looked down at him, the concern probably evident on my face. "I'm not sure I understand you, Daryl. You told us you were ready to shoot him without warning out there in the desert with your rifle that day."

Jackson nodded. "Yeah, I know, but I could see the threat to you guys right then and there. He was going to shoot two cops and I couldn't let that happen, but don't forget, I hesitated at the last second. I think I *would* have shot him, but I keep wondering. I mean if those cars hadn't happened by at that second, would I have pulled the trigger in time?"

I squatted down and looked into his eyes. "Would-a, could-a, should-a. What happened, happened. You can't worry about what *might* have been and we don't have the time to debate it." My tone was deadly serious. "You listen to me good, both of you. It's real simple and you need to get it through your heads. This guy is a killer. He's ruthless and proficient. He's probably a true sociopath if not an outright psychopath. I've seen and dealt with people like this before. A person like this doesn't think like you or me. Their brain is just wired wrong, who knows why? If you give him any warning, and I mean *any* warning at all—" I nodded at the Calico. "—or hesitate when you have the chance, *or* miss your shot, he will kill us. Do you understand what I'm telling you? He will kill us all without hesitation, without pity, without concern of being caught, and without any remorse. He'll kill us and give it no more thought than stepping on a bug."

I looked away for a moment. I'd already come to a decision and it was time to tell them both. "This is going to sound cold and cruel, guys, but it's a cold and cruel world. If you are not up to this, either of you, I need to know it right Goddamn now! I intend to do *whatever* it takes to at least try and survive this. If you can't get your mind wrapped around that, or you just don't have the stomach for it, then we'll divvy up the ammo, food and water, and we'll go our separate ways right here and right now with no hard feelings. When he gets here you can deal with this guy however *you* want. I want an answer and I want it right-the-fuck now! What's it gonna be?"

Jackson was surprised by my stern admonition. Sanchez not so much. *Frank's already come to the same decision*, I thought. I reminded myself that Sanchez was no babe-in-the-woods when it came to survival. He'd told me early in our relationship, and much to my surprise I might add, that he'd grown up in one of the meanest barrios in east Los Angeles and had fought to survive nearly every day of his life before his father moved their family to Texas when he was sixteen.

After a few seconds of inner conflict, I saw Jackson set his jaw against the unpleasantness to come. "Okay, I'm in."

"All in?" I pressed.

"I said so, didn't I?" he replied, clearly irritated at my insistence.

Sanchez gave me a look of what I'd always called determined resignation. The same look SWAT cops had right before they went through the door of a barricaded suspect's place. The same look soldiers had as they prepared to storm up an enemy hill or take out a bunker. The look of men knowing, and even expecting, that what they were about to do could very well be their last act on this earth, but had decided to do it regardless.

Sanchez had made his decision and was now mentally prepared for whatever may come. He nodded and said, "Let's do this, *veterano*."

The human brain was an amazingly complex organ. The body an equally amazing machine. I was certain that after all these passing years, the combat training, survival instincts, and experience I'd developed as a young man in that far away Asian land so long ago had faded forever, but I was wrong. Old memories, instincts, and hard lessons suddenly came flooding back. I was much older now, of course, and while not terribly out of shape, my body just couldn't do the things it used to be able to back when I was nineteen.

Well, I wasn't nineteen anymore and that was a fact, but my brain apparently still retained the skills, even if my body wouldn't cooperate at times. Standing there watching Jackson trying to get comfortable, I noticed my senses were actually changing second by second. They were suddenly heightened. My hearing was vastly improved. I could hear the slightest noise. My nose was more sensitive. I could smell the soil, the sage and cactus, and the coppery smell of our blood in the plane some yards away. My eyes now caught even the slightest of movements. Ants crawling on the Mesquite tree trunk and the single flitter of the wing of a small bird in the branches. I was amazed and somewhat surprised how easily I slipped into "the zone." Completely in touch with my surroundings. *It has to be some primal animal survival thing*, I thought briefly. This was not the usual fight-or-flight instinct. This was kill-or-be-killed in its most raw form.

I began to implement my plan. "Daryl, you stay here and cover us. Keep your shit together and your eyes open. Frank, since you're ambulatory and you have one good arm, you come with me. I know it hurts but we're short on time and I'll need help."

Jackson settled into a shooting position on the ground and pointed the ugly snout of the little Calico in the direction from which the OHV would most likely approach.

Watching him, I said, "Two things, Daryl. First, don't get directional fixation. The threat can come from anywhere in a 360 degree circle, not just from down this trail. Use your ears as well as your eyes. Second, there are animals that have better eyesight than humans, but the human eye is absolutely the *best* in the animal kingdom for detecting motion. Particularly sudden motion. You're fairly well concealed here. Try to keep your movement to a minimum. Move your eyes and not your head to look around. If you have to move or turn your head, don't turn it any farther than necessary to see and do it *very* slowly. We'll be over by the plane for a few minutes."

Sanchez moved to retrieve Jackson's bags with the food and water from the plane. We realized the two of us were not going to be able to retrieve Johns's body, however. Injured as we were, there was just no way we could maneuver his 185-pound weight out of the rear seat and through the door of the damaged plane.

I removed his personal belongings and his badge, then placed one hand on his shoulder and wiped the blood from his face with the other. "Goodbye, bro. Odds are I'll probably be seeing you again *real* soon," I said to him.

I'd never been very "religious." Never bought into the religious mumbo-jumbo that men have made up over the centuries to excuse their evil ways. Religion was all bullshit as far as I was concerned, but that was not to say I was not *spiritual*. I did believe in divine presence, a supreme being as it were, though I didn't necessarily think he was an old guy with a beard and white robe.

As I looked at Johns's pale and bloody face, I offered my own prayer for his soul. "Mike here was a good man and a good cop. He died trying to catch an evil son-of-a-bitch. Do me a favor and set an extra chair for him at the table, will ya? Oh yeah, and if you could see your way clear to give us a hand here, I'd appreciate it. Otherwise, you might want to keep three *more* chairs handy. Amen."

Unknown to me, Sanchez had been watching and listening. "Amen," he said.

I climbed out, opened up the side storage compartment in the fuselage near the tail, and removed Jackson's second bag which contained the snack food and water bottles. I then noticed in the same confined space, a small tool kit, two compact emergency blankets, two quarts of engine oil as well as two of hydraulic fluid, and a 20mm emergency flare gun kit.

"Listen!" Sanchez said suddenly.

The sound of the Razor's engine could once again be heard, this time much closer. I saw Jackson tense up and point the Calico in the direction of the sound, but once again after a minute or two, the noise faded. As I retrieved the flare gun kit, I looked at Sanchez and nodded toward the compartment. "C'mon. I've been timing him. We've only got about 10 minutes. He'll probably find the plane on his next pass. If not then it will, for sure, be the one after that." Seeing the extra oil and fluid had given me an idea. "Grab those containers of oil and hydraulic fluid, Frank, and pour them over my clothes. Everything except for my head. Hurry!"

Sanchez looked astonished. "What? Why?"

I motioned for him to hurry. "Quick! You'll see. No time to explain."

He un-capped the containers and started to pour.

"That's it. Use your good hand and spread it around on me."

I held my hands up high so they would not be covered. Jackson was watching us now. They both must've thought I'd gone crazy, but Sanchez complied and started spreading the combined fluids on me. When Sanchez had used up everything but a small amount of the oil, I stopped him. I was now covered in a sticky dark brown goo from neck to boots. As they both watched with confounded looks, I lay down in the sand and dirt and began to roll back and forth. The gooey sticky mess immediately picked up everything off the ground. In just a few seconds all of my clothing and exposed skin was completely covered with sand, dirt, small rocks, and leaves. I took the last bit of oil with my fingers and repeated the process with my head, face, and neck. Soon my eyes were the only thing that made me discernible as a human being. I looked more like a sand monolith or some creature from a science-fiction movie.

"Man, you are one crazy son-of-a-bitch," Sanchez said.

Walking over to some brush, I lay down, instantly becoming one with the landscape.

Jackson chuckled from his hide. "Yeah, crazy like a fox. I get it. An instant ghillie suit."

Sanchez shook his head. "I'll be damned! I *never* would have thought of that," he said. "You blend right in with the dirt."

I stood up and walked over to his left shoulder. "If you liked that, you're gonna love this."

I reached out suddenly, jerking the bandage off of his shoulder and tearing away the scabbed dried blood along with some flesh from the edges of his wound. Blood began to immediately drip from the open wound onto the ground.

Sanchez grimaced and yelped in pain as he jumped out of my reach. "What the fuck, man? That hurt like hell."

"Sorry, bro," I apologized. "But I need you to bleed as you walk. I want him to think you're hurt. It might make him less wary."

"What do you mean *think* I'm hurt? I am fucking hurt! Now I'm hurt even more—and what do you mean 'walk'?" he asked. Angrily, he touched the area around the wound. "I thought we were going to try for him here."

"Careful," I cautioned. "Don't get your grimy fingers in that wound. No need to compound the infection problem. Here." I handed him the First Aid kit I'd retrieved from the plane. "I noticed when I got into this kit before, it's a good one. There's new compress bandages, along with a couple packs of blood coagulating powder. Keep an eye on your bleeding. I don't want either of you passing out from loss of blood. Patch yourself up again if you need to, otherwise I'll do it for you when we meet up, assuming we're all still alive that is."

I handed Jackson Johns's pistol and ammo, telling him, "Here, take this, and leave the Calico here on that rock right there. I'll grab it in a minute." I laid out my new plan to them. Turning to Sanchez, I told him, "Frank, help Daryl walk. I want both of you to head off through the brush right there." I pointed to a gap in the cactus and sage. "I want you to keep walking North in as straight a line as possible. Make as many tracks in the sand as you can and make sure you leave some big

drops of blood along the way. I want your tracks and your blood to be
visible and very easy to follow."

Sanchez now understood. "We're bait. Not sure I like that much."

"Exactly," I told him. "I'm going to make sure our friend finds the
plane and then starts to follow your trail. I won't be far behind you
and, with a bit of luck, I'll get a shot at him."

"Before he catches up and shoots us both I hope," Sanchez muttered.

"That's the plan," I replied.

Jackson didn't look convinced. "You're assuming he'll follow on
foot. What if he follows in the Razor and runs us down? It would only
take him a minute to catch us in that machine."

I smiled at him. "Well, then in that case, your next-of-kin will have
a good time spending your retirement money. You let me worry about
the Razor. I want you guys at least ten minutes out when I start this
show. Now get going and don't stop. I'll catch up."

Shaking his head once again and mumbling his opinion of my lineage, Sanchez walked over and helped Jackson up. After switching
weapons, once again leaving the Calico for me, Jackson picked up the
bag of food and water as I helped myself to one of the quart containers
of water and stuck it in the side pocket of my utility pants. Sanchez
supported Jackson as best he could with his one good arm and, together, they limped out of the clearing, leaving a trail of blood and shoe
tracks through the brush, sand, and dirt that a blind man could follow.

I walked over picked up the Calico, making sure it was ready to
fire. I did the same with the Model 459 Smith & Wesson compact .45 I
was wearing in the Kydex holster on my hip. I was now glad that I had
opted to carry the larger caliber pistol, instead of the little Kahr PM9
that usually accompanied me. Looking at the large black bore of the
.45 before I slipped it back into the holster, I smiled as I was instantly
reminded of the old saying, "Make sure the caliber of the gun you carry *always* starts with a four."

I always kept it loaded with Black Talon ammunition. In 1991,
Winchester Arms pioneered a new hollow-point bullet. Designed primarily for law-enforcement, it was also available on the open market
as well. It was a devastating bullet. Upon striking tissue, the bullet
opened up into what is best described as a flower-pedal-like pattern
The sharp, pointed pedals opened outward, almost doubling the size of
the bullet as it passed through tissue. Add to that the rotation of the
bullet already in progress from its flight and you ended up with a real
buzz-saw. In .45 caliber, it would stop any man, anywhere, anytime.
Winchester named it Black Talon. They even anodized the bullet itself,
coloring it black. Due to some bad press a few years later, the company

was forced to remove the black coloring and re-designate it the ranger SXT. *A rose by any other name*, as the saying goes. My pistol was loaded with original black anodized version. Hold-overs from another time.

When I was satisfied that neither weapon would fail me at a critical moment, I waited for the remaining minutes of the allotted ten to expire. I then walked over to the Cessna. Removing a large Phillips screwdriver from the tool kit, I stabbed several holes in the bottoms of the aluminum wings, penetrating the fuel bladders in both. Aviation grade gasoline began pouring out onto the ground. Backing off to a safe distance, I again waited in silence until I heard the faint sound of the Razor's engine approaching.

Opening the flare gun kit, I removed the red colored pot-metal flare pistol from the case, then broke open the action, and dropped a flare cartridge into the chamber. It looked like an oversized shotgun shell. Closing the gun, I held the flare-pistol at arm's length elevating the barrel, attempting to estimate the arc of flight of the projectile, and pulled the trigger. With a loud pop and an ever-so-slight recoil, the 20mm red flare arched upward in ballistic flight, then dropped out of the sky and bounced off the far wing of the plane into the desert sand beyond, burning furiously with bright red incandescence.

My aim was off. I'd wanted the flare to pass under the wing and into the fuel now pooling on the ground, but it didn't happen that way. Instead, the flare ignited a small bush on the other side of the clearing.

"Shit," I muttered, but it turned out my bad aim didn't matter.

The dry bush now burned furiously, and the end result was the same. People never gave gasoline the respect it deserved. We all had become so casual to the use of this liquid, filling our cars, trucks, and big-boy toys every day as we did, we forgot the danger it holds. It was actually the fumes that were generated by the evaporating liquid of the gasoline that were the real hazard, the explosive power of the vapor being much greater than the liquid itself. The destructive power of gasoline fumes had to be seen to be believed.

As the fumes from the leaking Av-Gas reached the burning bush, I, again, got a reminder of that power. My ears registered the chain reaction as one gigantic whoosh-BOOM! The whoosh having been made as the fumes from the leaking gasoline reached the burning bush and flashed, igniting the gasoline saturated dirt on the ground.

In an instant, flames raced across the soil to the fuel streaming from the holes in the wings and ignited the rivulets of streaming fuel. *Gold-colored chains hanging from the wings to the dirt.* A nanosecond later, the flames reached the confined fumes and fuel in the wing tank bladders creating a massive explosion, thus the resulting BOOM.

The explosion blew the wings off of the small plane, raising the fuselage three feet off the ground in the process. A tremendous wave of heat washed over me and, although I was a good thirty yards from the blast, the shattering effect of the explosion knocked me back three feet and hard on my ass. My eyebrows were singed and several small bushes were now burning nearby. I was amazed that the homemade oil/sand concoction covering my skin and clothing had not ignited, but it was that very paste that had saved me from serious flash burns. I picked myself up. *Guess I was a smidge too close*, I thought dryly.

The small plane was burning furiously now, the plastic, rubber, aluminum, and the body of Michael Johns all contributing to the column of black smoke rising into the clear desert sky, creating a directional arrow to the crash site. I knew it would draw the man driving the Razor like the proverbial moth to a flame. I had only minutes before he came snooping around. I moved quickly over to my "hide" and lay down. Covering myself with more dirt and sand, I positioned the ugly little Calico so I could use it quickly, making sure the safety was off but keeping my trigger finger away from the trigger. I didn't need an accidental discharge should I be startled or have to move suddenly.

I'd been lying motionless there for no more than five minutes when I heard a small stick break in the brush off to my right, accompanied by a single quiet crunch of gravel. *Sooner than I thought. He's here right now.* My heart began to race. I could feel my blood pressure rising. My grip tightened around the assault pistol.

I hadn't heard the approach of the Razor's engine and I chastised myself for expecting that kind of a warning. I'd underestimated him. *This guy is a pro, you dumb-ass! He's not going to drive up and announce his arrival with the noise from his vehicle. You told Jackson to get his shit together. You're the one who better do just that or you're dead meat!*

I quickly thought over my options. The killer would obviously stay concealed as long as possible and observe what he could. He would only move in on the plane when he felt comfortable in doing so, but by the same token, he could not take all day. Staying totally motionless, I closed my eyes and listened. Soon I heard another scrape of a boot against the soil, this time more to my front, but no closer to my concealed position. He was circling, approaching from the other side of the plane. I saw some movement at the edge of the brush on the opposite side of the clearing and, suddenly, there he was, moving in a crouch, slowly, steadily, his head on a swivel. *Damn! The plane is between us!* All I could see was the top of his head and his feet. I realized there was no way I was going to get a clear shot at him from here, not without exposing myself.

The breeze had picked up now and it was blowing toward me from the man's position. *That's probably why I was able to hear him,* I thought. The wind had carried the sound to me. I could see the man's back was to me and I could tell he was trying to get a look into the cabin. The smoking plane and the brush between us still blocked my shot. The breeze was now rustling the nearby brush. Between that and the crackling of the retreating flames, I was certain I could move out of my position and not be heard. I was equally certain that if I moved right now, I wouldn't be seen, either. I made the decision to circle around, find, and disable the Razor. I had to guess at the killer's path of approach, as best I could, by the sounds of his movements.

I was quietly backing out of my hiding spot in a low crawl on my belly away from the clearing when my knee touched a Cholla pod that I hadn't seen laying loose on the ground. The long and thin barbed thorns immediately penetrated my pants and pierced the skin. Involuntarily my leg recoiled, shoving gravel and dirt and making a loud scraping noise that I knew was too loud for the man to miss. I froze. The killer was still now also. *Shit! He must've heard me.*

I lay there motionless, hardly daring to breath. I was sure the pounding of my heart could be heard fifty feet away. After a long five minutes passed, I saw movement on the ground nearby in the clearing, It was a desert kangaroo rat darting from a bush to my left. The man's head jerked toward it. He'd seen it also. The killer relaxed, then returned to examining the cabin of the charred plane. I slowly turned in place and continued my crawling escape, giving that Cholla pod a wide berth.

When I'd put some distance between myself and the plane, I stood up in a crouch and crept slowly in a wide half circle behind the man's line of approach. It didn't take long to cross the tracks of the Razor. I followed them for only a few yards before spotting the parked machine. It was at least 100 yards from the plane. *You* were *being careful, weren't you*? I mused. I stood for a moment listening. When I heard nothing to indicate any approaching danger, I took out my knife and slowly walked around the Razor slicing several half inch long cuts in the sidewalls of all four tires. Air immediately began hissing out of the multiple openings in the rubber.

My original thought was to stage an elaborate accidental flat tire scene, using a sharp stick or some such, and then try to erase my own tracks around the vehicle and ambush him when he came back, but I immediately discarded these thoughts. This particular man would see right through such a charade. Now my intent was to slow him down and put him on foot, but I knew that simply slicing the tires was not a guarantee. I reached under the dash and ripped a handful of wires loose also, throwing them as far as I could into the brush. It wouldn't matter now if he discovered, when he returned, that the damage was man-made. I crept away as quietly as I'd approached, staying on the hardest ground possible to avoid leaving many tracks.

Once clear, I took off at a slow jog, again circling away from the plane. It was time to catch up with Sanchez and Jackson. The slow jog was all I could muster, injured and tired as I was. I began to get a bit worried when after fifteen minutes, I had not seen their trail, but my concerns ceased five minutes later as I came across the disturbed soil and blood indicating their passing. I turned up their back trail and add-ed my tracks to theirs. It took another fifteen minutes of jogging and limping for me to catch up with them. I was making too much noise moving this fast, but it was a calculated risk. The killer couldn't be behind me this quickly. I was sure he would return to the Razor and upon discovering it disabled, would then set out on foot after us.

I was wrong.

CHAPTER 51

Smoke

Rocha heard the explosion and, from his zigzag search pattern across the sand, instantly spotted the ball of fire and the accompanying smoke. He was close. Less than a half mile by his reckoning. He briefly wondered why the plane had taken so long to catch fire. He turned the Razor toward the black pillar reaching into the sky. When he determined he was approximately a hundred yards from the fire, he parked the OHV, got out, and made his approach quietly, circling out and away from the Razor.

Only a fool would make a straight line approach from a vehicle that someone may have heard arrive, he thought. He crept to the edge of the clearing. From his vantage point, he could clearly see the remains of the burning plane. The explosion and subsequent flash-fire had exhausted the remaining fuel and it wouldn't be long before the flames burned themselves out. Remaining motionless, Rocha scanned the clearing with his eyes and ears. The wind had picked up considerably. After several minutes of observation, he had detected no threat, so he slowly moved to the remnants of the plane. It was still too hot to physically examine, of course, but he got close enough to recognize the shape and smell of at least one body inside. He was sure he'd seen four men in the cabin of the plane as it had flown over the house. One body here meant three of the occupants of the plane had survived.

Roca heard a slight scraping sound in the brush on the other side of the plane. Seemingly all in one motion, he crouched, whirled, and froze, his MP5 ready to spit death at any perceived threat. He saw nothing. There was no movement. No sound save for the wind through the brush and the crackling of the dying flames.

He crouched motionless for another five minutes, his eyes examining every inch of the brush surrounding the clearing. Suddenly, a small desert rat ran from the shade of a bush on the other side of the clearing, scampering to a new home. It was surprisingly loud in its travels, kicking up sand and small rocks as it ran and fishtailed like a racecar. Rocha decided the small rodent must've been what he'd heard. He eased into a standing position, took one more look inside the cabin of the plane, then began to look for tracks. Within minutes he discovered the tracks and blood trail left by Sanchez and Jackson.

Blood could tell an experienced tracker a lot. By examining blood that fell vertically and struck a hard surface, the trained eye could easily tell direction an injured person or animal was going. One could also roughly determine the speed at which they were moving. The consistency and chemical makeup of a blood droplet as it hit caused the droplet to spatter out from its center, forming tiny spikes in every direction.

If the injured person or animal was standing still or nearly so, the spikes would all be roughly the same length out from the center of the droplet in every direction. However, if moving, the spikes would be longer on the side of the droplet in the direction of that movement., The length of the spikes and the frequency of the droplets could sometimes allow a tracker to roughly estimate how fast the prey was traveling as well. The faster the movement, the longer the spikes. The directional blood spatter in this instance was not of importance to Rocha. The softer areas of sand and dirt held the two men's shoe tracks quite well, making their direction of travel obvious. He was more interested in the extent of their injuries and how long it had been since their passage. The blood would also tell him some of this.

Both men were bleeding, of this he was sure. The blood they'd left behind was not bright red, which meant it was not arterial. Neither would bleed out soon. He reached down with his index finger and touched one of the larger droplets that had been shaded by a small sage bush. The top of the blood drop was dry and crusted, but as he pushed down through it, his finger came up with a moist red stain on the tip. He smeared the red liquid between his finger and thumb, studying it. *Still fairly fresh,* he observed.

Rocha squatted down and examined the shoe tracks. He was encouraged by what he saw. One man was assisting the other. *A leg wound, perhaps? That would slow them considerably and limit the mobility of at least one of them, though both seemed to still have use of their upper bodies.* He reminded himself that both would, in all probability, still be armed, and that he must use caution. Wounded animals could be the most dangerous. *Where is the third survivor?* he wondered.

Rocha was contemplating whether or not to retrieve the Razor before following the tracks when his attention was suddenly diverted by the sound of an aircraft flying low and to the south.

That was the second time he'd heard a plane's engine today. Although he could not see it, he suspected they must be searching for the missing Cessna, and it would not be long before they spotted the still smoldering wreckage. As he continued looking at the sky, he realized there were not many hours of daylight left. He was running out of time.

He decided not to return to the OHV. The two injured men could not have gotten far. Rocha now followed on foot, moving silently and swiftly up their trail. Focusing on the two injured men, he was certain that at this pace he should be able to close the gap quickly, kill both hopefully finding the third with them, then escape under the cover of the approaching darkness. He was only a few miles from the interstate. He could easily hike out of here. As he pursued the two injured men, he decided in retrospect that attempting to kill these deputies had been a mistake, an impulse of personal pride that should have been ignored. *Live and learn*, he thought.

He knew that after all of this, he would have to hide in Mexico for a few months before he could sneak back across the border under Obama's new Let-anyone-in-who-wants-in-so-they'll-vote-for-me immigration policy. Through his connections with the cartel, Rocha had seen with his own eyes the nearly daily influx of criminals, drug smugglers, and men of Middle-Eastern lineage cross the open border into the United States. *What a fool this American President is.* He smiled to himself. He was growing confident now.

Twenty minutes of swift hiking later, Rocha suddenly froze and stepped off the trail. He'd heard the sound of low voices. Circling out to the side, he crept through the brush and cactus slowly, until he had two men in sight. Both men were injured and were resting in the shade of a large Mesquite tree, but they were now preparing to move out again. He was concerned as to the location of the third survivor, but these two were here now, and he could not let the opportunity pass. Rocha raised his MP5 sub-machine gun. He wasn't sure how many rounds he had left in the 100-round drum and he was disgusted with himself for rushing away from the Razor without taking any extra magazines for the weapon. He had plenty of loose ammunition back in the OHV, but that was of no help now that he had abandoned it.

He'd have to hit both men with what was left in the weapon now, then rely on his revolver if necessary. He wasn't too worried, however. He was an expert marksman. Rocha aimed at the two men, flipped off the safety with an audible click, and squeezed the trigger. Dirt jumped around both men and large chunks of bark flew from the Mesquite tree behind them. He could tell both had been hit hard as they toppled over backward, but to his surprise, one deputy immediately spun where he lay and returned fire with his handgun, the bullets striking dangerously close.

Rocha ducked and was turning when movement very close to him on the left caught his eye. He suddenly realized his error as the shape of a man in some type of strange camouflage appeared very close to him, an apparition rising from the sand itself. *So, there had been three survivors! Who is the fool now?* he thought briefly as he whirled to face this new threat.

CHAPTER 52

Pact

Both Sanchez and Jackson were resting in the shade of a large Mesquite tree. The ominous black muzzles of both their pistols were trained on me as I moved up their back trail.

"Whoa, boys," I said quietly and held up my hands. "After surviving all this shit, I'd hate to get killed by my own guys."

They both lowered their weapons.

"We were pretty sure it was you," Sanchez said. "We could hear you huffin' and puffin' like a train, but it still pays to be careful."

I tossed the flare gun and the extra flare I'd been carrying onto the ground in front of them. "You guys made it farther than I thought you would."

"We've been pushin' hard, but I finally had to rest," Jackson replied. "My leg was about to give out and I had to re-bandage it, unless you want more blood on the trail."

"No. You've given enough for the cause," I said, looking at Sanchez's dripping shoulder. "So have you, bud. Bandage yourself up, too. You guys drink any water?"

"Yeah, just now. Both of us drank a quart."

"Not enough with your blood loss," I told them both. "Pound down some of those crackers for the salt, and another quart of water each." I woofed down a packet of crackers, pulled a quart of water for myself from the carry bag, and began sucking on it. The warm water and food rejuvenated me somewhat.

"Here's the deal," I said and gave them the details of the burning of the plane and the disabling of the Razor. "I think that slowed our friend down and put him on foot, but as soon as he's confident we escaped the plane crash, he'll find your tracks. He's probably on his way already." Jackson looked around pensively. "We should have a little time," I said to ease his mind. "I don't think he could get here this quick. He probably doesn't know for certain how many of us got out of the plane. I tried to jog where the ground was the hardest until I crossed your trail so I wouldn't leave many obvious tracks. Hopefully he's in too much of hurry to look very hard for any other tracks but yours."

I turned to Jackson. "Sorry to get you into this, Daryl. I sure wouldn't have had you and Mike along it if I'd known how this was going to end." My thought drifted back to Johns's body. "You're buddy is going to be righteously pissed at you about his plane, I'm guessing."

Jackson managed a smile for the first time. "Hey, I'm a big boy. You didn't force me to come along. I'm always up for adventure. That's why I fly. Granted, I did get a little more out of this trip than I bargained for, however. As far as the plane goes? Bryce, that's my buddy's name, always insures stuff for more than it's worth. I'm sure he'll get the insurance company to buy him something bigger, better, and newer."

It was then that a small plane crossing the sky in the distance caught all of our attention.

Sanchez glanced around the sky. "We've only got a few hours of daylight left. You think they are looking for us yet?"

I nodded. "If I know Sonya, she's already all over Davis about us." I nodded toward the fading sound of the plane. "I think they're looking for us right this minute."

Jackson looked down at his bandaged leg. "I don't know how much farther I can go. It's really starting to hurt."

"Okay," I said. "Sit tight for just a second while I have a look up ahead."

With that, I walked away from both a few yards then worked my way through the brush trying to see what lay ahead. A small area of higher ground was visible a quarter mile distant. The small rise had several large boulders on top and looked to be a much more defendable spot than it was here. I turned and quietly picked my way back through the cactus and mesquite. I had Jackson and Sanchez in sight when I heard a mechanical click in the brush off to my right. I recognized the sound instantly as the safety of a weapon being flipped off and it was close. It was *very* close!

I'd underestimated him again. The killer had closed the distance much faster than I thought he could. *Shit, I'm dead*, was the instantaneous thought that flashed through my mind as I subconsciously braced myself for the impact of bullets. What happened next was a blur, yet as always, time seemed to stand still. My lips opened to shout a warning to my two companions, but I already knew it was too late.

The killer's MP5 muzzle sparkled brightly and was instantly followed by fast and multiple pops. I saw the dirt suddenly fountain up around both Sanchez and Jackson—ugly dirt stalagmites created by impacting bullets. The sound of the weapon's firing seemed tremendously loud being this close to it. I could feel the heat of the muzzle blast. The yellow-red flame spitting out the end of the weapon silhouetted the outline of the man standing no more than ten feet from me. Bark chips flew from the trunk of the Mesquite tree behind and above Sanchez and Jackson as they both fell backward and collapsed onto the ground. I was sure that neither escaped the barrage of deadly 9mm projectiles. Both men had indeed been hit, but to Sanchez's credit, he immediately flipped prone onto on his stomach and was returning fire with his pistol.

Shocked that I was not cut down in the first few seconds, I suddenly realized the killer did not know I was there. The gooey ghillie suit had done its job. I turned slightly and raised the Calico, letting my finger slide down to the trigger. The motion must've caught the eye of the man. The killer turned and pointed his MP5 at me.

His lightning reactions surprised me as both our weapons came to bear. He was a half-second quicker and I, again, saw his muzzle flash as I squeezed my own trigger. The Calico repeatedly jumped almost pulling itself out of my hands. Jackson had not told me he had converted it to highly illegal fully automatic, and I had not taken the time to examine the weapon closely enough to notice the selector switch had an added full-auto position. The Calico had swiftly spit out fifteen rounds from its fifty round drum when something slammed hard into my left side, spinning me around and knocking me to the ground. I lost my grip on the Calico as I fell onto my side with my back to the man.

Again, I expected the impact of bullets, but none came. I lay on the ground stunned. My left side felt as if it was on fire. I knew I'd been hit. I knew because it had happened to me once before.

The smell of cordite from all the gunfire hung thick in the air. There was nothing but silence. My left side ached badly now, and I could feel the warm and sticky liquid that was my blood creeping around my back and down onto my butt cheek. I heard a scraping, dragging sound close by. I painfully shifted my position to see what it was, just as a hand grabbed at my boot.

The killer was there, one hand on my boot, the other holding a large folding knife, raised to stab at me. Summoning what strength I had left, I lashed out at him with my other foot, catching him in the face with the sole of my boot. It wasn't a very hard kick. I just couldn't get much behind it in the position I was in, but it was enough to make him turn loose of my boot temporarily. I rolled onto my back, the pain from my side making me cry out. I clawed at my fanny pack trying to get at my .45.

The killer's knife hand lashed out as quick as a snake and he buried the blade into my left calf above my boot just as my Smith & Wesson came free of the pack. The man was close enough to me now that I could see that his chest and stomach were covered with blood. It occurred to me then that he'd also been hit in our exchange of gunfire.

As he tried to retrieve his knife from my calf, I again cried out. The pain was excruciating as he pulled and twisted on the knife trying to extract it so he could stab me again. The knife was slippery with blood, however, and it kept slipping through his hands. He couldn't have known that no matter how hard he pulled, he would never have been able to retrieve it. The blade had gone all the way through my calf, penetrating the edge of my shinbone as it passed. Bone and the swelling tissue had it locked in place like a vice.

The killer looked up and we locked eyes. There was a slight smile of confidence on his face as he reached for the revolver in his shoulder holster. His expression didn't change, even as he stared down the half-inch diameter black hole of my pistol barrel two feet from his face. I stared back into his eyes. There was no emotion there. They *were* black, like doll's eyes. He let his bloody hand slide from the butt of his own pistol not having the strength left to pull it free. I stared back at him and said quietly, "Smile, mother-fucker, wait for the flash."

I pulled the trigger and the Smith jumped in my hand. The Black Talon performed flawlessly. The dark-colored bullet leapt from the barrel and tore through the man's right eye near the bridge of his nose. The two-foot-long flame of the muzzle blast blackened the flesh on his face. Small black flecks of unburned gunpowder penetrated his forehead, both cheeks and lips. In a nanosecond, the ballistic bubble surrounding the bullet liquefied his brain tissue as it passed through. The flower pedals of the Black Talon hollow-point had only partially opened when the bullet blew a two inch hole in the back of Rocha's skull as it exited, splattering blood, bone splinters, and gray brain matter, which covered the dirt and surrounding brush.

The bullet itself, having spent most of its energy, now spun off into the air, traveling another hundred feet before it struck a Cholla cactus and was deflected, falling harmlessly to the hard desert sand. My head flopped back into the dirt. I was suddenly very weary, becoming weak from the loss of blood and shock. My side and my leg both ached badly but were starting to numb as my body tried to defend itself against the damage and accompanying pain.

I couldn't understand why it was so quiet. I couldn't hear the wind, or any birds, for that matter. Nothing but complete and total silence. It didn't dawn on me that my hearing had completely shut down due to both the auditory overload from all the gunfire at such close quarters and my brain's reaction to shock. I turned my head as best I could to see if Sanchez or Jackson were alive. I could only see one of Jackson's boots sticking out from behind the Mesquite. Frank was face down in the dirt next to the tree. Neither man moved, and I was unable to make my mouth work to call out to them. I closed my eyes against the late afternoon sun. *So this is how it ends*, I thought. *After all the hard work, just to die right here in the West Texas dirt.* My thoughts wandered. I thought about what I'd always told others, "There's no good way to go, but there are some truly shitty ways to go."

This wasn't so bad, I decided. *Better than fire, or suffocation, or getting eaten by something. I just wish I could see Sonya one more time. Tell her I love her.* I heard a muffled pop from the area where Sanchez lay, but I was too tired to open my eyes to see what it was. I drifted along the edge of unconsciousness. A shadow passed over my closed eyelids. I opened my eyes briefly, but saw nothing and closed them again. *Probably just a circling vulture or two waiting for the dinner bell.*

I inwardly laughed at that thought, but no sound left my lips. Time meant nothing now and I lay there, slowly slipping into darkness. *Wait, wasn't that the title of an old song?* I couldn't remember. I knew was dying. The shadow came back, passing swiftly over my face, once, twice, but I just didn't have the energy to open my eyes a second time to look for its source, though I was certain it was more of those bastard scavenging birds come to call. It was much easier just to drift.

I was delusional. Sometime later, my mind registered that the wind had *really* picked up and was whipping my face with pebbles, sand, sticks, and dirt. Then the vultures came back. My eyes remained shut, as if glued, but my hearing had partially returned. I could hear hundreds of the scavengers flapping their wings in unison. Flap, flap, flap, flap, flap.

The scavengers shook the ground as they landed around me. They tore at my clothing, ripping it away. I could feel the sting of their beaks as they repeatedly pecked at the wounds on my leg and side. One even had hold of my neck and throat. I felt myself being rolled onto my side, helpless to stop them. Finally, clutched in their talons, I was lifted off the ground as they began to fly. Darkness then washed over me like a wave. It carried me away from the hideous sounds and the pain.

CHAPTER 53

The Light

I'm dead, I guess. Where's the bright light? I thought *I am supposed to see a bright light or get sucked into it or some shit. Whoops! I guess I'd better not be swearing since maybe I'm going to be meeting the Big Kahuna as soon as I find that damn light everyone is always talking about. Crap! There I go swearing again. Oh, well, if you go to hell for swearing, then my soul has already had it. Hey, there it is. What the hell is Sonya's face doing in the light? She didn't die. Oh no! Olsen too? And Davis?*

I could see Sonya, Olsen, and Davis all standing together in a semi-circle staring at me, surrounded by the brightest light I'd ever seen. Suddenly there was sound. A *lot* of sound and it was uncomfortably loud. Chimes, voices, and a continuous and an annoyingly constant beep. There were smells also. That unpleasant hospital odor I'd smelled so many times in my life. That mixture of anti-septic, medicine, plastic, stainless steel, urine, and feces. The smell of the sick and the injured, and even the dead. Dimly, I could see Sonya was staring at me as if through a frosted window.

"Jason?"

Her voice sounded distant though I could see her face was close to mine. *What the fuck is going on here? I'm dead. I'm not supposed to be able to hear, or smell, or see, or think!*

"Jason? Answer me. *Jason!*"

Yep, definitely Sonya's voice. Then like a train suddenly rushing from a tunnel, or maybe like a new born baby exiting the birth canal, I was thrust into the world of light and sound, but to my surprise, it wasn't the bright light cast off by the glory of God or the sound of Angels singing. It was the hideous light cast by fluorescent bulbs in the ceiling of a hospital room. People surrounded my bed. A nurse fussed with a blood pressure reading from the monitor, then hurried from the room to call the attending physician.

I looked around the room, groggy and confused. Davis and Olsen were both there. Tammy stood against the back wall, watching. Sonya was bending over me, her face close to mine. My eyes locked with hers, then wandered down the low cut top she wore.

"Nice hooters," I croaked hoarsely.

Her chin dropped to her chest as she closed her eyes and whispered, "Oh thank God."

Olsen stepped over and I could feel his hand on my shoulder. "Glad to have you back, buddy."

The doctor and the nurse both rushed back in and both began poking and prodding me, with the doctor shining that obnoxious penlight in both my eyes. "Mr. Douglas, can you hear me?" he asked loudly.

"Of course, I can hear you," I replied. "And you don't have to shout. I'm right here, and get the friggin' light out of my eyes, it's annoying as hell."

"Sorry," the doctor said as he slipped the light back into his pocket. "But I needed to check for the response of your pupils. How do you feel?"

"How do I feel? That's a ridiculously rhetorical question, don't you think, Doc? My side hurts, my leg hurts, my dick hurts from the tube that's shoved up it. My throat is killing me. My neck is killing me. My back is killing me. I'm hungry. I'm thirsty, I need to take a crap, and it stinks in here. All in all, Doc, I feel like shit. How long have I been here?"

He made some notes on my chart. "Three days, Mr. Douglas."

I gaped at him. "Three days?"

"Yes, three days. You were in surgery most of the first day and in an induced coma for two more, until right now that is. Actually, it's had us a bit worried that you didn't wake up sooner. Your wounds were serious but not as bad as they could have been. The knife wound to your leg was a bit dicey due to the tissue damage from the blade being twisted. That had to hurt a bit, I assume."

"You assume correctly, Doc. It hurt more than a bit."

"Yes, well anyway, like I said, that damage was fairly severe but we got it repaired. Your side was less serious. You were extremely lucky. You were hit by two bullets. Both glanced off your ribs, after breaking several, of course, but the bullets never penetrated into your chest cavity. Both just exited out the meat of your back. Like I said, *extremely* lucky." He and the nurse finished checking my vitals, the monitor, and my IV drips. "Well, you try and get some rest," the doctor said as he cast a disapproving eye at the visitors in the room. "I'll look in on you later."

"Thanks, Doc," I said to him as he walked out.

The nurse followed him out telling everyone else, "Except for his wife, all of you out."

Davis stepped up to my bed. He was all business. "As soon as you can, Douglas, we need a statement on what happened out there."

I nodded. "Three days, eh?"

Davis nodded.

I shifted in the bed, which reminded me why I was here. Pain shot through my side and my leg. "How did I get here?"

Davis looked around for the nurse but she had left the room. "Here's the short version. One of the CAP planes spotted the wreckage of the Cessna and the Razor. Then a few minutes later he spotted the flare, then Sanchez and Jackson. He just kept circling you guys until the Highway Patrol plane took over, but we actually didn't get to you or the suspect Rocha until the Border Patrol SAR guys landed in the chopper twenty minutes later."

I suddenly remembered the shadows of the circling vultures, the flapping of their wings, and being carried away. Obvious to me now, it was the circling aircraft and rescue helicopter.

Davis broke my chain of thought as he continued. "The doctors here said you almost bled out. They had to put several units in you. Lucky for you guys the SAR helicopter was a paramedic bird. They carry plasma and lactated Ringers on board. Only thing that kept you alive."

I was confused by what Davis was saying, the morphine causing my mind to drift and my eye lids to get heavy. I heard the nurse then. "Okay, everyone, except his wife, out!"

Sonya bent over me. "Sleep now, honey. We'll talk more later."

As I drifted off to sleep, my last conscious thought was, *Flare? I didn't fire any flare. You guys? What did he mean by you guys?*

Blackness once again overtook me.

CHAPTER 54

Time Travel

Six days. I was told later that was how long I'd been lying in that hospital bed, totally immune to any of the trappings of the outside world. I was aware only of the clinical sights, sounds, and smells of my immediate surroundings.

Sonya never left my side, except to eat small solitary meals in the hospital cafeteria. She slept in a recliner that the staff had moved into the room. Doctors and nurses came and went. I never knew what time, or even what day it was. I was only aware of daylight and darkness.

Looking back on it weeks later, I couldn't help but think how much it resembled the portrayal of actor Rod Taylor's traveling through time in H.G. Wells' *The Time Machine* film, watching the days and nights pass while my body just stayed in one spot. Of course, the alteration of time and space in my mind was enhanced through the power of the pain-killing morphine.

Davis came in daily. He would greet Sonya then talk to the doctor, asking how I was, but not out of real concern. His inquiry was only in reference as to when I would be available for questioning. Then he'd leave. Olsen and Tammy visited whenever they were allowed. Sonya told me the sheriff came by once and that I talked to him briefly, though I didn't really recall our conversation.

On day four, the nurses cut back the IV drip morphine. They shut it off completely on day five. I was ravenous and the hospital food just wasn't cutting it. Olsen, Tammy, and Sonya all conspired to sneak me some In & Out. I pounded down the burger, fries, and chocolate shake with delighted gusto. My happiness with the change of diet was short lived, however, as my thoughts returned to what had happened six days prior.

I turned to Olsen. "So the services are all over with. I'm assuming were they nice?"

"Services?" Olsen replied. "There was only one."

"Mmmmm. I would've thought there would have been one for each," I mused. "Anyway, was it nice?"

"Very nice," Olsen answered but seemed a bit puzzled at my statement. "Everyone was there for him. The tribe had a special Indian ceremony also, full dress, tom-toms, a special dance, songs, the whole deal. Yeah, it was nice."

"So they did all three at the same time? That seems a bit odd," I told him.

"All three?" Olsen was totally confused now, which irritated the hell out of me for some reason.

"Funerals, Jim. Not just Johns's, but for Sanchez and Jackson," I said to him more harshly than I meant to.

Sonya came to Olsen's rescue as she suddenly realized what was happening. She turned to me. "Jason, honey, Frank and Daryl are alive."

Olsen's expression changed to one of surprise as he suddenly understood.

"Bullshit," I blurted out at her. "I saw them killed with my own eyes."

I was getting pissed now, thinking that for some reason, they were keeping it from me, but to what end I couldn't imagine. Sonya was patient. Being a nurse, she knew the lingering effects of the morphine were still affecting my reasoning ability.

"Jason, listen to me. Frank and Daryl Jackson are still alive. They were both shot, yes, but they survived. Frank is the one that shot off the flare. That's how they found you all. They flew Daryl to a hospital near his home three days ago for some additional surgery on his hip after he was stable, but Frank is right down the hall. He's been asking us every day about you."

This was too much for my drug addled brain to absorb. *Sanchez and Jackson both alive? It can't be. I saw them both killed with my own eyes.* To say I was stunned would be an enormous understatement. Stupefied would be more accurate.

"W—what? H—how?" I stammered. "Someone tell me what the hell happened."

"I already told you what happened on *our* end, Douglas."

Davis was standing in the doorway and had overheard the last part of the conversation. As he entered, Sonya reached into her purse and fiddled with something. The motion went unnoticed by Davis but not by Olsen, who raised an eyebrow at her. She gave him the slightest shake of her head in return.

"I know," I replied. "One of the CAP search planes spotted the wreckage of our Cessna, etc. I remember all that, Lieutenant. I meant how is it that Sanchez and Jackson are both still alive? I saw them shot to pieces with my own eyes."

Davis turned to Olsen and said sternly, "Hit the bricks, Deputy."

"Yes, sir." Olsen turned and walked out, probably heading for Sanchez's room.

"Mrs. Douglas, would you please excuse us," Davis asked Sonya. "This is now an official investigation interview and you can't be here, sorry."

Sonya looked at me. I nodded that it was okay to go then gave a quick and almost imperceptible glance down at her purse. She gave the slightest nod in return, setting her open purse on the chair next to my bed. She then got up and walked out the door, Davis shutting it behind her.

He turned to me. "Sanchez and Jackson were both hit multiple times by that MP5, but they didn't die. Almost bled out, though, blah, blah, enough about them. You can get the details from the doctor later about their injuries. Right now, I want to hear about everything that happened out there, including everything you know about all of these murders."

My wits were returning to me rapidly now that I wasn't on the dope any more. *Lots of compassion for your injured deputy,* I thought. *What an asshole.*

Davis glanced at the monitor then tapped the glass face. "You know, Douglas, you should have done me a favor and died a hero's death out there like that Indian cop did, but no. Instead you just made one hell of a mess which now I have to try to clean up. The FBI was already investigating the cartel connection between Lopez and those guns, and now they want to know how this Rocha character that you blew away is tied in and why we didn't bring them into the loop on the homicide investigation of those two biker assholes. Technically they're 'assisting' us with the Lopez killing, but really they've taken over the whole case and pushed us to the back of the bus. Now it seems this Rocha may be good for several contract killings down El Paso way, so the El Paso homicide cops have invited themselves into our little party.

"The FBI, the Department of Indian Affairs, and the local Native American Tribal Counsel are all up in arms about your Indian buddy getting himself killed, and they're demanding to know what the hell he was doing up there in that plane with you guys. *Everyone* wants to know how the two dead bikers and those skeletons are involved with this. They think we were blowing smoke up their ass with *that* initial investigation from weeks ago, which, of course, we were, but I can't tell them that." He chuckled. "Can I?"

Davis' voice started to once again climb in both volume and oc-
tave. "No less than five investigators from both the FAA and two insurance companies want to know what the hell happened to that fucking airplane. The FBI has also taken over the investigation of your
little wild-west show out there in the desert. Shit, they've still got people out there sifting through pebbles and sand. The Department of
Homeland Security and the Border Patrol have agents investigating
why and how two now-dead Mexican citizens, Lopez *and* Rocha, both
came to our attention while they were in the US and why we hadn't
notified them of what we knew and when we knew it. This, of course,
has drawn the attention of the Mexican Charge de Affairs and the
Mexican Federal Police. Oh yeah, and there's some supposedly hot-
shit *Magnum P.I.* type from up Dallas way, a retired hard-ass NYC
homicide cop who now works as a gum-shoe. He's been hired by that
missing surgeon's family. He's tenacious as hell and he's poking his
nose into everything!

"If that's not enough, there's satellite trucks from all the major
networks parked up and down the street in front of the jail with the
reporters sticking microphones and cameras in my face every time I
move. There's even reporters camped out in the lobby downstairs waiting to get a crack at *you*. The Fox News guys aren't so bad. At least
they're just trying to find out what actually happened, but the other
major three networks are leading every broadcast with their bullshit.
'We know you white people are fucking over the Indians again' stories, and then, of course, there's the lawyers!"

Davis's face was turning that purplish red color I had become so
fond of. He looked like he was teetering on the edge of a full blown
heart attack or stroke.

I knew what the answer would be before I even asked, but I
thought I'd needle him a bit for his "You should have died a hero"
comment, so I innocently asked, "Lawyers?"

His head snapped up as he stared at me in anger. "Don't give me
that crap! You know exactly what I'm talking about!" The lieutenant
was almost shouting now. "This story is attracting every asshole ambu-
lance-chasing lawyer from all over the western half of the country like
sharks to a dead fucking whale carcass, and they're all lining up to see
who can get their lawsuits filed first." Davis closed his eyes, rubbed
his temples. "Christ on a crutch. How did this ever get so out of control?" he asked no one in particular. He opened his eyes and looked at
me. "All-in-all, Douglas, this is a foot-long shit sandwich and we're all
going to have to take a bite."

I decided to see if I could actually push him over the edge. "I
thought you thrived on all this attention and press coverage, Lieuten-

ant. Getting up there in front of the cameras and all. It seemed to suit you."

"Still wise crackin', eh, Douglas? Laughing in the face of danger. You think you're such a smart operator. I'm gonna throw you to the wolves, wise-ass. All of these people, the Feds, everyone, are trying real hard to find a scapegoat to blame this entire mess on! They want very badly to hang someone for the plane crash, the shoot-out, and the bodies. I intend to make sure you're gonna get the blame for all of it, the death of Johns, the plane crash, and the wounding of a deputy and a civilian. Hell, they'll probably even hang you for killing Rocha who's a Mexican citizen! All I have to do is say that I did not authorize any of you to take that plane flight, or even better yet, say that I gave you an order *not* to do it. You are on your way to federal prison for a long time, smart-ass."

I had known all along that Davis was going to save his own ass by laying this all on me. I snorted. "That's true, Lieutenant, you could try to lay it all on me, but I'm thinking you'll have a hard time explaining why one of your senior deputies was right there with me. Especially since it would surely come out in the investigation and any subsequent trial that Deputy Sanchez talked to you on the cell phone, not just once but twice, and told you what we were doing with that plane."

Davis chuckled smugly. "Douglas, if Sanchez wants to keep his job *and* his pension, I'm sure he can be persuaded to see things my way."

"What about Olsen?" I asked.

"Olsen is a new young cop. You know how it is. He'll go along to get along. He's not going to jeopardize his career for a has-been like you."

"And Jackson?" I pressed.

He smiled. "Mr. Jackson has no firsthand knowledge of what was actually talked about on the phone between Sanchez and myself. Jackson is a civilian, recruited by you, who was not supposed to be there in the first place, and was only doing what *you* told him to do."

Davis smiled. In his mind he probably saw it as such a simple solution. He would blame it all on the retired rogue detective from California. Oh, he knew he'd take some heat for giving me the "provisional deputy" status, but it was a small price to pay to make everything go away, including me.

He stood up and smiled. "I need to go talk to the sheriff. I'm sure he'll see it my way, also. I'll see you around, Jason," he said as he walked toward the door.

As he reached for the handle, there was a quick knock and the door was pushed open from the outside. Three lean and efficient-looking men in dark suits entered the room.

CHAPTER 55

The Suits

Two of the men appeared to be in their early-thirties. The third man, the obvious leader of the group, was somewhere past 40, though it was hard to pinpoint his exact age. All seemed to be trim and in good shape. Their expensive, tailored suits fit them well, but the telltale bulges visible on their right hips under their unbuttoned coats made it obvious who paid their salaries.

Sonya stood in the hallway just behind them. One of the men produced a small black leather identification wallet from his inside jacket pocket. He opened it and held it out for inspection. The gold colored U.S. Department of Justice shield was unmistakable, as was the ID card opposite it on which the letters FBI. were printed in large bold type.

"Gentlemen, my name is Special Agent Daniel Johnson." He then introduced the men on his right and left. "This is FBI Special Agent George Von." The man on his left nodded and held out his ID. "And this is Department of Homeland Security Agent Alfred James." The DHS man repeated the same action with his ID. Agent Johnson smiled at me. "I guess we have some things to talk about." He then turned to Davis. "No need for you to stay, Lieutenant."

Davis was not happy at being dismissed, no doubt wanting to know what I would tell the FBI agent. He shot one more hateful look at me and walked out.

I motioned Sonya to come in past the men. "Excuse me, gentlemen, this is my wife Sonya." The three men turned and nodded to her politely. "Agent Johnson, since I have the feeling we'll be in here for a while, my wife needs to get her purse off the chair there." I gestured to the purse.

"Of course." Johnson moved aside but as she reached for it, he asked, "You are not carrying any weapons in your purse, are you, ma'am?"

Sonya reached for her purse. "Heavens, no. My husband is the only gun guy in our family."

Yeah, right, I thought.

As if reading my mind, Johnson smiled. "Somehow I doubt that, ma'am."

Sonya gave him one of her best coy smiles, batted her eyelids at him flirtatiously, then held her purse open for him to look inside.

He held up his hand. "No need for that, ma'am, I trust what you say to be true."

She looked past the FBI Agent to Davis, who had stopped just outside the open door, obviously attempting to overhear what he could.

Smiling sweetly as she squeezed passed Davis, she addressed Agent Johnson over her shoulder. "Besides, my husband, the ex-detective there, told me that he *never* allowed anyone to have a cell phone that can record voice or video in the room when he was interviewing someone."

Johnson looked at me then shot a quick glance at Davis. For just a brief second, the corner of Johnson's mouth twitched into a knowing smile. It was gone an instant later.

"That's a good rule for sure," he said. "Nice to have met you, ma'am."

"Call me Sonya."

Johnson nodded. "Nice to have met you, Mrs. Douglas—Sonya."

As Agent Johnson and Sonya exchanged these minor pleasantries, I watched Davis. His face was pale. He knew he'd been had. Everything he'd said to me, every threat he'd made, his acknowledgement that he'd known about the flight, and his intention to orchestrate hanging it all around my neck, had just walked out the door on Sonya's smartphone.

No sooner had she walked out than Agent Johnson turned addressing his partners. "Gentlemen, I want to speak to Mr. Douglas in private. Please see to it that the lieutenant out there finds his way *all* the way out."

Agent Von turned toward the door. The DHS agent raised an eyebrow, hesitated for just a second, but said nothing, and also turned to walk out. It was obvious that he was confused by the tact taken by Johnson. Both men posted themselves just outside the door. The lieutenant wanted to protest, but it was evident to him that both agents would be more than happy to "escort" him from the hospital if he didn't leave on his own accord. He turned and walked away.

Agent Johnson walked to the window and looked out, saying nothing for a full minute and placing his hands together behind his back. *Aloof indifference.* I immediately recognized the interrogative technique. When he finally spoke, it was in a quiet, calm tone. Still looking outside, he said, "I can only assume that whatever is recorded on your wife's cell phone will implicate Lieutenant Davis in some- thing...untoward, shall we say? Would that be an accurate assumption on my part?"

"Your assumption would be accurate," I replied.

"You are aware, I'm sure, Mr. Douglas, that recording someone without their knowledge is illegal." It was a statement rather than a question.

"That's what they say," I replied. It wasn't true. Recording a con- versation was legal as long as one of the participants knew and agreed, but why argue semantics?

"Still, that would be the state's problem, not the federal govern- ment's," he mused. He still hadn't turned to face me. "I can also only assume that whatever the lieutenant said to you is of a serious enough nature, for you to risk prosecution for making the recording."

"Do you really need to ask?" I asked in return.

Johnson sighed. "I suppose not. Well then, we'll set that aside for the moment."

He turned and pulled up a chair very close to me, leaning forward, making direct eye contact, and placing his hand on my shoulder. Again, I smiled inwardly as I recognized this interrogation technique for what it was. He was taking "control" of the conversation, or so he thought. Speaking in a monotone yet sincere voice he said, "Jason, I need you to tell me *everything* about this incident. From the time you and your wife stumbled across the skeletons a few weeks ago to wak- ing up in this hospital bed."

I looked at his face. "That's going to take some time."

"I've got nothing but time, Jason," he replied with sincerity. "Oh, and by the way, do we need to go into Miranda, etc.?"

I shook my head. "No, not right now anyway, providing I set the ground rules for our little chat."

Now it was his turn to raise an eyebrow. "What did you have in mind?"

"I tell the story from beginning to end, one time and *one time only,* with you sitting, quietly taking your notes. There will be no questions during. Zero, none, or I'll lawyer-up. When I am done with my initial statement, I am done. If you want to play twenty questions *after* I fin- ish, I'll lawyer-up. Don't waste your time trying to interview Sonya. She's a cops' wife and she knows you cannot compel her to say any- thing. If you bug her, I'll lawyer up, and so will she. Besides, there's plenty of others involved in this deal for you to interview for confirma- tion of my story without me answering a million questions. Also, I talk only to you. You try to tag team me with one of your buddies out there, I'll lawyer up. Finally, no recording my statement. If you want to officially record my statement, I'll—"

Johnson interrupted." I know, I know. You'll lawyer up."

I smiled at him. "Well, actually, I was going to say I'd set the rules for that, but since you brought it up, yeah, I'll have a lawyer around for that also."

The FBI agent grimaced at his error in jumping the gun in our little game of wits. Johnson thought about what I'd said for a moment, then asked, "I suppose asking to get on the box would be a non-starter?"

"Gee, ya think?" I replied sarcastically.

He shook his head but smiled, knowing we had reached impasse. "Jason, you just made me fifty dollars richer."

"How's that?"

"Agent Von bet me that the first words out of your mouth would be to ask for a lawyer. I bet it wouldn't, at least not right away."

"Good for you," I replied. "You can use your newly acquired funds to have one of your minions out there go get me a Starbucks."

Johnson smiled. "By the way, Jason, and I hope you don't mind me calling you Jason?"

I smiled. *Another investigative technique right from the playbook. Establish a personal relationship.* "Not at all, *Daniel*."

Johnson gave me a surprised look for using his first name. This wasn't going the way he wanted. I was supposed to be intimidated by his FBI status. His facial muscles tensed but only for a split-second. "Touché."

I looked out the window. "It's gonna be a long evening, Daniel. How about that Starbucks?"

Johnson nodded and I gave him my order. He walked to the door and opened it. After a brief, low-volume exchange with the other two agents, Agent Von turned away and walked down the hall. The DHS man now stood guard just outside the door. He would insure that no one except medical staff entered the room while the interview was in progress.

"I have a concern," I said.

He shook his head. "If it's about Davis going down to sweet talk Sanchez while we're in here, don't worry about it," he replied. "I have another agent on his door as well. No one will talk to Sanchez until *I* do."

Is he already suspicious of witness tampering? I wondered. *Or just being thorough.*

"I'm just trying to be thorough," he said as if again reading my thoughts.

Holy shit, this guy is sharp. Ah well, he's an ivy leaguer and I'm just a junior college guy.

"By the way, have *you* talked to Sanchez?" he asked

"Me? No. Hell, I didn't even know he was still alive until a few hours ago."

Johnson was eyeing the pocket recorder he had in his hand. It was a mini-cassette type.

"I wish you would re-consider allowing me to record this," he said, looking at me. "It would really save me a lot of time and trouble, and save you from having to repeat it all later."

I nodded. "I tell you what I'll do. You round up another recorder just like that one, and we'll record on both of them. When you leave here, I keep the second cassette, just to make sure it's all on the up and up, so to speak."

Johnson stood up. "Why not digital? Like your wife's phone."

"For the same reason you don't use one. Too easily manipulated, and I want a physical tape of our conversation."

He nodded. "I have a back-up in the car. I'll be right back."

Within minutes he was back in the room, as was Agent Von with my coffee. I thanked him as he silently set it on the table and left.

"Doesn't talk a hell of a lot, does he?" I waved toward the door Von had just closed behind him.

Johnson snorted. "You don't know the half of it, but that's why I like him. Not jabbering all day." After making sure both recorders were working properly, Johnson began the process that I'd been through so many times before, when I sat on *his* side of the interview table, or in this case, hospital bed.

Turning on both recorders, he began. "This is Special Agent Daniel Johnson. I'm interviewing retired Vista California Police Detective Jason Douglas in his hospital room 23A at the Revas County Hospital. The time is 13:30 hours. The date is…"

And so it went. When all of the recording preliminaries were out of the way, I began my story.

Much to the chagrin of the medical staff, it took four hours for me to walk Johnson through the entire affair from beginning to end. To my surprise, he didn't stop me to ask questions, although I knew it was killing him not to. He did switch tapes in both recorders several times, however, numbering each tape in each set identically. I was pleased that he set the full tapes on the table next to the recorders. When I'd finished and he'd turned off both recorders, it was only then that I added two additional pieces of information that I did not want recorded. First, I related everything Davis had said to me, which, of course, I now had recorded on Sonya's phone. The second was that fact that I knew the exact coordinates of the murdered surgeon's body. This surprised Johnson.

He sat there in silence for a moment, then said, "To be honest, I don't know where this will all lead, Jason. It is one hell of a mess. Where's the doc's body?"

"We'll talk about that tomorrow," I replied.

Johnson didn't like that answer much, but finally nodded. "Well, okay. It's not like either he, nor you are going anywhere tonight. On that note, there will be an agent outside the door tonight, just in case you decided to go for a um…walk, shall we say?"

I snorted. "I'm not going anywhere, Daniel."

He stood up, reaching for his pocket recorder and the used tapes. Before he could pick them up, I snatched all from the table.

"What are you doing?" he asked, a bit startled.

"Just making sure we practice safe sex," I replied.

I popped open both recorders and removed the cassettes. I handed him all the tapes in my set, and kept all of his

He shook his head. "You are a distrustful son-of-a-bitch, Jason," he said, pocketing the small plastic cassettes I offered him.

I shrugged. "I just don't want to be the only one without a chair when the music stops."

Johnson turned to walk out. "You don't need to be so suspicious, Jason," he said. "I am really here to try to help you."

"Uh-huh."

Shaking his head again, he said, "I'll be in touch. Get some rest."

"One last favor, Daniel?"

"What's that?" he asked, walking toward the door.

"Could you have Sonya come back in, please, and, umm, tell those reporters waiting out there in the lobby that I might feel well enough for an interview, you know, to answer *all* their questions by tomorrow."

Johnson stopped in his tracks, his back stiffening at my not-so-veiled threat. He turned and stared at me for a moment, then put his hand on the door handle.

"One of my agents will be outside your door should you need anything. I'll be in touch."

I winked at him. "Don't wait too long, *Daniel*."

Shortly thereafter I heard voices speaking outside the door and a few seconds later Sonya walked in followed by a nurse and a food service technician. I was exhausted and it showed. The tech placed the tray of that wonderful hospital food on my table and left. The nurse went about her duties of checking my vitals, drawing blood, adjusting the anti-biotic drip, and insisting I take my pain pills, cluck-clucking about my not using my Spirometer enough.

"No more visitors for you today, Mr. Douglas. You need to get some sleep."

I just nodded. Sonya settled into her recliner. When the nurse had gone, Sonya asked with concern in her voice. "What's going to happen, Jason?"

My eyes were starting to close, the pain pills kicking in. "Don't worry. Something tells me they're going to want to be rid of us real soon. You stash your phone?"

"Yes. I talked the cafeteria lady into giving me some foil and I double wrapped it just like you taught me. I'm the only one that knows where it is."

"Good girl. Here." I handed her the cassettes. "Go put these with it."

I was asleep before she got to the door.

CHAPTER 56

Sanchez

*H*ospitals *suck*! It was the first conscious thought I had every morning, so I knew I was getting better.

Bright and early, the day shift nurse whom, much to her chagrin I'd nicknamed "Nurse Ratchet," decided it was time to torture me by getting me up to walk a marathon. For several days now, the medical staff had already had me up and moving about for short periods of time on bathroom runs, which had been fine with me as I hated the whole bedpan and catheter thing. I wanted to get that behind me, no pun intended, as soon as they'd allow it.

The food sucked, the TV channels sucked, the boredom sucked. The only thing that was even remotely enjoyable were the sponge baths given to me by the young and reasonably cute female nurse. That small pleasure ended after the second time I started sporting wood as she deftly used her warm washcloth. Nurse Ratchet said it was time to start bathing myself with Sonya's help, but to this day I think Sonya had something to do with the young nurse's sudden departure.

On this particularly fine morning, I trundled down the hall with the assistance of Sonya, holding onto the rolling IV rack. Sonya pointed out Sanchez's room. There was no agent presently guarding at the door so the two of us went in. Frank was lying in bed staring at the ceiling. His eyes lit up when he saw us. "Holy shit, *vato*! It's good to see you," he exclaimed. "I keep asking about you but no one will tell me shit."

I walked over and grasped his right hand with both of mine. "Glad you made it, buddy," I said, my eyes tearing up. "Last time I saw you, you were laying in the dirt, tits up. I was sure you and Jackson were dead. I was dumbfounded, and ecstatic I might add, to hear you were alive."

He laughed. "What's that old expression? 'Word of my demise has been grossly overstated.' We owe you, I understand, for taking that asshole Rocha out."

"*Por nada*, my friend. Just pure luck. He had me, or I should say we had each other. I still think he was a fraction of a second quicker on the trigger than I was. Never know why I came out on top."

"Bullshit," Sanchez exclaimed. "You have it, *mano*. '*El sobrovivir desaro, mi amigo.*' The desire to survive, my friend. That's what gave *you* the edge."

"Whatever it was, it worked out, I guess," I told him. "He's smokin' a turd in hell and we're still here." I looked around the room, embarrassed by his praise. "Let's change the subject. So how are you feeling, really?"

"Like I got dragged backward through a knothole by my asshole."

"Wow! That good, eh?" I chuckled. "Have the Fee-Bees been in to talk to you, yet?" I asked.

"Yeah. Been grilling me for a couple days. They really want to know where that dead doctor is, but I told them you're the only one who knows. To tell you the truth, I don't think they know what to do with me, or any of us, for that matter. I heard that Johnson guy talking on the phone to his boss in Washington. Seems they don't want any of this information getting out to the press. Did you fuck with that guy about talking to the reporters? He made it sound to me like you did. Davis is beside himself. He's been trying to get in here to talk to me, but those Bureau guys have shut him out and have clamped down on him big time. I heard it's the same with Jim, Daryl, Williams, that highway cop chick, everyone. Bureau has a lock on us all. They got some Federal Judge to issue a gag order on everything connected to the case."

Sanchez chuckled again. "Man, both Davis and the sheriff don't know whether to shit-or-go-blind over the whole deal because the Feds won't tell either of them anything. Who would have thought that some old bones in the desert and a couple of dumb-ass bikers getting themselves killed would have stirred up such a hornet's nest?"

Sanchez, Sonya, and I sat there for an hour before Agent Von came barreling through the door.

"You can't be in here!" he almost shouted. "How did you get in here?"

I grinned at him. "Well, which is it? How did we get in here or we can't be in here?"

"Both. You're all material witnesses in this case, maybe even suspects. No one is supposed to be talking to anyone about anything!" Agent Von was not a happy guy. He knew he would be in trouble over this

"Relax Von," I said. "Tell you what. You don't tell anyone we were here, and I won't tell your boss the door was unguarded, how would that be? Where'd you go, anyway?"

"I went to the can—excuse me—" he said to Sonya. "—the men's room."

"For an hour?" Sanchez asked. "What'd you have for dinner last night, *vato*?"

After a few seconds thought, Von gave a curt nod. "I won't say anything, but you need to go back to your own room right now."

"Okay, don't get your panties in a wad," I said to him.

I then bent over and whispered in Sanchez's ear. Sonya gave him a kiss on the cheek and we both turned toward the door.

"Get well, spic," I said over my shoulder.

"You, too, hick," he shot back as we trundled out the door with the IV rack in tow.

Early the next morning, Johnson came to see me again, and to my surprise, he was accompanied by the sheriff, Texas Ranger Captain McBain, and a third man I hadn't seen before.

Johnson spoke first, nodding at Sonya. "Jason, could we speak to you in private, please?"

"I don't think so, Daniel. Sonya is my wife. I'm going to tell her everything anyway, so she stays."

Johnson looked at the unidentified man who nodded. Johnson then introduced him. "Jason, this is United States Attorney Frans Creedor."

Uh oh, I decided. *This can't be good.* But then I'm not partial to attorneys. Particularly the federal prosecuting kind. The man reached out his hand to shake mine. I tried to show no reaction as I shook it.

"Good poker face, Mr. Douglas," he said. "But you and I both know your heart rate just increased."

I smiled. "Not as much as you'd like."

CHAPTER 57

Accord

W ell, don't worry too much about my presence here." Creedor's smile faded as he withdrew his hand. "I'm not here to indict you. In fact, I'm not here *at all,* if you get my meaning." I nodded, still giving him nothing. He pulled up a chair. "Mr. Douglas, we have a…a situation here. Unbeknownst to the sheriff and his department, the US Department of Justice and the FBI have had multiple investigations on-going in this area for quite some time now, delving into the workings of the Mexican drug cartels, some of which, of course, have come into public view. I'm sure you're aware of the 'Fast and Furious' gun-walking case that has been in the headlines?" I nodded.

"Do you follow the news, Mr. Douglas?" He didn't wait for an answer. "I'm sure a fellow like you does, so you know that the ATF has egg all over its face for that one, and by association, so does the entire federal government. I'll be direct here, Mr. Douglas. We, and when I say 'we' I mean the Department of Justice, do not want any more of the facts of these investigations being made public. If the details of the homicide cases you and your partner were working on, and your subsequent shooting incident got out, it could and probably would, jeopardize several of our on-going investigations. Agent Johnson is here today to make you a one-time offer and—"

I interrupted him. "Wait, let me guess. Get out of town by sundown?"

When Creedor smiled, it was like looking at the business end of a Crocodile. "Actually, you don't know how close you are with that one."

Johnson spoke for the first time. "Here it is, Jason. We'll let you leave town on your own accord. No charges, nothing. You just walk away, or drive away in your case, but *only* if you agree not to talk to the press, or anyone else for that matter, about this entire affair."

I glanced at Sonya, winked, then turned back to Creedor. "I'm guessing any involvement by me in any of this gets swept under the table, never to be heard of again, is that correct?"

Creedor nodded. "In a word? Yes, and, of course, we want the location of the surgeon's body and the recording you made of Lieutenant Davis.

I paused and thought for a few moments. "Mr. Creedor, I was born at night, but it wasn't *last* night. We both know this mess coming out has very little to do with your on-going investigations. 'Fast and Furious' went south and your boss, Holder, doesn't want another major scandal hanging around the president's neck." He didn't reply, so I continued. "Tell you what. I'll agree to your deal, but only under the following conditions."

He raised an eyebrow. Clearly Creedor didn't like me dictating terms. "Go on," he said stiffly

"Whenever and however you spin this shooting story, Deputy Sanchez gets the credit and commended for dispatching a dangerous outlaw, or whatever you're going to make Rocha out to be. Officer Johns gets honored posthumously for being killed in the line of duty in the pursuit, with Olsen granted the same honors for being injured." I then looked pointedly at the ranger captain. "*No one* gets transferred to a beat in outer-fucking Mongolia just because they happen to know the story and you want them silent. Of course, I'm particularly referring to Troopers Williams and Baker. You can make them sign a non-discloser agreement or whatever it is that you do, but no transfers and no retaliation. In fact, I want some kind of commendation in their file, also. They were instrumental in helping get this guy." I turned back to Johnson. "Fix the plane deal with the FAA for Daryl Jackson. No fault of his and no insurance holdups on the plane for the owner. I keep all the recordings." *Including the one my wife is making right now,* I thought.

These demands startled the sheriff and the ranger, but the Feds seemed unmoved. Creedor glanced at Johnson and I thought I detected a twitch of a smile.

"What guarantee to we have those recordings won't find their way to the press?" Johnson said.

I smiled at him. "The only guarantee is my word, which I will gladly break if you don't live up to your end of the bargain. If you keep your word, then those recordings will die with me."

Creedor looked at Johnson and nodded. "That's a lot to demand, Mr. Douglas," Creedor said.

"High stakes game, gentlemen." I then added, "Oh, and one last thing. This—" I waved my finger around the hospital room. "—all this, gets taken care of for all three of us. That's what I want for keeping my mouth shut."

Creedor didn't need to consult any of the others. He didn't even give the ranger Captain or the sheriff a glance. That told me he had obviously been given "Carte Blanche" by his boss to make any deal, or threats, he wanted to make.

"Mr. Douglas, I think we have an accord." Creedor then stood up, shook my hand for the second time, and walked out, followed by the sheriff and the ranger captain.

Johnson hung back a moment. "Where is the surgeon's body located?" he asked.

"Sonya, give my Garmin to Daniel here, please." I could still tell my calling him by his first name bugged him. I found it quite humorous. As Sonya handed him the small device, I told him, "The coordinates are in the Landmarks file, under Waypoint 3."

Johnson made a quick note then took the device. Just before he left, he said, "If asked, I'll deny I said this, Jason, but you did a hell of a job taking out Rocha, a hell of a job, and well played with Creedor, by the way. Maybe we'll meet again sometime."

"FBI Special Agent Johnson?" I said, giving him back the respect due him. "Do me a favor. Keep an eye on all this and make sure the sheriff and the rangers hold up their end of the bargain. Sanchez, Olsen, and Johns are—were—good cops."

He nodded. "I will. I noticed you didn't include Davis in your list of demands."

I shook my head. "He's a piece of work, that guy, but he's the sheriff's problem. I don't give a rat's ass about him one way or the other. My recording him was just a means to an end."

The FBI agent stood up and moved to the door. "Goodbye, Jason."

"Goodbye, *Daniel*."

He smiled, shaking his head as he walked out.

Later that afternoon, a deputy US marshal showed up with several non-disclosure forms requiring my signature. He also had a copy of the court order outlining the terms of the gag order. The next morning I was discharged from the hospital, being told that all the proper paperwork had already been completed. It seemed like a long ride back to the ranch and the RV. The ranch owner, Frank Rollins, had returned and came over to introduce himself, telling me I could stay as long as I needed.

I didn't ask, but it was obvious the Feds had paid him a visit also. We invited him, but he had no inclination to sit and chat over drinks, explaining that he was flying out again, this time to Austria to look at some Lipizzaner stallions. Sonya and I took him up on his invitation to stay. Over the next two weeks as I healed up, Sonya split her time between nursing me and helping Juan tend the horses. He and the Dobermans seemed to enjoy her company as well. Although still sore, I was able to function well enough to slowly get the RV ready to roll again. The doctor would have preferred we stay another week before moving on, but I assured him I'd take it easy.

The evening before we left, as I sat in my patio chair outside the RV, a sheriff's patrol car pulled into the gravel driveway. The speaker mounted to the front push bar clicked loudly, then blared, "Freeze, you hick! Step away from the RV!"

Olsen was driving. Sanchez sat in the passenger seat. I laughed and flipped them my middle finger. As both got out, I could see what looked like brand new sergeant's stripes sewn to both sleeves of Olsen's uniform shirt. Sanchez was dressed in civilian clothes and still moved gingerly. Sonya had heard the crunch of tires on gravel and the speaker. She stepped out of the trailer, wearing her favorite Daisy Dukes and a tank top with no bra. Olsen's face immediately lit up as he once again was privy to her female attributes.

"Hi, Jim! Hi, Frank!" she said, bouncing down the steps and giving each a hug, which, of course, Olsen enjoyed immensely, considering my wife's attire. Sanchez groaned as she squeezed him.

"Ooooh, sorry, Frank. I forgot you're not healed up yet," she said.

"No problem," he replied. "Just a little sore still. Jim! Goddamn it, quit looking at her chest!"

No embarrassment this time. "Sorry, Frank, can't help myself."

Sonya loved the attention. Women always do, no matter what they may say.

I looked at Olsen's sleeves. "Wow, sergeant now, eh? I didn't think you'd even be back on duty yet, and with a promotion no less."

Olsen smiled and held one arm out for inspection. "Yep. Brand new stripes. I'm actually on light duty for another month or so, but we heard you were leaving and my lieutenant said I could come say goodbye."

I was surprised. "Davis actually let you come see me?"

"Oh, hell no! *Former* Lieutenant Davis is now Retired Lieutenant Davis," Sanchez interjected.

"No shit?" I asked a bit surprised

He winked. "Yup. The sheriff 'suggested' it was time for him to retire."

"I now have a new boss." Olsen smiled as he jerked his chin toward Sanchez. For the first time I noticed the gold lieutenant badge clipped to Sanchez's belt.

"Well kiss my sister's black cat's ass! 'Lieutenant' Sanchez?"

Frank nodded. "Yup. Got my Laurel-and-Hardy handshake from the sheriff yesterday. In fact, coming out here to see you is my first official out-of-the-office trip as lieutenant."

"Damn, man, congratulations to you both!" I exclaimed and shook both their hands.

"Listen, Jason." Sanchez suddenly became serious. "A lot has happened since you've been out here hiding out. Davis retired. Those two highway cops, Williams and Baker? Well, they both got promoted to corporals and I heard they got to pick their next assignments. Heard they are dating now, also. Daryl Jackson got an offer to be a VIP pilot for the Bureau of Indian Affairs, hauling government officials around all over the place. A little bird in an FBI suit told us it was all you're doing. That true?"

I stared down at my shoes. "Don't know what you're talking about, Frank."

Sonya snorted.

"Yeah, I thought you might say that. Look, we ah…took up a little collection, the five of us, you know? To help out with some of your travel expenses. The sheriff was even able to get the county supervisors to chip in from our Crime Stoppers' Rewards Program." He handed me a thick manila envelope. "I hope it helps out."

I held up my hand. "Frank, I can't take your money—"

He cut me off. "Jason, we insist. It's the least we can do. It's the least *I* can do after you saved my ass out there. Now take it! I insist. I won't take 'no' for an answer."

I looked at the envelope, then reluctantly took it from his fingers and handed it to Sonya.

"I've got to get back to the office, Jason," Sanchez said. "The sheriff doesn't know I'm out here. He'd probably jerk my promotion if he knew. He doesn't like you very much."

He held out his hand. I took it but then pulled him into a gentle hug. "Goodbye, buddy," I said, my eyes watering. I did the same with Olsen. Tears rolled down Sonya's cheeks. Looking between Olsen and Sonya, I said to him, "You best get one last eye full and cop one last feel since it'll probably be your last."

Sonya slapped me on the arm and wiped her tears away, then hugged both Olsen and Sanchez. We shook hands one last time, then both men climbed back into their patrol car. As it turned out onto the gravel ranch road, the light bar flashed and the siren made a single, "Yelp!"

Early the next morning, we said our goodbyes and expressed our sincere thanks to Juan and, of course, the Dobermans, then the two of us climbed into the cab of the truck. Sonya opened the manila envelope and gasped.

"Jason! There is a *lot* of money in here!"

The truck and the trailer were rolling on the gravel as I told her, "Don't count it. Let's just enjoy it until it runs out. In fact, I don't want to go to Yuma and park the rig right now. We've been sitting too long in one place as it is and the weather is going to be good for some time to come. Let's head north and see some of the country in that direction, maybe Wyoming or Montana."

I pulled onto the interstate and accelerated. The odometer had just rolled passed the two mile mark when a TSDPS patrol car pulled up next to my driver's window. I looked over at the cop driving. Mark Williams and Samantha Baker were riding together, a double unit. They had obviously been waiting for us in one of Mark's favorite hiding spots. Williams pointed to his new corporal stripes and gave me a thumbs up. Sammy held up her left ring finger.

Sonya immediately spotted the diamond engagement ring. *Women can spot that stuff a mile away. How do they do that*? I wondered.

Sammy pointed to her new stripes also then leaned over the console and hugged Mark's right arm, smiling at both of us. I guess she had decided to "break the glass case," after all. We both laughed, waved, and nodded our approval. Sonya blew them both a kiss.

We saw Mark reach for his microphone to answer a radio call. With a final wave, he then turned on his overhead lights and mashed the accelerator. The cruiser shot forward and was soon out of sight.

EPILOGUE

The four Mexican men sat facing each other around the circular table in a small cantina just outside Ciudad Juarez, Mexico. All were in their mid-fifties. No less than thirty, heavily armed bodyguards were stationed both inside and around the outside perimeter of the cantina. There was no need for any additional privacy, as they were the only four patrons. When several of the bodyguards had entered the premises first, the other customers fled in a rush. These men were well known. No one wanted to be anywhere close to where they were.

One of the four men at the table spoke in Spanish, thus beginning the conversation. "Our asset in El Paso has been eliminated. We will need a replacement."

"What do we know about his death?" said a second man

"It seems he was killed by a retired policeman," replied the first.

"How can this be?" asked the third man. "A former Special Forces soldier, highly trained with combat experience and numerous contracts under his belt, killed by an old, fat, lazy, retired policeman?"

The first man rebuked him. "You are thinking too much of our own country's retired policemen. Maybe this American policeman is something special. Maybe he is not old, or fat, or lazy. Maybe our asset became lax himself. More likely overconfident." He shrugged. "Or maybe it was just bad luck."

The fourth man, obviously the senior of the group, spoke for the first time. "This is my fault. I should never have given him permission to soothe his injured pride and go after those policeman in the first place. Although things worked out in the end with the killing of the two bikers and Lopez, it was too costly. I should have thought this through much better. Let this be a lesson to you, my friends. Rocha allowed it to become personal. That is what got him killed. We will need to start a recruitment at once. Do we have any applicants?"

"Yes," the second man replied. "Several that look promising."

"Excellent. Begin vetting them at once. Regarding this retired policeman, it would not be a good thing to allow Rocha's killing to go unanswered. I want all the available intelligence on this man, his family, where he lives, etc. If the opportunity arises in the future to make an example of him, we will take it."

The third man spoke up. "Did you not just say to not allow things to become personal?"

"This is not personal," replied the senior man at the table. "It is business. If we do nothing about Rocha's killing, it will appear as if we are weak and that we allow our soldiers to be killed whenever someone has the inclination. No one will want to do the 'wet work' we require on occasion. We will meet again soon. gentlemen."

The meeting was at an end.

About the Author

Douglas Durham was born and raised in the Central Valley of California. During the Vietnam conflict, he served in the US Army as a Military Policeman. With his final posting being the Presidio in San Francisco, Douglas opted to stay in the San Francisco Bay Area where he worked as a Police Officer. In the early '80s, Douglas moved to the Coast of California near San Luis Obispo, but the Central Valley was not yet ready to turn loose of him. In 1988, he and his wife returned to Fresno, California, a city of over half a million people, where he worked in the Investigations Division of the Fresno Police Department as a Crime Scene Investigations Supervisor assigned to the night shift for 23 years, retiring in 2011. Always the aspiring writer, Durham kept notes over the years of his adventures and real life cases and, finally upon retirement, had the time to start his writing career. *Death in the Desert ~ A Jason Douglas Novel*, is his first. There will be more to follow.

Durham resides the majority of the year in Yuma, Arizona. He and his wife travel during the summer months in his RV and on his motorcycle, both for new project research and just to see America. He is still married to his wife of 30 years and has two grown daughters both of whom still live in California.